THE LOCO LIFE OF
DOCTOR TACO

THE ROAD LESS TRAVELLED
LEADS TO STRANGE ADVENTURES

IRV DANESH, MD

The Loco Life of Doctor Taco, Published February, 2014

Interior Design and Layout: Howard Communigrafix, Inc.
Editorial and Proofreading: Benjamin Snedeker, Karen Grennan
Photo Credits: Author photo, Lou Goodman

 **SDP Publishing**

Published by SDP Publishing an imprint of SDP Publishing Solutions, LLC.

For more information about this book contact Lisa Akoury-Ross by email at
lross@SDPPublishing.com.

SDP Publishing
Permissions Department
36 Captain's Way, East Bridgewater, MA 02333
or email your request to info@SDPPublishing.com.

Library of Congress Control Number: 2013957929
ISBN-13 (print): 978-0-9911597-9-6
ISBN-13 (ebook): 978-0-9913167-0-0

Printed in the United States of America

To the loves of my life:
Some of you lived the experience with me and are no longer here,
and
some of you are with me as a result of that experience.

To my bashert, *Fanny, you have always backed me no matter
what* mishegas *I wanted to do. You are my muse, my friend, my
anchor.*
*To Sam, Zach, Max, and Jake, my proudest accomplishments.
Each of you is a gem to my eyes.*
*To my parents who wanted their son to be a doctor.
Your love and support got me here.*
*To my brothers who still think I'm smart, even though
both of you are smarter than I'll ever be ...*
*Finally, to my friends and colleagues from Mexico,
New York, California, and Boston ...*
I think the jail time was worth it.

The United States already faces a shortage of physicians in many parts of the country, especially in specialties where foreign-trained physicians are most likely to practice, like primary care. And studies predict that shortage is going to get exponentially worse when the health care law insures millions more Americans starting in 2014.

For years the United States has been training too few doctors to meet its own needs, in part because of industry-set limits on the number of medical school slots available. Today about one in four physicians practicing in the United States were trained abroad, a figure that includes a substantial number of American citizens who could not get into medical school at home and studied in places like the Caribbean.

–New York Times
August 12, 2013

Chapter 1

Sunshine, Palm Trees, and Open Sewers

1975

Tampico, Tamaulipas, Mexico

"What do you have there, gringo?" The federale stood tall in front of the American, his black hair glistening with Brylcreem and khaki shirt sporting huge wet spots at the armpits. The sweet smell of Polo cologne emanated from his slick body like the fetid fog off a swamp. Sam, the gringo in question, instantly recognized that this man was a federale. Who else wears mirrored sunglasses at ten o'clock at night? The pearl-handled .45 bulging at his hip was the other clue. Definitely *Fist Full of Dollars*.

"Oh, just some presents, nothing more," Sam said. The federale smiled for the first time, amused it seemed, by the shakiness in Sam's voice.

"Presents for whom?" He asked, still smiling, fingers twitching by his gun. "Maybe you have a girlfriend here? There are many beautiful girls on this street."

"Yeah, for a girlfriend. I have a girlfriend here." Sam felt like his shorts were saturated in his own sweat—or worse, any other body fluid he could muster.

"You know, señor, I have a girlfriend, too. She is—how do you say it, very demanding? Maybe you can show me what you got for yours. I am always looking for ideas to keep her satisfied."

"They're just trinkets, really. Nothing much."

"Oh, I insist." With that the federale pulled the large bag away from Sam's sweaty hand and dumped the contents onto the unpaved street creating a small cloud of dust. Dozens of lipsticks, sample perfume bottles, and unmarked plastic packets now littered the street.

"Look at all these things! What a lucky girlfriend you have! But what's this, señor?" The federale picked up one of the packets. "Not drugs?"

"Drugs, NO! No drugs!" Sam could sense that he was about to reenact the lead role in *Midnight Express.* How had he done something so fucking stupid in this shithole of a country?

"You have no girlfriend here, do you, gringo? All these girls are *putas*, no? Prostitutes. I have never heard of a gringo making an honest woman of one. I think you are selling these trinkets and if— as I suspect—these *bolsitas* are filled with drugs, there will be muchas problemas. Of course, you realize that you are under arrest," he said as his hand idly caressed the gleaming white pearl grip of his .45.

"Arrest?" Sam cried.

"Your clothes, your car, and your apartment will be searched for contraband. You are taken into custody for smuggling contraband into *El Estados Unidos Mexicanos de America.* Hope you enjoy our Mexican jail hospitality."

Six months earlier ...

Sam loved her. She had saved him from the lovelessness San Diego had always represented to him.

She challenged him to be smarter, to listen to the things she said and come back with thoughts of his own. She came from a good family, an educated family, and Leah was a nice Jewish girl. Coming from a good family who lived in the flat part of Beverly Hills, she was tall, with dark eyes that always seemed to bore into his heart. Her dark hair fell straight, framing blood-red lips that easily smiled or pouted depending on her myriad moods. As far as he was concerned, she was perfect. He couldn't stand to be away from her.

Tonight he intended to tell her that he planned to face the world with her, to support her, help her, love her till death do them part.

At least that was what the romantic part of his brain told him. But, Sam's rational mind was giving him problems.

At twenty years old, and halfway through college, he was a failing premed student. His future was looking pretty bleak. He didn't know what next year would bring him. He'd probably be working at Kinko's or the supermarket in his Podunk of a hometown. Even next week wasn't so certain. He thought his only chance for med school admission was if he could get the recommendation of the professor who taught a class that Sam was currently failing.

What could he offer her? What would her father say, an accomplished and published Professor of Medical Toxicology, revered by every medical society in San Diego. At the current rate, Sam would never be a man he'd trust to provide for his daughter.

Just as he began to despair, Sam's resolve stiffened (among other things). He loved her more than life itself. Love would conquer all, as the song said. They'd live on love, God damn it.

"Schmuck," his doubting Sam chimed in, practically aloud. "Love doesn't put a roof over her head, food on her table, or even cover the cost of condoms. And don't forget those, pal, because God knows babies cost a fortune."

———— • ————

She looked beautiful in the light coming through the car window from the streetlamp, even when she wasn't smiling.

"We can't have a future together at this point. You're going off to medical school and I'm going to Israel for a social work program. How are we going to commit to each other from half a world away?"

"We can be together even if it means we will only see each other a couple of times a year. Love will hold us together, sweetheart, can't you see that?" Suddenly his romantic brain was sounding less brainy, but it wasn't down for the count just yet.

"Sam, I do love you, but we're both starting new chapters of our lives. How do you know you won't meet someone else? Besides, I understand that the nurses are pretty sexy and I can't expect you to handle a long-distance relationship with those kinds of temptations."

Sam felt as if he were sinking into mud and he was having problems breathing. "You're the only one I could ever love."

"That is a lovely sentiment," she said sadly, "but we're too young. You know I love you, but we both have our own dreams to achieve and we can't do it together. Good luck, my dear sweet boy." With that she walked off into the night leaving him to his dark thoughts and the feeling he'd never see her again.

———— • ————

He always dreamed of being a hero. As a child he would tie a towel around his neck, a superhero out to save the damsel in distress.

Eventually, his hero dream led him to medicine. What did biochemistry, organic chemistry, and calculus have to do with patients bleeding from holes, fevers with no known cause, or helping a baby breathe? Sam was smart enough to realize his lack of experience in the medical arts. Maybe the Krebs cycle was something a doctor used everyday. In the end the embryonic doctor within him could not believe that college premed courses weren't a waste of time, and studying them was not keeping him from becoming the next Ben Casey or Jonas Salk.

His life was a study of not sweating the details. Only in his love life was this pragmatism lacking. He couldn't shake this overwhelming—and utterly illogical—belief that love would overcome any obstacle to his happiness.

"Sam, I don't think we should be doing this," she said, squirming away from him. "I want to be friends with you, but that's it. You have your dream and I'm going in an entirely different direction. I like you, maybe even love you, and hope we never leave each other's lives, but this can't go any further."

It was the first time he had tried to make love with her. Leah, always the practical one, took a deep breath and said, "Besides, don't you have that biochem exam in the morning? You look like you need to get some sleep or at least cram for the test some more."

"No, I studied all afternoon," he lied, trying to rekindle the passion by finding her clavicle with his mouth. "I'm as ready as I'll ever be."

Leah disengaged once again. "Well my frisky boy, take some of that energy and turn it into an A for me on the exam." With that she straightened her clothes and got out of his car.

Fuck, this was the saber through the heart. He began considering which friend would mend his broken heart best: Johnny Walker, Jack Daniels, maybe Don Q? Even getting stinking drunk had a romantic overtone. She would find him on the street, filthy, smelly, and fall deeply in love with him.

As their bodies disengaged, he wearily remembered the exam. What time was it? Shit, five hours from now—a sigh and loneliness again. It always ended this way. Being a romantic gave him an excuse for denying the here and now, always aspiring to a future of perfect love and not the mathematics of quadratic equations or biochemical reactions.

The next morning Sam woke up to a beautiful day that seemed to mock him. Shower, breakfast, and hit the road. "Good morning, Sam," said a voice in his head. "Up and at 'em. It's time to get moving." Maybe today would be the day he would get his act together. Besides, tonight would be a fresh night, offering the possibility that maybe, just maybe, she might change her mind about leaving.

"Good morning, Sam," the voice in his head repeated. "Up and at 'em. It's time to get on the road to success."

Fuck that.

Stuck here in a suburb of San Diego, going to a university and studying subjects that were increasingly irrelevant to him, there didn't seem to be any success awaiting Sam. Great prospects in the future? Probably zilch. Romantic commitments, definitely zilch. Sam was going nowhere and he was getting there fast.

What happened to him? He was smart, got good grades in elementary school, was valedictorian of his eighth grade class. With pubic hair, things got a little tougher, sure, but he managed to keep his grades up in high school (except trigonometry—that one eluded him). Parents intervened on the math stuff. It's amazing what a willowy blond with long straight hair, shiksa nose, Harris Tweed jacket, jodhpurs and the smell of horse liniment could do for obtuse angles.

"Let's go, Sam." There was that voice again, interrupting another reverie. "You've got classes to attend, volunteering to do, and all the other things that a medical school demands you succeed at." Honestly, he was beginning to hate that voice.

———◆———

University of California, San Diego was Sam's third college.

When he attended high school he simply ran out of "good, challenging" classes. The counselor arranged for him to take classes at the junior college. One of the classes was great—Philosophy 101 taught by a hero. He was a former priest from a small church in Chile during one of their periodic violent upheavals. As a priest he had suffered for the poor as part of their revolution. Sam could imagine standing with the man at the barricades fighting the just fight. And here Sam was learning from the great man. The class was wonderful. He received a high grade and started applying to colleges. By the time his two semesters at the junior college were over he would be ready to enter a four-year college as a sophomore.

Off he went to LA, but instead of going to UCLA with its city environment he ended up at Occidental, a small liberal arts college. To make matters worse he had no car. Oxy's campus was famous for being used as a "college set" in multiple old movies. For the aspiring spy or diplomat, the college offered an exceptional Russian studies program. He was interested in neither. He found that he didn't fit in with the other students. They were mostly from LA, had money, cars, and a common background. Some had known each other from childhood. While they were friendly enough, it was he who never felt part of their college experience.

What made life worse was living in this section of LA. Sam was so far from any civilization, that even leaving campus was daunting for him. He spent every weekend he could at his parents' friend's house, dropped off by one of his classmates. He eventually brought his bicycle up from San Diego and spent the weekend riding around the West Valley.

It was a limbo time and he eventually found himself disinterested in most everything. His grades slumped and he realized that his dream of medical school was not going to happen.

Just as Sam started college, his parents decided to relocate to the Caribbean to start a more lucrative business. As hard as they tried the business failed and they found themselves back in San Diego. Tuition for a private college was not financially in the cards so in an unspoken agreement it was decided Sam would come home and attend the state school. There were advantages to living at home with his parents, though. They had a TV, a well-stocked fridge and his laundry washed, folded, and put away by his ever-loving mother. Things became easy. He could wake up whenever he wanted to with breakfast waiting, shower, dress, and out the door to class.

He was surprised to find himself doing well in the arty classes. English professors found him competent in the language. History, non-analytical psychology classes, and those fillers of the college curriculum—creative this and creative that—were all easy street.

His problem was the sciences. Biology was OK. He could understand the applications for the future and so he did well. General chemistry and organic chemistry, on the other hand, were sheer torture; they were humorless classes taught by professors and teaching assistants who hated most of their students. These classes were just a waystation on the path to medical school. The professors knew that the thousands of pishers in these classes could care less about discovering a new rubber or artificial sweetener. Everyone knew that the ones who made it through med school and residency would, in a few years, make more money than over 90% of these professors. Who said learned men couldn't be insanely jealous?

Sam even had the dubious honor of taking his class in biochemistry from the author of the textbook. The professor would enter the class ten minutes late, open the book and start reading the day's chapter, and then leave. Questions to be answered by the teaching assistants.

Sam filled his days, one after another for three years, accumulating more than enough credits to attain his Bachelors, but not enough credits in any major. He switched from Psychology to Biology and back to Psychology, wandering intellectually and never quite connecting socially.

Sam now found himself in the middle of his junior year with an ex-girlfriend, a broken heart, and one last very slim chance of becoming a doctor. He had to will his legs to keep moving forward into a lecture hall that had become synonymous with the killing room of a serial murderer.

———◆———

"OK, hand them in; pencils down … now!"

Sam jerked out of his lack of sleep-induced stupor. The paper in front of him had chicken scratches and vague equations, which he was sure were wrong. Had he actually fallen asleep during the test?

"God," he prayed, "please let Professor Goldman release me from this useless college and deliver me to super hero doctor's coat status." Sam passed in his test, gathered up his things and walked straight out of the classroom towards Goldman's office for his appointment.

"I have an appointment with Dr. Goldman."

"Name," the secretary said without even looking up. She knew he was just another of the hundreds of premeds on pilgrimage to Dr. Goldman's office begging for his letter of recommendation. It was she who typed up exactly two letters per year recommending the top two premed students. Dr. Goldman only wrote the letter if the student was going to med school to do research, not for direct patient care. "Sit over there," she said. "Dr. Goldman has a very busy schedule today and he will see you as soon as he is finished making his calls."

Sam sat as instructed. The office was one befitting an honored professor. Dark wood, sumptuous leather, and framed certificates adorning the walls.

He was anxious. There was nothing to read and he hadn't brought anything with him. He expected a quick meeting to obtain Goldman's approval to apply for medical school. Besides, the office was way too warm and the haughty secretary made him uncomfortable. Soon Sam was sweating and fidgeting.

There was a soft buzz and the secretary picked up the phone. Sam could hear a murmur of words, but couldn't make out anything distinct. Without saying a word herself, she put the receiver down.

"He says he can give you only five minutes."

"Five minutes?" Sam repeated.

"Or, you can re-schedule," the secretary dryly replied.

"No, I'm sure five minutes will be enough." Maybe this was a good sign. Goldman would certainly tell him that he'd be proud to write a letter of recommendation.

Sam gently knocked on the door and entered the office. Maurice Goldman, five foot five in shoes, bald and paunchy, was sitting behind his desk. The desk was composed of enough wood to build a small house. Behind him were pictures of the great man and famous scientists: Einstein, Carson, Maiman, and others. Certificates of his genius and accomplishment. Awards lauding his philanthropy. Maurice Goldman's life was out there for all to see.

"Cohen, you're here for my blessing to apply to medical school?"

"Yes Pro … "

"You have got to be kidding," Goldman barked out. "You'll never be a doctor, no way, no how."

Sam's face lost all color and was replaced by a sheen of sweat. He had never been kicked in the balls, but was sure this felt worse.

"If you had come to me and said you wanted to go to law school to be a gut-sucking, piece of shit, shark lawyer I would have been happy to write you a letter, but a doctor? Let me put it to you like this: I wouldn't take the chance that you could be the on-call surgeon who does my emergency triple bypass. Look at you! You're not a scientist and you sure as hell aren't a good student." And with that, Goldman punctuated his insult by picking up a file folder and tossing it at Sam.

"Look at your academic career. The best grade you've yet achieved in a science was a B in biology—basic biology! At the elementary level a course of gross memorization, no reasoning, no logic and no requirement to actually figure out a problem."

"But ... " Sam stammered.

"But what? You think this is because I hate the premeds in my classes? You think I prefer the chemistry majors? Well that's true, but there's another reason I only give two recommendations to medical school each year."

"But ... "

"There's that 'but' again, a sure sign of inferior logic. My recommendations are sacred. When a school gets a recommendation from Professor Maurice Goldman it means something. I'll even admit to a selfish motive. My father had heart disease, hypertension, and prostate cancer, all of which I can and probably will inherit. Do you think I want to take a chance that someone who got a D in Organic Chemistry would be my treating physician? Not a fucking chance in hell!"

"But, I worked for your wife ... "

"So get a letter from her. I'm sure she'll say you're a nice schlub.

The kids loved you. You probably walk old ladies across the street. That letter will get you into the convent of your choosing! ... To be a nun!"

Sam was about to totally break down. Without this recommendation, he wouldn't even get to the interview stage. He was numb and unable to speak.

Sam felt like he was in the presence of his executioner. He saw no compassion in Goldman's face, just a frozen expression that signaled disapproval and disrespect. Sam couldn't decide if he had a knife, whether he would slit his own wrists or slit Goldman's fat stump of a neck. "You couldn't give me a break; not an ounce of compassion for me and the great things I'm trying to accomplish, you fucking asshole," he thought. Sam's breathing went ragged and his eyes took on a cold squint. He was sure his blood pressure was way up as his brain felt congested with too much blood.

"Sam, I'm sorry I upset you. You need to look at another career. According to your record you do well in subjects that don't have hard science or math in them. Maybe law school; forget my comments about gut sucking and sharks. Obviously, law is a fine profession. If you really want the joy of treating patients, try clinical psychology. You care for patients with problems and help them. If you go on and get your PhD you can even call yourself a doctor. Think about it. I would be happy to write you a letter for almost any other post-graduate study, but please don't continue with the fantasy that you can be a doctor."

———•———

Sam left Goldman's office shell-shocked. His bowels were twisted into knots and he felt the urge to vomit and have diarrhea all at the same time. He needed to get air. The halls in the university were oppressive and the fluorescent lights were causing his eyes to sting and tear. There was pressure in his chest. The smells from the organic chem labs were noxious, worsening his claustrophobic feeling. He started walking very fast and then broke out into a full run, bursting out of the building like a missile seeking its target.

"Hey Sam, what's happening?" called out a passing blond. He turned his head to see who it was and slammed into a decorative light pole that was festooned with handmade posters, handbills, and advertisements that documented daily life at the university. It was a head-on collision and Sam was the loser. Down he went, the papers tacked to the pole flying around his head like those birdies that circled Wile E. Coyote's head every time the Roadrunner dropped something on it.

The blond came running over. "Sam, are you OK?" Sam painfully moved his arm and took the piece of paper that had stuck to his forehead after landing on him. He looked at her blearily. "Are you an angel sent here to take me to heaven?" The girl saw a large bump on Sam's head and thought it might be a good idea to call for help.

"Sam, lie still. I'll be right back."

"You're all the help I need," Sam said as he forced himself into a sitting position.

"Don't move, you could be seriously hurt. I'm going to get Campus Security."

"No, sweetheart, don't need them, just you. Maybe you could help me to my apartment. Or yours if it's closer?' he said with a grin.

"Yeah, I guess it's true what they say," she said.

"What's that they say?" Sam replied.

"Men don't need their heads, because all their thinking occurs much lower and in a smaller space." With that the blond took off leaving Sam sitting on the walkway.

"How many failures can I endure today? God must hate me," Sam thought. He was about to toss the piece of paper in his hand when he noticed the word Medical on it. He started reading.

New Medical School Opening

The Benito Juarez Abraham Lincoln School of Medicine in beautiful Saltillo, Coah., Mexico invites applicants to this very rigorous program in the medical arts.

A four-year program leading to the Degree of Medico Cirujano (Mexican equivalent of MD) based in the City of Saltillo, the Denver of Mexico.

MCATs are not required.

Please contact:

George Romney

52-555-234-1

Or

97 Avenida de Revolucíon

Saltillo, Coah., Mexico

Apply now for our January Class

Sam just stared at the handbill. Was this a sign from God? Did the Lord have mercy on his soul? Was this the path he had been looking for? But, you could get killed or raped in Mexico. Still? Looking right and left to make sure no one watched him steal the handbill, Sam ran back home.

———•———

"Hey, Sam," his father yelled from the living room. "Get in here. I'd like to talk to you."

Sam barely registered his father's voice. Sam was still in a funk from this afternoon's encounter with Goldman, and he really didn't want any interaction with the civilized world. With his future going down the drain, he wasn't interested in pat advice about "buckling down" or "less time chasing girls" or "don't worry, it will all work out."

"Sam! Get in here!"

When the master bellowed, the servant must respond. Sam shuffled into the living room where his father was pacing.

"Listen," he said. "I was just talking to Solly Shwartz about his son Dustin. He's back."

Sam mustered a single grunt in response.

"Jesus, Sam, Dustin Shwartz, almost Dr. Dustin Shwartz. He's back from medical school."

"And this helps me how, Dad?"

"He just graduated from Guadalajara, off to do his residency."

"Where, in a Tijuana hospital?" Sam asked sarcastically.

"No, smart ass, somewhere in the States, probably New York. You should go and talk to him."

"OK, I will when I get a chance."

"You have a chance now; get showered and get up to his house. I called him. He's expecting you."

"Dad … "

"Listen Sam, this lying around in the fetal position and moaning about the world being unfair is doing you no good. You want something? You want to be a doctor? Then go get it. No one is going to give you what you yourself won't fight to get. If you don't want to go to med school, tell me now and I'll leave you alone. We won't ever have this discussion again."

His father was right. A visit to this guy wouldn't hurt. He got up and got showered.

———— ◆ ————

Dustin Shwartz was a dark-haired, tired-looking kid. His hair cut short, a thin moustache adorning his upper lip, his clothes hung on his frame and he had dark circles under his eyes. His skin color was unnaturally pale, as if he hadn't seen the sun in years. Bela Lugosi had more melanin in his skin than Dustin did. Every unexpected noise induced rapid eye movement and a twitch. Dustin was obviously a very stressed guy.

Sam and Dustin were sitting on the patio of the modest Shwartz home. As usual, it was a perfect day in San Diego. The sun bright, but the temperature cool because of a salty breeze coming in from the Pacific. Sam was looking at the glass of beer that Dustin had provided, the condensation providing a focal point as he tried to formulate what he wanted to ask Dustin. Fortunately Dustin broke the ice.

"Hey, what's up man? My dad says you're interested in med school and thinks you are going to have problems getting in?"

"Yeah, that about sums it up." Sam started.

"Sam, hang on a moment. Let's talk grades. I'm sure you feel uncomfortable discussing them, so let me start off by saying I was not a brilliant student."

"How not brilliant?"

Dustin started chuckling. "Let's see. I try to put that dark period in my life in a small smelly corner of my brain. I got a C- in calculus, a B in biology, a C in physics and, the kill shot, organic with Professor Goldman, a D+."

"Shit, I am doing somewhat better … "

"So, let's hear what somewhat better is?

Sam went on to relay his sordid educational history. "What the hell," he thought. Dustin sounded like he was a worse student then Sam was, and in math Sam was proud to mention that in calculus he had earned a B.

"A math genius, Mazel tov."

"Well, I started in the premed calculus class and was getting an F, so I dropped that and took the calculus class in the engineering school … "

"Med schools are going to notice that; it may not help your cause."

"C- in general chem, and … "

"Look, Sam, there are probably a thousand applicants for every opening in an American med school class. Of those thousand, there are probably at least five that are batting a straight A science grade point average. Why would they take you?"

"Well, I have some recommendations from when I volunteered at the VA hospital, teaching Hebrew school at the Temple, good grades in other subjects."

Dustin sadly nodded his head, noting that nothing that Sam had told him improved his already abysmal chances of US medical school admission. He gently broke the news that in his opinion Sam ought to be looking at going to a medical school that was out of the country.

"Sam, while there is always hope, there is also a reality. Your grades won't cut it. That's OK. You'll apply to med school and see what happens. Maybe I can help you with the backup plan, the J-I-C."

"J-I-C?"

"Just In Case. Everyone needs a Just In Case, even those guys with a straight A average. Do you speak any foreign languages? French maybe? Do you have relatives in Ireland?"

"I don't want to go foreign. I speak shitty Spanish. Enough to say where's the bathroom or give me another tequila. I have no relatives anywhere outside of San Diego and New York, and I think I still have a chance of getting into an American school."

"Stubborn, that's good, but stubborn without being realistic is not good. When I knew I wasn't going to be accepted to an American school I searched for foreign ones. Each school I looked at had its pluses and minuses."

"There are pluses?"

"Some. Ireland is the best. They teach in English, though it can be a bitch understanding the accent. The medicine they teach is first world and the schools are well-equipped. Negatives, most Americans have to apply to a six-year program and it is almost impossible to be accepted there without some tie to Ireland."

"So, it's hard to spend six years in a pub, right?" Sam asked sarcastically.

Sam listened to Dustin droning on about six-year programs in Belgium and some in France. He sensed that the reality of a European education was not as easy as he thought it might be. "Christ, this bastard was forced into a Mexican medical school." Sam's depression deepened. If Dustin couldn't make it, how was he going to be Sam Cohen, MD.

"So far you're not convincing me," Sam broke in. "You went to Mexico, that must have been a treat."

"I'd be lying if I said it was great. Guadalajara is a gigantic school that has hundreds of Americans. It is easy to get to and even if you only have some rudimentary Spanish you can make it through. The living conditions in Guad are not horrible. In fact apartments are relatively cheap. Food, you bring your own, I'll explain that later. The worst part of Guad is the politics.

Guadalajara was in fact under pseudo-military control. The Deans of the various schools were hard-line conservatives worried about a communist takeover of Mexico. By their thinking the US had shirked it's duty to nuke the communists back to the stone age thereby allowing the domino effect to possibly take place. They saw the American students as hippies, representing the weakness in America. Mexico had to be defended and so military type guards carrying rifles were on campus. The med school administrators went further by allowing no student to walk on campus with long hair or full beards. Only the pencil thin 'stash was allowed.

Most of the Administration would have been happier without the gringos in their midst, but the gringos brought in lots of money.

The school could charge five times or more tuition than they could the average Mexican student. As is always the case, capitalism will always triumph over fear of communism. The Americans were welcomed with restrictive rules and then bled of as many dollars as possible.

Sam was wide eyed. "Shit, and you lived with that?"

"I did and so did many others. The plus is at the end of four years you will be a doctor. IF, and this is a big if, you study your ass off becoming as prepared as you can to face the American medical system."

"Armed guards, tonsorial restrictions, it sounds like a nightmare. Pardon me for saying so, but look at you. You look like crap."

"Thanks, man. Becoming a doctor is not the romantic life you see on TV. You sweat blood and then pray that it all works out OK. Anyway you're just catching me after a thirty-six-hour shift on a trauma surgery elective. The jungle has been active the last couple of days."

Dustin's smile was weak, though Sam thought he had a confidence and maturity that was well beyond normal for a guy in his mid-twenties. Dustin's radical new life intimidated him. He didn't think he had the backbone to survive, let alone prosper in such an environment. He wouldn't sacrifice what Dustin had sacrificed. He'd do something else; besides he believed that he would get into an American school.

"Listen," Dustin said, "think about what I said and if you have further questions or come to New York, I'll be starting my internship at Brookside Hospital. You'll find me there. It's in the shittiest part of Brooklyn."

Sam drained his beer. "Thanks, Dustin. After this talk I hope the torture you're going through is worth it. I guess I have to decide if being tortured is for me."

Dustin gave Sam a knowing smile. "I agree, Sam. For me it's worth everything. If you don't think the same way now stay out of medicine because the capital you spend trying to achieve an MD will always be too much."

———•———

There was no one in the house besides him and the wrinkled handbill in his hand.

> Medical School …
> Call …
> Saltillo …
> Mexico!

Back in his bedroom, he sat on the edge of his bed, the crumpled flyer in his fist. He knew he could be killed—or worse. Mexico: the water gave you incurable diarrhea, not to mention the tropical diseases. Then there were the corrupt government officials, the police, and just plain citizens that were out to rob you blind. Did he really want to live in such a place? He had comfort, familiarity, and most of all a life that took very little effort to lead. Why in god's name would he leave this? To be a doctor? To save lives? To be a hero?

OK, say he wanted to be a hero. Say he wanted the adulation of the crowd, the cheers, the fingers pointing at him. There goes a hero, a man of worth, a leader.

Mexico would be his only chance, and let's face it. To become a hero took sacrifice and courage. The sky darkened and inside his house Sam continued to ruminate on his career.

———•———

Sam spent the next day carefully composing a letter.

Dear Mr. Romney,

No, that's not right, it's Mexico.

Dear Señor Romney,

Romney is not a Mexican name, besides if he's the contact at the school it must be:

Dear Doctor Romney,

OK, good start. Next …

My name is Sam Cohen.

"No, that's not right."

Throughout the afternoon Sam wrote, erased, wrote some more, erased some more, finally writing a letter of inquiry that would also serve as a letter of introduction. He hoped it would impress George Romney as to his sincerity and intelligence in undertaking a medical education in a foreign land. He put the letter in an envelope and started putting on stamps. One couldn't be enough—two, three? He walked down to the mailbox with an envelope bedecked with stamps. With a quick prayer, *Baruch ata* … he threw the letter in and hurried back to the house.

———•———

The next day started uneventfully. Sam put the letter out of his mind. He needed to finish up his classes for the semester but meanwhile, he could start making other plans, "just in case."

He arrived on campus, showing up in body, but not in spirit to the lectures. Hypotenuses and Krebs cycle, it was all the same to him. He was more interested in the stacked redhead in abnormal psych class chewing suggestively on her Bic pen. As much as he wished to pursue the redhead, he knew he didn't have a chance in hell so he met up with some guys in his science fiction literature class for lunch and then drove home about three. He knew the house would be empty since his father and mother would both still be at work. He looked forward to peace and quiet, maybe a beer and a nap.

Sam got to the house and opened the door at the same time as he reached into the mailbox. It was empty and that was unusual. He walked through the door only to be bowled over by his mother, crying and hugging and kissing him.

"My Doctor, my Doctor," she cried. She was so excited that her already thick Polish accent became even more guttural and strained. She was hardly understandable. "Sam, you got the letter from the University of California Medical School. You can learn to be a doctor and stay here with us."

Sam could hardly believe it. A letter of acceptance already? He had just finished and sent all the forms in two weeks ago. Maybe there was such a thing as a miracle. His mother shoved the letter into his hand. "Open it, open it."

Sam disengaged from his mother's embrace. "Thin letter," he thought. "Maybe good things come in small packages."

He slipped a finger under the envelope flap and ripped open the letter causing a paper cut. "Ouch," he suppressed the obscenity he was going to utter as he bled. He didn't care as he smeared blood in his haste to read the letter.

Dear Mr. Samuel Cohen,
We regret to inform you ...

The words triggered a shot of adrenaline in his heart. He couldn't breathe, and for a moment the throbbing he heard in his ears was all that existed as his body went numb.

"Sam, what's the matter? Are you alright?" His mother was confused as to her son's reaction to the letter. Her love and absolute faith in her son and his future as a doctor, blinded her to the possibility of his defeat. Slowly Sam regained his ability to react. He took a deep breath and collected his thoughts and speech. He knew this was the end of his dream. He was seeing it play out before his eyes.

He turned to his mother and with a deep breath told her that he had failed to be admitted to the University of California. For a moment he thought his mother had stroked but then he heard her begin to sob. He wished he could do the same, but he knew this was only the beginning of a prolonged catastrophe. He just didn't have the strength at this time to mourn his non-existent future.

The next day he left in the morning to go to classes and returned home to find the mailbox holding another rejection letter from Creighton Med. As the days went by, he would come home to more rejection letters. The days in which there were none only intensified the agony of what Sam knew to be the inevitable ending.

On top of the daily torture of checking the mailbox, he was subject to his parents' reactions to the rejections. His mother would come in the door first, her eyes seeking a sign that there was success. On finding failure she would give him a brave smile and murmur that all would work out the way God wanted it and then flee to her room where she could cry in private. His father, an hour later, would put on a brave front, clapping him on the shoulder and telling him not to worry as the next medical school would appreciate what a fine doctor he would make. Each time the flame of hope in their eyes would dim when he told them that either there was no news or bad news. Soon he was down to one school.

One of his uncles was positive he could get him into medical school. He told Sam that with the contacts he had, admission was a sure thing. Sam had sent him his file of grades, recommendations, and applications.

Sam prayed much like the lifelong atheist who has been told of his imminent death, but so far he had heard nothing from God except his uncle's voice on the phone telling him not to worry. It was a done deal.

The phone rang in the background, but Sam didn't have the strength to go answer it. The ring stopped and then his mother bellowed from the kitchen, "Sam! Phone! It's long distance from New York."

Sam went to the kitchen where his mother met him, cradling the receiver to her breast. Her eyes wide, she whispered, "It's someone named Hurwitz. Maybe it's your uncle's contact at the medical school."

Sam took the receiver. "Hello, this is Sam Cohen."

"Mr. Cohen, this is George Hurwitz, one of the trustees of the medical school at Yeshiva University. I am a friend of your uncle. He has explained to me your deep desire to study medicine at YU."

"I am very eager, Mr. Hurwitz."

Yeshiva was an institute that trained rabbis, but also had a medical school in New York.

Sam, desperate to succeed, verbally pushed every button he thought might ensure his admission to the one religious medical school he had applied to. "I am very excited that I can not only earn my medical degree but I can also dual major and become a rabbi ... " Sam was making it up as he talked. He felt like vomiting—a rabbi, him? Even his parents, having seen first hand how poorly rabbis were treated by their congregations, would prefer he contract gonorrhea than become a rabbi. In addition, the last thing in the world he wanted to do was add on extra work and take classes to be a rabbi. He had enough problems academically as it was. Oy vey, God was going to give him the plague.

"I didn't realize you had that interest, Mr. Cohen. Your uncle never mentioned that you wanted to dedicate yourself to the rabbinate."

"I wanted to surprise him, you know how pious he is." Sam thought, "I am going to burn in the eternal fire of hell ... wait ... Jews don't have hellfire."

"Mr. Cohen, I can help you achieve one of your dreams."

Sam broke out into a big smile. "I'm going to be a doctor, I'm going to be a doctor," he thought.

"The rabbinate is looking for men to assume ... "

"Wait, what's that," Sam broke out into a sweat. "You mean I not only got into med school, but into rabbi school, I'm so-o-o hap ... "

Please let me sound sincere, he thought. Oh well, I'm a doctor ... fuck it. Yippee!

"No, Mr. Cohen," Hurwitz interrupted. "I'm sorry, I tried my best, but I wasn't able to get you into the medical school."

"But ... "

"It was impossible, your grades, MCAT scores, well it just wasn't enough for our regular students. If you had been a minority ... "

"I am a minority. Jews are less than 2% of the population here in the States," Sam cried out.

"Mr. Cohen, you are not an under-represented minority for American medical schools. We just can't take you based on your grades and test scores. I'm sorry."

"I'm sorry, too, and I'd rather be a priest than a rabbi. Priests dress better!" Sam yelled angrily into a dead phone. His mother, who had been standing near him in the kitchen, started crying quietly.

———— • ————

He needed another way into medicine. He frequented McDonalds often as a customer, but being a line cook just didn't look like a good career choice and the employees all smelled like cooking grease. Maybe Hurwitz was right. "Hmm, clinical psychology," thought Sam. He already pictured himself with a beard and small black round glasses à la Freud. A large office dominated by a leather couch, the tasteful coffee table, box of Kleenex, and his great chair with reading light. He would treat the rich, the famous, and hordes of beautiful, distraught, vulnerable women. Maybe this wasn't such a bad idea. Was it hard to be admitted to a program? Sam had to find out. With new hope he hopped in the car and went to the university library.

First, it looked like he had to complete his major in psychology … shit!

Now where were the programs? He went through the usual grad school references listing the programs for PhDs.

"Experimental psych, experimental psych, and another experimental psych program. Crap! All the programs are experimental psych programs. Where are the programs that teach patient care, not rats (or lawyers)," he thought. "This sucks. I hate rats. They have beady little eyes and those teeth." He shivered with the thought.

Wait, here are a couple of programs. "A new clinical school in San Francisco." San Francisco, very nice. I'll get an apartment in the Haight District. Patients from Nob Hill. Life will be good. Uh oh, "this school is not yet accredited." Hell with that.

Finally, Sam had a list of five programs, three in New York that concentrated on clinical psychology. All accredited and all having clinics in the city. He wrote down the address to apply for the Graduate Record Exam and the American Psychological Society. He also made a note to stop shaving and grow a beard.

Sam continued in his classes and tried hard to be interested in the psych ones. It was hard going. The reality was that psychology at the undergrad level was mostly about rats running mazes and experiments in human behaviors. He was bored to death. But, he also knew that if he didn't get through this phase his chances of being anything except a nine to five office worker, or worse, a "Pickles with that … ?" at McDonalds were pretty low. Worst of all, his depression was getting worse. He searched through his psych textbooks and found himself described on page 131. *Depression is more than just sadness.* He was really worried because the text stated he would eventually become overweight from stress eating and wouldn't be able to get laid because his equipment would cease to work ... shit!

He considered going back to the VA to do more volunteer work on the psych ward, but he just couldn't bring himself to do it. The endless hours of sitting in a stuffy room with chain-smoking veterans was just too horrible to bear. He wished that he could be allowed to be in on one-to-one patient sessions, but that was not permitted as those meetings were deemed too intimate.

The day was moving on. Finally he was in the car driving himself back to the house. "Another day closer to some goal," he hoped, without any self-awareness that he had accomplished nothing except to begin another fantasy that he would not turn into a reality.

The house was quiet as he made his way to his room. On his desk was the stack of rejection notices that taunted him cruelly. He grabbed them up and went to the kitchen to put them in the trash compactor. He was so intent on this task that when his mother said hello he jumped, scattering the letters all over the kitchen floor. His mother, superstitious Eastern European that she was, began poo-pooing to ward off the evil spirits. "Too late for that," he said. She looked him in the eye and poo-pooed him, too.

His mother stooped and helped him gather the papers, pausing to study one that caught her eye. "Sam," she said, slowly, still reading, "what's this?"

"Another letter of rejection. Give it here. I want them out of the house. It's time to move on."

"No, this one isn't a rejection. What is it?" she asked as she handed him the paper.

Sam took it and looked it over.

New Medical School Opening ...

"It's nothing, Mom. It was a flyer I found hung at school. I wrote to them, and the bastards didn't even have the decency to write back. It wasn't worth the postage."

"Sam, you can't write a letter to Mexico and expect an answer. It can take months to get there, if it gets there at all," she cried. "You need to call this George Romney person. Call him now."

"What do you mean, it takes months?"

"I lived in Latin America, mail doesn't show up. It gets held up, lost, in someone's pocket. You need to call, call now."

"But, it's late in Saltillo. I'm sure there is no one in the office."

"Call," she demanded.

Sam, defeated, did as he was told. He had nothing to lose. The ringtone was odd, but eventually there was a click and an American voice answered.

"Hola."

Sam looked at his mother, fluent in five languages. "Spanish speaker, can you ... ?"

"This is George Romney. Can I help you?"

"Oh Dr. Romney, this is Sam Cohen from San Diego."

"Can I help you?"

"I sent a letter about the school ... "

"Never got it. Are you calling about admission into the first year class or a transfer from another medical school?"

Sam wondered who would call to transfer from an American medical school to a Mexican one? Well, different strokes for different folks.

"Admission into the first year class. I am at the University of California ... "

"You need to get down here right away," Romney said urgently. "The class starts in four weeks and it is filling up fast. Do you have funds to pay for at least the first semester? Eventually you'll be eligible for Department of Education loans, but we are still working out the paperwork. Can you be here by next Wednesday? Señora Morales has office hours to speak to you then. Make sure to bring a check for $2,000 and another for $1,000, plus all your premed transcripts."

"About grades, I don't have the typical GPA for acceptance to ... "

"I'm sure. You did take premed subjects didn't you?"

"Yes, but I ... "

"Can you get here by Wednesday?"

"Uh, I guess, but don't you want to look at my ... ?"

"Great! We'll see you Wednesday, Seth."

"Uh, it's Sam."

Click! With that the line went dead.

Sam's mother was agitated. "What did he say? Can you get in?"

Sam was numb with shock. He had just been invited to his first medical school interview and he didn't even know if it would be conducted in English.

———•—•———

The next days were very complicated. His father with his engineering logic usually handled research and decisions for the family. Fortunately for him, and not so much for Sam, he was in Japan on business for his company and was unreachable. Sam called the major airlines flying into Mexico. None flew into Saltillo and most of them didn't know where or how to get there. He finally got hold of someone at AeroMexico who laughed and said the only way was to take a commuter flight that would get him to Monterrey and then he had to get to the bus station for the hour ride into Saltillo. "Buena suerte, the flight leaves from Tijuana International Airport." After all his years of goofing off in Tijuana, Sam had never known that there was an airport there.

Most of the residents of San Diego knew that to take your car into Tijuana was an invitation to have it ripped off. When driving down for the day you parked at a lot on the American side and then walked across the border. Sam couldn't contemplate leaving the family car there for a couple of days, so he'd need a ride. His mother bravely volunteered. This was a stretch for her since she drove an average of three miles a day. Driving to Tijuana involved getting onto a freeway and then driving thirty miles. Not to mention that she would then have to drive home alone. Despite this, she seemed eager to do it. He guessed that no matter the hardship, driving far away from home on her own, sending her son into an unknown place with unknown dangers, and not being able to see and talk to him everyday as she had done all his life became secondary to making sure she helped him achieve his dream.

Next, a quick trip to the Mexican consulate, where for a small sum, an expedited tourist visa could be obtained. While no paperwork was necessary for a trip to the border towns, any trip beyond the frontier required the red-printed piece of paper, stamped appropriately.

———◆———

Sam was scared, but that wasn't bothering him as much as the fact that he had no girlfriend who cared about him enough to share it with. This was momentous. He was about to reach for a real future that a man and a woman could build on together.

He phoned Leah when his mother was out of the house. "Hi, how are you doing?"

"Oh, Sam, what's going on?" she asked. "I haven't seen you at school lately." Leah was nonchalant in her tone compared to the exuberance he felt just being on the phone with her.

"I just wanted to tell you I got an interview for a med school. I'm leaving tomorrow. I just wanted to share this with my best … "

She cut him off, "Sam, I'm so happy for you. You must be walking on the ceiling."

"Look, maybe we can get together tonight, celebrate?"

There was a silence at the other end. "Sam, you are wonderful and deserve this. I'd love to get together with you, but I'm leaving tonight."

"Leaving? Where?" Sam was confused. She was leaving San Diego?

Leah tried to keep it light but firm. She was going to Israel to start her master's degree in social service. She once again stressed that they were on different roads and that she for one was up for a new life, one that didn't include Sam Cohen.

"But, we are supposed to be together forever … "

"Oh Sam, we were never supposed to be together in that way. I love you, but it would have never worked. I wish you success and happiness. Have fun down there … especially with all those pretty nurses."

His old life ended with the click of the phone.

———— • ————

They pulled into a strip mall parking lot. Cars sporting license plates from California, Arizona, and New Mexico were mixed with plates that had larger letters and numbers and points of origins such as B.C., Mexico or Sin, Mexico. Both Americans in shorts and t-shirts, and Mexicans, mostly in button-down short-sleeve shirts and jeans, were shopping in the Seven Eleven, hardware store, and the electronics shops.

Sam, nervous but eager to start his journey, embraced his mother. "I guess this is it, Mom. You sure you're OK getting back home?"

His mother held him tightly. He knew she would have held him there forever. "Sam, go safely and come back safely," she murmured in Yiddish. It was a phrase he had heard her say to him since his first day in kindergarten. "I love you, now go." She pushed him away and moved to get into the car. "I'll see you in a few days."

Sam watched her as she took off in the direction they had come from.

As he crossed the border, he instantly realized what a foreign land Mexico was. He looked up a hill to the fence separating the American side from the Mexican side of the border.

The grass on the American side of the fence was green while the Mexican side was brown. The Americans had landscaped their side of the border with expensive plants and irrigation. The hill looked like a park with flowers and bees and sweet fresh air. The beautiful scenery abruptly ended at a very tall chain-linked fence. Dead plants, dry dirt, and the occasional overgrown weed sprouted among broken bottles, used papers, and mangy looking dogs that defecated anywhere and everywhere on the hill. He was surrounded by dust and noise.

Sam hailed a cab.

"Can you take me to the airport?" he asked the cab driver in the bright red car decorated with Christmas lights.

"Hey amigo, you are on the wrong side of the border. Lindberg Field is 20 miles north and I'm not allowed past the border checkpoint."

"No, Tijuana International, can you take me there?"

"Why the fuck do you want to go out there? The planes are flown by children," the cab driver laughed—another crazy gringo, probably all drugged up.

"Look, my flight leaves in an hour. Can you take me or not?"

"Sure I can for $30 American, but you are nuts."

"$30? That seems a little high."

"Look *maricón*, $30 or find another cab. I'm busy." With that the cab driver pulled his hat rim down over his eyes and reclined in his seat.

"OK, let's go."

"It's your funeral."

———◆———

Flight 5951, or Vuelo 5951, was a local. Tijuana to Hermosillo. Hermosillo to Chihuahua. Chihuahua to Monterrey. Six hours and the sun quickly dropping in the sky as the plane headed east. The ground below was tan dirt and scrub brush. There were occasional cars on the roads, but otherwise very few signs of life. Occasionally a few lights appeared from what seemed to be no more than three or four buildings. He was lonely already. What had he gotten himself into?

Around ten p.m. he arrived in Monterrey, collected his bag, and went looking for a cab.

"Excuse me, Inglés?" he inquired at the first cab he came upon.

"Sí, I speak American. Do you need a cab?"

"Yes, I need to get to the bus station."

"Which one señor? We have two, Norte and Sur."

"I don't know. Which has a bus going to Saltillo? I need to get on the 11 o'clock bus or I'm stuck here till the morning."

"Which bus station do you want to go to, señor? I take you to either one."

"But, I don't know which one to go to. Wait, I'll ask someone in the airport."

Sam ran back into the terminal and at this time of night found the airport almost shut down. He finally found a custodian mopping the floor.

"Inglés?"

"Sí," the custodian replied.

"Do you know which station has the bus to Saltillo?"

"Sí, Saltillo," came a smiling reply. "Saltillo oeste."

"Huh, Saltillo bus?" Sam made sounds that he thought approximated a bus. The custodian looked at him like he was a moron, but started mimicking the noises back to him.

"Oeste, sí, Saltillo," he grinned.

Sam looked around, praying there might be someone else there, but no luck. He thanked the custodian and walked back out to the taxi stand where another cab had shown up. Thinking he might have better luck, he approached the second cab.

"Inglés?"

"Sí, I speak English, where do you want to go?"

"The bus station that has the bus that goes to Saltillo. I need to catch the 11 p.m. bus.

The bus driver slowly looked at his watch. "You'll never make it. I'll drive you to Saltillo, $100 American."

"One hundred dollars, are you kidding? I don't have that kind of money. Now can you take me to the bus station?"

Hearing the commotion the first cab driver woke up and started over to Sam. "Hey, you're not allowed to take his cab. It's illegal, I'm the next cab in line."

"But you don't know which bus station I need to go to."

"Hey, *mierda*, *chupame*! You should know which bus station for Saltillo. What are you, retarded?" He got out of the cab.

"You called me mierda, you *pendejo*. You steal a fare from me? I'll castrate you."

"You are a *cabron* and your woman is a *puta*. I know, she blew me last night."

Sam was stuck between the two of them as they started pulling out knives. He ran for it, neither of the cab drivers paying attention. Within a block he noticed a brightly lit building with a sign, Estacíon Autobus Oeste. West Bus Station. Sam ran in and found a ticket agent who was happy to sell him a one-way ticket to Saltillo, Primier Classe. As he settled himself into a frayed, poorly padded seat, among people, chickens, and crying children, he realized he had just survived his first cultural hassle.

The bus looked much like the one the Partridge Family used. As it pulled out of town, the streetlights fading behind them, Sam was struck by the darkness. The sky was dense with stars, more than he had ever seen in California. It was quite beautiful and very lonely. The only noise was the occasional brief stirring of a baby who was quieted at the breast. Even the snores from sleeping passengers were muted by the grinding drone of the bus's diesel engine, it's pungent fumes diluted by a rush of crisp cold air as the bus labored up the hills. An elderly Mexican man wearing a frayed sports jacket and ancient homburg murmured in Spanish in his sleep, his head finally resting on Sam's shoulder. Soon Sam's eyelids became heavy, and he too joined the rest of the passengers in sleep.

———◆———

The bus shook to a stop and the dim interior lights flashed on. "Saltillo," the driver called. Sam thought he had only just closed his eyes, but it was 12:30 in the morning and cold outside. He followed a line of people through a mostly deserted bus station to find the recommended hotel across the street. The lights of the hotel were off and the door closed. He pressed the doorbell, but, discovering it didn't work, knocked on the heavy oak door; its weathered and chipping black paint chafed his knuckles. His effort was in vain. No one came to open the door. He was cold and tired. All he wanted in the world was a bed on which to rest his head. It was 1 a.m. now. Sam reluctantly went over to a rusty, advertisement-papered phone booth, its door long ago rusted in the semi-open position, and light bulb dimmed by age. He slid in a peso, found the paper on which he'd written Romney's number, and dialed it.

One-ringee-dingee, but nothing like the rings in the States. Two, three, four and then "Hola?"

"Hi, Dr. Romney, this is Sam Cohen … "

"What time is it? Wait, aren't you from New York? Do you know what time it is here? Wait, it's later there. What do you want?"

"San Diego."

"What about San Diego? Did it drop into the ocean?"

"No, I'm from San Diego. I'm sorry. I know it's late. It's now one thirty in the morning."

"Well, call me when it's ten in the morning. Good night!

Romney was about to hang up when he heard a screech on the line. "WHAT!"

"I'm here, Dr. Romney. In Saltillo, but the hotel is closed. I don't know where to go. I'm sorry I'm disturbing you but if you can just tell me where another hotel is … "

"Another hotel, where do you think you are, Manhattan?"

There was a silence on the line. The bus station, its massive overhead lights going out one by one, was closing and the temperature was dropping. He could see his breath fogging up in front of him. He hadn't seen this since he had been a little boy in Chicago.

"I'll come and get you, stay where you are."

"Thank you, Dr. Romney. Oh, I'm about 6 foot … "

" … and probably the only American waiting in front of the bus station. Be there in twenty minutes."

"Thanks … ," but the line had already gone dead.

Light spilled through the mud-spattered windows as roosters announced the morning. Trucks with failing mufflers rattled down the street outside. Sam stretched but found the couch was too short, so he got up, feeling stiff, and looked around. Romney's apartment was concrete with old clay tile, painted in a peeling, institutional green color. The little bit of furniture looked like it came from donations to Goodwill. There was a radio, but no TV, and the window curtains were faded and dusty.

Romney stuck his head into the room. "*Bienvenidos a Mexico*! The bathroom is down that hall. Meet me in the kitchen when you're through. Breakfast will be served," he smiled.

After his morning routine, he walked into the kitchen grateful to be alive. Foreign smells, at once spicy and smoky, greeted him from the kitchen that was unlike any that would have been built in San Diego. The rudimentary stove was hooked up to a propane tank and bare wiring powered the electric service to a small refrigerator. No American safety standards there. He nervously wondered how many kitchens suddenly exploded on any given day.

"How do you like your eggs?" asked Romney. "I got chorizo and some bacon if you want."

"Just coffee would be great—and the eggs, thanks. I'm sorry about last night. I just didn't know where else to go and there weren't a lot of people around to ask."

"Yeah, Saltillo closes down after nine. Gotta get your boozing and whoring in before that."

Sam laughed uncomfortably. "Dr. Romney ... "

"First of all, Sam, I'm not a doctor just yet. I was the first American down here, so I sort of coordinate between Señora Morales and the American students. If you need transcripts, emergency leave, someone to talk to, I'm the one you come to."

"Well, that's cool I guess, but don't we have direct contact with the administration? I mean at UC San Diego, any student with problems in a class goes directly to the Department Head. This allows the departments to get to know you."

"Sam, remember this is Mexico; you're not in the States anymore. In the eight months I've been here we have averted most of the problems those poor bastards in Guadalajara have." He paused to sip his coffee, wincing, as if anticipating it would scald his lips. The eggs on his plate had most certainly gone cold.

"The students here come to me and I negotiate with Morales. So far it has been working out great. Don't worry, when you start classes you'll see how smooth life can be here." As if to prophesize the future, a truck backfired sounding like a shotgun had just fired a warning shot at Sam's life.

"You talk like I'm already accepted. I haven't even had my interview yet."

"You'll find Morales is pretty liberal with admissions and that unlike the States, getting into med school is easy. Making it through can be a challenge. They don't coddle in this country, they don't offer any special help, no special aides. It's usually you and a book. To make matters worse that book is in Spanish."

Sam felt the weight of the world on him. "You make it sound impossible. Studying medicine is hard. The education comes from experienced professors who want to train the new generation of doctors. This sounds like a correspondence course."

"I guess in some ways it is; the first two years is in the standard texts. The key is the second two years where you start seeing patients. That's when it really starts getting tough. In the first two years if you don't buckle down and study like you mean it, you will fail. Guaranteed. And you have only yourself to blame. The subjects are usually rote memorization. There are various study aids that pass from class to class, student to student here. The aids help you get through American testing."

"But, I don't see a hospital. Every medical school catalogue I ever read touted their great affiliated hospitals. Where do we practice on patients, assuming we even make it to the third year."

"That, my friend, is a matter of negotiation, and right now, you don't have to worry about that. In the meantime, why don't you go out and see the town. Get its flavor. You can also walk around and see about an apartment."

"I don't know if I have time for all that. What time is my interview this afternoon?"

"Morales can't see you for two days. You're scheduled in right after siesta ends."

"What! You told me the interview was set up for today. I can't hang around for two or three more days. I have classes and other obligations. Jesus, I'm scheduled for a flight back tomorrow afternoon!"

Romney's face clouded. "Look Sam, I know I've said this before but if you want to study medicine here, you'll have to remember this is Mexico. Remember that. You have to schedule yourself around a Mexican schedule. This isn't the US. Morales is the one making the rules. You have to play by those rules or you'll never get anything accomplished. I've seen people who couldn't figure that out. They got so frustrated they quit. All that time and money wasted and no MD after their name. I'm warning you."

Sam panicked. While Romney was sure he'd be admitted, what if he wasn't? He couldn't just skip his college classes. If this didn't work he was still minus a bachelor's degree. He then thought about home. With Dad out of town his mother was alone. He knew she was unused to dealing with the day-to-day all by herself and he felt guilty about not being there to help her.

"George, please, can you try to get me in today? It's important. I have classes to attend and other family responsibilities. I have to leave tomorrow."

Romney thought about it, scraping his fork across his plate, spearing the last of his eggs in its tines; finally, he shook his head. "I don't know, Sam. Morales is at the school, but frankly she does this as a power trip."

Sam was confused. "What do you mean?"

"There is a psychology here. The Mexicans have some sort of inferiority complex in all dealings with Uncle Sam. Something about them thinking we stole California and Texas. This even flows down to the personal level. Morales always needs to feel she has the upper hand on the gringos. Tell you what, do you have those checks I told you to bring?"

Sam dug out the two checks he had prepared in San Diego. Tuition for $2,000 and the other for $1,000 in administrative fees. Sam couldn't figure out what the $1,000 was for until Romney just laughed and told him to think of it as rent for living in the Mexican territories of California through Texas. Morales imposed the fee on all gringos that wanted to become doctors.

Romney told Sam to show up at the school in three hours. "Maybe this will be a lucky day for you."

***

With nothing else to do, Sam spent the next three hours exploring the town. The buildings were all poured concrete with shutters over the windows. Each was painted a bright color that the weather had faded over time. The town was beautiful in a European, old world sort of way.

The people were dressed in layers of cheap clothes. On most of the T-shirts were ads for American brands of food or sporting equipment.

The people were friendly and welcoming. Here in Saltillo, unlike most of the border towns he had visited, a lot of people did not speak English.

He had lunch at a small hole in the wall and was introduced to *rajas*, a tortilla filled with cheese and sautéed cactus that was delicious. In broken Spanish, Sam had explained to the waiter he wanted something meatless. He was afraid of what he had seen walking the town. The butcher shops were mostly open-air affairs with little or no refrigeration. Beef hung from rafters, either in strips or as gutted carcasses. Flies circled the offerings with impunity looking for a place to eat, shit, and lay eggs. The waiter was confused. He probably thought Sam was a nut job, as it was rare in Mexico to not have meat at a meal. Vegetarianism had not made much headway in Saltillo, but Sam really didn't want to spend hours on a plane with tainted meat trying to escape his colon in the worse way.

At the appointed time he was in front of the school and his heart sank. This was a medical school? The entrance was a gate that was built into a wall that went all around the school. Over the arch a sign proclaimed:

Escuela por Estudios Español

Tacked on underneath was a hand painted sign that looked like a bed sheet.

Benito Juarez-Abraham Lincoln Escuela de Medicina

Sam entered and found a postcard-perfect courtyard with planter boxes full of bougainvillea. The floor was composed of dark brown hexagonal clay tiles and the walls had mosaics of grouted multi-hued broken ceramics with the occasional mirrored piece thrown in. The classrooms circled the courtyard. Most of them had blackboards and student desks. Only one bore any resemblance to what he thought a medical classroom should look like. It had a dozen old-fashioned student microscopes, some in disrepair, and boxes of slides. He did not see a slide projector, lab, or even a door that indicated there were bodies for dissection inside.

How was he to learn medicine in such a place? Sam felt like he had wasted his time and was ready to walk out the gate when he heard footsteps.

"Here you are, Sam!" Romney had found him and was smiling. "I have good news. Sra. Morales will see you now. You did bring the checks?"

"Checks are here. She'll interview me now?"

"Let's go. Remember, I'll talk if there are any weird questions … "

"Weird questions? I don't understand, what kind of weird questions?"

"You'll see. Come on, she won't wait."

Romney led Sam down the hall to a heavy, dark brown, carved wooden door labeled Administrative Offices. He pushed the door open and a beautiful, dark-eyed Mexican girl not more than eighteen was sitting at a receptionist desk. She saw Romney and greeted him with a big smile.

"Jorge, she is waiting for you. You know she doesn't like to be kept waiting."

Romney smiled, "I know, Amor, but this candidate needed some instructions on how to get around the town. This is Samuel Cohen."

The secretary gave Sam a once-over with her eyes and smiled. She seemed to like what she saw. "Hola, Sr. Cohen. I am Rosa, the secretary of Señora Morales. Welcome to Saltillo and the Benito Juarez-Abraham Lincoln Escuela de Medicina. I trust you had no problems getting here."

"Well, it was sort of difficult," Sam started.

Romney immediately broke in, "But he was so pleased with how accommodating the people are in this town. Isn't that so, Sam?"

Sam slowly nodded, "Uh, yes, it was great."

"She is expecting you, Sam, but have a seat as she is on the phone with a very important official in the US Government. She knows you are here."

Sam and Romney sat and waited. Sam couldn't argue with the scenery. Rosa's full lips, her dark, downturned eyes steadily on her work, and her fine breasts, swelling with each breath, could have—under other circumstances—held his attention all day, but after a full forty-five minutes he just couldn't sit anymore. He started to rise, but was quickly shoved down by Romney.

"Sit still, Sam, this is all part of the process here in Mexico."

"What do you mean?"

"I mean this is where you wait with respect for Morales. When she decides you've waited long enough, she'll invite you into her office."

"You mean she's not on the phone?"

"I doubt it. She's probably doing her nails. She and Rosa both love to do their nails. I think they have a club."

Sam looked at the beautiful secretary, and, sure enough, bottles of garish colored nail polish were set out on her desk along with various used cotton balls. At least she smiled as she looked at Sam.

A phone rang and Rosa answered in Spanish. "Señor Cohen, Jorge … you can go in now," Rosa said as she gestured toward the door. Sam's stomach dropped and he felt lightheaded. It wasn't the way he had envisioned it happening, but it was happening now. In the next half hour his future would be closer to his dream or his future would smell like stale beer and vomit.

George whispered, "Remember: Take your cues from me." Sam was about to ask him what cues exactly, but he found himself in a room that could have been a copy of Maurice Goldman's office back in San Diego. The desk was massive with dark wood, and instead of the pictures of celebrities, Señora Morales had a large tapestry of the crest of the school hanging behind her desk. It was the strangest thing Sam had ever seen. There was the profile of Abraham Lincoln and another profile he supposed was Benito Juarez, both facing each other. Romney later told Sam that President Benito Juarez was considered the Lincoln of Mexico, both having been born poor and self-educated. Romney thought that Morales added Lincoln to the school's name as a signal to Americans to come to this "American" medical school. The tapestry also had a red cross and a dove and reminded Sam of a box of Smith Brothers cough drops.

"Jorge, *quien es*?" came a voice from a large leather chair behind the desk. The chair swiveled around and Sam saw a small, broad woman about sixty years old. Shit, she looked like Maurice Goldman, with hair.

"This is Sam Cohen from San Diego. He wishes to study at your school," George replied.

"Ah Señor Cohen, welcome to Saltillo. Have you been to Mexico before?"

"No, Señora Morales, it is quite a beautiful country. The people are friendly." He nervously started to say, "I'd like to explain my organic chemistry grades ... "

"Sam, Señora Morales wanted to know what you thought of the school's facilities?"

"Well, I haven't seen anything but one classroom with some old micro ... "

George cut Sam off again. "The building is beautiful, isn't it? It also houses the language school ... "

Sam, puzzled, didn't know what to say and was frozen, looking intently at Señora Morales. There was an uncomfortable silence in the room.

"I think you will do very well here. You have the deposit to hold your place in the class? We start in three weeks," Señora Morales smiled.

"Don't you want to know anything about me? My grades? Why I want to be a doctor?

"Sam ... Señora Morales knows you from your application probably better than you know yourself. She prides herself in knowing people," George said quietly. "You would consider it an honor to study at her school ... am I right?" He asked, with a big smile.

Morales looked at Sam, nodding, "Es verdad, it is true?"

"I ... " Sam paused. "I want to be a doctor ... "

"Of course you do, Señor Cohen. Do you have the check for the January semester?" She stood with her hand out.

"Sam, give Señora Morales the checks and you'll be in medical school," George whispered.

Sam set the checks in Morales's waiting hand. He realized that this was a momentous occasion.

"Congratulations, Sam. You're on the road to a long and satisfying career in medicine."

Morales continued nodding, "Es verdad."

———•———

Sam and George walked out of the school. The sun seemed brighter, the air fresher, and everyone they passed appeared to have a smile on their face.

"I can't believe it," Sam was in shock. "She didn't ask anything. Why didn't she want to know anything?"

"What does it matter? Morales just wants to fill her classes with paying customers, translate that to students. You're an American, brought money, and don't look like a troublemaker. You're exactly the type of student she wants here," George said.

"But, my grades, what I want for the future, admission tests ... "

"Sam, you've got to get it into your head that it's different here. When you're in class on day one, look at the person on your right, then look to the person on your left. I guarantee you won't see them at graduation. In other words, this was by far the easy part."

"The easy part, huh. I'll make sure to attend classes and study ... "

"Well, there are a lot of distractions down here. The bars are open twenty-four hours a day, women are available on a fee for service basis and just sitting in the classes and studying for the school's tests is not going to get you through the American Board exams. You'll have to do two times the studying for them."

"I can do the studying, and as far as the rest ... well, I can become a monk, if need be. I'm going to just study. I still can't believe it. I'm actually going to be studying medicine."

"Yes, you are," but George didn't seem enthused. In fact he seemed depressed. He couldn't make eye contact with Sam. As they walked, George's end of the conversation became more monosyllabic, and then he would just grunt at appropriate times. Sam didn't notice that the signals being broadcast by George were not positive. Sam was just too proud of his future. At this point Sam thought, "Damn the torpedoes, full speed ahead."

"Come on. We have to get your stuff and get you on that bus back to Monterrey." George grabbed him by the arm and pulled him down the road.

———•———

Sam had put together lists of objects necessary for living in the third world. Clothes, books, typewriter, candles, sheets, towels. "Maybe we should just hire a moving van to get all your crap into Mexico," Sam's dad, always the practical one, said as he looked over Sam's list. George had told Sam that buying anything in Saltillo was expensive and the quality wasn't the same as the States.

"Tuna? There is an embargo of canned tuna in Mexico? What, the Mexicans only eat tacos?"

"Pop, George said that canned food is three times as expensive in Mexico and canned is good because most of the places to live don't have refrigerators."

"Hmm, well I'll get your mother started on these lists," he said, reading through them with an intensity that should have been reserved only for reading the *New York Times*. "You know how she loves shopping and finding a bargain. Sonia!"

"Harvey?" His mother walked into the room, a smile on her face. "Yes dear, you bellowed?"

"I need you here for a small ceremony," Harvey looked very serious as he turned to Sam.

"Your mother and I wanted to tell you how proud we are that you have been able to fulfill a dream."

"Thanks Pop, but if it weren't for Mom and you, well none of this would have happened," Sam said quietly. "Thank you for being there. I don't think I would have been able to get through the rejections without knowing that you still had faith in me."

"No, we are the proud parents of a son who didn't give up.

Anyway we just wanted you to go to Mexico with a few tokens of our pride and love."

His father pulled a bag out of the closet. "Now close your eyes!"

He started giving things to his wife who then went over and "dressed" Sam.

Sam still obediently had his eyes closed. "Hey, what's going on guys?"

He felt a jacket being pulled on over his shoulders and things being placed in pockets and finally something being placed around his neck.

"OK, now keep your eyes closed. We are going to lead you," his father laughed.

Sam felt himself being tugged down the hallway.

"Harvey, get the camera."

"Oh, Mom, not the camera."

"Shush," his mother admonished, "he is so excited, he couldn't even sleep last night."

"OK, the camera is ready, Sam, open your eyes," his father said.

Sam opened his eyes and was immediately blinded by the flash. As his eyes cleared he saw both parents beaming at him with pride.

"Oh Sam, my doctor, so handsome." She immediately came over to hug and kiss him.

"Sonia, give the doctor some room to breathe."

Sam found himself in front of the full-length hallway mirror. He was in a long white coat, crisply starched. In the front breast pocket were a pen and penlight. In another pocket was a blood pressure cuff and around his neck was a fancy Harvey triple-headed stethoscope, which he took off and held tightly. This would be his talisman through the rest of his life. His eyes welled up. Embarrassed, he was unable to stop an errant tear running down his cheek.

His parents had always been supportive, but this culmination of a horrendous year of uncertainty, failure, and just plain bad luck always had the cushion of his parent's love and unwavering support to soften the blows. He had come to expect the support and like most emotions in life eventually under-appreciated it. He just didn't have the words to tell them they meant everything to him, that he could never have gotten through this without them, that he owed them so much. As he responded to their presentation he knew that whatever he said was inadequate.

"I don't know what to tell you guys. Thank you, I love you so much," Sam stammered. He really didn't have the words to tell them how much their love, support, and confidence in him meant. As he looked at them, seeing their joy he realized that he really didn't need the words, they understood.

"The clerk in the store said this is the best stethoscope they have," his father grunted. "He said he thought Dr. DeBakey, the famous cardiac surgeon, had one. I told him that my son needs it in order to send him off to be the best doctor he can be."

Chapter 2

The Presidents of Saltillo

On the wide and open road, Sam imagined himself as George Maharis driving a 60s Corvette in *Route 66*. "Cue that iconic music," he thought.

Sam drove east through the suburbs of San Diego and then through the wilderness and desert. The day was sunny, his thoughts were cloudy. The one constant in his life was his parents. Unlike many of his friends and classmates, Sam didn't have major problems with them. They had always had his back. The year he had gone away to school hadn't afforded him any more personal freedom than when he lived at home. They tirelessly supported him, and he surprised himself as he realized they had become more to him as an adult than he had expected. They had become his friends.

The car radio began to lose the rock station, turning to static, and he worked through the stations he could now pick up, finding only country music.

Federal Highway 8, San Diego to Casa Grande, Arizona. Then hang a right and get on Federal Highway 10, Casa Grande to Van Horn, Texas. There were miles and miles of empty desert. Sometimes a brightly lit gas station beckoned and sometimes it was a tourist trap rest area hawking silver and turquoise made in China.

By now the only music on the radio gave him the message that Jesus saves and his best friend was that mangy dog on the porch.

The sunsets were beautiful, as were the sunrises. He continued moving east.

From Van Horn he made another right and started down Texas Route 90. He was in a foreign land. He drove through dozens of little towns, each proclaiming "Potable water."

Del Rio, Texas border town. He was about to enter Mexico. He found a rest stop and placed a quick coded long-distance phone call to his parents before he crossed into Mexico. He didn't know when he'd actually be able to hear their voices again. His new life was about to begin. Was there a sign somewhere that said, "Abandon hope all ye who enter here?"

Mountains, rain, clouds, slick roads, and mud. Roads full of potholes, little shacks that sold Coca-Cola and unidentifiable meat cooked on a fire-pit grill reminding Sam of Memorial Day barbeques at home. Corn tortillas crisping and flies and bird droppings everywhere. The entire establishment under a sparse thatched roof, open air stand. He drove and drove. There was no place to stop and rest anyway on Highway 57 Mexico.

He reached a crest in the road just as the sun was going down. Twinkling lights in the cool air. Just down the road was Saltillo; the capital of the State of Coahuila is considered the Denver of Mexico because of its height above sea level. At one time it had been the capital of the State of Coahuila y Tejas, before the gringos from the North did a land grab and re-named the area Texas. This was to be his future home. He had made it.

Sam pulled up to a large house on a side street. He re-checked the sign on the corner and it matched the paper that he had stuffed in his wallet. Avenida del Revolucción No. 19. This was the home of his host family. Señora Morales hadn't yet figured out where to build a dorm and charge the students an arm and a leg for room and board. In the meantime, Sam was sure that whatever he was paying these people for a room, there was a kickback ending up in Morales's pocket.

"Bienvenidos, Señor Cohen. Welcome to our home." Señor Rudolfo was a large, happy, fortyish man who had signed onto the school's "Family for Students" program. He had two younger children and a plus-sized wife who spoke no English, but always had a smile on her face.

"We have prepared your room and dinner will be ready soon. You must be hungry and tired after the trip from California. I can help you unpack your car after dinner. You don't want to leave your belongings outside after dark."

"Gracias, Señor Rudolfo, maybe I can … " Sam was interrupted as the most obese man he had ever seen entered the room.

"Another gringo has arrived. Well Rudolfo, there goes the neighborhood. Hi, I'm Marvin, your new roomie. Welcome to Mexico," the man burst out.

Sam was transfixed. Marvin was short, maybe five foot five, but he must have weighed close to 300 pounds. He had a cherubic face with ruddy cheeks and a toothbrush mustache. His arms and legs were logs and his abdomen made him look eighteen months pregnant. His eyes twinkled. He seemed to be a happy soul.

"What, you've never seen a fat man?" Marvin asked.

"I … I … sorry, I wasn't staring," Sam stammered.

"Of course you were … "

"No, I … "

"Don't worry about it roomie, you aren't the first and won't be the last. Come on, let me show you the digs. Rudolfo, when's dinner?"

"*Media hora*, half hour, *mas o menos*."

Marvin said to Sam, "OK, twenty minutes to get you situated. I obviously don't miss a meal for anything."

As they walked through the hacienda, Marvin said with

a falsely formal tone, "I'm Marvin Goldberg. Welcome to the possibility of a future."

"Well, I'm Sam Cohen, and I hope this works out."

"Amen brother," Marvin said with a sigh. "There are now about thirty ex-pats that are hoping the same thing you are. I didn't realize that Romney had targeted the west coast also. Almost all of us come from the New York area. Strangely for an Irish guy he targeted mostly Jews to come down here."

"How is the school? The little I saw … well it seemed a little primitive," Sam said tentatively. "Maybe I'm wrong. I mean this was obviously the only school I could get into."

"Nah, I think primitive is a good word. Maybe non-existent. Look, all the Americans that came down here were desperate. None of them had another choice. It wasn't as if Harvard had invited any one of us to matriculate and we picked Ol' Benito-Abe Med School. This is everyone's last chance. The only thing that everyone here has in common is desperation. We are all goddamn desperate to be doctors. We'll see how many go all the way."

"What about you, Marvin?" Sam was curious. Marvin was not exactly what Sam thought was the med school type. Aside from his obesity, he was old. Sam guessed if he was not already forty, he was knocking on that door.

"Me? I'm here for the exotic lifestyle and the Latina women. They say Latina women like big men."

———

20 years before …

"Marvin, I'm sorry," his mother cried, blubbering. "It's just that your father had planned to make sure that you had enough for all your schooling, but when he died unexpectedly there wasn't anything left."

"Yeah, and the little that was left you spent looking for a new man," Marvin thought blackly.

"We don't even have enough for next semester's tuition and as much as I would like a job, you know how my back is."

Marvin pushed any thoughts of his stepmom on her back away. He wanted to continue college and get away from this bitch, but it seemed as though he was stuck. Besides, despite how she screwed up his life, Marvin had promised his father that he would take care of her.

"Don't worry about it. I think I have lined up a job that will keep us sheltered and fed. I'm interviewing for it today. They said they're looking for intelligent guys that are in shape and could use their muscles if need be."

Marvin was just barely twenty, 165 pounds, handsome and well-muscled. He grabbed his coat and headed for the biggest employer in this part of the Bronx, the Bronx-Lebanon Hospital.

---

15 years later ...

It was a raw day. Grey, damp, windy, befitting the funeral of the woman he had supported for 15 years. She had never once made it easy for him. Alcohol, drugs, a succession of "uncles" and one night stands for cash in hand. He had stayed with her, keeping his promise to his long dead father. That was done, but the damage was done, also. The handsome, athletic boy had become the bitter, out of shape wreck. He never succumbed to the greater vices that his stepmother used to cope with the pain, but he had retreated into himself, caring little what the world saw or how he would survive.

The rabbi gave the last benediction, Marvin grabbed the shovel, scooped the earth up and dumped it on the box. He took one last look, gathered his coat lapels together against the cold, and walked off to his job. He would never come back to the gravesite again.

His days were all the same. Get up, eat, food shop, read sci-fi or mystery novels, a little magazine porn for relief before the nap, and off to work on the night shift as a Psychiatric Attendant at the Bronx-Lebanon Hospital.

It was midnight on the ward. Marvin was sitting behind his desk watching the few psychiatric patients who never seemed to sleep. He was friendly with the crazies. Depressed, schizophrenic, bipolar, they were all more palatable as companions than the other inmates of the ward. Those inmates were called doctors and were only incarcerated for eight hours at a time. They were supposed to be a help, but they never seemed to care enough to do their exalted job.

"Hey Marvin, can you get outta that chair long enough to make some fucking coffee? I swear you are the laziest SOB I have ever met."

"Dr. Schwartz, you know it's not my job to make coffee. There is stuff in the pantry to make it if you want to."

"Marvin, I don't give a shit if it's in your job description or not. Go make the fucking coffee," Schwartz yelled.

By this time the antics of the doctor were agitating the patients. It wasn't fair to the patients and he didn't want to clean up a potential battlefield. When this group of patients got agitated they had a tendency to start fighting and Marvin didn't want to call an emergency to restrain them. Besides the paperwork was a bitch.

Marvin got up to make the coffee and when he got back he found that the asshole doctor was mentally torturing Mr. Kelly. Kelly was a big Irishman who was depressed. His depression stemmed from being molested as a child by a succession of priests. He had tried to tell his parents, but the simple religious folk had called him a liar and placed him in the tender care of the Church for more hours of abuse.

Kelly had received strong medication and electroshock which made him quiet and very forgetful. He had become Schwartz's favorite whipping boy.

"Hey Kelly, tell me again about being an alter boy. Where did you put the candles?" Schwartz laughed.

"Dr. Schwartz," Marvin said quietly. "You're agitating him, please let him rest."

Dr. Schwartz now found a new target. "Excuse me Dr. Marvin, are you offering some medical advice?" he roared.

"I'm just saying he is getting really agitated and sometimes has problems controlling his anger. Maybe for everyone's sake you should let up. Kelly, take it easy. Dr. Schwartz didn't mean anything by it. Come on, why don't we see if there is any ice cream left in the freezer."

"Yeah Kelly, why don't you go with Marvin? Marvin, you like an occasional fag encounter don't you? I'm sure Kelly can explain how it's done."

Kelly attacked. Marvin tried to get him off Schwartz, but instead he was flung off and smashed into the wall. The lights went out.

As he opened his eyes he saw Kelly pounding Schwartz into a pulp with his fists. Marvin tried to get up but his head spun when he tried. He finally crawled over to Kelly imploring him to stop and then physically tried to stop him. Marvin was flung across the room again. His last thought as he again lost consciousness, was that there was going to be an opening for a competent psychiatrist on the ward.

———◆———

Marvin was in traction for two weeks. Dr. Schwartz had been killed, but thanks to Marvin's account, Kelly was sent to a secure ward for the psychiatrically dangerous and not to jail.

Eventually Marvin went back to being an attendant, but he had changed. He wanted to be a psychiatrist. After seeing incompetents and outright sadists like Schwartz, he knew he could help these patients; maybe he could even help himself. He started taking classes he had missed by not finishing college. He took classes by day and worked by night. His diet seemed like one long greasy fast food burger, no exercise and little sunlight. The stress was also starting to get to him—he ate more and more, his weight ballooning past 300 pounds.

A couple of the nurses tried to help him with his ward duties but it didn't work. He finally finished his BA five years later. He registered with the premed office to get his application and recommendations together.

Mr. Smith was a nice, older man who taught general chemistry. He had been saddled with the responsibility of premed advisor. Smith's job was to help the applicants achieve medical school admission, but so far his success rate was about 2%. He hated the disappointed looks, the quiet tears. What could he do—there weren't enough schools in this country and they all demanded straight As and a "well-rounded life." Jesus, what did the med schools think, that perfect grades and being a football star equaled a good doc? Bullshit! But Smith was a small cog and the schools chose the ones they thought fulfilled this template. He was left with the psychological aftermath.

"Here is another disaster in the making," he thought as he picked up Marvin's file. "Science GPA of 2.96 and he is thirty-nine years old. What the hell has he been doing all these years?" He read Marvin's personal statement and was moved. A man who cared for a mother with substance abuse becomes a caregiver for the mentally ill, then kills himself to get a degree while still working. Now he finds that no med school in the US will take him.

Marvin knocked on the open door. "Shit, not only too old, but also too fat; certainly not a Dr. Kildare or Ben Casey," Smith thought. "I can't help him, but maybe?"

———•———

Marvin was hopeful and felt alive for the first time in a long time. He appreciated Smith's honesty. He knew it would be difficult getting into a US medical school. He just didn't realize that it would be impossible, but he still could be a doctor. It would take a car and a visa, then a lot of luck. He went directly to the bank. There was a 1968 Lincoln Continental he was dying to own.

———•———

The sun came up late and it was cold. Frost painted the dirty window panes sending rainbows of color into the room. The ubiquitous roosters announced the morning in a cacophony of screeching across Saltillo.

The first day of school. In a moment of weakness he remembered how, as a child, his mother took him to the store to buy pencils, paper, notebooks, and pens. Who would walk him to school his first day here in Mexico? He had imagined independence would be synonymous with self-confidence. Not so, he realized, as he ran his hands through his hair and down over the stubble on his cheeks. Shit.

Sam got out of bed seeing that Marvin had already showered and was probably eating his double breakfast and downing gallons of coffee. He jumped out of bed, showered, and shaved. He smelled the breakfast of bacon, hot spices, and eggs and knew he couldn't eat a thing.

Marvin was on his second round of eggs, coffee, chorizo, and tortillas. Bright pieces of yellow egg dotted his mouth and chin. "You're up early," he said, lifting a forkful of chorizo to his lips.

"What do you mean, early? It's eight-thirty. If we don't pick up the pace, we'll be late. Do you have any idea how they dress for school here? I have some button-down shirts and khakis. I really want to make a good impression." Sam was fidgeting with excitement.

Marvin started laughing. "Oh, my God, you have so much to learn about this place. Nine means ten thirty, possibly eleven. Nine in the morning I doubt Morales's maid has even opened Madam's blackout curtains yet."

"So why are you up if it's too early to get to the school?"

"Food, baby, food. It takes a lot to keep this magnificent body fueled up and raring to go. Grab a cup of coffee and I'm sure the Missus will make you a hearty breakfast. Then we can browse through a five-day-old copy of the *El Paso Times*. We leave here and go to the school in an hour and a half. Now, what do you want in your eggs?

They stepped through the bougainvillea-decorated gate at precisely ten forty-five. There were about twenty Americans loudly complaining that they had been here for over an hour and a half, to which Marvin sagely nodded his head at Sam. "See, right again."

Sam decided to seek out some of the other students to expand his social life. Most of the students were his age with a smattering of oldsters in their mid-thirties, and a couple of youngsters under twenty. Many had the same story as Sam—grades not good enough. Some believed they screwed up the interviews as they were straight A students. Sam thought that most of them had probably screwed up the interview, as they all seemed to be uncomfortable interacting with the other students who were there.

The majority of the older students were second or third career people. They were PhD candidates in the sciences who had wised up when it dawned on them how little they would make as scientists. The smell of Porsche leather became the attainable dream. The social workers, most of whom had been in their respective fields forever, finally tired of beating their heads against the wall trying to "cure" the incurable of drug addiction, or chronic non-employment due to lack of education. Maybe becoming a surgeon and taking out gallbladders would compensate for all the pain they had had to deal with in their lives.

They were all in the central courtyard standing around waiting for the start of class. Tables were brought out with little cakes, coffee, and tea. Suddenly, a group of six thug-like, burley Mexican males entered the room followed by Señora Morales.

"*Jovenes*, welcome to your school," she boomed. "You are all very fortunate to be in the first class at the Benito Juarez-Abraham Lincoln Escuela de Medicina. You will be offered a first-class education comparable to the Harvard in Estados Unídos."

"As good as Harvard. I'll be glad to get an education comparable to Moose U. in the States. Bizarre," Sam thought.

"We will start with Spanish language classes for the next weeks, till we are ready for the first medical class. All classes will start at … "

"Señora Morales, is there any word as to completion of the accreditation process?" one of the younger men asked.

Morales looked icily at the student. The courtyard went silent.

"We will be fully accredited very soon. Now your Spanish classes … "

"How soon Señora Morales? I would really like to start my medical school classes."

"Soon! Class is dismissed." Morales marched angrily to the exit, but the students were now murmuring and not listening to her instructions.

"What do you mean a week? Why aren't classes starting tomorrow? We're here, the professors are here, aren't they?" Lots of heads nodded agreement, but what most of the students didn't notice was that the thugs who had initially surrounded the class in the courtyard looked like they were about to pounce.

From next to Sam came a loud voice, "Come on everyone. It's not so bad. We just got a week's vacation in a town with a lot of bars and cheap beer! Let's start the drinking. God knows I'm thirsty!" Marvin laughed and began heading for the gate. The recommendation broke the spell and some of the students started moving out.

Sam turned to Marvin. "What are you doing? I'd like some answers. What's this accreditation? Isn't the school accredited? Shit."

"We have to get everyone out of here. See the bullyboys?" Marvin whispered, pointing to the thugs. "If we don't clear out and play by the rules, they'll start swinging. After that La Policía arrives. You don't want that."

Sam, aghast, looked at Marvin.

"Let's get out of here and get a beer. We'll talk then."

———◆———

They went to a local bar. Day went to night as the only illumination inside came from dim bulbs and neon signs advertising Tecate beer. The sawdust on the scarred, wood floor smelled of stale beer and urine and the three patrons appeared so drunk they barely raised their heads as Sam and Marvin entered.

"I don't understand. What just happened?" Sam felt like he had been kicked in the groin. It was obvious he was not in medical school at this point, but what was he doing here?

"The reality of trying to go to medical school in Mexico became apparent. Like the States, all these schools are supposed to be accredited by one of the National University accrediting sources. This being

Mexico there are ways to start admitting students and calling yourself a licensed school before formal accreditation is conferred."

"But, how does this happen?"

Marvin chuckled, "Same way we got accepted to the school; they paid."

"You mean Morales paid someone off at the National University?"

"Probably, but not only can you not prove it, it really works against you to protest. The way these things work she could still get accreditation and all your paperwork would just be backdated."

"So she will get accreditation," Sam sighed in relief.

"No, I actually think she won't. The process that she has been going through has been taking too long. According to the snooping I have been able to do this is the sixth 'next week' she has told everyone. That means she has suddenly fallen into disfavor at the National University or, and this is a big one, she can't come up with enough pesos to pay the bill for full accreditation."

"Full accreditation?"

Marvin became pensive, "Yeah, full accreditation, hence Romney."

Sam was confused, "Romney? What does he have to do with this?"

"He was her best chance for muchos Yankee dollars. He lured desperate students down to Saltillo and then helped her shear them of their money."

Sam started hyperventilating, "Oh fuck, I might as well leave now. Maybe applying to psychology school wasn't such a bad idea. Do you think I can sue Morales for fraud? Shit, I don't even think I have enough cash to pay for the gas back to San Diego … "

Marvin firmly told Sam to calm down. "You're not going anywhere yet.

"But Marvin, I feel like I was violated. She screwed us."

"Yeah, and you didn't even get kissed first, or maybe you did. You still have a chance of going to med school. It just might take some extra work. Come on, we have things to do."

"Where are we going?"

Marvin smiled. "To see a friend."

———•———

Andy Blumenkranz was in his rented house surrounded by boxes and listening to the soundtrack of his life for the last decade: his wife's constant shrieking.

"Andy, this house isn't big enough for us. We don't have a bedroom for each of the girls. They're seven and five now—they need some privacy."

Andy sighed knowing this was not the start of anything pleasant. "Why, Marla? They're kids and both girls. What kind of privacy could they need? Besides, this place is more than we can afford already."

"Yeah, and whose fault is that?"

Andy knew he had lost once again. How do you reason with someone who has no concept of economic reality? A knocking on the door saved him from more complaining and brooding, neither of which he needed if he wanted to get all moved in by tomorrow.

"Come on in," Andy said, "door's open."

Marvin and Sam walked into the house. "Hey Andy, how's it going?"

"Andy you miserable a-hole, did you find the can opener yet? The kids are hungry," Marla screamed from the other room.

Andy smiled at Marvin and Sam. "Couldn't be better, I know where the pacifier is. Give me a second." Andy reached into a box and came up with the can opener. "I found it dear," he said, as he trotted into the other room.

"Jesus, who is this guy?" Sam asked, amazed.

"One of the smarter ones here. Unfortunately he got smart after he married the bitch and knocked her up ... twice."

Andy returned. "So what can I do you for Marvin, and who is your partner?"

"This is Sam. We need some help. I think you need to become Moses and start the Exodus."

Andy looked at both of them and smiled. "Marla, stop unpacking."

"You fucking bastard!" a shriek came from the other room.

Sam, Marvin, and Andy went to the back yard with bottles of cold Dos Equis.

Marvin started, "I think Morales is stringing us along."

Andy took a pull on the beer. "So, what else is new. I'm guessing there is more than the usual bullshit going on? What happened at the opening festivities today?"

Sam exploded, "She brought us down to a school that is worthless. She took money from us for nothing."

"Hey, calm down youngster," he said firmly. "The first principle of foreign medical schools is that if they can fuck you for more money, you can bet your last dollar that they will. Better get used to it. Now what happened at the meeting that I didn't attend because of, how shall I say it? Spousal maintenance?"

Marvin and Sam related the high points of the meeting as Andy absorbed the information. He didn't appear upset or surprised. Andy was used to disappointments. He also knew that for every problem, if one were flexible, a solution could be found. Andy was older and knew that this was just another bump in the road of his life. He had had bumps before, way more bumps.

10 years ago …

"Oh God baby, it's sooo good … "

Marla was exciting him like no other woman had and he couldn't believe that on their fifth date he was actually getting laid … and re-laid. The woman was insatiable.

"Marla, are you on something … ?"

"Go for it, stud, I want it."

And that was all it took.

———

There was something to afterglow. Here he was in bed with this hot woman who was snoring quietly beside him, warm and loving. He was happy. He met Marla at a family event. She was the unmarried cousin from the other side of the family. The unmarried girl who was invited to mix with the single guys. Maybe they could hook her up and create another family event.

Andy bit. He had just obtained his teaching certificate and had landed a great starter job as a high school biology teacher. The pay wasn't great, but he was single, with no college debt thanks to part time jobs and the City College of New York. Life was great. The only problem was his love life. He had had the usual girlfriends and one-night stands, but nothing really stuck. Because of school and work he really never had the time or money to have a long-term relationship. Now he needed someone in his life. He wanted a wife, kids, and the American dream, or at least the Brooklyn dream.

Maybe Marla was the one. She was OK looking, a bit on the loud and coarse side. He was excited by that. He too could be the same way. Now he found out she was a sexual dynamo. Man, there weren't many Jewish girls like that in his experience.

Marla stirred beside him. "Hey, stud," she said as her hand found ground zero, "think you can rise to the occasion?"

"Shit, yeah!"

---

3 months later ...

"Crap," the phone rang. He had almost escaped from the apartment. The ringing phone kept him from leaving. He knew it was Marla and he felt guilty. He couldn't stand her anymore. But what did he owe a woman who gave him sex whenever he wanted it, any way he wanted it? She was just so crude and demanding. Then there were the conversations. If he had to listen one more time to how her cousin married a doctor and now had a big house in the Five Towns he was going to kill himself. He picked up the ringing phone.

"Hello."

"What the fuck took you so long to answer? Were you in the can playing with yourself?"

"No Marla, what's going on?"

"We need to get together. I got a problem and you're involved. I'll be over in a half hour."

"Look, I was about to go out ... "

"To meet up with another woman, you fuck."

"No Marla, to pick up some groceries."

"Well, this is more important. I'll see you in a half."

Andy hung up the phone and put his coat away.

"Hey, stud, big news."

Andy was dreading what was coming next.

"You knocked me up. I'm going to have an Andy Jr."

He started to sweat and couldn't catch his breath—a baby. He was going to be a father.

"Are you sure? Maybe you aren't."

"I went to the clinic and the rabbit died. Congrats hubby."

Marriage, how could he get married to Marla?

Andy had a sense of responsibility, but how could he be so stupid. He had trusted her. He should have known better. It was no longer just his life, there's a baby, my baby.

"Are you sure you want to continue the pregnancy?"

Marla started to scream at him, "What are you saying? Do you want me to kill your baby? You are a bastard!"

"No, I was … I mean it's going to be tough, with what I make."

"You should have thought of that before you knocked me up. When do you want to get married? We should do this before I start showing. "

Andy felt the floor dropping out from under his feet. "My family, my friends … Yes, we should do this as soon as possible.

———•———

The wedding was a sober affair. His parents tolerated it. They couldn't understand why he would marry someone like her. Six months later they understood. He was in a funk. The bedroom acrobatics stopped immediately. "I'm pregnant, you'll hurt the baby." She was also gaining a hell of a lot more weight than the doctor recommended.

She kept complaining about the lack of money, the small apartment, and finally the job he loved.

———•———

He loved his daughter. She was a happy child, always smiling and blowing spit bubbles. She was the only thing making him happy and for her he tried to keep Marla as satisfied as he could. She complained that she didn't have support, the baby needed the most expensive clothes and strollers. He tried to explain that there just wasn't the money for these things. Maybe his mother or (he shuddered) her mother could come and relieve her a couple of times a week. None of this remedied the circling of their marriage down the drain.

Andy, in their seventh year of marriage, became one of the school's counselors. Aside from being happy about a raise, he loved helping kids troubled by drugs, pregnancies, and sexual identity problems. He loved that he was put in a position where he could make a difference in kids' lives.

Marla still gave him hell at home bringing up his brother-in-law, Zach. Zach was married to Marla's sister who was the polar opposite of Marla. Calm, petite, and refined she had married a psychiatrist. Marla always pointed out that if she had married Zach (as if Zach would have given her a second look) she would be the Queen of the Five Towns by now.

Andy wondered if training to be a psychiatrist was for him. If he loved counseling, maybe this was his next step. Maybe a little private confab with Zach without Marla's screeching voice … ?

———•———

"You're a little old for this you know," Zach said gently. "Even with credit for the premed classes you've taken, you're short a few more science classes. Then you'd have to take the Medical College Admission Test. Jesus, Andy, it will be two to three years till you can even apply for a position."

"So you don't think it's possible?" Andy was disappointed. Reality revealed another brick wall.

"I didn't say that. I said it would be a long haul with a wife who is difficult, to say the least, and a couple of kids. I don't think you can survive three years in your current situation. You need something life changing now or you might get so depressed you start having suicidal ideation."

"It would never come to that, besides I'm happy, I got a good job, the kids … "

Zach looked sadly at him. "Andy, you're a nice guy that got railroaded by a shrill woman. It is hard to believe that your wife is from the same gene pool as my wife. You're depressed and up to now had nowhere to go. I'd prescribe medication, but it's not appropriate in your case. I think I have a way to get you out of this rut, make you a psychiatrist, and finally contain Marla to a certain extent. But it will take a lot of hard work."

"How?"

"Ever been to Mexico?"

A year and a half later Andy, now owing money to his brother-in-law, father-in-law, and the Dime Savings Bank of New York, loaded up his short school bus and started driving down the road.

———•———

Andy had a grim smile. "Our first task is to get confirmation that the school won't be accredited. If that's true we need to find a new school."

"We need access to Morales's office. My guess is there's a load of documents in there we've got to see," Marvin was already thinking.

"I want to help also. What can I do?" Sam demanded.

Andy started laughing., "Oh, we have a great job for you Mata Hari."

Sam's face went blank, "What do you mean?"

———•———

Mexico ran smoothly according to the Latin time clock. Siesta is a wonderful idea: It affords the working man time to go home during his workday, have lunch, get laid, nap, and then return to work refreshed and ready to take on the world. It's a wonder the rest of the world has been reluctant to adopt this model.

At ten minutes to one Sam entered the reception area of Morales's office. Rosa was sitting at her desk filing her nails. The minute Sam walked in she turned on a dazzling smile.

"Sam, *buenas tardes*! How are you doing?"

Sam just couldn't get over those lips wet and swollen with anticipation and those breasts bobbing in the waves of her breathing.

"*Hola*, Rosa. I just came by to see if all my paperwork has been filed, but I see you're busy."

"No, I am bored. The Señora is away at a meeting and I have nothing to do but guard the fort," she said with a smile. "Let me check for you."

Rosa got up and went to the file cabinet to open a bottom drawer. The skirt pulled taut across her buttocks.

"Man, what an ass," he thought, when she disappointingly straightened up leafing through a file.

"Yes, it seems all is in order. Is there anything else?"

She went back to her desk and started arranging nail polish bottles.

"Hey, you seem to like the more exotic colors. Are they from the States or here?" he started.

"Oh, they are from here and very expensive. You know they tax everything here that is made outside Mexico. When I go to Texas I usually buy a few bottles, but I haven't been able to go for a while."

"Today might be your lucky day."

"What do you mean?"

"Well, I was unpacking and somehow a bag of nail polish bottles was in a box. I think my sister put it in as a joke, who knows? There are like half a dozen bottles in some pretty far out colors. Want to take a look?"

"Oh Sam, I'm sure I can't afford them at this time."

"Afford them? You'd do me a favor if you simply took them. I was going to toss them anyway, but it seemed a shame. They're brand new. Come on down to my locker and take a look."

"But I can't now. I have to watch the office."

On cue, Andy strolled into the office. "Hola, Rosa. What's going on?"

"Nada, Andy."

"I need to speak to Señora Morales. Is she available?"

"No Andy, she is busy all day."

Sam broke in, "Hey Rosa, Andy can watch the place for a while, can't you Andy?"

"Well as long as it's not too long … Yeah, I can sit here for a bit."

Rosa looked concerned. "I don't know if I should. If the Señora finds out she will fire me."

Sam looked concerned. "Who's going to tell her? Besides, it will be ten minutes. Come on."

Rosa hurried out of the office with Sam.

Andy immediately went into Morales's office and started carefully looking through papers on her desk. Nothing was there. He tried to open a drawer in the desk but it was locked. Try as he might he couldn't jiggle the lock free. So intent was he that he didn't hear the door creak open.

"Find anything?" Marvin whispered.

Andy jumped. "Shit! You almost gave me a heart attack."

"Whoops! Something we don't know how to take care of yet."

Andy kept jiggling the drawer. "Damn, I can't get this open. This stunt was for nothing."

Marvin moved over to the drawer. "Go keep guard on the door. Let me see if I can open it."

"Marvin, I've been trying but it won't unlock."

"Door … now," Marvin commanded.

Marvin started whistling the *Mission: Impossible Theme*. He grabbed two paper clips from the desk and straightened them.

Andy looked back, "Come on, you really think you're going to open that, or do you watch too much television?"

Marvin continued, softly whistling, and then a click was heard as Marvin opened the drawer.

"How did you do that?" Andy was astonished.

"Learned it from hanging out with the criminally insane on the ward. Never turn down an education," he smiled.

Andy came back and started rifling through the files. "Here is something." Like most official documents it was embellished with stamps and ribbons. Andy spent some time reading through them, his face becoming grim.

"OK, I'll get Rosa back. See if you can spread the word to our future classmates to meet up at my place at seven p.m. Don't let Romney find out."

———◆———

Andy found Rosa and Sam in a dark alcove by the lockers. They were giving each other mouth-to-mouth resuscitation while doing a simultaneous physical exam. He coughed discreetly.

"Uhh, Rosa … ROSA!"

The couple quickly disengaged. "Oh Andy, we did not hear you. We were talking about lipstick," she blushed.

"I can see that," Andy said as he looked at Sam. "Oh," Rosa went from red to a hot red when she saw Sam's face covered with her lipstick. Sam wore a shit-eating grin.

"I have to get back to my family, Rosa. Are you guys finished here?" Andy asked with a smile.

"Oh Sí. Gracias Andy," and she ran back to the office.

"Sorry I had to put you through that. Hope it wasn't too unpleasant. We've got to go."

"Did you find out anything?" Sam asked.

"Yeah, meeting at seven, my place. Don't tell Romney."

———•———

Andy's place was mobbed at seven. It was strictly standing room only with students from the school representing three or four countries of origin, white Jews and Italians, blacks from both the States and the Caribbean, Hispanics from the States, South America, and Cuba, and finally Asians, the real surprise Sam thought. All the Asians he knew were straight A and high med school entrance exam scorers. Weren't they all supposed to be in American medical schools?

Soon, even with the fans overhead and on tables revolving at full speed, sweat was dripping off everyone and the smell of deodorant failing was musky in the air. Marla grudgingly gave in to Andy hosting the meeting at their place, saying as she left him for the evening, "You better clean up after all the assholes you've invited here."

"Can I have everyone's attention? I'm Andy Blumenkranz and I've been waiting for official medical school classes to start for two months. Has anyone besides George Romney been here longer?"

There were looks and whispers among the students, but no one came forward.

"OK then I'll start the meeting by calling it to order and asking if anyone else would like to lead?"

Again whispers, but Andy had no challenger.

"As you all know, we came to Mexico to learn medicine. I think it's safe to assume that no one came to this school to practice in Mexico. With the information we were able to obtain, not only will we not be able to go back to the States as doctors, we won't be able to practice here in Mexico even if we wanted to."

There was a loud murmuring.

"What do you mean, Andy? There are plenty of guys I know from Guadalajara that are in residencies in the States, and there are even some that are in an actual practice."

The noise level went up appreciably. They were confused and they were scared. This was the end of the line for a lot of them. Either they achieved an MD or it was back to slinging hash at home.

Andy let them get the noise out of their systems for a minute.

"OK, everyone calm down." He answered the question, "The difference is that Guadalajara was accredited by the National University or UNAM many years ago and was functioning as a medical school for Mexican nationals before the first Americans got down here. Morales on the other hand had a private language school for American teachers teaching Spanish. She figured out that she could make a fortune by opening up a med school. The difference is she never understood that even the Mexican government requires some sort of minimum requirements to train doctors. Now she has no accreditation and probably will never get it."

The students were all shouting at once. There was movement and more clamor in the back and suddenly the students parted to let Romney through.

"Crap," thought Sam.

"Never get accreditation? What kind of nonsense are you peddling Blumenkranz?"

"George, welcome. I asked the class over to discuss new information about the likelihood of school accreditation. According to information I recently obtained it seems to be a forgone conclusion that this place will never get its accreditation. We need to discuss what this means for all of us."

"That's bullshit. Señora Morales has told all of you that accreditation will be finalized by next week, two weeks at the most. Your information is phony or you made it up. Why are you getting all your classmates anxious about this, Andy? Morales has people in UNAM who are finalizing the paperwork now."

"UNAM already sent papers to Morales confirming that she will not get accreditation, at least this year. I've seen them," Andy said. "Think about it, George. She has been lying to you, and she'll throw you under the bus to keep up this charade. Join us. We need to figure out what to do now."

"Fuck you, Andy, and fuck any of you that listen to him. Where are these documents? Has Blumenkranz shown them to you?"

"Has Morales shown you any documents that prove that the school is going to get accredited? Give us something tangible; that's all we're asking for. George, we need a plan now ... "

"Screw yourself." George walked out of the house. There was absolute silence. Sam felt a palpable chill come over the room, the faces of his fellow students frozen in a rictus of disbelief. Sam also felt the freeze and shivered. It was like a vacuum in the room, sounds muffled, breathing ragged, even the lighting appeared dimmed. Who was right, who was full of shit. While he inherently believed Andy and Marvin, he also thought Romney was a good guy trying to help his fellow Americans through the difficult process of med school in a bizarre world. Sam believed that most of the students still had some faith in Romney. In the end it was Romney who got them down here to study in a medical school, but very few of the students, including himself, would take a chance on the accreditation of this hybrid of a school, and would seek a situation somewhat safer.

Marvin took a deep breath and then addressed the students. "Let's take a ten-minute break. Then those who are interested in exploring new avenues in the pursuit of a medical degree can return here." The crowd started to go outside for some air. The air came rushing back into the room with all the outside sounds. The grumbling and worried voices of the students were the background music and there was a stink of collective fear.

Marvin, Sam, and Andy gathered in the living room to plan some sort of strategy.

"Shit, that was a disaster," Sam said. "Romney is going to make us look like we don't know what's happening. I wish we had been able to Xerox that document."

"Yeah, Xerox it, show it to the class and Romney and immediately go to jail when Morales calls out the federales on us for breaking and entering. Right now he has nothing on us. He probably thinks we may have bribed someone at UNAM," Andy said.

"But we have no proof to show the class. Most of them will believe Romney; it is the easier way."

Marvin put a hand on Sam's shoulder. "Sam, you can't save everyone. Look at it this way. There were thousands of students in the States that were rejected from a spot in a med school. A small percentage didn't accept that failure and ended up here. Now it looks like another move has to be made in order to become an MD. A percentage of our group will now take the next step. I hope there aren't many more steps after this."

The students reconvened, their numbers diminished by half. Their faces stone, they were angry and wanted to do something now. Sam could see a lot of the students clenching and unclenching their hands, frustrated that once again the way to a future was uncertain and failure was possible.

"OK, I call to order the first meeting of the Survivors of Saltillo," Andy said looking around. "Our first order of business is forming a committee to find a new school. Anyone have any contacts or ideas?"

The crowd looked at each other, but there didn't seem to be much in the way of a Savior.

"OK, there being no instant cure for our problem I'd like nominations … "

A small, thin student with a thick Brooklyn dialect called out, "Andy, why don't you just pick some people to figure this out. We'll support you." There was a lot of affirmative murmuring.

"OK, in that case I'd like to nominate my cabinet and ask for volunteers. Marvin Goldberg and Sam Cohen will be my assistants, but we need one or two others to … "

"Yeah, be your wet work guys, the guys that do the dirty work but are never seen. Agents 005, 006, and 008," a black-haired man, muscled like a swimmer, said. He was a kinetic individual, all tics and gestures.

"Yes, I guess so, but I doubt that wet work will be required. What's your name?"

"Bennie Frankle," he cried out, affecting a pseudo-military posture, "late of Baldwin, New York, by way of the world. I bring many skills, expert SCUBA diver, motorcyclist, poet, lover … "

"Bennie, I'm sure no one is interested," came another voice in the crowd. "I'm Sayeed." He was very Middle Eastern looking, dark, deformed nose from an old injury, sensuous pillow lips, with a slight accent that wasn't quite foreign because it had an overlaid New Yorker twist. "I volunteer and my major qualification is to keep an eye on Bennie. I'm from Brooklyn and am the finest cab driver in the Five Boroughs."

"So we have a two for. I think that is enough for the time being." Andy looked out at the crowd. "Everyone OK with my assistants?"

There were a lot of nervous glances at Bennie, but everyone seemed OK with the group.

"Now, I propose we attempt to find another school in Mexico instead of widening the search. I don't think Europe is a viable idea, though that is the second largest concentration of Americans in med schools."

Bennie started jumping around, "Why not Belgium, Andy? Good beer, drugs, proximity to London, France. Wait, what about looking in France, babes that are sexy, though they don't shave their pits, but man oh man did I mention sexy ... "

Sayeed grabbed Bennie. "Bennie, some of us are trying to get a degree and get back to the States as soon as possible. Focus!"

Andy just smiled at Bennie. "As I was saying I think we should stick to this country. Most of us don't have the money to make a European move, plus there are a bunch of kids here that had to transfer here from Belgium because they couldn't advance in a Belgium school. Their rules are much different. So, I make a motion to proceed with the selection of another Mexican school and to try to make a deal for the entire group of us to get admitted as soon as possible. Anyone in disagreement?"

The crowd voted in agreement.

"OK, the working group will continue and the rest of you can go home. Let's say we meet again in four days here at Casa de Andy."

———— • ————

Andy, Marvin, Sam, Bennie, and Sayeed sat at the kitchen table getting to know each other. There were the usual bottles of Dos Equis on the table, and as a tribute to their shared birthright (Jew) or birthroot (sons of Abraham) or home place (New York) a beautiful Hebrew National salami was being carved to go along with the beer and Nathan's mustard.

"You're kidding, Baldwin on the Island? You must have lived five minutes from my house. You could have even been one of my students at some time," Andy said.

Bennie, fidgety like a perpetual motion machine laughed, "Yeah, but chances are you might have been on some committee that kicked me out of the school. I never completed more than two years at a public school and once my father started shelling out to the private schools, it was on a month-to-month basis. My father got me into Princeton, thanks to the Frankle wing of the physics facility, but I was bored."

"Wait, let me get this straight. You were at Princeton because your father had pull and you left because you were bored?" Marvin was amazed.

"Well, bored, and Princeton really didn't want me there."

"What happened?" Sam asked.

"He was caught fucking the wrong woman," Sayeed said with a smile.

"There is no such a thing as the wrong woman," Sam said. "How do you know about it?"

"I am Bennie's Man's Man, his driver and bodyguard. I am responsible for him and for that I get to go to medical school."

There was just silence in the room.

———◆———

Bennie Frankle, of the Baldwin Frankle's, was born into wealth. He could have become a captain of industry much like his father, grandfather, and great-grandfather before him. He would have had his time on the cover of industry trades, then *Businessweek*, and then maybe as *Time's* Man of the Year. This wasn't to be as Bennie was born to be different. Who knew what caused it?

It could have been that Bennie's mother, a fragile girl, not used to being with someone who ignored her, found companionship in a bit too much alcohol. It might have been a genetic legacy from the crazy brilliance of a great, great uncle in the Russian Pale back in the 1800s. Who knew?

Bennie was different from Day One.

At the age of six he was reading at a high-school level. He created and wrote up his own science experiments by the time he was nine. He was interested in everything, but his intelligence was accompanied by a social retardation that was impossible even for the hardiest of teachers to accept. Bennie was passed from classroom to classroom. Eventually he would find a home outside the Vice Principal's office to while away the hours while his classmates participated in activities together. In the inability of the teachers to deal with Bennie they made him a social outcast.

High school was worse. Bennie tried hard to be social, but his social skills hit all the wrong notes and actually scared a lot of his age group. He was way too knowledgeable to be part of a gang of tweens. Puberty made it even worse. No girl at that age wants to deal with a boy who understands not only the biological mechanics, but also understands the biological imperative.

Throughout the difficult years his father had consulted with multiple psychiatrists who used poly-pharmacy to "normalize" Bennie. Bennie hated the medication and eventually refused it. His father wanted to give up on the psychiatrists but the schools insisted on them. The schools threatened to kick Bennie out, so there was yet another round of psychiatrists and another round of newer, better drugs. Bennie was delivered from this torture when he graduated from high school.

He wouldn't touch another pill or allow a syringe to enter his body for a long time.

After years of being analyzed and medicated, and then analyzed some more, Bennie became interested in the reasons for the failure of his treatments. Bennie was also concerned about the "cured of what." Was he bipolar, schizophrenic, major depressed, borderline? At one time or another in his life he had been diagnosed as each. What kind of doctors could so disagree with each other, but all agree that one cocktail of psychotropic meds or the other was necessary?

Bennie was finally accepted to Princeton. His father had the pull. Princeton, while certainly not lacking in alumni contributions, could always use a few more million dollars just to babysit a "friend's" son. The school was just far enough from his father, but close enough that when trouble came and his father was called, a personal assistant could easily come get him.

Bennie had one hobby. Women. Tall women, short women, padded women, skinny women, red, brown, and white women. He loved them all. The best part for Bennie was that most women couldn't resist his curly black hair, fabulous physique, and that bad boy, crazy twinkle in his eye. Bennie was a stud.

Bennie loved the college. A lot of the stress between his father and him was put to rest. His father almost forgot he had a smart, but mentally troubled son who was an embarrassment. For Bennie the air was clear and every day was sunny. Bennie could do pretty much anything he wanted to do, and what he liked to do was sleep late, take only psychology and a smattering of science classes he was interested in, drink, and fuck. Not necessarily in that order. Sometimes he liked to fuck first. Bennie had many takers in the years he was there.

One fine fall day Bennie was sitting in the local coffee shop/ bookstore when he spotted a beautiful, older, raven-haired woman who looked like she was transported from the pages of *Playboy* with *Vogue* overtones.

"Did I just die and go to supermodel heaven?" he wondered. He planned his "chance" encounter. What would be better than starting up a conversation about the latest book in the stacks? Maybe "have you tried the quiche here? You must try a piece of mine." He was so intent on his planning he didn't notice a shadow cascading over him.

"Are you Bennie?" A bouquet of Chanel No. 5 penetrated his nostrils and he quickly looked up. She was at his table. He started to stand up.

"Relax, besides you'll need all your energy soon. By the way, I'd love to hear your next line."

"Uhh … ?"

"Damn, just not good enough. My friends said you were witty and a cunning linguist. Guess they were wrong." She smiled and turned away.

"Wanna fuck?" Hey, it was a Hail Mary pass.

She turned and flashed Bennie a naughty smile. "Maybe you will do. Come on and we'll see."

———◆———

They were together in a Holiday Inn twenty miles out of town. The woman was insatiable. Unlike all the countless others, she had an understanding of the act that no woman his age had ever been able to express. He learned as a joyous participant that sex is a sport to be enjoyed slowly, building up points so that in the exuberant end both parties won.

———◆———

"You're incredible," Bennie gasped, sweat pouring off his body, still ablaze from his marathon.

"Again, not enough. Where did my friends get the idea that you were quick … "

"Quick? Look I'm sorry, but I mean I never … "

She smiled, "No dear, not that kind of quick. You were more than adequate for a boy your age. In fact you could probably teach a man twice your age and the best part of you is that you are definitely teachable."

"I want to marry you," Bennie was smitten. He had to have this woman in his life forever.

She laughed, but then stopped. Her face took on a serious and longing look. "Oh, Bennie, you're serious aren't you? This can never be, but I think you are interesting enough for return bouts as long as we want. The moment we don't want … well, we will come to that bridge eventually, but not today."

"But, I lo … "

"Don't!" She was now angry. "Let's have fun. Fucking, little talking, more fucking, and fun. That's what this is going to be. Nothing else … ever."

"But … " Bennie pleaded.

"Massage my butt, that last position was a bit strenuous for a woman my age. Please," she said firmly.

This was not some lovesick kid, nor was she a desperate woman. She just wanted it her way and he decided he was lucky just to get what he was getting. Maybe this was the time to keep his mouth shut and enjoy the moment.

"I see you recharged," she said wickedly.

Bennie lustily agreed.

———•———

Bennie spent the next year enjoying life. While still a wild man, the rougher aspects of his personality calmed. He showed up for tests, never for classes, maintained a high B average (if he cared it could have been straight A), and had regular sex and an amorous relationship with the woman. He called her Kat, which she loved, because she was so like a cat. She wanted to be touched, but only when she chose. She had a feline grace and was ferocious in bed.

It bothered him that she never wanted to go to a public place with him. She always called him and he had no way of knowing how to get ahold of her. He suspected she was married, or at least attached to a man in some way, but he wasn't sure.

As with relationships that transition from pure lust to love, Bennie became dissatisfied with the limitations of their affair.

"There is a great movie playing. Why don't we make a night of it? You know, dinner, movie, and drinks. Maybe just dinner if the movie doesn't interest you." "Bennie, if we do the classic boring dating thing there is less time for fucking. I know how much you love the fucking. Why waste time?" she asked in a tone that didn't encourage more discussion on the matter.

Bennie was desperate and so in love. "But, maybe just once. Come on, I'll spring for a great dinner, we'll forget the movie."

"Tell you what, next time I call you have take-out here and ready. We'll have a picnic in bed."

"As much fun as that sounds, I really want to take you out like normal people do."

Kat got out of bed and started getting dressed. She was plainly mad and did nothing to hide it from Bennie.

"Where are you going? I thought you had the afternoon? Please don't go."

"I did have the afternoon," Kat put on her coat. "I had the afternoon for fucking and playing, not for boyfriend and girlfriend, not for puppy-dog looks, not for planning how many kids we'll have in the house with the white picket fence. None of that is on the table. It will never be on the table."

She turned to leave. Bennie jumped out of bed and grabbed her by the shoulder. "Please don't go. I don't want you to leave me."

She stared at his hand on her shoulder. "Let me go, now."

He was in shock. What had he done? He released her.

"Kat, please," he pleaded.

"You are a sweet boy, Bennie, but you are a boy. With the next special someone make sure she can appreciate your love before you show it."

With that she walked out of the room.

———•———

He walked around in a funk. He missed tests. He confined himself to his room. He missed her and he realized what a mistake he had made. He didn't even know her name let alone phone number or address.

"What a shmuck."

His few acquaintances called to get him out of his apartment. He turned them down. He stopped going to take tests at all and generally withdrew from college life. When the apartment became too oppressive, he started going out to their old haunts, trying to find her to no avail. A month passed and Bennie was barely hanging on academically. The phone calls asking him to rejoin the world dried up.

———•———

"Bennie?"

Bennie had answered the phone at the un-godly hour of 10 a.m. on a Saturday. Shit, it was his father.

"Dad, why are you calling so early? It's barely dawn."

His father's peeved voice answered, "Even on a Saturday very few people would consider midmorning as dawn. I got a phone call from the dean."

"Yeah? What about, and can this wait till I get up later? I'm pretty bushed."

"No Bennie, this can't wait. The dean tells me you haven't taken a single exam for over a month and he will have no choice but to dismiss you from the college. Fortunately, he is a reasonable man and understands your problems."

Bennie was awake now. "And what problems might those be, Father of Mine?"

"You are off your meds, aren't you? The prescriptions haven't been refilled for a long time. I am not a stupid man and can add one plus one and it equals you are sick again. I want you to start taking them today. One of the office workers is driving up to hand deliver your pills. I expect you to take them. In addition I want you to attend a party tonight hosted by the dean as my representative. "

Bennie sighed. "How much did it cost to pay the dean off and keep me up here?"

"Too much and frankly I'm getting tired of it. One of these days you'll get yourself into a mess that I won't be able to buy you out of. It is fortunate for you that that day has not come. You will go to the party and present the dean with a check to sponsor a Chair in Clinical Psychology. You will be clean and you will be normal."

Bennie had had enough. "I think not. Not to the meds, not to the payoff. I'm coming back to Long Island."

"That would be inadvisable."

"What?"

"Bennie, you are not welcome back here without meeting these demands. If you get yourself cleaned up and back in good academic graces," he paused, "well, we'll see."

Bennie was shocked. His one safety net had always been his room at home, surrounded by his books, music, videos, and especially his privacy. It was a place he could always count on to be able to calm the chaos in his head.

"I—I don't know what to say."

"You say nothing. The meds will be there in two hours, I'm sure your apartment has running water to shower and shave. Make sure you are at the party at eight p.m. sharp. Now get moving." The phone clicked off. Two hours to the minute the doorbell rang and one of his father's assistants delivered his meds.

A tasteful quintet from the music department was playing at the dean's residence when Bennie got there. The mood was depressingly light and airy. Most of the guests were department chairmen who wanted to get on the dean's good side and grab what they could of the donor's contributions to the college. Normally Bennie would find the begging and genuflecting hilarious, but he just wasn't in the mood.

"Bennie," the dean called. "How is your father?" It's showtime Bennie thought. "Shit, I think the asshole is actually drooling. Maybe a little fun … " But no, this wasn't the time or the place. Bennie had a straightforward mission. Pay the bastard off and retreat back to his safe apartment. Hell, after this he could probably stay home and still get his degree.

The dean led Bennie to an unoccupied corner. "You know, son, I had a lengthy conversation with your father. He told me about your problems and begged me to keep you enrolled here. I wasn't convinced at first, but because of our old friendship you'll be allowed to remain as long as you shape up. You will attend all the classes, take all the tests, and as a punishment, I am requiring that you put community time into the college."

"Community time, what's that?"

"Oh, I think there are various things you can do; help police the grounds, mow the lawns, paint the walls where needed. Mostly chores of that sort. It will demonstrate that you want to be here and want to take part in what the college offers."

Bennie was angry. Free labor? Bennie didn't mind physical work, but to put the time in so this bozo could score points, Fuck Him!

Bennie pulled the check from his pocket. "So you're saying this is not enough to keep me here?"

The dean went to reach for the check, but Bennie kept it out of his grasp. "That check, young man, was from your father for further research in the psychological fields." He chuckled. "Maybe that research will one day cure your problems."

Bennie saw red and was ready to kill.

"Dear, would you help me for a moment," a sultry voice said.

That voice, the perfume … "Oh My God, Kat?" he loudly exclaimed.

"Kat, who is Kat?" the dean was confused.

There was an uncomfortable silence in the room, until Bennie finally couldn't take it anymore. She was with this asshole?

"You're married to him?"

"Bennie, please go," Kat was clearly embarrassed.

The dean's comprehension of his wife's infidelity was instant. His face was red with rage and his eyes were bulging out of their sockets. He looked like a cartoon character who had been kicked in the testicles.

"You and this loser? How could you? He is a child and not a very bright one at that," barked the dean.

"Kat, you can't love this malignant prick," wailed Bennie. "He can't be any fun. I doubt he can keep it up and, most importantly, he can't really love you like I do."

"Give me that check now and get out," commanded the dean. "You will do as I say and keep quiet about all this. Attend your classes and keep out of my sight or else."

"Look at him, Kat. He cares more about the money than he does about you. Please come with me, I love you," Bennie cried.

With that Bennie looked at the dean. "I could care less about being at this college and this money ... " he held up the check.

"Before you do anything, realize this. I will make sure my wife is disgraced. I will make her life miserable."

"She is miserable now you impotent, pompous ass," Bennie's voice had now reached the higher decibels and the guests at the party were noticing. "She was out seeking love and a friend. Obviously you were providing neither." Bennie looked at her. "Kat, please come with me. We'll have fun enjoying all the good things together."

"My dear," the dean hissed, "tell your friend to give me the check and leave."

He looked angrily at Bennie. "As for you, let me spell it out. You are a student here. My wife is part of this college and would be disgraced if it were found that she was fucking a student."

He sneered at Kat. "Tell him how you would be disgraced. You see, Bennie, Kat as you call her, has no money of her own and if this scandal became known, she would never get another job in an academic situation. I will make sure of that. Now give me the check and get off the campus. You just spent your last minutes here as a student and if I can help it, anywhere else."

Bennie looked longingly at Kat. "You'll always have someone who makes you his universe."

Kat, tears running down her face whispered, "Just go, Bennie. Go and don't come back here."

Bennie's face dropped. He took a breath as he ripped the check into a million pieces. The dean screamed at him to stop. There was sudden silence in the room. By now everyone was riveted on the drama taking place between a very angry dean, his sobbing wife, and a tough-looking young man who looked like he was about to break the dean into small pieces.

"Call my father for a replacement, but if I hear that Kat's reputation is impugned in any way, I can assure you my father will come after you personally. I wouldn't take that as an idle threat," Bennie said hotly.

With that Bennie walked out of Kat's life.

———◆———

His father made a deal with him. Go away. Far away. He would supply Bennie with a very generous allowance on the condition he didn't see him for a long time. That amount of time was left open. Bennie agreed, but only if his father agreed to protect Kat. As distasteful as it was for Mr. Frankle to get involved with Bennie's sordid affair, he also was impressed as to the length Bennie would go to protect a friend. Maybe Bennie was joining the human race. Besides, while Mr. Frankle had not been a great father or husband, he did listen and agreed that the dean was a malicious piece of shit. He quietly agreed and told Bennie he'd have a talk with the dean.

The door to his father's office opened and a young exotic-looking man came in. He stood quietly waiting for Bennie's father to address him.

"Bennie, as independent as you have been, that independence usually led to problems I've had to fix. I would like you to meet Sayeed. Sayeed is going to become your driver and right hand man. He is also going to attempt to keep you safe wherever you travel."

Bennie looked over to the expressionless man. "Don't need him. Anyway what difference does it make? You don't want me here and I don't want to be here. I'll take care of myself."

"You may find this hard to believe Bennie, but your mother and I do love you and want you safe from the world and from yourself. Sayeed is a resourceful young man. I think you'll get along well with him. It will also ensure that you have financial resources from me. Sayeed is a transportation expert." His father smiled. "Sayeed is considered one of the best cab drivers in Brooklyn. He also knows how to handle himself in interesting situations."

Bennie looked at Sayeed and grinned. "You'll be Kato and I'll be the Green Hornet."

Bennie took the deal. He packed a couple of T-shirts, boxers, a pair of jeans, and a toothbrush. He was gone by the end of the day.

———•———

Bennie traveled. He stopped his meds and had his crazy days, but was able to control himself. The allowance was enough to give him some independence but not enough to get him into trouble. He had to occasionally work odd jobs. They traveled out of New York and into the Southwest. Many times he worked with migrant workers where he developed a respect for their labor on the farms. He also learned that when they got sick there was very little support to help them. He heard of rumors that there were medical schools in Mexico where he could study. They didn't care if he had a degree or if he had been kicked out of college. Just bring cash. This he understood very well. He made a phone call to his father and worked out a deal that included "his right hand man." At the start of winter they crossed the border into Mexico.

Bennie had heard rumors that there was a small language school in a little village that was starting a medical school. Sayeed had met some Americans in El Paso that were studying at La Guad. They had told him of a paramilitary presence and very stringent rules on American behavior. Sayeed already knew he could not allow Bennie with his "quirks" to get anywhere near this school. He doubted Bennie would last a month without getting, at best, kicked out, at worst, shot. When Bennie told him of the Saltillo school, he thanked Allah, Moses, and even Ahura Mazda that there was a place in Mexico he wouldn't have to worry about being jailed or killed and agreed to set out to the Mile High town of Saltillo.

———————•◆•———————

So the team was formed. Bennie and Sayeed would make contacts with the various schools in Mexico.

Sam and Marvin would liaise with the class and get them ready for a move. Almost all the class had been accepted by Morales at the same time. They had all dutifully given her deposit checks at that time. Fortunately, this being Mexico, none of those checks had yet cleared the American banks. Word was quietly circulated to contact the banks that the checks had been drawn on and have them held. Most of the banks so far had been cooperative when told that it was felt that the students had been scammed. None of the banks wanted to get in the middle of a legal fight so they made a note to tag those checks when they entered the system.

Andy, of course, coordinated his two teams. He also kept his ear to the ground for possible trouble from either Morales or Romney. He was worried that if word leaked the class was going to move en masse, Morales would try something "legally." Legally in Mexico meant paying off an official to put them all in limbo, if not in jail. They had to work fast.

———————•◆•———————

The team met at Andy's house. Marla exited the room as they gathered with their Dos Equis bottles.

"I better not find a fucking mess here in the morning and if you fucking smoke, do it outside!"

She left and Andy whispered, "And away goes the Wicked Witch of Saltillo … "

"I heard that, you asshole," came her voice from the other room. "Why don't you just spend the night with your queer friends?"

Andy mumbled, "It would be a relief." He then smiled at the group. "OK amigos, what's the story?"

"Well, as you ruled out Europe, which takes all those great looking French babes out of the picture … "

"Bennie, focus," said Sayeed.

"As I was saying, in Mexico it appears that there are two or three places willing to make a package deal for admission. Cuernavaca is a beautiful town near Mexico City. For Mexico the town is clean, seems to be gringo friendly and has two schools running at the start up stage."

"Two schools? Seems like we have a good chance to at least get out of Saltillo. We could make it more competitive by adding fifteen to twenty students as a bargaining chip," Marvin said.

"I agree, but," Sayeed said. " … and this is a big but … the schools are run by two brothers that are warring against each other. One of these guys is called the Communist. This is the last title you want in Mexico. The other brother split off from his brother over money matters and it looks like he may not have his shit together when it comes to accreditation. The town is perfect for us, though. It takes about 45 minutes to get to Mexico City's airport. A great 'just-in-case' situation for us."

Sam was worried about even considering Cuernavaca.

"Communists and no official accreditation. Isn't that the same situation we have here, minus the Communist? What else is there?" Andy asked.

"Sayeed and I rejected all the border schools … "

"Wait, there are border schools? Where?" asked Andy hopefully. Maybe this was a chance for him and the other married students to get into a stable situation as far as family life went.

"Tijuana, Matamoros, and Juarez all have them, meaning at least theoretically we could find housing in San Diego, Brownsville, or El Paso."

"You mean I came all the way here, when I could have stayed in San Diego?" Sam cried.

Bennie clucked sympathetically, "Yeah, maybe. The problem is none of these schools have Americans enrolled. I think this might be too big a hurdle for the schools as they all are state supported and the Mexican states are usually touchy about Americans making inroads on their institutions."

"Slim pickings so far," said Andy. "You mean to tell me out of one hundred plus schools here in Mexico, this is the best we have to pick from?"

Bennie smiled, "Naw, we left the best for last, and I mean this is a story befitting Hollywood. This guy was a general contractor making no money. One day he decides to take his last centavo and spend it on a lottery ticket. Much to his amazement he wins a couple hundred thousand in real American money. Now this guy wants to become very rich. He looks for a way to invest his money. He makes friends with the local surgeon, who it so happens trained in Chicago. This surgeon remembers the desperation of the gringos trying to get into med school. He is also familiar with the hundreds of thousands of dollars Guadalajara is raking in. So he forms a partnership with the contractor. He tells the contractor, 'You build the physical plant. I'll put together the curriculum, the professors, and run interference for accreditation. We split the profits.' The rest, as they say, is the whole enchilada."

"I think the expression is the rest is history," Marvin said dryly.

"Not down here my rotund friend. Here the enchilada is the story and how after awhile it can stink."

Skeptical, Andy asked, "Is this a good deal for us or not? I mean if it stinks … "

"Everything stinks South of the Border, but at least there are schools here you can buy your way into. It's our best chance, Andy. It is accredited, has space in classes with actual teachers, the town has an airport, and maybe the best part is they're looking for infusions of cash, which we will provide. I think we should negotiate with them.

"OK, Marvin and I will approach them. Let's hope it's all you say it is." Andy got up to end the meeting.

——————◆·——————

All the students who wanted to leave were notified. The banks had been told to put a stop on checks for the school. Everyone would meet one mile out of town and caravan the rest of the way to their new home. Sam and Marvin would bring up the rear of the caravan with their cars.

When they met at the meeting point a lone car was already there. Romney stood in the middle of the road. Sam, Marvin, and Andy got out of their cars in anticipation of trouble. How did Romney find out?

"George, what are you doing here?" Sam asked.

"I came to wish you guys the best. I'm sorry you all are leaving."

"Is that all, or can we expect problems from Morales?"

"She doesn't know. I figure she won't really have an idea until her bank notifies her of the cancelled checks."

Andy, suspicious, said, "Come on George, what's really up? I can't believe you've been hanging around in the middle of the road, just waiting to wave goodbye."

George looked sad. "No, I came to apologize. I did a little investigation of my own after your meeting. You're correct, she'll never get accreditation. Worst part was when she got the official first report. The National University had major criticisms and it looks like she decided it would be too expensive to fix. That didn't stop her from continuing to have me recruit in the States and take tuition money. I think she was going to let the farce go on as long as possible and then disappear with the money. I am responsible for some of this. I want to make amends."

Marvin looked at Andy and Sam. "You did us a favor, George. You got us down here to begin with. We'd all be back in the States still searching for a medical school that would take us. Do yourself a favor and join our group."

Romney looked sad, but relieved at the same time. "I can't. I'm going to continue recruiting for her for another couple of weeks, but can stop the process before more kids show up. I'll try to intercept the mail for as long as I can. You need to go wherever you're going and finalize the deal with the new school as fast as possible. If she comes after you, the next school will protect you. They want the tuition money for themselves, right? Now git," he said with a smile.

Sam knew it was time to move on. "Thanks for everything, George. Try to join us as soon as you think you can." Sam, followed by Andy and Marvin, shook George's hand.

Sam drove away, but kept an eye in his rearview mirror as George, looking very much alone, got smaller and smaller.

Chapter 3

Sunshine, Palm Trees, and Open Sewers

"What a town Tampico."

— The Treasure of the Sierra Madre

Tampico, from the Indian word "a place of otters," is famous for beaches, petrochemicals, and the birthplace of Mexicana Airlines and Coca-Cola of Mexico.

"Señores, this is where the famous actor Humphrey Bogart sat on a bench in our beautiful park," said a cab driver. Tampico was probably most famous for Humphrey Bogart sweating to death during the filming of *The Treasure of the Sierra Madre*.

Sam looked around, already miserable in the heat and stench at the center of town. Unlike Saltillo, Tampico was more like a city than a village. There were palm trees and buildings made of old cracking cement and faded marble covered in deep green moss. The central square had an ancient-looking gazebo that hosted the town's many mariachi bands. Surrounding the square were government buildings and department stores. The walls of these buildings were plastered in old political posters encouraging the people to vote for Mexico's dominant political party. All the posters had a man with black hair, brown skin, and usually a black, thick moustache. Tampico even boasted a satellite town, Madero. There were shops, movie theaters, and an airport with connections into the States. He knew he should be happy as life would be easier, but God, was it hot, and the smell, you just couldn't get away from it. Shit and gasoline, plus all the things that were rotting in the soggy heat.

Tampico was the headquarters of Pemex, the Mexican National oil company. It was rumored that Nixon had come down here to negotiate with the President of Mexico about oil deliveries. Maybe they sat together on the same bench that Bogart had. The town looked like it had open sewers and garbage rotting everywhere.

The caravan had arrived yesterday afternoon, so the priority was to get everyone settled. Unlike when students had arrived in Saltillo, there hadn't been enough time for the school administration to figure out where to place students with families or to find enough apartments. Marvin was sure this was sticking in their craw. Morales had been making a tidy sum getting kickbacks from the placement with families in Saltillo. He was pretty sure this administration would have loved to do the same.

As the caravan entered town and drove past the airport they saw a Holiday Inn on a hill. The caravan stopped and after a quick vote decided that Andy and Marvin would try to get a good group rate for at least a few weeks' lodging. It was already anticipated it might take a while to find enough rentals to house everyone because the school was so new and the town wasn't ready for the influx.

They entered the hotel lobby where they found a desk clerk manning a quiet lobby. The clerk called the manager and after the usual dickering a deal was made. The Saltillo group had found their temporary home in the "no-tell hotel" rooms of the Holiday Inn of Tampico, Tamaulipas, Mexico.

The next day was hot and humid. The smell hadn't gone away, but in general the group was feeling very hopeful. The school was actually walking distance from the hotel. A lot of the families were happy that they would have the leisure of finding alternative housing over the next four weeks.

The students met in the lobby of the motel. Andy led the walk over to the school.

"OK everybody, remember when we get to the school try to keep the chatter as low as possible. Sam, Marvin, and I will talk to the administration and get us all squared away. Let's go."

The procession walked across the street to the large lot in front of the school. The school looked like a Spanish mission. Painted white, it had a large archway leading into the building and a mission motif over the arch where two columns bracketed another arch. There were no crosses, so at least the Jews in the group were feeling a little more comfortable. As is typical in Mexico, the building appeared new with fresh paint, but if one looked closely the walls were unfinished, bare brick missing plaster in patches. The pipes were jutting out of walls hooked up to nothing and bare wires were waiting for electrical fixtures. At the front of the building Andy reminded everyone to "keep it down." Most of the group went over to a small sandwich truck.

"We are here to see Sr. Adolfo Garza," Sam told a receptionist who was stationed in the lobby."

"Sí, do you have an appointment?" The young male receptionist was dressed in a white shirt with a red handkerchief tied around his neck. Sam was reminded of the stories his mother told him of the young communists in Russia. God, he hoped this wasn't an indication of what awaited them here.

"Come this way, please," the young man gestured. They were led into an office that looked amazingly like Sra. Morales's. It had a similarly gigantic wood desk that certainly had contributed to the deforestation of some small country to the south. There were the same heavy velour drapes, but instead of the great seal of the Benito Juarez-Abraham Lincoln School, a large crimson Universidad del Tampico tapestry was hung in back of the desk.

Garza was a short, squat man who looked like he had worked in construction all his life. His hands were large and calloused. His skin was the color of deeply stained walnut, old and weather beaten. "Welcome Estudiantes, I am the Chancellor of the Universidad del Tampico," Garza said in heavily accented English.

"Sr. Garza, we are pleased to meet you. I am Andy Blumenkranz and these are my fellow students, Sam Cohen and Marvin Goldberg. We represent about twenty students who would like to gain admission to your first year class. All are premed in the States and all are financially able to pay tuition for the four years."

Garza's eyes lit up, already figuring what an increase of twenty students would do for his net worth. "Ah, twenty students. That is quite a lot of students. I am not sure we will be able to accommodate all in our first year class." Garza paused and gazed up at the ceiling. He suddenly had a great idea. "Why don't we create a one-term Spanish and cultural class and start your medical studies in six months. This way I can guarantee in four and a half years you will all get your *Titulo*, your diploma.

Sam was about to start shouting. Between Mexico and Bennie he should have known this was nowhere near a done deal. God knew how many weeks, possibly months would elapse before he even started school.

"Hmm," Andy said brightly. "I'm sorry Mr. Garza, we must have made a mistake. We thought you had room for us in this class. I'm sorry to have wasted your time." He nodded to Sam and Marvin.

"Andy, we just … "

"Sam," Andy said, "Bennie must have been confused by a Spanish idiom on the phone when he told us someone at UT had said they would welcome all 20 of us into this class. We should go and not waste any more of Sr. Garza's time."

Andy started moving Marvin and Sam out of the room. Marvin said to Sam quietly within earshot of Garza, "We're lucky Sayeed made that deal with Cuernavaca to enroll us. He has the deposit money ready to wire right now."

Sam wailed, "But I can't drive anymore and this looks like a nice clean town."

Marvin put an arm around Sam. "Well, I suspect we can squeeze in a few days vacation here at the beautiful Holiday Inn's pool before we start driving. I'm sure everyone could use the rest before starting medical classes in earnest."

Sam walked out of the office with Marvin, Andy bringing up the rear. Andy noticed that during Sam's little breakdown, Garza was mentally taking down every word. Andy turned around to face Garza. "Thank you again for your time and sorry for the misunderstanding. Thank God, we all have a place to start school. I understand Cuernavaca is a lovely town. Goodbye, maybe we will see each other in the future at a medical convention."

"Adios, Sr. Blumenkranz. Your group is staying at the Inn across the street, sí?"

"Yes, I think we will take advantage of the pool and relax before heading down the road. The manager of the Holiday Inn will be disappointed losing the long term rents, but there is nothing we can do."

"I know the manager, I will call him and make sure your group is treated well. It is the least UT can do."

Andy smiled, "Gracias." He walked out to catch up with Sam and Marvin.

———•———

"Did he take the bait?"

Andy gave Sam and Marvin a big smile. "Were you two theater majors? Sam, 'a clean town'? Tampico? Hilarious! You guys were great."

"But Andy," Sam asked, "do you think he is going to do anything?"

"I'll let you know in about two or three hours if Sayeed is as good as he says he is."

Sam reminisced about a previous episode with Sayeed. "I think he is good, very good … In fact I think he has the exact skill set we need here. Sayeed is a phreaker."

———•———

Sam, in the caravan, had been driving hours on the road to Tampico when Andy's bus ahead of him started honking and signaled a turn into one of the few gas stations they had seen for hours. Sam breathed a sigh of relief as his back and legs were cramping from the strain of the long twisty, bumpy road that was a collection of potholes and debris due to minor rockslides from the hills bordering the road. He felt homesick and depressed because of the guilt at leaving Saltillo without getting word to his parents that he was on the move. He felt that his parents should know what was going on. If they tried to get ahold of him at Señor Rudolfo's house or the school they would worry when they found out he had disappeared. Unlike San Diego there were very few pay phones in Mexico and so far there had been no phones on the road to Tampico.

The students got out to stretch and buy Cokes and cakes like the Mexican equivalent of Twinkies and use the lone outhouse that nauseated most of them with the smell. Sam spied a payphone hanging on the side of the service station with a small group of students clustered around. He approached the phone only to hear angry grumbling from one of the students attempting to use the phone.

"Fuck this fucking shithole of a country and the fucking phone system," yelled a blond-haired, red-faced boy. He slammed the handpiece onto the hook. "Fucking thing is broken, the coin slot is blocked, and the operator won't put a call through, even reverse charges." He strode away cursing. The rest of the crowd dispersed muttering curses that echoed the blond kid's frustration.

Sam went over to the phone and picked up the handpiece and rotary dialed the operator. "*Sí?*" replied the operator.

Praying, Sam responded, "*Operador Internacional por favor.*" Sam heard the familiar clicks and buzzing on the receiver.

"Operador Internacional ... " came a voice.

"Yes, I need to place a reverse charges call to San Diego, area code 714 ... "

"You need to deposit *cinco pesos, securidad ... ,*" the operator interrupted.

"Listen, this phone is broken, the coin slot is blocked. Can you please just reverse the charges?"

"Cinco pesos ... "

"Look, I told you the slot ... " There was a click as the operator disconnected, but Sam didn't notice as he was still yelling into the phone in frustration, his face red just like the other boy's. Sam also started slamming the handpiece onto the hook.

"Hey, slow down Sam, you'll break the phone that way." Sayeed had walked around the building and observed Sam's attempt at a call.

"The operator is demanding five pesos, but the slot is blocked. I need to call home and let them know what's happening," he yelled.

Sayeed grabbed Sam's hand to prevent mayhem to an innocent phone and said calmly, "So let's make the call."

"Didn't you hear what I said? The phone is ... "

"Yeah broken, I heard. Let's make the call anyway."

Sam moved away from the phone. "What are you, a repair man for Bell telephone?"

Sayeed took the handset once again off the hook. "No, not a repairman, a phreaker."

"Huh? What's a freaker?"

"Oh, it's someone who is aware of switching devices and electronics," he said as he started rapidly tapping the phone's hook up and down in a specific pattern. "What's the number?"

Sam told him and after a few moments Sayeed gave Sam the handset where he heard his mother saying "Hello?"

Sam blurted out, "Mom, hang on ... Sayeed, how did you ... ?"

"It's like Morse code. The opening and closing of the phone's switch in a specific pattern tells the phone to allow the call. No money involved. Don't tell anyone as I don't need a line of students wanting me to set up free calls to the States. Now talk to your mom, we will talk after." Sayeed moved away to allow Sam some privacy.

———•———

It is tough being a kid thrust between opposing loyalties. Sayeed never belonged to any Brooklyn gang. Then again, Brooklyn itself was never comfortable with the multitude of gangs that resided in its streets. Sayeed was a citizen of Brooklyn, hailing from Palestine. His father, Mahmoud, was a Muslim from Palestine who married a Christian from Lebanon. Mahmoud found himself in the crossfires between Fatah, who didn't trust him because of his wife, and the Jews who didn't trust him because he was automatically labeled a terrorist. The poverty in which he lived on the West Bank was the last straw. He ran for it. Like the immigrants before him, he was lured to the land where the streets were paved in gold.

What Mahmoud found was not gold and the factions in the streets were still warring. Still, on the whole, no one was putting bombs in cars or walking the streets with RPGs. In fact life wasn't that bad. He opened a small hardware store with money borrowed from relatives and discovered over time that Muslims, Christians, and Jews frequented his shop for the best bargains in the five boroughs. In commerce, the war was won by making and accumulating money. Over the years Mahmoud found that his neighbors were good people and that he was accepted. He was happy he had relocated his family to Brooklyn.

Sayeed came of age in this melting pot of a city, the tenth largest in the United States. As a child he played with Christians, Jews, and Muslims. He went to school, learned, and got into the same minor trouble that all the other kids did.

Sayeed's mind was fast and he learned certain subjects very quickly and thoroughly. He learned everything there was to know about cars. What made them run and run faster. He learned about electricity and how circuit design worked, but what he loved most in school was physiology and how the body worked. It wasn't long until Sayeed knew he wanted to study to be a doctor, specifically how to treat cancer. He wanted desperately to save his mother who was diagnosed with metastatic breast cancer when she was in her forties. She lived just long enough to make Sayeed promise two things ... to help his father and to become a good doctor.

Sayeed promised, but he was still young and for the most part unsupervised. His father loved him dearly, but the death of his beloved wife made him retreat into his business. He had time for breakfast with his son and an occasional dinner, but Sayeed looked too much like his wife and poor Mahmoud could only take so much heartbreak in a day.

Sayeed didn't resent his father. He knew Mahmoud loved him. He also knew that Mahmoud missed his mother dearly and was in mourning. Eventually the street kept him company. He was popular with the Irish, Jews, Poles, and even the Muslims. His quick mind, strong body, and fearlessness made him an easy pick in most situations.

He made good use of his electronic and car skills. When he turned fifteen he got involved with a street gang. Petty theft was on the agenda of the "Club," but mostly it was about boosting cars and taking joy rides. Because of his electronics skills and more importantly his skills with automobiles, Sayeed became an expert driver and there wasn't a car he couldn't start up. Life was good and he was relatively happy.

The other part of Sayeed's life was making money. Sayeed never had the hunger to accumulate great sums of cash just for the sake of accumulating cash. He wanted to make money to have more fun. He could have worked in his father's store, but the atmosphere was so morose. Sayeed had skills and those skills led him to telephones.

Most people in the neighborhood had family in faraway places. The Muslims had family in Northern Africa and the Middle East, the Jews in Europe and Israel, the Italians in Italy, and the Irish in Ireland. All his neighbors had family, all wanted to be able to talk to them, but no one could afford international long distance. Sayeed saw an opportunity.

Thanks to his interest in electronics shop in school, he continued his education in the library. Soon he was able to modify a person's phone or the telephone-switching device for that phone. In other words Sayeed learned the art of free phone calls to foreign (or domestic) lands.

He became popular and always had money in his pocket. There were no worries about getting caught. The customers were grateful and kept their mouths shut. Moreover Brooklyn was so large, how was Ma Bell going to figure out which phones had been altered.

The cops arrived just as he was putting back the final wires to reconnect the phone. Sayeed was read his rights and handcuffed. Being a minor, he was placed in a small holding room by himself.

His handcuffs were removed and he was offered a Coke. Mahmoud was brought down to the station and told about Sayeed's business. Mahmoud looked grey after the District Attorney told him what the possible consequences could be if Sayeed was found guilty. He was also told that during a police surveillance of gang activity, Sayeed's name came up in association with an underaged gang that boosted cars. The D.A. was waiting for the detectives to come in with more information. If it were found that Sayeed was part of the gang, these charges would be added on.

When Mahmoud walked into Sayeed's detention cell he looked like he had aged a century. Sayeed started crying immediately. "I'm sorry Aby, so sorry."

Mahmoud was scared, "Sayeed how could you do such a thing? Telephones and cars?" Tears started running down Mahmoud's face. "My beautiful wife has left me and now they will take my only child." He put his face in his hands and his sobs could be heard down the hall.

The door opened and the District Attorney entered. He looked at the scene. He looked at Mahmoud. "Have you obtained a lawyer for your son? If you can't afford it the State will appoint one for him."

Mahmoud looked bewildered. "No, I ... I don't know who can help ... "

The D.A. had a lot of cases pending. He could tell there was a lot of love from the father and a lot of respect from the son even if the son was a delinquent. It was also obvious the son knew he had screwed up and was angry at himself for hurting his father. Maybe this kid could be turned before he ended up a statistic. "We are going to go before the judge where an attorney will make sure Sayeed's rights are protected." He looked at Mahmoud. "Will you be responsible for making sure he stays out of trouble and that he gets to his court dates?" Mahmoud could only nod.

The D.A. said to Sayeed, "If you can give your word as the son of your father, that you will stay away from phones, cars, that gang you run with, and generally stay out of trouble, I will recommend to the judge that you be released on your own recognizance. Sayeed, do you know what that means?"

"It means that on my honor I will come back to trial."

"Smart, where did you learn that?" the D.A. smiled.

"Perry Mason."

"Come on, we have to see a judge."

———◆———

It worked out. Sayeed was put on probation. His father, who felt he had been given a warning from God, made sure Sayeed stayed on the straight and narrow. He was around for breakfast and they had lunch together in the store when Sayeed was not in school, and dinner was either in the store or at home. Their relationship deepened and a relative calm prevailed.

Sayeed took an afterschool job in a mechanics business and soon he was one of the top mechanics in the place. Everyone went to Mahmoud's son for the tough electrical problems. His father thought he would make a great electrical engineer, but Sayeed was still fascinated by the human body. He wanted to study medicine, but as good as his grades were, money was a problem.

Mahmoud's business made them enough for a roof over their heads, food on the table, and clothing on their backs. It did not cover more than a city college degree let alone a medical one. Even if Sayeed received a scholarship, he knew he'd never be able to swing the tuition and incidentals.

When Sayeed became eighteen he enrolled in the City College of New York as an engineering major, and took premed courses on the side. It was impossible for him to totally dismiss his dream. To help pay for the college extras he started driving a gypsy cab. He soon made himself a reputation as the best driver in Brooklyn. There wasn't a shortcut he didn't know or a street he couldn't get to.

One day he was sent by the dispatcher to pick up a Mr. Frankle. Mr. Frankle was desperate and fuming. "Fucking assholes, couldn't come to a decision and now I'm going to miss the plane. Goddam it!"

"What time is your flight?" Sayeed asked quietly trying to calm this irate man.

"Shit, in 40 minutes, it's fucking rush hour and I'm sure the highway is a parking lot."

"We'll make it, don't worry. I would buckle in though."

They made it with time to spare. "Hey kid that was some driving. What did you do, take a course at Bondurant driving school?"

Sayeed said, "No, I just know these streets. Have a safe flight."

Frankle took out his wallet and pulled out a hundred dollar bill. "Thanks. Do you have a full time job or something?"

"School. This is to get me through college."

"Got a number in case I ever find myself in Brooklyn trying to get to Kennedy?"

They didn't exactly become friends over the years, but over time they learned about each other's lives. Frankle was a businessman who helped small companies become big companies. He was always scouting for the next big moneymaker. He had a wife whom he rarely saw. They had lost interest in each other years ago, but neither was that interested in divorcing. The Mrs. enjoyed her social position and the money that came their way and the Mr. needed someone to man the home front. Mr. Frankle had a son who was a handful. He told Sayeed that the son tested genius plus, but had personality problems that no psychiatrist had yet been able to diagnose let alone treat.

Sayeed asked if the son seemed happy to which Frankle replied, "Maybe too happy."

"Maybe," Sayeed said, "you should leave him alone. It looks like he is smart enough to at least figure his way out of trouble."

Frankle laughed, "Sayeed, when you have kids of your own, and God forbid one of them is like Bennie, you'll know the heartache I have from him."

——— • ———

He graduated from college with decent grades. It wasn't enough to apply to medical school. He was without a steady girlfriend, though there was a string of conquests in every religion and color. He didn't care; it all was good and felt good. No promises were made to any of them. The ladies knew his reputation for the two-week relationship. Mostly he was just responsible for himself and he had no big ambition to make a lot of money. His relationship with his father was perfect except on this one point. Mahmoud could not understand why a boy like Sayeed with brains, personality, and looks was satisfied doing nothing with his life.

Sayeed had decided to go back to being a grease monkey. It was a life until it all changed.

——— • ———

Mahmoud had been having pressure in his chest intermittently a whole week. He didn't think about it too much. He thought that his stretching made his muscles lock up.

That evening he closed up the shop. He pulled the shades and started the quarterly inventory. He listed all the boxes of nuts and bolts, tools and other items, in his notebook. After toting a particularly heavy box, he started getting the pressure. This time he broke out in a sweat and couldn't catch his breath. Just to move was almost impossible. He never made it to the phone.

Sayeed got a call at ten in the morning from Mr. Kimmel who owned the coffee shop next door to his father's store.

"Sayeed, is your father sick?"

"Not that I know. Why? Is he acting sick, Mr. Kimmel?"

"No, no it's just that in the thirty-five years of being neighbors I have never seen your father playing hooky. The store is closed."

It was like ice water had started to run in Sayeed's veins. He thanked Mr. Kimmel and told him he'd be right over and hung up. He raced upstairs to his father's room. There was no one there, the bed still made. Frantically he ran to the hardware store. He opened the door and screamed at anyone to call 911. The whole neighborhood turned out for the funeral.

———◆———

The imam conducted the service that was attended by the neighborhood. Everyone's life had been touched by Mahmoud at some point, whether it had been to discuss the weather or to get advice on a plumbing problem. He was a respected man.

It comforted Sayeed and made him proud that his father had been held in such high esteem. He turned around as the imam finished the last words and faced Mr. Frankle.

"Mr. Frankle, I didn't know you knew my father," he said with surprise.

"I didn't, but I know his son and thought I'd pay my respects. From the turnout your father was well-loved."

"Thank you," said Sayeed, choking up. "I will miss him so much."

Mr. Frankle hugged the boy, murmuring, "Don't worry, it will all work out."

———◆———

The months passed and Sayeed made the decision that he never wanted to take over the hardware store. He talked to Mr. Frankle who advised him whom to contact and how to sell the store. Its sale left him a small nest egg. He again spoke to Mr. Frankle about the best ways to invest it. Sayeed wanted to just give Frankle the money, but Frankle would have none of it.

"You need to learn how to handle your own money, how to make it grow, how to invest and what to do if you invest poorly. I will give you some names and some titles of books. Read, research, and then make your own decisions."

It seemed good advice so Sayeed parked the money in a short-term account and taught himself economic basics from the books Frankle advised him to read. He never got interested enough to pursue a business career, but he took enough interest to learn the basics well. The money grew and he felt he had some security. He went back to the garage and kept taking driving jobs, especially those for Frankle. Their time on the road was full of conversation about business, art, and music, and when the last of the personal barriers went down they spoke about family, love, and life in general. It was here that Sayeed learned more of Frankle's only son, a son with problems.

Frankle, for his part, learned about Sayeed's love of the sciences and medicine. He respected this boy who was smart and could look out for himself.

Sayeed dropped Frankle at the airport. Frankle had looked very agitated. Unlike all of their previous trips there was no conversation this time. As Frankle got out of the car Sayeed wished him a safe journey. Frankle just grunted and slammed the door. It was the last Sayeed saw of him for six months.

Sayeed was worried about Frankle, but he let it rest. He didn't know if it was anything he did, but he figured that Frankle would be back soon and hopefully whatever upset him could be straightened out.

The weeks turned into months and eventually Sayeed ran out of ways to try to get to the bottom of the mystery. He had called Frankle's secretary multiple times to no avail. He was either out of the country or in a meeting and he couldn't be disturbed.

Sayeed continued his life, puzzled yet sad by the disappearance of a man he considered a friend and mentor.

———◆———

The phone call came at midnight. Sayeed woke up immediately worried. He never got phone calls this late.

"Sayeed, Frankle here."

"Mr. Frankle, what's the matter? I haven't heard from you for ... "

"Listen, I'm sorry about that. There is no excuse ... "

"I'm just glad you're alright," Sayeed said with relief. "I don't care about that. I'm just sorry if this was my fault in any way."

"Sayeed, it had nothing to do with you. I need your help with my son Bennie."

"Anything I can do."

"Get to the airport in the morning, there will be a corporate plane waiting for you. One last thing I need to know."

"Yes?"

"Do you want to remain stuck in Brooklyn?"

Sayeed became Bennie's Man's Man, driver, friend, and protector.

———◆———

Sayeed was at the telephone junction box waiting. He hoped that Garza had been baited enough to check up on the group from Saltillo.

Sam whispered to Sayeed, "Any contact yet?"

The line became active. Garza was making a long-distance call. Sayeed smiled. He hoped his college Spanish was enough to get him through this conversation.

"Hola," Garza said, "I need to speak to the Jefé of the School of Medicine. My name is Adolfo Garza and I am checking on recent admissions."

Sayeed needed this done now, he couldn't hang out behind the building forever.

"Sr. Garza, I am Dr. Castro, how may I help you?" Sayeed mentally sighed with relief.

"Sr. Castro, Yo soy El Decano de Universidad del Tampico. It has come to my attention that a group of students that had applied to our school was in contact with you about admission to Cuernavaca. I am trying to confirm this."

Sayeed smiled to himself. "That is a very strange piece of information you wish to know Sr. Garza. Is there a reason this is important to you?"

Sayeed could hear a hesitation in Garza's voice, "Sí, I am trying to track down this group as I believe they may be attempting to defraud independent escuelas de medicina en Mexico."

"Hmm, well normally I would not care to discuss internal business operations of the school, but I have a question. Has this group actually signed the admission registration papers with you for the Universidad Nacíonal?"

"Well, they came here to sign, and … "

Sayeed fought to contain his laughter over Garza's attempt to dodge the question. All Mexican students in the university system were required to submit paperwork to the National University system offices in Mexico City. It enabled the government to keep track of who was enrolled and who might be a problem. This was the first clue that Morales in Saltillo may not have been honest in her dealings with the Americans.

"I'll take it that was a no, Sr. Garza. At this point it would seem that these American students are not trying to defraud anyone, but trying to get the best deal they can. As far as I know this is not against the law in Mexico. If I may ask, what kind of a deal did you offer them?"

Garza's voice was quaking with anger, "That is confidential and I believe you are wrong about the fraud ... "

"Sir, I believe we have nothing more to discuss, good afternoon."

Sayeed hung up the phone smiling. That fuck Garza was trying to get info about a deal in Cuernavaca. Time to go in there and low-ball tuition. He could tell Garza didn't want to lose tuition worth hundreds of thousands of dollars plus whatever else he could screw the students out of. "Come on Sam, let's go into Garza's office and do what all Semites do the best."

"And what might that be, Sayeed."

"Negotiate a great financial deal," Sayeed replied with a gleam in his eye.

Now to find Andy and Company.

———•———

The Holiday Inn had become the American student headquarters. The hallways were crowded with students on their way to classes or errands. Their spouses would gossip in the halls and their kids thought it was great to run up and down the long carpeted hallways. The pool area was command central despite the splashing tourists and sunbathing executives. It was here Sayeed and Sam found Andy and Marvin drinking beer and talking strategy. Bennie was Bennie, performing acrobatic feats off the diving board, entertaining the young, pretty, and flirty Mexican girls hanging poolside watching his every move. Maybe they hoped to catch a rich American to take them to the America of *Rich Man, Poor Man*. Sayeed made a mental note to talk to Bennie about the consequences of fucking one of these chicks. Their fathers had semi-automatic weapons and very sharp knives. The "Poppis" would think nothing of avenging the honor of one of their daughters. God, he promised Mr. Frankle he'd keep Bennie safe. He hoped that was possible.

"Have a beer, Sayeed," Andy said, pulling a bottle from the crate beside the table. "Tell me some good news, like Garza got the message."

"I believe that it might be time to think about a wonderful deal for us poor gringos. Garza thinks we are all about to pull out … " There was a commotion at the entrance to the pool area. The receptionist they had met at the school was looking around the pool area for someone. "It seems we have a visitor," said Sayeed, nodding in the direction of the Mexican.

"Show time," Andy said, lifting his bottle and finishing it in one deep draught. "How about we let him sweat a bit?"

Sayeed smiled. "Why not," he said, lifting his bottle for the four conspirators to clink.

The receptionist, looking very confident, came over to their table. "Sr. Blumenkranz, Buenas dias. I am Ramon from Sr. Garza's office."

"Yeah, I remember you. How about a beer?"

"No thank you, we have to go over to the school. Sr. Garza would like to speak to you about your group's possible admission to the school. Come with me please."

Andy took a long swig of the cold beer. "Sure you don't want one of these? Mexican beer is pretty good."

"I'm sorry, we really don't have time. Sr. Garza is a very busy man. He has time for you now."

Andy took another swig. "I'm really sorry, but we are also busy. Most of the group has to pack it up. We think we will probably start driving to Cuernavaca in the morning. Shame, most of us sort of like the looks of this town."

"Please Sr. Blumenkranz, Sr. Garza needs to speak to you."

"I guess you don't understand what I am saying. We are leaving tomorrow. I'm sure Sr. Garza had some good reason for not negotiating with us. Sr. Castro in Cuernavaca wants to provide us with a reasonable cost medical education. Maybe he understands that this group will supply four years of revenue for his school. Maybe Castro also understands that we could draw revenue from students in the coming years from our recommendations." Andy smiled, "But I'm sure Sr. Garza had his reasons. Maybe he has guarantees of a student supply from the States for the next four years and counting. I hear that's how Guadalajara started. Now you sure you don't want that beer?"

Ramon looked like he was about to vomit.

"Please Sr. Blumenkranz. I can't go back to Sr. Garza and tell him that you have totally disrespected him. Please come and speak to him."

Andy looked at the group. "Can I have a private moment with my colleagues, Ramon?"

"Of course." Ramon walked away.

Andy adopted a rigid demeanor, and took on an air of maestro conductor. "Marvin," he whispered, "start looking angry and shout that you had enough of Garza, then Sam, try to calm Marvin."

Marvin did as Andy said, waving his arms, his face becoming red. Sam, on cue, tried to calm him saying the place sucked, but maybe they should listen. Marvin just started swearing louder.

Andy let this go on a few minutes, adding pointed comments every once in a while. He finally told Marvin that he should tone it down. "Sayeed, now look at me and tell me to fuck off as loud as you can."

Sayeed started swearing in English, followed by impressive Arabic, topped off by Yiddish. He then knocked the bottles of beer off the table and walked away followed by Marvin and then Sam shaking his head and sighing loudly as he too walked away from the pool. Andy looked like he was ready to have a stroke. He took a couple of deep breaths and picked up the unbroken beer bottles, and with his shoe, carefully piled the glass shards of the broken ones.

He motioned Ramon back over. Ramon was ready for the worst.

"Look, my friends aren't really in the mood to fuck around. I'll do what I can, but it is going to be tough. You can tell Garza that we are scheduled to get on the road by ten a.m. If I can, I'll come to his office at 9 to say goodbye."

"Please come tomorrow. I'm sure Sr. Garza would be grateful." Ramon went back to the school to face the music and tell Garza what happened.

Andy waited till he thought Ramon had left the hotel and then went to find the rest. Sayeed was in his room with Sam and Marvin drinking some cold ones.

"So what happened?" Sayeed asked?

"Did you have to destroy perfectly good cans of beer? Well, maybe it's for the best. I can't go over there to get us enrolled with a hangover," he smiled.

Sayeed raised his can in a toast and the rest followed. "To the future of medicine, and to you, Andy."

———————

And so it started, classes with a Mexican twist. Sam had his usual first day jitters. He had never gotten used to first days. Just waking up and getting out of bed for school took monumental effort. He figured it stemmed psychologically from kindergarten. His mother used to regale family members with stories about Sam's first day of school. She couldn't get Sam to even approach the building. He clung to his mother, fearing if he let go he'd never see her again. It took the kindly principal, a Texan, to get him to separate and join his classmates. He never thought he had enough water in his body to support the continuous waterfall of his tears.

He tried to get out of bed and couldn't. It took repeated pounding on the door and Bennie's offensive requests to know "if he had finished fucking her yet, so they could get to class," that forced him out of bed.

Bennie looked around and, scratching his neck, told Sam he was disappointed to discover that he was alone. Without another word, Bennie sipped on one of the cups of coffee he had brought, leaving one on the nightstand for Sam, who took the coffee, gulped half of it down, and then went to the shower.

"You OK, Sam?" Bennie finally asked. "I mean it is some exciting shit we are getting into, isn't it?"

"Yeah, sure. I'm excited, I'm excited, OK! You sure class starts this early? I mean this is Mexico. Maybe nine a.m. means eleven a.m. and we will be sitting around. I could have had two more hours to prepare myself."

"Prepare yourself for what? You sit in a chair with a writing surface in front of you and eventually fall asleep. You did go to college didn't you?"

Sam came out, dressed, and looked longingly at the bed. He finally said, "Let's go."

"You got it, Almost Doctor Cohen!"

Chapter 4

Clase Uno: Anatomía

In hundreds of medical schools across the United States smart students were calmly sitting in large, antiseptically clean lecture halls listening to the wise, welcoming words from some anatomy professor. Usually dressed in a long white coat with button-down shirts and ties, these professors lectured the future doctors of America on the importance of intimately knowing every cell of the human body. The professor would explain that learning the secrets of the human body was the bond that linked countless generations of healers. He also explained that to do this each student would dissect a human body. The body, generously donated by the deceased or the family of the deceased, would be treated with the reverence due it. With these profound, important words, the students would take their first steps toward the goal of becoming surgeons, internists, pediatricians, but most of all, first class healers.

Sam was ready to be awed as he walked into the giant lecture hall of the school. "Agh!" What was that smell? He gagged. Had the sewer backed up? Maybe something died? The place was being cooled by one wheezing wall air conditioner and the paint job was incomplete. Black mold was evident in the areas around the cooling unit. Was the entire class breathing that shit? The seats were unpadded stadium seats with a small shelf built in front of each seat as a writing area. There were about

50 students, roughly half American and half Mexican. Predictably each group stayed with their peers. As Sam walked in he saw some Mexicans wearing red shirts. They were the proctors and were taking everyone's names and assigning seats. It felt like first grade.

As the last of the class assumed their seats, the proctors all reported to the master proctor at the front of the hall who started writing on a large piece of cardboard. When the proctor finished he motioned to one of his underlings to dim the lights except for a spotlight at the lectern. Quiet came over the class.

The door near the lectern banged open and He walked in. The professor was the antithesis of Sam's imaginary professor of anatomy. Professor Valdez was five foot two with jet-black hair dyed with shoe polish and slicked back with Valvoline. He had no neck and wore black sunglasses. His skin was pockmarked from adolescent acne. An evil grimace showing nicotine-stained teeth completed the nightmarish image of the professor they would all endure.

"Vamos aver," his gravelly sly voice boomed in the cavern of the hall. This *vamos aver* would be repeated by Valdez hundreds of times over the next months. It was the signal that someone was about to be embarrassed—usually in the Spanish language, an American the victim.

Valdez looked at the cardboard mat the proctors had written on for him.

"Alvarez, Simon."

"*Presente*," said one of the Mexican students who jumped to attention like a recruit before a General, his starched, white shirt and rep tie beginning to look wilted in the thick humidity.

"Altagracia, Linda," he went on, checking off the students one by one.

"Ko-haan, Samuel." Valdez looked around, "Ko-haan?"

There was silence in the room, students looking at each other.

Valdez looked up from the chart, "Ko-Haan, no esta?"

"Hey Sam, I think he means you," said Marvin.

Sam suddenly realized that Valdez had been calling him: 'Cohen.' "I'm here, Professor Valdez."

Valdez looked up and stared out into the sea of seated students. "*Ko-haan ausente!*" he barked!

Sam looked panicked. "What did he say, what's going on?"

"Silencio!, one of the Proctors roared at him."

Sam, who hadn't been chewed out in a class since he was ten, was in shock, but he stood up and said, "Hey! I'm clearly here. I didn't understand the Professor's pronunciation of my last name. I'm here."

There was an ominous silence in the room as Marvin and Andy tried to get Sam to sit down. "Sr. Cohen," Valdez's voice boomed out. "You didn't respond to your name when I called it. You are not present if you do not respond."

Sam angrily answered, "But I'm obviously here. I just didn't understand you."

"You don't think I can enunciate Sr. Ko-haan? I speak Spanish very well I am told ... "

"I'm sure you do, but Cohen sounds different in English and I just didn't understand you."

"Oh, that's the problem, you didn't understand the Spanish."

Sam was confused, "Well, maybe?"

"Sr. Ko-haan, where are you now?"

"In your class, Professor."

"And where is this class?"

"At the Universidad del Tampico. What does this have to do ... ?"

"Indulge me a moment. Where is this school?"

"Mexico."

Valdez looked intently at Sam, "Now, this is important. What is the language of Mexico? Wait, I'll answer that for you as I truly don't think you know."

Sam was now pissed. "Of course I know it's Spanish."

"But obviously you don't understand Spanish. You don't even understand your name when it's called. If you don't understand something as simple as your name in Spanish how will you understand the names of the chambers of the heart or the ventricles of the brain? In this country we speak Español. You would do well to learn it, preferably before the next class."

Sam felt all the energy drain out of him. He stood silently as Valdez just smirked at him.

"Ko-haan, ausente! Now get out of my class that you are not here for!"

"That son of a bitch," Sam screamed. Sam was pacing in his room, its walls closing in on him. He felt as if the air conditioner was broken and now was pumping in hot, steamy smog.

"Sam, you have to calm down. This is Mexico, not the States. You can't get into confrontations with these assholes. You'll lose." Marvin looked at Sam sympathetically.

"The shithead just wanted to fuck with me. What do you think it was all about?"

Marvin leaned back into his chair. He felt for his friend, realizing that the younger American would have a hard time understanding that Mexico was different than being in the States. It could be a short medical school career if they didn't start playing the game by Mexican rules.

"You're right Sam. He did want to make an example of you."

"See, I was right. Now where do I go to get satisfaction?" he asked heatedly.

"Nowhere. You cool off and then you try to go and apologize for not listening carefully. You humble yourself. Valdez has nothing to lose. You, on the other hand, have everything to lose. Now chill in that chair and listen."

Sam took a deep breath and sat quietly.

"That's better," Marvin said pensively. "If you ever read any of the history of Mexico you would realize that most of the Mexicans have an inferiority complex when it comes to Americans. Our shared history is brimming with the United States taking something from them, usually territory. Let's face it, most of California, Arizona, New Mexico, and Texas were Mexican territory at some time. It is a poor country while America is rich. A lot of its population has to sneak into the US to feed their families. Now they feel that the US dictates to Mexico what this hemisphere's policy should practice at any given time."

"Great, so Mexico is a loser country, no shit. What does that have to do with me?"

"You need this country and the people that are running the school if you want to practice medicine. In fact, if I were Valdez I'd be running to Garza to tell him that you're a troublemaker, typical American. I'd tell Garza that if I were him, I'd kick you out. It would make it easier to control the rest of the Americans and the cost would be minimal. Don't think that if you get kicked out any of the Americans will leave to back you up. They came here to get an MD. For the majority that is the most important thing."

Sam was silent. He knew that Marvin was right. This wasn't the States and he couldn't expect that he would be able to slide through like he did in San Diego. He knew that in the US students held the upper hand. If a professor sucked as an educator or, God forbid, an entertainer you didn't go to his class. Drop it and pick another professor teaching the same subject. Hell, if he really sucked, write into one of the student-run publications rating the professors and their classes. Make him look like a real dick. He doubted that the Mexican students had any such publications. They'd probably be shot by the military.

"Fine. Touché. I guess you're right, Marvin. Wonder how I'm going to apologize to him."

"I think offering him a blow job might be too extreme, but offering him an apology and maybe a small token of forgiveness might just do the trick."

"Token of forgiveness?"

"Come on, I think by his smell I might know just the thing."

Sam approached Valdez's office and knocked tentatively on the door. He was shaking inside from anger, but knew that Marvin was right. This was a no win and if Sam wanted out of Mexico with a MD in hand he'd have to shut up and fake eating crow.

"*Venido adrento.*"

Sam opened the door and went into the office. He looked around and he was drawn to the empty bottles of scotch thrown on the floor, sitting on the desk, and laying on bookshelves. Papers were everywhere, as were books and even dirty shirts and socks. In the corner, Sam couldn't believe his eyes, but was that a pile of dirty undershorts?

"Professor Valdez, I have come to apologize."

"Ko-haan, you are no longer in my class. You do not understand my Spanish and think you can fake your way through this class."

"Please Professor, I understand I was wrong and will try harder to understand you and pay better attention. *Lo siento.*"

"Lo siento, huh. Well at least you have started to speak in the proper tone. You are still docked an absence. The school requires attendance to classes. If you do not attend classes you fail. One more time and you will fail. Do you understand?"

"I do. I will not miss another class and I will study harder to understand Spanish." Sam pulled out the "token of forgiveness" that Marvin recommended. "Professor, I would like to present this to you as an offering of my appreciation that you have let me back into the class.

Valdez took the bottle. "Hmm, Johnny Walker Red, a very honorable present." Valdez's face cracked into a crooked smile. He gripped the bottle as if it were a final railing saving him from oblivion. He gazed lovingly at the bottle, Sam but a memory. "Though next time if you feel the need to bring a present, I prefer the Black. Forget about the absence. Now go and study. There is a test tomorrow."

Sam left immediately. Johnny Walker Black. Well at least he now had some idea of the price of a bribe.

———•———

Classes began and a routine started up. The living situation was not ideal as it was expensive. On the other hand, as the Americans soon realized, the town had not quite caught up with the idea of student rental housing.

Garza kept talking about building dormitories, but he didn't have the cash or time to start building. He was too busy figuring out how to bribe officials for a dental and veterinary school, the latter very much in demand in the States.

For Sam, it was just a lot of effort to "go native." He liked the comfort of the maid coming in and cleaning. He liked the American-style restaurant that served breakfast, lunch, and dinner. There was also the camaraderie of having other Americans down the hallway. Parties were always popping up in one room or another and study sessions could be found in the "ballroom" of the hotel that the night manager let them use.

He got up a half hour before he had class, showered, and rolled across the street to class. The Boys even had a meeting place in the morning. Marvin, Sam, Bennie, Andy, and Sayeed began referring to themselves as "The Boys." Whenever they went out, they called together the Boys. They studied together, relaxed together; they may have been the closest thing to a fraternity on this primitive campus. In another one of Garza's architectural plans, he had envisioned a wall surrounding the school. Like everything else at the school the wall had never been completed, so the half-painted, half-completed, four-foot eyesore was out in front of the courtyard. The nice thing about it was it was also right in front of the *torta,* or sandwich truck, that sold hot Mexican coffee and simple ham and cheese sandwiches with the wonderful Mexican rolls. In the morning the Boys gathered in front of the truck to get coffee and a sandwich and shoot the shit about the coming day or how it would be when they all were doctors in the States.

———•———

"Vamos aver!"

Valdez was in his usual mood and dress. With a sour face, dark sunglasses, and greasy slicked-back hair, he looked like a very short gangster.

"Class, next week we start the laboratory of this course. You will need to come prepared for dissection and you will need bones to study."

The class became very excited that "real medical school stuff" was about to start.

"Silencío!" he commanded, his face red and saliva sprinkling the first row of students. The class quieted immediately. "You will all buy my approved dissection sets that the proctors will sell in the courtyard and you will be given information about the bones. Anyone not prepared for laboratory by next week will fail this class. Now … Vamos aver!"

Valdez's proctor turned down the lights in the auditorium and a large discolored movie screen with a torn corner lowered behind him. A second proctor came in with a carousel cartridge for a projector and started up slides. The first slide showed the structures of the heart. The names of the structures had been blacked out so only numbers and arrows appeared.

"*Torres!*" Three students answered, "Sí, Professor." Valdez looked annoyed. "Torres, Maria. *Que es el nombre de Numero Tres?*"

Two of the students rapidly sat down leaving a young 16-year-old girl to respond. "The aorta, Professor?"

Valdez smiled, "*Muy Bien, Amor.* Very good, my love."

Sam thought that a Professor who addressed any student with the moniker of "my love" would probably find himself on a fast trip to the honor board at the U of California, but this was Mexico.

"Vamos aver, Ko-haan!"

Sam quickly snapped to attention; he wasn't going to screw up again.

"*Que es Numero ocho?*"

Sam looked at the structure numbered eight. Was it pointing to that small thing that looked like a blood vessel or the roundish thing next to it? Maybe the hole in that reddish thing … shit who could tell?

"Ko-haan, did you study these structures?" Valdez asked with his hungry wolf grin.

"Sí, Professor, it's the pulmonary vein." Sam was sweating.

"Oh ho, the pulmonary vein. Class, Doctor Ko-haan says it is the pulmonary vein. As his Professor I give him 50% credit. He did get one word right." Valdez looked up into the air and cocked his head as if he were listening to someone. "What did you say, Doctor Ko-haan operated on you and you didn't make it? You think he should be flunked?"

The Mexican half of the class was laughing now and Sam was becoming red-faced both from embarrassment and anger. He wasn't used to being put on display like this.

"Doctor Ko-haan I gave you 50% credit because you said pulmonary, but the patient you operated on said to flunk you because of the small mistake you made when you operated on his pulmonary artery and thought it was his pulmonary vein. *Que lastima*. What a small mistake that cost your patient his life."

"But, Professor, it is hard to tell where that arrow was pointing to," Sam stammered.

Valdez again cocked his head as if listening to something, "The patient doesn't give a shit. You fucked up. Now sit down. Vamos aver, Smith."

Sam took his seat, embarrassed and knowing in his heart that on many levels Valdez was right. He hadn't studied very hard, much like college, and this was important material. He might one day kill a patient with these mistakes. He resolved to start putting in the time. That resolution bolstered him to the end of the class.

The proctors had set up a table in the courtyard where they had boxes of anatomy dissection kits. Each kit consisted of a leather portfolio with elastic straps that held an old fashioned scalpel handle, a tweezer (or as Sam would later learn was a "pick up" in surgical terminology), an object that looked like a dental pick, a wire probe, and a box of scalpel blades.

"Hey, Sr. Proctor, I need one of those kits."

"Momentito," the Proctor said, taking a long drag of his cigarette.

Sam, bored of the whole mañana thing, replied, "You know those things will kill you."

The proctor just looked at him and blew the smoke his way.

Marvin was standing near Sam. "Hey, Marvin, don't you think this guy looks a little cyanotic?" Marvin looked at the proctor and sagely nodded his agreement. Sam said to the proctor, "I think you really need to see a doctor, Jefe."

Of course this whole conversation was lost on the proctor whose command of Spanish let alone English was suspect. He ignored Sam and Marvin until he finished his cigarette and downed a bottle of Coca-Cola.

"*¿Qué quieres gringos?*"

Sam, losing his patience, was ready to explode. Marvin placed a restraining hand on his arm.

"We need two of those kits, please," Marvin said sweetly.

"Two hundred."

Marvin and Sam started counting out the bills.

"Not pesos, dollars."

Marvin looked at Sam. "How much is 200 pesos in dollars?"

The proctor broke in, "No, the kits are 200 dollars gringo."

Sam couldn't believe it. "$200 for two kits that have $10 worth of tools, you have got to be kidding. This is robbery. I won't pay it. I'll get the stuff from the States … "

"Do what you wish," the proctor smiled, "but Professor Valdez is starting dissection next week and it will take you two days round trip to get to the border and back. Think of the money you'll spend on gas."

Marvin sighed and then took out $100 American. "I'll take one."

"What are you doing?" Sam demanded angrily.

"He's right, we don't have the time and this stupid kit will cost us twice as much to get ourselves. Just pay him."

Sam stood there infuriated. "Pay him," said Marvin quietly.

Even though Sam resented getting screwed by the system in Mexico, he loved the dissection kit. It was the first piece of medical equipment that he was going to be able to use. He practiced putting on the blades for the scalpel handle and pretended that he was doing his first surgical case.

By the time Marvin came back into the room, he was feeling happy and more positive that he might realize his dream one day.

"God fucking dammit! That guy is the biggest piece of shit … "

"Whoa, buddy. What's got you by the short hairs?" Sam started laughing. He decided for all of Marvin's age and wisdom, he still had some hot blood running through his veins.

"Did you read the info in that kit?"

"What info?" Sam started looking through the kit finding nothing except the instruments. "Nothing in here."

"Wonderful quality control, just like the rest of this toilet of a country. Here, read this." He handed over the paper.

Attention

Skeleton Requirements for Anatomy 101

Skeletons are required for class starting next week. You may team up with 6 classmates in purchasing a skeleton, disarticulated with at least one set of arm/hand/wrist bones and one set of thigh/knee/lower leg and ankle/foot bones. Rib bones must include at least the first rib, second rib and two other ribs.

These bones must be in sanitary condition.

Sets of bones are available at the bookstore.

$2,000.00 per set (US)

This is a requirement of the course. Any student not having these bones by next week will fail the class.

Sam was almost hysterical. "Two grand! Even if we split it six ways, that's still over three hundred bucks per person. That was my eating money for the next month. I can't just keep asking my parents to cough up this money."

"I think we need to go native," Marvin had a weird expression on his face. "You aren't a VERY religious Jew are you?"

Sam, processing this, came back with the most intelligent answer he could come up with. "Why?" he replied worriedly, "we aren't going to have to convert are we?"

Marvin told him, "Let's find the rest of the boys. We're going to need the man power."

———— ◆ ————

"Are you fucking kidding me? Jews aren't allowed in there!" Sam looked panicked. The sun was high in the sky, it's blinding light making it difficult to read the arch over the entrance of the *Cementerio Municipal de Ciudad Madero*. Beyond the gate were acres of dry scrub grass, dust, stunted trees with dry, grey-green leaves and tombstones that were placed every way except straight up. He was never one for funerals and what was planned for today had him sweating and his stomach turning.

Marvin smiled at him. "Didn't realize that you were that religious. Why don't I play rabbi for you and give you a Papal dispensation. You need to participate in this because one day it may save a life."

Andy didn't look too happy about all this, either. "Marvin, is this even legal?"

Bennie was excited, "Come on, this will be fun—like a group project in school. By the way, I want the wishbone."

Sayeed was just disgusted. "Bennie, the human body doesn't have a wishbone and I agree with Andy. Isn't there another way?"

Marvin sighed, "Look, we could all split the $2,000 tab and give it to that asshole Valdez, but frankly, aside from Bennie, none of us can really afford to pay him. All the Mexican students do this, according to the info I got. It just has to be done with a certain finesse. Now do you all want to pay the shithead or should we do this?"

The friends all looked at one another and nodded agreement.

"OK, how do we go about this?"

Marvin led them over to the caretaker's hut for the town's main cemetery. "I guess we ask the boss undertaker where we start digging."

"Buenas días amigos," the undertaker said. He was a large man, brown from working in the sun, with dirt under his nails and nicotine stains between his fingers. "May I help you?"

"Hi," Marvin said. We are from … "

" … the new medical school. It is 20 pesos to enter per person and another 20 pesos to rent a shovel, per shovel."

"Wait a second," Sam said. "How do you know why we are here?"

"I officially don't, "the undertaker said with a straight face. "So that will be 100 pesos for your group and I might recommend two shovels for another 40 pesos, 140 pesos por favor. Oh, by the way, any packages that leave this holy ground are taxed another 500 pesos, but you can pay that before you leave. Also we offer advice as to the best place to pick up your package for a small surcharge of 1,000 pesos payable now. This includes the help of the staff here."

Andy was confused, "Packages that you help us pick up?"

Sayeed grimaced, "Andy, he will show us the best place to dig."

"Dig? I can't know about the digging. The staff will show you interesting places in the old cemetery."

"Look man," Bennie was about to go ape. "We're here to dig up a skeleton. What's this package and what's with the tour?"

The undertaker looked shocked. He looked around to see if anyone might be listening to the conversation, though no one was even close to the cemetery. "Señores, grave robbing is a crime in Mexico. If you attempted it I would have to contact the Policía immediamente. The tour service we provide is to find the grave of your ancestor, Señor Hueso, sí? The rental of the shovels is for gravesite cleanup for your loved ones."

"And of course if we don't pay, the police get notified," Sam said.

"Oh señor, do not look at it this way. Professor Valdez has requirements that if not met mean dire consequences … for you. I am just a humble caretaker of honored remains, who wants to see young men such as yourselves be successful in their career choices."

"Christ, let's pay him and get this over with." Marvin was already sweating bullets from the heat and the dust.

Andy gathered money from everyone and paid the undertaker.

"Come with me," said the undertaker, pointing. "Gather up those shovels and I will show you where your Great Tio is buried." They trudged off toward the lone hill of the cemetery. The grave robbers were all wondering if they should have just paid Valdez the $2,000.

"Ahh, the final resting place of Tio Hueso. You may start cleaning up and I will meet you later at the office to check your package. Remember, do not remove any nails."

"Nails, what do you mean nails?" Sayeed asked, but the undertaker had already taken off.

"Well boys, who wants to start digging?" Andy was trying to get this over with quickly. Cemeteries gave him the creeps and besides, God, was it hot and smelly.

"Me, Me!!" Bennie was manically jumping around with his hand raised. He grabbed a shovel and started moving earth near a headstone.

———•———

The sun was unmerciful. Near the friends there were numerous holes in the ground, all approximately six feet deep. They were frustrated, hot, smelly, and thirsty, just like the land they were digging into.

"I'm going to that bastard in the shack and tell him that if he doesn't come out here and help us I'm going to … "

"Do what, Andy? Go to the police? That seems to be counterproductive. We need to keep at it."

"Fuck! How many more hours are we going to be here?" Sam, who was scorched from the sun, kicked at the ground. "God fucking dammit!" He started hopping around on one foot. When he calmed down he went over to inspect whatever his foot had run into only to discover it was buried wood. Curiously, his foot forgotten, he started brushing the earth he had loosened from around it. It was the corner of a box.

"Oh my God, a coffin."

The rest assembled around the box.

"It can't be a coffin. It's supposed to be at least six feet under." Sayeed started carefully digging around the corner, as did Bennie. The outlines of a coffin eventually appeared.

"Who'd just leave a coffin on the surface?" Sam thought the very idea that people were so irreverent to the dead was appalling.

"Earth probably shifted. Look at this place, no sprinklers to keep the ground damp. Over there is a dry riverbed. No drainage was ever planned. Half these boxes have been shifting position since they were planted," Bennie said sagely.

They all looked at Bennie as if he were possessed by a spirit.

"Wha'? In my travels through the States I worked landscaping to stay close to the little people," he grinned. "Kept my physique at fighting trim."

"Looks like it's ready to lift out." Andy got down on the ground and managed to get his fingers under the coffin. Bennie, Sayeed, and Sam got down and took the other side.

"OK boys," Andy said, "on the count of three, lift. One, two, three."

The box popped out of the ground and they went sprawling.

"Shit, look at these scrapes," Sam said. "Can I get leprosy or rabies from this?"

Marvin looked at the scrapes and said dryly, "It's possible. If you start foaming at the mouth or your dick falls off let us know; we'll take you to one of the local hospitals. And may God have mercy on your soul."

"Smart ass," Sam said, pissed.

Andy had been looking at the box with Sayeed. They were searching for a way to open the coffin and get the skeleton out.

"It's REALLY nailed shut. There must be thirty or forty nails here," Andy said curiously.

Sayeed, trying to decipher the carvings on the lid, said, "wonder what all this means. It's like a faded cross or an "X" or … I just don't know."

"Maybe he was the King of Mexico and we're about to get the Royal Bone," Bennie laughed.

Sayeed eyed Bennie. "Why does everything that comes out of your mouth seem vaguely sexual?"

"That's easy. I haven't gotten laid for twenty-four hours."

"Oh fuck, would you just shut the fuck up."

"Jealousy ill becomes you my man from the Levant."

Sayeed gave up.

Sam, tiring of the verbal battle, said, "I'm going to the undertaker for a crowbar."

"See if you can buy some beers. I'm in need," Sayeed begged.

Sam returned shortly with the undertaker. "He wouldn't loan me a crowbar and insisted on returning with me to, as he said, to inspect the merchandise."

"Hola amigos," said the undertaker. He started inspecting the coffin. The expression on his face changed visibly as he inspected the carvings. He looked up, fished a handkerchief out his pocket and tied it around his lower face. He then crossed himself.

Bennie laughed, "Whatcha going to do, rob us or pray on us?"

It suddenly dawned on Sam, "Oh fuck we're all going to die. It's the plague isn't it?"

There was a general panic as the boys tried to put space between them and the box.

"Relax amigos, it's not the plague."

There was a sigh of relief from the friends.

"It's leprosy."

Sam started whimpering, "I'm too young for my dick to fall off."

"No, I think your dick will stay in its intended place." The undertaker got down on his knees, mask in place, and carefully inspected the seams of the box. "See, it is sealed with wax. I doubt if the disease could seep out of the box. Even if the box wasn't intact the disease is probably dead with its host."

Sam said, "Well aren't we lucky. You could have warned us. Maybe this box could have contained plague and we'd all be dead."

"No amigo, the plague boxes were painted black with a huge red cross."

Sam became agitated and looked at his friends, "He really doesn't get the concept of warning us does he?"

Marvin said, "Calm down Sam, the Gods have spared us once again."

Andy became impatient, "Well Señor Undertaker, what do we

do now? We've been here hours and still haven't had the necessity of paying you anything besides an admission charge."

The undertaker looked around and then down at the empty space where the coffin had been. He smiled.

"Oh, I think I will earn my fee yet," he said, nodding to the hole.

———— • ————

The boys formed a circle, gaping down at the excavation.

"A fucking condominium, how modern these Mexicans are," Bennie laughed.

"You've gotta be kidding," said Andy, "a coffin buried under the coffin we dug up?"

The undertaker said, "Well, this cemetery has never had enough land, consider yourself lucky."

"What if this coffin has a plague victim in it?" Sam decided this being a doctor thing wasn't worth his life or his dick, not necessarily in that order."

"Well, it's a possibility … " the undertaker said gravely, "but I doubt it."

"How can you be sure?" Sam asked.

"It doesn't say the plague on the coffin. See you later amigos." He walked off.

It took them another hour to finally clear the coffin of its attachments to the soil. It was an old, moldy pine box and looked like it had rotted in one of the corners.

"OK boys, pray to whatever Gods you believe in," Sayeed said seriously.

"Why? Do you think this box has anthrax?" Sam asked seriously.

"No anthrax, I hope just all the bones in decent shape. Stop worrying about the plague. Anyway you can cure anthrax with antibiotics. Smallpox on the other hand … " Sayeed said to Sam and frowned.

"Smallpox! I've had enough of this." Sam was ready to run for it.

Marvin and Andy started laughing. "Sam, you gotta chill. There is nothing that can hurt you in these boxes." Andy picked up the crowbar they had borrowed and started working on the lid. It suddenly popped open revealing a medium-sized skeleton. The bones were not shiny like he imagined they would be. Dirt, mold, and moss clung to them, and they were draped in remnants of rotted clothes. The only smell coming from the coffin was that of ancient mustiness. The sight of the skeleton neither nauseated him nor scared him; instead he thought about the human being these bones represented. Was he or she a farmer, a thief, or a revered leader in the distant past? Dust to dust was a biblical phrase that didn't yet apply to these poor souls, but "maybe if we had left them undisturbed," Sam pondered.

"Be careful and take the socks out first. Shit, I wish they buried these guys with gloves on," Sayeed said fervently.

Sam chuckled, relieved that no one had abruptly toppled over dead or had their face melt off. "What are you, a fetishist?"

"No, schmuck. We are trying to get as complete a skeleton as possible. If this person was buried with socks all the foot bones will be loose, but contained there … "

"Unless he was an amputee," Marvin said smugly.

"Uh, right."

They carefully lifted out the individual bones and with a page ripped out of an old anatomy book tried to compare the bones to the picture. It was slow and tedious work. There were at least 206 bones, some said 208, but the friends decided that they'd never find the ear bones in the coffin and would be lucky to find all the finger and wrist bones. Hopefully some of the other students would find extras and be willing to part with them.

"God, these bones are disgusting. What's the brown stuff and that smell?" Andy looked pale as he handled the bones. He kept wiping his hands on his pants.

"Petrified meat and probably mold. Some of the Mexican students told me the kids at the State medical school take the bones and soak them in a bleach solution and then shellac them."

Sam sighed, "Looks like we're going to do the same. I mean old petrified muscle and mold. That can't be very healthy."

"Yeah, I agree. I think I have an old tub that will hold all these bones. After we leave here let's stop and get a jug of Clorox and about a dozen six-packs of beer."

They wrapped the bones in an old bedsheet and gathered up the shovels to take back to the undertaker.

"Finished? I take it you found the treasure," said the undertaker.

"Uh, treasure, sure," Sam replied.

"I believe there should be 1,000 pesos that Tio Hueso left me," the undertaker smiled and put his hand out.

Sayeed, already hot, smelly, and stinky with absolutely no patience left, exploded. "What the fuck, you told us 640 pesos total. We're not paying a penny more."

The undertaker pointed to the hole left in the ground. "Surcharge for earth replacement. We do it for cost at 360 pesos."

The boys looked at each other. Sam grabbed the shovels back from the undertaker. "Let's go," he said wearily as he started trudging back to the gravesite.

———— • ————

"Get that fucking shit out of my house you fucking grave robbers!"

Marla was definitely not happy. Her incessant bullying could either go down in the *Guinness Book of World Records* or enable her to be enlisted as a Chief Petty Officer in the US Navy. Sam shook his head in sympathy for his friend, Andy. His life was a living hell.

"Boys, we'll have to do this in the backyard. Why don't you take the bones and a six-pack outside and I'll find the tub and put the rest of the beer in the fridge."

Soon they had the tub out and filled it with bleach and water. They carefully laid the major bones in the solution. Andy found an old colander with small holes in which he placed the hand and foot bones. That, too, went into the solution. Soon bottle tops were popped and Sam had procured a couple of cigars which Sayeed and he indulged in.

"Christ, can you imagine all the fun the guys in the US med schools miss by not having to supply their own?" Sam chuckled.

"Yeah, they haven't had this much fun since the 1800s. In those days they snatched fresh bodies from the graves and got paid by the medical schools for their trouble," Marvin said.

"How long do we soak the bones? I have to keep Marla and the kids away from the tub."

"Maybe twenty-four to forty-eight hours, then I'm guessing we'll have to let them dry and we'll need a place to shellac them," Sam said.

Bennie, who had been lying on the patio floor, suddenly sat up. "I think I know what to do. Sam, let's go back to the hotel. I need to talk to Carlito."

"Carlito, the gay waiter?" Sam asked.

"Oh, don't even intimate that he is gay. Down here you're not officially gay unless you either come out or they catch you," Bennie said.

"But, he's obviously … "

"A little effeminate and I wouldn't drop the soap around him. Let's go."

———•———

Sam and Bennie found Carlito back by the malodorous garbage dump at the rear of the Holiday Inn. He was a tall, dark man—a cross between Tony Curtis and Jack Palance, but with lipstick.

"Hola, Bennie my darling, what can Carlito do to you today?"

Bennie grinned as Sam's eyes got wider and wider. "That's do for me today, Carlito."

"Ohhh, amor, my English isn't too good."

"I'll say," Sam said sarcastically.

"And who is this little bird, Bennie?"

"This is my friend, Sam. Sam, this is Carlito. Besides being a topnotch waiter he virtually runs the kitchen."

"Him?" Sam asked?

"Yes, I run it so be careful what you say. One never knows what I might stir the sopa with. Comprende amigo?"

Sam started laughing, "I am forewarned, Carlito." He stuck out his hand and Carlito smiled and shook it.

"So what can I do for you?"

Bennie started, "We need a little private area with a dry heat source and a place that is well-ventilated."

"Well-ventilated is easy. We have a screened porch that we can curtain off for you, but dry heat. That might be tough."

"We don't need much space. Maybe two meters by one and a half meters."

"No, that's not the problem; how high off the ground?"

"Maybe four to five centimeters."

Carlito smiled. "I have just the place for you. 140 degrees C OK?"

"I think so."

Carlito had a wicked smile on his face. "Now what's in it for me?"

"Ahh, Andy told me to tell you he has saved the best for you. He'll take care of you."

"Oh, that poor dear man. He should leave that bitch. I'd take care of that man."

Sam gulped to suppress a laugh. "We're sure you would, Carlito."

———•———

So Tio Hueso was delivered into Carlito's tender loving care. This being Mexico the kitchen's oven was powered by propane and was always hot. Carlito took the damp bones from the Clorox bath and placed them on the floor under the oven.

"Dry heat, no? I think your Tio Hueso will like it here."

Sam couldn't believe these bones were allowed in a kitchen. Wasn't this a public health hazard? Bennie told him to get real. "This is Mexico, do you think there are public health inspectors here? If there were would they allow those taco carts to operate the way they do?"

Sam knew what Bennie meant. Most of the Americans crossed the street to avoid those carts. As far as Sam could tell the vendors made the tacos with meat from the head of a cow or a horse (he suspected horse from the partially stripped skull that was left). The skull gaped blankly at anyone who walked by. The worst part was the stench and the flies that collected around these skulls left on the ground next to the cart. Hygiene did not seem to be a big priority here in Mexico.

Sam and Bennie thought that leaving the bones here for 24 hours would be enough to "cure" them.

As they left, Sam thought that whoever the bones had been, they enjoyed the warm, dry heat after the cold, damp coffin they had been in.

———•———

"Vamos aver!" Valdez bellowed.

Sam was definitely hungover. The lack of sex was the problem, and alcohol was a poor substitute. He wasn't a stud muffin, but dammit Sam missed even the opportunity to try here in Mexico. Sayeed had told Sam that one of his prime functions was to keep Bennie from sticking "it" where it had a good chance of getting chopped off. As a teenager, visiting his relatives in Puerto Rico, the lesson was taught. *You Catholic girls start much too late* might be something to fight against, but in heavily Catholic countries not only did the girls believe in virginity, the parents (and brothers) took personal offense. There were plenty of students like him, and they all met at the pool area for ten o'clock cocktails to lament their lack of sex.

So now, here at nine in the morning and hungover, he had to keep from falling asleep in Valdez's class. It was a losing battle.

"Ko-haan, vamos aver," Valdez called. Shit, now what was he talking about.

"Ko-haan, do you know this structure? Stand up and tell your classmates. I'm sure you know, as you seem so bored to be here. You know how I can tell, Ko-haan?"

"No Professor, I am not bored. I think that structure is … "

"I can tell you're bored because your eyes were closed and your mouth open. I believe I spied drool."

"Fuckhead," Sam thought.

Valdez smacked the tip of the pointer on the screen showing an opened chest and abdominal cavity. "What is this, Ko-haan? Quickly, the patient is dying, what is this?"

"Come on, Sam," he thought to himself. His mind went into overdrive and nothing was coming up. "The inferior vena cava," Sam said with conviction.

The room went silent. "The inferior vena cava? Sr. Ko-haan, in what part of the body is the inferior vena cava?"

"In the chest, Professor," Sam said confidently.

"Oh, in the chest, Doctor. Then how does the blood from the legs return to the heart?" Valdez asked sarcastically. "Maybe the blood … hmmm, how do you say, beams up."

The class started laughing and Sam just got angry.

"I know the vena cava is also in the abdomen, you just didn't give me a chance."

"Sr. Ko-haan, rarely will disease give you a chance, you must know these things like you know your girlfriend's body. You do know your girlfriend's body, do you not Sr. Ko-haan?"

Sam was ready to explode, his face felt like a furnace and his fist was clenched. The class once again started laughing.

"Well, maybe it has been a long time since you knew your girlfriend's body. Sit down."

Sam was about to give Valdez hell, but Marvin and Sayeed dragged him down into his seat.

"Shut up and try to cool down. Valdez is just looking for an excuse to wipe the floor with you," Marvin said quietly.

"That fucking … "

"Enough, cool down."

Sam had had it.

———— • ————

"You need to start studying, not drinking after class," Marvin told Sam. "I know the classes are bullshit, but you still need to learn the material or you'll never pass the Boards or any other US qualifying exam."

"I'll pass. The classes down here are bullshit. I can't believe it. We are all adults, but in physiology class today Professora Rincon made us draw a *dibujo*, a picture of a cell using crayons. Crayons in med school. I'm sure the National Boards expect us to bring a Crayola #16 set along with our #2 pencils."

Marvin laughed, "Yeah, I doubt that, but what's the harm in the end. You have to learn the parts of a cell and if you do this, you may remember all the parts. You really are being too tight on this. Loosen up and do as she says. It's just another learning method."

"You know," Sam's eyes misted, "I folded up one of the precious dibujos, put it in an envelope and sent it to my mother to hang on the refrigerator. This way when one of her yentas comes by she can display it and say, see my son is studying to be a doctor."

Sam hung his head, disheartened. Marvin came over and patted his back. "The insults, the crap all seems so important when you're in it. It's only when you step back you realize there was no reason to get upset. Sam, just put the bottle away and study. The rest of the problems will take care of themselves." Marvin walked slowly out of the room.

———◆·◆———

Sam was in his room sweating over the Spanish translations of Valdez's class. On his right was *Grey's Anatomy* in English and on his left was the book in Spanish. He hated double studying, but Spanish was the language of instruction. Valdez had a point—their country, their language. Tonight it was giving him a massive headache. He had to get out.

Sam ended up at a bar and started self-medicating. He was three tequila shots in when he noticed a pretty Asian woman at the other end of the bar. She was a UT student who had already been enrolled when his group arrived. She was also making a dent in the bar's tequila supply when she looked up and noticed him.

"Hi, I'm Shey from San Francisco, come here a lot?"

"Hi, I'm Sam from San Diego and in the first year class."

"Ugh, Valdez. He's a creep and misogynistic to boot. A quarter of my class left this school just because of him. Rumor had it that Garza read him the riot act," Shey confided. "You know how Garza hates losing money.

"I hear that," Sam laughed. "How about another round? I'm buying."

Shey's lips curled up into a half smile and her neck and face reddened. "You got it, sailor." Sam moved to the barstool next to her.

Three rounds later, both agreed it was time to get out and go home. They tottered out of the bar and the cold wind took their breath away. There was a smell of burning mesquite in the air and the stars had a frozen, white appearance against the ink-black sky. The tropics of Tampico had turned into a frigid winter because of the cold winds from the north the Mexicans called a Noreste.

"Shit, it's cold," Shey said. "I hope the bus comes soon."

Sam looked at his watch. "Crap, I think the next one's in the morning." He looked through his pockets and found some pesos. "Shey, I'm sorry and wish I could be a gentleman, but the bar ate all my money except about eight pesos. You have some cash?"

Shey was slurring her speech as she opened her bag. "Yep, fifteen pesos more. I got you in my trap," she giggled.

"Trap?" Sam asked.

"You'll seeeee!"

Sam steered her to a taxi up the street.

They ended up at her apartment.

Shey was laughing. "See, you fell into my trap. Caught you, pretty boy. Come up for a drink."

Sam had no way back to the motel and it was getting colder by the second. It didn't matter, the booze had done its intended number on him. He was laughing and swaying with Shey. She smelled so good.

Shey grabbed him at her doorway and kissed him passionately. "Hurry, open the door," she commanded, handing him the keys.

They crashed into her apartment with Shey barreling into him. He kicked the door closed and soon they had wiggled out of their clothes while practicing mouth-to-mouth resuscitation.

"It's cold. Come over to the bed where it's warm."

Sam bowed to the inevitable.

"Grab that jar on the table … "

Shey grabbed it from him and with her two fingers plunged them into the jar. With the contents of the jar on her fingers, she rubbed her nipple. "Want a treat?"

Sam couldn't believe what was happening. He sucked on it as she moaned. "Oh so good." She dipped her fingers again and made a trail south.

"See what you can find," she challenged.

Sam searched with gusto and soon she was bucking and screaming, violently. "Oh my God!

That's when the bed collapsed and the power went out in the apartment, but neither Shey nor Sam noticed.

———•———

"Ohhh God," Sam whispered. He was freezing cold and his head throbbed. Where was he? Last night's sexual games came back to him as Shey stirred beside him and opened her eyes.

"Oh shit, what happened?" Shey groaned. "Oh no, I brought you home didn't I."

"Uh yeah, you invited me in and … "

"Oh no, please don't tell anyone."

Now Sam was starting to panic. "I won't but … I mean … "

"Sam it's OK, not your fault. I guess too much tequila, but I'm engaged.

"Engaged?"

"Yeah, he's in the States, a neuro resident. I came down here to get a degree and to become a neurologist. I guess the loneliness and the booze … " She started to cry.

"No, please don't cry. I swear I won't tell anyone. I'm so sorry." Sam was upset. He didn't know what to do.

Shey looked at him and gave him a little kiss. "This can't happen again. I'm so sorry. It was really nice last night."

She was feeling her body and grimacing. "Ugh, so sticky." She brought up some thick red liquid on her hand and her eyes went wide. "I'm bleeding?"

Sam looked and his nose twitched. He laughed and licked her fingers. "Not unless your blood is made of strawberry jam."

"Oh fuck," she laughed. "Gotta clean up. You relax Sam, I'm going to take a shower then make us coffee." She darted into the shower and Sam stretched and heard a horrendous scream.

"Shey, what's the matter? Are you OK?" He jumped out of the bed.

"The water is ice cold!"

She ran back, shivering in a towel, and flicked the light switch. No lights went on.

"We can't wash, the hot-water heater is electric," she wailed.

Sam, sticky and smelling of strawberries, growled, "Shit, even sex is cursed in Mexico."

———•———

The bones were ready for shellacking. Carlito led them to a large screened porch where they kept cooling racks for the tortillas.

"You're lucky that we don't need to make tortillas for the next 24 hours, otherwise the air would be filled with corn flour and your shellacking would be grainy. I recommend you do this today and it can dry overnight."

"Listen Carlito, thanks for all this."

"No problema, Andy. I expect a token of your appreciation."

Andy smiled and pulled a sack out of his backpack. "I think you will find this more than satisfactory. Just do me a favor and keep the stuff hidden since I am not ready for distributing yet."

Carlito was going to faint or reach sexual climax after seeing the contents of the sack. "Oh, you are too generous, my friend. This may keep me going for months."

"Well, thank's again for your help and remember, hide the stuff."

After Carlito had left, Sam asked, "What did you give him, Andy? Drugs, American dollars, more drugs?"

"No, nothing like that. I have stuff that a man in his position needs very much. That it is importado makes this stuff very valuable and rare. I daresay Carlito will be our friend a long time."

"Great, Carlito is happy. But, what did you give him?"

Andy just smiled at Sam. "Oh, something that with a little luck will support my family while we live down here. By the way I've got a proposition for you."

"Sure, anything except going out with Carlito," said Sam, puzzled.

"We'll talk later."

Chapter 5

If You Can't Be a Doctor, Start a Business

Sam and Marvin were sipping down two cold ones. Sam had been depressed since his night with Shey. The weather didn't help as it continued to be cold and dreary. Shey was unavailable and anyway it wasn't Shey he missed. He wasn't like Bennie, all fun, and ready for any kind of a woman. Even Andy had that bitch of his, but at least he was warm at night.

He couldn't get Leah out of his mind, her smile, her wit, the way she nervously laughed when she had scored a point in a conversation. He just couldn't understand, with a love as strong as he felt for her, how could she reject him so. He had written letters in care of her parents' house, but so far he hadn't gotten a single response. When he tried to call her, no one picked up. It was as if a cold lump of emptiness sat at the center of his chest. How could he study, even concentrate, when she was so much on his mind?

"Hey Sam, where are you?"

"Here. What's the matter?"

Marvin sighed. "Forget her, Sam. Your priority is to study, study, study. You have to pass the National Boards to get out of here next year and you also have to pass your classes at the school. No excuses."

"Yeah, I know," Sam was plainly annoyed. What did Marvin know about his love for her? In fact how could an old guy like Marvin know anything about love.

"OK, stay focused. Wanna go get some tacos and then hit the books?"

"I'd love to Marvin, but Andy wanted to talk to me about some help he needed. I'm supposed to go over there in an hour."

"Some help? Did he say what kind of help?

"Not yet, but he sounded like it might be an adventure."

When Sam arrived at Andy's place, Andy took him to a back room covered in laundry waiting to be folded. "So you know that I left a low-paying job—don't sit there, those are clean—I had to borrow money from every available source open to me to go to school." Andy was sitting in an easy chair that had been cast off from a previous renter.

"I figured that studying here while supporting your wife and kids meant either you were filthy rich or that you were in hock to guys with crooked noses."

"Well it's not that bad, but I owe the in-laws, including a brother-in-law, a lot of green. There is also the Dime Bank of New York. I owe them more than a couple of dimes. This brings me to my proposition. You're a smart, good-looking kid. People like being around you."

"Wait a second Andy, this isn't illegal is it?" Sam was worried. He liked Andy a lot and probably owed him his medical career, but he also knew the stories of Mexican jails. Besides, he didn't think he wanted to be used by a big hairy Mexican named Juanito.

"No it's not illegal," Andy said. There was a silence. "Well it's not majorly illegal."

"It's not drugs is it?" Sam asked wide-eyed.

"No, no it is definitely not drugs, in fact I think it's a public service. One that will allow you to meet interesting people, provide a

public service, and maybe—and this is a big maybe—find a little lovin'
on the side."

Sam was now intrigued. "What are we talking about, Andy?"

"Hmm, the best way is probably to show you. Come on, I'll show
you the stash."

Andy stood up and led Sam toward the rear of the house. "Quiet,
or the bitch will know what we are up to."

"I heard that, you eunuch!" Marla bellowed.

The back of Andy's house led into a cavernous garage that held
sealed boxes of various sizes, some marked with mysterious code titles
in English, some in Chinese. They were stacked along the walls and
divided into sections like the warehouse for a department store. "What
is all this stuff and how did you get it here?"

"It wasn't easy but thanks to strategic packing and good luck from
the Lord I got it all here from the Lower East Side. It's products that
women like," Andy said with a smile.

"Perfume?"

"Oh, that and so much more. We are going to sell this stuff at
tremendous profit to a certain concentrated segment of Mexican
society."

Sam's mouth dropped open.

Mexico imposed exorbitant taxes on anything that was imported
for sale to its citizens. This meant that only the very rich could afford
to buy imported goods. Mexican industry, which was perceived to make
inferior goods, had a virtual monopoly on necessities and comfort
products like cosmetics. Many women's magazines had internationalized
so that *Vogue*, *Harper's Bazaar*, and *Cosmopolitan* were now published
in multiple languages and were distributed throughout Mexico. As
demand for foreign cosmetics grew, so did a black market.

Women are women everywhere in the world. They want to look

nice. They want to know what the world is saying about fashion, make-up, birth control and the "10 Sexy Things You Can Do in the Bedroom to Make Him Yours Forever." Mexican women were no exception.

There was one small problem. The goods and services advertised and written about in the magazines were either unavailable in Mexico or were so expensive, being importado, that only the richest women in Mexico could afford them.

Andy was a smart guy. He realized that in addition to his payments on various educational loans he also had to house and feed his family. Money would still have to come into the household while he was in school.

Andy spent countless hours in the library studying Mexican life and business. He learned about the horrendous taxation that was imposed on foreign imports and he learned about supply and demand.

The more Andy read the more he realized he might have hit on a surefire business. He needed only to find a way to bring merchandise into Mexico. The other problem was to find a market that would absorb a lot of merchandise quickly and quietly to avoid the Mexican authorities. This required Andy to become a smuggler. He went back to the library searching for answers to his distribution problems.

One day in the library, despondent because he just couldn't find an answer, Andy read an article in an obscure sociology journal that pointed out the answer. It was as if God Himself had told Andy to go forth and make the women of Mexico happy. So what if it was only a small percentage of a certain sociological segment of women. Andy smiled and started looking through ads to purchase a vehicle and then make a trip to the Lower East Side of Manhattan. His smile became bigger. This was going to be a blast.

"Douche!"

"Well, that's not all there is. There are lipsticks, perfume, cologne, eyeliner, and mascara in addition to flavored and un-flavored douche."

"Jesus, where are we going to sell this stuff? We can't just go door to door. The cops will be on to us in thirty seconds flat."

"Ahh, my boy, this is where the genius of research comes in. Ever hear of Boy's Town?"

"Boy's Town? What's that, a prison?"

"Oh no, it's a wonderful place filled with the stuff wet dreams are made of."

———————

Andy had it figured out. For sociological reasons Mexico's men needed a legal source of women. The Catholicism of Mexico kept unattached men from "sowing their wild oats." Society, recognizing this need, set up a system whereby these men could visit special areas of town where they could purchase the services of women. In this part of town the women who sold their services could earn money while being protected by the local police. It was a system that was widely accepted. Prostitution was tolerated in these commercial areas, usually called Boy's Towns.

The Boy's Town in Ciudad Juarez across the border from El Paso, Texas was legendary. Because of the large Air Force facilities in El Paso, Boy's Town was big enough for its own zip code.

Tampico's Boy's Town was in Ciudad Madero, a suburb of Tampico, and accessible by a two-lane, unlit, unpaved road in a corner of the city limits. It contained bars, jukeboxes, and women. The bars all had small rooms attached to the buildings and were run by a Mamacita. There were women who catered to every socio-economic class of Mexicans and foreigners.

Andy had made multiple trips to the Lower East Side of New York where knock-offs were the specialty of the area. There, the beauty supply stores catered to women of color and those with very little to spend on luxuries.

Lipsticks in garish colors, perfumes with strong floral components, and of course products that "ensured he'd always come back for more." Beer flavored douches and brightly colored condoms were among the most interesting.

Andy made deals for lipsticks that cost him 10 cents a stick and colognes that cost a buck or two a bottle. Within a month, having spent almost $300 for boxes of these products, he was on to the next problem—getting his supply into Mexico.

He finally found exactly what he needed.

"Jesus, how long did it take you to build this?"

Andy showed Sam the interior of the yellow school bus he purchased back on Long Island. "Oh, about a month to figure out how to give myself the maximal space and build the lockers. The interesting part was building the fake crate fronts, and piling toys and household goods into the small spaces."

Sam was amazed as he inspected the school bus. Lockered cabinets were built with false fronts that jutted out about two inches from the locker. The false fronts looked like the sides of crates on tops of crates that didn't fully close. Toys and household goods jutted out. "Man, this is incredible."

Andy smiled, "Yeah, I'm pretty proud of myself. I loaded all the merchandise in and then filled the rest of the space with boxes of our household goods, clothes, and food. With the kids running around creating their usual ruckus, the border patrol was glad to take a quick look and get us out of there. My kids. Aren't they great?"

"So Boy's Town is where you're going to sell the stuff? Why do you think that's safer than finding a person in the neighborhood who will help sell it door to door?"

"Well I have already made the excursion to Boy's Town a couple of times and there is a small contingent of police, but they seem to be there to keep the drunks from breaking up the bars or hurting the girls too badly. I think the girls themselves will protect us when they find out how much cheaper this stuff is compared to buying in Mexico."

"How much cheaper?" Sam asked.

"A lipstick down here is about five to ten dollars. Mexico doesn't really have a lipstick factory so almost all of the products are brought in from elsewhere. I bought these as 10 cents per stick 'seconds'. They come in colors that only the Caribbean girls living in New York like. I'll sell them for the equivalent of a buck fifty. My guess is I'll get rid of them immediately. Pricing will be similar for the other items I have."

"So where do I fit in?"

"You, my friend, are both driver and salesman. Obviously, I can't drive the school bus there and I can't take all this stuff by cab. You have a car, and more importantly you have that sweet, innocent, All-American Jew Boy look that women love."

"So you are basically using me," Sam said with a laugh. "Why not Bennie? He is more charming."

"And not stable. The key to this whole thing is quiet charm, stay under the radar. That's not Bennie's forte. Look, I'll give you a percentage of the sales; this way you have some entertainment money to use in the Town."

"I see what you mean. OK. I'll do it. When do we start?"

"How about in a couple of days. Weekdays are best because the girls are not as busy. "

"I doubt I'll ever need to use the services of the Town."

"Well, we'll see. There aren't a hell of a lot of other outlets for a dick here in Mexico, at least safely."

———•———

"Vamos aver, Rodriguez."

The usual four students got up to present to Valdez. Valdez with his customary shaded eyes could never figure out why they couldn't read his mind and know which one of them he wanted. Sam was slouched in the uncomfortable chair trying to see through blurry eyes. Last night he had promised himself no more than a couple of beers. Unfortunately, one of the more financially secure students brought over some killer mezcal that Sam just had to try. Try he did and now he had a tremendous tequila headache. Maybe it was true that one shouldn't mix alcoholic beverages.

He had sent the fifteenth letter to Leah last night before he started his introduction to mixed drinks. He hadn't heard from Leah since leaving San Diego. To be fair, she was in Israel. Did mail get to Israel from Tampico?

She was a million miles away, and not only hadn't she promised that they would get back together, but also said in no uncertain terms they would be reduced to mere "friends" when she got back. The realistic and mature posture to take was to forget her. She wanted a new life. How much clearer was that? Unfortunately, Sam knew his heart always had control over his mind, so the depression became worse.

Andy's extra money for Boy's Town … it wasn't love, but it might be relief.

"Vamos aver, Ko-haan!"

Shit! Couldn't Valdez leave him alone? "Sí, Professor?"

"What is this I am pointing to?"

Sam looked at the slide for the first time since having taken his seat. It was a blown up picture of the pelvis. He was pointing to a pelvic structure that looked like some vessel leading deep into the pelvis, maybe running anterior?

"Ko-haan, stop stalling. The patient is waiting for his great doctor."

The class started laughing. "Silencio! Ko-haan, now!"

"It is the testicular artery, Professor?"

The class again laughed, and this time Valdez laughed with them.

"You should tell your patient she is a man in real life. She won't believe you because she has felt balls, but never on herself you idiot. Sit down now."

Sam's face once again reddened. This time he wasn't angry at Valdez, just at himself. He wasn't ever going to become a doctor if he didn't get his shit together.

<hr />

Sam slammed the door to his room in the hotel. He was so angry that the room appeared as one gigantic blur, like an op-art poster whose details you think you know but really can't make out. He threw his bag at the desk knocking off the water bottle. The bottle smashed against the wall sending splinters of glass and drops of water flying, each creating a rainbow in the bright sunlight streaming through the window. A loud knock came from the shut door. "Leave me the fuck alone!" he yelled.

A muffled voice replied, "Open up shithead or I'll get Carlito to open this door."

"Fuck," he replied and opened the door letting Marvin in. Marvin took in the room, noting the broken glass and spilled water.

"What the fuck is the matter with you, Sam?" Marvin was very pissed off. "Look, I can guess what's going on in your head. We were all your age at one time, but she isn't worth it. She left you, she never wanted to see you again, you weren't good enough, she didn't want to fuck before the first anniversary. Whatever it was, I repeat, she isn't worth it."

"She was everything." Sam was stone faced. What did Marvin know about love or about her for that matter? She wasn't a Marla. She was sweet and beautiful and full of love and …

"Stop that NOW. Whatever your relationship was with her it's finished. She's on the Moon as far as you are concerned. Unobtainable!" Marvin looked at Sam realizing that he was in major trouble unless something changed the equation right now.

"Sam, her father is a doctor, right?"

"Yeah, so what?"

"I know she's Jewish. She give you the line she was always looking for a professional, a doctor or lawyer?"

Sam was now amazed. "How did you know?"

Marvin laughed. "Those Jewish girls always give us Jewish boys that line. It's fed to them in their mother's milk. OK, so here is how it goes and you need to think about this. You want her?

"Of course, more than anything … "

"Save it. Her father a doctor?"

"Yes."

"He give her a good, and by that I mean she never wants for anything, life?"

"Yeah," said Sam suspiciously.

"Well, this is the future. Step One. You keep doing what you're doing here in this shit house and you will never be a doctor. No MD, no professional. Step Two. You keep fucking up you'll never go back to the States for a residency. No residency means no profession, no profession means no money. No money means Daddy tells her if she marries you she will never have the House in the Five Towns, never have the Saks charge card, never vacation in Aruba, never have the 3.8 carat F, VVS1 diamond, never be able to buy La Perla. You get the idea."

Sam looked at Marvin intently; slowly a smile broke out. "I graduate, I get the girl."

"Buddy, only if you want her after all this. In the meantime, cut out the booze, try the local talent, and study, study, study."

———•———

Sam started studying and as time went on Leah was less on his mind. He still wanted her, but knew Marvin was right. It was the only avenue open to him. Returning to San Diego with no degree confirmed that Professor Goldman was correct. Only A students became doctors. It was time to grow up. She was either missing him or boinking every stud Sabra that smiled at her. It was time Sam buckled down and got his priorities straight.

But first he had to help Andy.

———•———

"We're loaded up, Andy."

They had loaded a couple of boxes with lipsticks, cologne, and douche. In addition Andy had made up two string bags filled with samples that they could take from bar to bar, showing off their wares.

They drove into the night down streets that were poorly lit but paved, then streets paved and unlit, and finally pitch black and unpaved. The stars were bright in the sky. Sam, having lived most of his life in cities, had never seen a night sky so beautiful and awe-inspiring. Finally, there was a glow on the horizon and small buildings with garish neon lighting came into view. The music of multiple jukeboxes and the sound of drunken men staggering from building to building signaled Sam and Andy they had arrived.

———•———

"Which direction do you want to go?" Andy asked.

Sam looked around. "Uh, I guess that way," he said, looking up the street. "What is that smell?" There was a pungent, musky, sour smell that hung in the air, unpleasant but not overwhelming.

"My guess, the smell of hundreds of desperate men with their cocks up and alcohol in their bellies. Of course, the rotting horse meat isn't helping, or the hibachis, or the open sewer system. Why don't we plan to meet back here in an hour and a half and compare notes."

"OK," Sam said. "You sure this is safe?"

"Yeah, I think this is safer than using a toilet here. Remember, just in case, cover that rascal first." He pointed at Sam's crotch.

Sam laughed, said "Fuck you," and walked up the street to the first big bar.

———•———

The Casa Blanca was the name in red, white, and blue neon. Next to the name also outlined in neon was a very buxom woman in a "come hither" pose. The noise of the men inside and the jukebox was deafening as Sam walked into the bar through swinging doors like the ones hanging on saloons in Westerns.

Before him was a cavernous room, dimly lit. The cigarette smoke was so thick the far edges of the place were hard to make out. At one end was a large bar made of old distressed dark wood. Dilapidated stools, the seats covered in a red plastic, were placed along the bar in a haphazard fashion. The men were mostly Mexican wearing cheaply made clothes, their black hair slicked back with Brylcreem. There was also a smattering of Americans and Europeans that sat or stood, most with a tequila or a beer in front of them, uncomfortable in the setting, but like the Mexicans their eyes locked onto a doorway ejecting women wearing tight dresses that showed a lot of skin up top and down low. Coming from an ancient jukebox, half it's neon lights dead, Elton John sang about not breaking his heart.

He walked up to the bar and motioned to the bartender.

"*Sí Señor, Que quieres?*"

"I would like to speak to the manager," Sam said, figuring this was the way to make a pitch and get out.

"Manager," the bartender said, "you just came in and don't like something already?"

"No, no I don't want to complain, I'd like to show him some very special merchandise."

The bartender went on alert. He whispered, "We don't sell drugs here. It is illegal in Mexico, gringo!"

"Jesus, keep your voice down," Sam said, now nervous and looking around for any police. "I'm not selling drugs of any kind. This is stuff for women. You know, personal stuff that only a woman would use."

A deep, gruff voice from the end of the bar said, "What kind of stuff, gringo?"

A tall, busty woman approached from the end of the bar. She was sporting 40 DD's, a skin-tight dress, and a five o'clock shadow.

"What are you selling, my beautiful amigo?"

"Uh," Sam stammered. While not caring what guys did for kicks, he didn't have a lot of experience with full-blown transvestites. "Mostly cosmetics, cologne, other things that you probably wouldn't find useful."

"Oh, you beautiful man, let me see the cosmetics." The transvestite reached over and patted Sam's hand. "You know lipstick is so expensive in this fucking country. What's a girl supposed to do to be beautiful for her man?" She smiled, "Or men."

"Right." The transvestite looked at the bartender with a perplexed look. "Your friend is a brilliant conversationalist isn't he?" Maybe you should find Lola. She might want to see what this hombre has to sell." The bartender smiled and walked off.

"What's the matter, amigo? Are you uncomfortable sitting with a beautiful woman? Maybe my tits are too big and luscious for you?"

Sam was now blushing crimson and sweating, "No, I, uh … "

"Maybe he is not used to the stubble of a beard on a woman who might want to give him a blow job?"

"Oh Lola, you bitch, you have arrived," the transvestite said smiling. Nodding to Sam he said, "This beautiful boy may have some merchandise to show us. Maybe I can get it cheaper for a favor." He reached for Sam's crotch.

Lola blocked the transvestite's hand. "You have no class, Brunhilda. Have you even introduced yourself properly, cabron?"

Chastened, Brunhilda turned to Sam, "Perdone me Amigo, my name is Brunhilda and this is my puta friend, Lola. Can we see what you have brought?"

By this point Sam was hardly listening. Lola was a knockout, somewhat like a live Barbie doll. She was tall, blonde, with luscious red lips, mammoth firm breasts, and a valentine shaped ass. All thoughts that Sam had for the love of his life disappeared with the appearance of this woman who was built for sex. He had problems keeping his eyes off her chest. Her breasts were mesmerizing.

"Hi, I'm Sam. I represent a service that can bring you cosmetics at a price that is affordable. These cosmetics will enhance any woman's beauty. We also supply other products of a more personal nature to women in your business."

"Hey Sam, since you want to sell me something and I am not selling you anything at this time … UP HERE."

His eyes snapped to her face, his cheeks now the color of apples. She started laughing.

"Don't worry, *joven*. It is a common reaction." She felt herself up, lifting and separating her rack. "They are beautiful ... no?"

"Y-Yes," he stuttered, now more embarrassed than ever.

"Bring him una cerveza," she ordered the bartender. "Now let's look at your goods. You looked at mine long enough."

He gave up. She was definitely too much for him. He handed over the bag, which she started going through, taking out things that interested her.

"I love these colors, joven. They are from the States, sí?"

"Yes, all the way from New York City. Did you see the cologne?"

She took out the sampler and sprayed a little on her delicate wrists and aired them, then she smelled the cologne. "Hmm, a little heavy for me, but ... " she looked around. "Brunhilda, try this. I think it would go good with your chemistry."

She continued going through the odds and ends of the bag, finally finding white, minimally labeled packets containing liquid.

"What are these, joven?"

It was the question Sam was dreading. "They are packets to clean the ... the, you know ... uhh ... down there ... the privates," he stammered.

"The privates? Private what? I don't understand," Lola said. "Explain better, what do you clean with this."

"It is to clean ... you know, down there. After a woman bleeds or has intercourse," he continued.

"Oh, it's douche," Lola said happily. We make our own to keep clean, what's so special about this?"

Sam answered uncomfortably, "It's ... uhh ... flavored."

Lola, Brunhilda, and the bartender all started laughing

uncontrollably. "What flavors, joven?" Brunhilda laughed even harder and Sam became even more uncomfortable when she asked, "Have you tasted them?"

"No, I haven't tasted them, but the flavors are printed on the packet. I believe that one is cherry ... "

They were splitting their sides with laughter now and the bartender choked out, "I don't think there is anyone here with a cherry, maybe we need a few dozen of that flavor."

Sam ignored this while the others could barely stand up, " ... grape, strawberry, and I think root beer."

Lola tried to get control of herself. "Root beer, now that's not decent."

Sam soldiered on though he was so embarrassed he just wanted to get out of this place and go back to the hotel. "The lipstick goes for two dollars, or the equivalent in pesos, the cologne for five dollars, and the douche for seventy-five cents a pack. You can let me know on my next visit if you are interested or if there is anyone else interested. I can pick up orders later in the week."

"Joven, when can you deliver?" Lola put the samples back in the bag.

"Uh, in a few days. What do you think you want?"

Lola looked at Brunhilda, who nodded. "You bring us 100 lipsticks of various shades, twenty bottles of cologne and as much douche as you have that's not root beer flavored."

"Wait," Brunhilda blurted. She was almost purple in the face from laughing. "Bring the root beer also. We will buy it all if you can bring the merchandise in a week."

Sam was in shock. "I'm sure I can arrange this with my friend. Do you really need all of this?"

Lola got up and started walking to the back. "I don't need much, joven, but … " she said, looking at Brunhilda, "I'm sure there are many girls here that do."

———◆———

"My God, the mother lode." Andy was ecstatic. "We might be able to get rid of this entire load within a couple of weeks."

"I guess. Now we have to get all the stuff here. Don't you think someone will notice?" Sam was happy that Andy would be able to support his family, but was worried that someone would be suspicious of boxes moving into the place.

"Sam, you're amazing. There'll be a couple of shekels under your Chanukah bush soon. We'll get the boxes here. Now let's vamos, class tomorrow. Do you know the bones of the wrist? Don't want to look bad in front of the class."

———◆———

The next morning Andy, Bennie, and Sayeed found Sam sitting on the wall wearing very dark sunglasses and snoring.

"Wake up Sleeping Beauty," Sayeed shook Sam's shoulder. "Wake up, come on."

Sam started batting Sayeed away, "leave me alone, I'm tired, Mom."

Sayeed shook him harder. "Come on, we have class."

Sam groaned, "Up all night, memorizing pisi this, trique that. Christ, where do they come up with these names?"

Bennie looked at Sam. "Scared Lovers Try Positions That They Can't Handle."

"Wha', I'm not scared and I don't have a lover, why would I care?" Sam said to Bennie.

"Hey man, it's a mnemonic. SCARED is the scaphoid bone, LOVERS is the lunate, TRY is triquetral, POSITIONS is pisiform,

THAT is trapezium, THEY is trapezoid, CAN'T is capitate, and HANDLE is hamate. It's a mnemonic, isn't that cool?"

"Yeah, cool," said Sam dully. "Why didn't anyone tell me about this stuff last night?"

They entered the school only to find the monitor barring them from the class.

"No school today, go home now," he said.

Sam smiled , "Hallelujah, I'm saved from another Valdez tirade."

Sayeed went over to the monitor, "Hey amigo, why no Professor Valdez? Is he sick?"

"Go home now. Leave the school immediately." The monitor looked worried. He was physically trying to move all the students out of the building. Sayeed went over to a group of the Mexican students.

Bennie was agitated. "Hey, what do you think is going on? Think that the school closed? Maybe there is a war?"

"Bennie, chill," said Andy as he saw Sayeed return. "Sayeed, what's going on?"

Sayeed looked worried, "Man, they are close mouthed, but from what info I could get, there is a rally for the governing party starting in an hour and they want all the Americans out of the school. One of the Mexican students actually thought it might be a good idea if the gringos stayed off the street."

"There has never been political violence here, at least that I remember reading about. What do you think is going on?"

Andy just sighed. "Who the hell knows? Remember in most ways the political situation here is just one step above a Banana Republic. I think we all should heed the advice for now. Go home and stay off the streets. Anybody wanting to hang at my place is welcome. You might bring some bedding as a just in case. Oh and a case of beer as a contribution would be greatly appreciated.

Bennie whooped, "Alright, sleepover!"

They gathered at Andy's house to ride out whatever political drama was at hand. For once Marla was somewhat civil. Andy told them when she left to get the kids bathed, that she was happy that Andy had brought backup. Just in case the Mexican soldiers decided to come to the door to rape and pillage.

"Well I guess we are useful for something," Sam said. "Maybe she will be grateful that we are here and not scream at us anymore."

Andy laughed, "Yeah, and it never rains in Southern California."

The evening was relaxed with Andy supplying the food and the rest supplying the beer. They heard music over loudspeakers and drums out in the neighborhood, but no one came up to Andy's house. Just before dawn the last vestiges of music, drums, and loudspeaker systems faded into the background.

Andy grunted and then belched loudly. "Well, I hope this blows over quickly. I have deliveries to make and a medical education to pursue."

Marvin looked annoyed at Andy. "You do realize how dangerous selling anything down here is? You're smuggling. God only knows what they'd do to you."

"They won't do anything to me or my friend Sam. First, we are careful. Second, the hookers love us for bringing them the finest in cosmetics and feminine hygiene products. Third, the money is big time for me, but in the grand scheme of things the federales are making a hell of a lot more shaking down the bars and the girls. We are not worth their time."

Sayeed, also concerned, broke in, "Andy, it just isn't worth it. You have a wife and kids down here. If you get put away they're fucked and you know it. Why are you dragging Sam into this?"

"Look, I need to do this. It is the way I keep the juggling balls in the air. Anyway, Sam is a great salesman and will make money off of this. Besides he volunteered."

"Andy, just take out another loan. In the end the debt won't matter, you'll make enough to cover it."

"You guys just don't understand. You are all single. A wife and kids are very expensive. I think I'm going to get some shut-eye, just in case we have classes later. Maybe we should all get some shut-eye."

They began to drift off to sleep, with the exception of Sam, who began to reconsider his newfound trade as a smuggler in Mexico.

———◆———

The political activity that had worried the school turned out to be much ado about nothing. The word spread immediately that classes would resume on their normal schedule. Sam felt he was prepared for once. He remembered something about lovers and sex positions, though he couldn't remember if the word sex had anything to do with the mnemonic. With the day bright and sunny and the smell of raw sewage and oil abated because of a prevailing offshore breeze, Sam enjoyed his coffee and torta and savored life. Marvin met him at the wall with a smile on his face.

"After living in the Bronx all my life, these days of sun and ocean air are a fucking pleasure. Like Paradise on Earth."

"Yes, it is beautiful out here. Wish we could play hooky, go to the beach and look at bikinis and what's in them."

Marvin chuckled, "Yeah, but the job awaits. We'd better get inside."

They made their way into the classroom and found Andy, Bennie, and Sayeed.

"Have you ever seen such a beautiful day? What say after we're finished with this BS we drive over to the beach and check out the native wildlife?" Bennie looked manic and ready to rumble.

Sam agreed. "That's a great idea. We can even work on our knowledge of human anatomy while we're at it."

"Vamos aver!" The grating voice of Valdez put an end to their good mood. Looking more bedraggled than ever, he was wearing a button-down shirt that was mis-buttoned and his complexion was more ruddy than usual. Even from the back seats the smell of stale alcohol was evident. When he came out from behind the lectern it was apparent he had spent the night in a gutter and had probably urinated on himself.

"Estudiantes, he burped, "vamos aver, … Sanchez!"

A cute little Mexican girl, probably not older than sixteen, rose from her seat.

"*Que linda,*" he leered. He was having a hard time keeping his balance. Sam knew that there wasn't an ounce of professionalism with Valdez, but to show up in class this drunk was a disgrace.

Suddenly the screen popped up with the new anatomic slide. It was a giant penis that had been partially dissected to show the working parts. The class was stunned and then began nervously laughing. The poor girl was mortified.

"*Que es esto?*" Valdez asked with a smile.

She just stammered, not being able to get the words out. Valdez started chuckling, "My dear, come on, you know what this is, or maybe your boyfriend hasn't shown you this part of his anatomy?" By now he was laughing uncontrollably while the poor girl was frozen solid.

"It's a dick, now leave her alone asshole!" Sam cried out, deepening his voice to hide his identity.

There was dead silence in the room. The Mexican girl ran out of the room while all the other students looked at the Americans to find the instigator of the challenge.

"Who said that? I will kill the fucker!" Valdez lurched unsteadily toward the Americans and ended up tripping and hitting his head on a seat, where he lay unconscious. There was pandemonium in the class as both students and monitors tried to reach Valdez, only to trip over each other. Sam and company quietly left the class when the monitor dismissed everyone.

"Are you out of your fucking mind?"

"Marvin, the asshole had to be stopped. The poor girl was about to break down in front of everyone," Sam said defensively.

"And that was your business how?" Marvin asked, good and angry. "Do you realize what problems you can make for the entire American class?"

"Uh, I guess I didn't think … Come on, man, what about justice? Is it all dog eat dog all the time?"

"Thinking is not one of your strong suits, is it? Well let's hope that Valdez was too drunk to remember exactly what happened or that he will be embarrassed enough not to want to relive it. Want to go to the beach?"

Sam smiled. "Only if you let me buy the beers."

It certainly wasn't the beach in San Diego and Marvin said it wasn't even the beach in most parts of Long Island, but there was sun, salt water, and girls in all manner of swimsuit attire, showing some skin. The men were looking and the girls were enjoying the attention.

Marvin and Sam found a beautiful observation spot after picking up a six pack.

"Did you hear the rumor about The Guad?" Marvin asked?"

"Which of the million zillion rumors is it?"

Marvin smiled. "Guad is letting its fourth year students go back to the States for electives."

"You're kidding. You mean they commuted the sentence. Where are they going? Guad has a hospital in the States?"

"I'm not sure of the details, but it seems that if those students can find a hospital to take them they can complete their education in the States."

"That's incredible." Sam was already envisioning treating English-speaking patients and being taught by English-speaking doctors. "Maybe we made a mistake coming here. We should talk to Andy about investigating the rumor and if it is true hauling ass to Guadalajara. Anyway, the little I heard, aside from the Neo-Nazi tendencies of the school, living in Guad is like living in New York."

"Whoa, boy. You are getting way ahead of yourself. We haven't even completed the first semester here. Besides you are thinking small."

"What do you mean?" Sam asked curiously.

"First, it's a rumor. Second, Guad just started this experiment. We have no idea if any of its students will be able to break into American hospitals. I'm sure that the AMA will have something to say about this development, and what they say will most probably be nasty. Third, if we go to Guad, saying that anyone actually has the money left for another move, it is three long years before we can escape, all the while being under martial law. Fourth, why do the work when the system will take care of it for us, provided the experiment is successful."

Sam was trying to make sense of Marvin's words. "OK, I understand the first three points, but I'm not understanding the fourth point."

"OK, as we are sitting on two ends of a log, let's try Aristotelian education. Admissions to medical schools in the States. Admission harder or easier?"

"I'm sure harder," Sam said confidently.

"One point to you. It is doubtful anything will change in the States. Being a doctor is a ticket to wealth and respect, something most people want very much. The AMA's sole job is to keep the numbers of graduating doctors to a minimum so that healthcare reimbursements stay at high levels. In other words, they don't want to share. Now for Question Two, number of medical schools in Mexico. Going up or down?"

"Uh, up?"

"You're on a roll. You think Garza is the only Mexican looking at the money Guadalajara is generating from letting gringos into its hallowed halls?"

"Uh, no," Sam said uncertainly.

"Believe me there are dozens of them thinking the same thing as Garza. Minimal cost for a building, a couple of used broken microscopes, second-hand desks and shit teachers. As the next cost saver maybe we'll let the fourth year students take care of themselves. It's the recipe for millions of dollars. I wouldn't be surprised if there isn't some American lawyer, right now in bed with a foreign governmental official, that isn't trying to start a foreign med school."

Sam nodded, "So basically we let Garza figure this out himself. But do you think that come fourth year I'll be back in California?"

"I think that if Guad's experiment works, the rest of these schools will be tripping over each other to offer a better deal. Yeah, I think we will all be back in the States. The question is when. Hey, look at that cute thing." Marvin was smiling as he pointed out the beauty who was walking the beach.

Sam tracked with Marvin, "Yeah, beautiful and young enough to be your daughter."

Marvin shook himself to get up. "Yeah, but my 'non-jail bait' daughter. In Mexico that's legal. Let's grab some more beers and head back to the hotel."

———•———

It was another night in Boy's Town. Sam took his bag out of the car to deliver to Casa Blanca. He had gotten used to the smell of stale beer with a hint of urine, the neon lights flickering at places signaling a lack of maintenance, and the clientele of the place desperate to fulfill sexual needs that wives or girlfriends wouldn't. The Casa Blanca in turn welcomed him as an old friend—after all, here he wasn't a medical student, but a lowlife black-market salesman; he fit in perfectly in Boy's Town.

"Sam, como esta?" The bartender set him up with a bottle of Dos Equis, the official beer of the red light zone.

"All good. Anything new here?"

"The usual, drunks, drunks and putas."

Sam chuckled. He actually liked the flavor of the place. There was a spice in the air that he had rarely experienced in San Diego. The bartenders were affable and had great stories when they weren't busy with drunks. The clientele were mostly friendly and sometimes bought a round in payment for the companionship of a like-minded amigo helping to scope out the women offering themselves. There were Americans, mostly students, mixed with the occasional international businessman, private plane pilots, and Mexicans—both the rich businessmen and the poorer farmers that arrived wearing denim coveralls and straw cowboy hats. Of course, the girls were the best part of the place. Every size, every shape, and every age, were all represented and here to give a man a few moments of pleasure while separating him from his money.

"Hey, is Lola here tonight?" Sam was now comfortable with the selling game. The girls wanted the cheap stuff that Andy had brought in from New York. It practically sold itself. In addition to Sam having a couple of extra bucks in his pocket, he now had the companionship of multiple young ladies who loved pressing their tits and asses into him. At first his prudish side didn't relish the contact, but as he got to know them he realized they too were in the selling game. As long as he kept that in mind and actually didn't buy the "product" he was allowed the "samples" that came his way.

"Hola, joven." Lola entered the bar area and all eyes at the Casa Blanca locked onto her walk. Her hips moved in a mystical kind of perpetual motion and breasts heaved under her dress with mesmerizing grace.

"Hola, Lola. How is it going this evening?"

"A little slow, but some gringo pilots are supposed to be coming in later so one is always hopeful. Are you here to make my life a little less dull?" She touched his cheek and looked into his eyes. "Tell you what amor, I am so bored that I'll give you a discount."

This wasn't the first time that Lola had been so generous in her offer to Sam. He just couldn't get past paying for it. It was obvious to him that Mexico was affecting him in strange ways. He was on his own. The moral and religious environment of his parents' home was slowly fading into the background. The conventional mores of upper middle class San Diego were disappearing. He was in Mexico, anything goes, everything goes, but don't get caught. Leah was in Israel, their relationship dead. A replacement for her was impossible. The Mexican girls in the classes were children and besides, between their fathers and brothers they were in virtual chastity belts. As beautiful as Lola was, he honestly didn't know if he could handle a woman like this. She seemed so ... advanced, and he still had Andy's merchandise to move and this would only complicate things.

"Maybe one of these days Lola, but right now I need to know if we can supply you with more of anything. I think Andy just found some new shades of lipstick and he had forgotten about a case of false eyelashes he had brought in."

"What are you, Amor? A *pato*? I offer you a gift and you turn it down?"

"Pato? A duck? I'm not sure what that means, but I'm sure you'll tell me."

"You know, Amor, a pato. A man who loves *verga*, cock and not pussy."

Sam laughed, "Oh, you mean a homosexual. No I'm not a pato, but for the time being I'm trying to concentrate on my studies and on selling this stuff."

Lola eyed him, "Hmmm, you are beautiful." She paused and eyed him more. "But, you are young and I think a bit of the romantico. OK, what do have for me?"

Sam sighed and started pulling out the samples.

———◆———

"Vamos aver, Class!"

Sam jerked to attention. It had been another long night and even with the best of intentions of study, study, study he just couldn't seem to finish his rounds in Boy's Town in time to do it. It might be that the beers and occasional Mexican brandy made him so sleepy. By the end of the evening he was lucky he didn't end up a statistic on the pitch black roads driving back to the hotel.

"Class, the day after tomorrow we will start dissection of the bodies the school has been so kind to find for us. Señor Garza has spared no expense providing this wonderful educational opportunity. Be ready to delve into the mysteries of the body."

The class applauded. Sam was ready. This was it, his real entrance into the world of medicine.

"Make sure to bring your dissection sets and dissection manual. We will start promptly at ten a.m. Now, vamos aver ... ."

After not hearing the usual "Ko-han," Sam tuned out.

"Hey Sam, wait up."

Bennie ran over to Sam who was trying to get back to the hotel for a little siesta before dinner.

"What's up, Bennie?"

"I think we need a bit of a celebration before the official start of our medical careers."

Sam was interested. "What did you have in mind?"

"I think a party in Boy's Town. You know, drinks, appetizers, more drinks, maybe more apps, followed by drinks in the company of women. What do you say?"

"I'm game, but it's a shame that Andy can't be with us. Marla won't unchain him and let him out of prison."

"Oh, she will this time. You know that big test that's tomorrow. Andy is going to the hotel for an all-night study session with us."

"All night, huh. You don't think that when he turns up at four a.m. reeking of cheap beer she won't figure it out?"

Bennie laughed. "That's the beauty of this. He'll shower, bring a change of clothes, and by the time he gets back from that 'test' tomorrow, she'll never know."

"Well, I hope he likes living dangerously, because if she even gets wind of this he'll have an ice pack where his balls used to be. OK, I'll meet up with you in the hotel lobby later. I'm going to rest up for tonight's festivities."

———•———

Sayeed was in a jovial mood. "Come on amigos, let's get a cab."

Sam, Bennie, Marvin, and Andy were all in the lobby of the hotel ready to go.

"Want to take my car instead of a cab?" Sam offered.

"Nah, let's get a cab so we can party all night and not have a designated driver. My treat." Sayeed was ready to party hard. He immediately went out to the street to find a cab. The rest moved to join him where they found him in a heated conversation with a driver.

"You fucking moron, Boy's Town. You know, Casa de Putas, cervezas, barras."

The driver looked scared and pissed at the same time. "Sayeed, it's a night for relaxation. Why don't you let me try," Marvin said, trying to diffuse the situation.

"Fuck this asshole. Come on, we'll find another cab."

"It seems a shame. This guy is already here. Why don't you cool off and give me a second." Marvin nodded to Sam and Andy who pulled Sayeed away while Marvin turned to talk to the cab driver. After a couple of minutes Marvin turned back to the group all smiles. "He says he will take us to Boy's Town. He just didn't understand your Spanish, Sayeed."

"Bullshit, he was just giving me problems because I look like a fucking Mexican and ... "

"Because you look like a Mexican," Bennie laughed. "Buddy, you look like a 'rab and your Spanish does suck big time."

"It does not! I speak better Spanish than you do," Sayeed yelled.

"Calm down now," said Sam. "Your Spanish is good, but you do have a heavy Brooklyn accent. Maybe that's what threw this poor cab driver."

"Well fuck him," Sayeed retorted, but the fire was going out.

"Come on, let's just get into the cab," Andy said.

They all piled in. Sam wondered about his friends. If the most mentally stable of them could be set off this easily, how was Mexico affecting the rest?

——•——

The bars were crowded with men in various stages of drunkenness. It seemed as if most of the Americans at the school had the same idea as Sayeed.

"Would you look at all the girls in here. Americans must be like chum to the sharks."

"Who cares," said a happy Sayeed. "Let's go get a beer." His friends followed him to the bar. Bennie had other ideas.

"I think I'm going to try my luck with the native fauna," he said happily.

Andy smiled, "You do realize the 'native fauna' are all hookers."

"Yeah, but that is what fantasies are made of." He took off in search of his fantasy.

The rest went to the bar. "Hey cabrons, what are you drinking tonight?" The bartender was ready for the influx of gringos and anticipating big tips.

"Whatever, but bring it now and keep it coming," Andy said.

"Tonight Dos Equis Especial."

"What's so special about our usual piss?" Sayeed asked.

"The piss is from virgins. What the fuck do I know? It seems to smell less like horse piss. Maybe the taste is less like rotting horse," he laughed and went off to get the bottles of brew.

"We all ready for our first body tomorrow? I know I can't wait," Andy said excitedly.

Sam said, "Finally I'll feel like I'm in a real medical school. I mean can you believe the histology class. I was ready for the final insult, expecting them to bring out the finger-paints."

Marvin shook his head, "Yeah, I know what you mean. I don't have as high expectations, but I was floored when they brought out the Play-Doh. I know I told you that the dibujos were just another way to learn, but clay and toothpicks?"

"Yeah, a weird educational philosophy here. I don't think Mr. Frankle ever realized what a shithole it was down here when he allowed Bennie to come to this backwater."

"I don't think Frankle cared where he sent Bennie as long as it was far from Long Island and all his business partners and friends. Less to be embarrassed about and less to have to deal with," Andy said knowingly. "Long Island society is a bitch. It's all about the house, the car, the job title, the bank account, and the vacation. You should see the train wreck kids I had to deal with and the lack of response from the parents about their little angels' problems. Bennie might actually be lucky."

"What do you mean, Andy?"

"You were raised in a close, loving family. Your success was the most important thing to your parents. As a result, when you didn't make it into an American medical school your parents took drastic measures, knowing full well the sacrifice that would be required."

"You mean money?" Sam asked.

"No, money was the least of it," Andy responded.

Marvin nodded knowingly. "They sent their son to a dangerous, backward country that might harm him because they wanted to support his dream. I'm sure it almost killed them to send you here. Frankle never had those feelings. He just wanted not to be bothered with his son."

Sam, Andy, Marvin, and Sayeed proceeded to pile up empty bottles of beer. The bartender obliged, occasionally sneaking them small shots of tequila as an aperitif for more beer. He liked to keep his customers happy. The girls would come over and try to get a customer, but had no luck.

Suddenly there was a loud disturbance from the rear of the bar.

"What the hell is that?" Sayeed cried.

Soon a very drunk familiar student came into the bar.

"I'm going to fucking kill that fag," the student slurred. The student was well known to his classmates. He was a pompous ass and the boys all knew him by the nickname that Sayeed had given him on day one of classes: Boushanab.

Chapter 6

The She-He Wasn't What He-She Seemed to Be

A stereotype of the student emerged in medical schools South of the Border. This type of student was typically raised by a father who believed in connections. Need a new car? "I have a guy in Bay Ridge." Need a loan? "I can talk to my dearest friend." Want a neighbor to stop a lawsuit? "Well, I know the best lawyer in town."

The father's connections were mostly fantasy. What was worse? The father felt he was better than everyone else. He raised his son in the same mold. When the father's connections all failed to assure his son admittance to Harvard Medical School, connections got him admitted to a Mexican medical school. The son came to Mexico vain, proud, and willing to tell anyone who would listen that he was the son of a man with important connections. The son never realized or admitted to being in the same fucked situation as the rest of them.

The son had a tendency to prance instead of walk, always with his chest out. He also sported a thick, black moustache. After speaking to Sam, Andy, Bennie, and totally ignoring Sayeed ("hey what are you guys doing hanging around with a 'rab?") Sayeed nicknamed him Boushanab.

The group decided that this wasn't the kind of person they wanted to hang out with and ignored any further invitations for camaraderie.

"Sayeed, why do you call him Boushanab?" Sam asked him one day.

"Because that is what he is. It is a slang word in my part of the world for a worthless, vain, playboy. Sometimes we use this expression for a very effeminate homosexual. In any case he is shit, from shit."

Boushanab's personality clashed with most of the students at the school and soon all knew the meaning of the nickname. Guys being guys, they told Boushanab that Sayeed was very impressed with him and gave him a great handle. Boushanab took the nickname as a tribute to his greatness and that of his father's greatness. What's more, his dad had gotten him a real cool sports car to make the trip to Mexico, which he drove all over town wearing very dark wraparound sunglasses. The students laughed their asses off. Tampico's roads were so bad that with every pothole that Boushanab hit, another piece of the car ended up on the street.

It was obvious that Boushanab was very drunk and had decided that he was not going to be celibate tonight. Through blurry eyes he picked a tall, dark, large-breasted hostess to accompany him to one of the back rooms.

One can only guess what ensued in that room, but it was clear that after the fee was paid and the meter started running, a lot of heavy petting was underway. After a very short time, with a lot of pleasurable moaning Boushanab stripped to reveal the Pride of Boushanab. Boushanab proceeded to lift the skirts of the lady for the final act. What he found did not please him. He started screaming at the lady, who was none other than Brunhilda. Now Brunhilda, under certain lighting, is very comely, but light or no light, he was still equipped with a "ready for action pole" between his legs. Boushanab, scared shitless of homosexuals under normal circumstances, was ready to stroke out, and with one hand grabbing his clothes his other hand shoved Brunhilda away. Brunhilda's head made a loud thud, which alerted the bouncer and bartender who started for the back rooms. Just then Boushanab came running out, naked and screaming about killing fags.

"Oh shit," said Andy. "The Mexicans are going to kill Boushanab."

"So what. He is an anti-Semitic, misogynistic, homophobe," Sayeed said. "Let the Mexicans do what they want with him."

"Look at the guy with the twenty dollar words ... misogynistic. For your information Boushanab is Jewish, he can't be anti-Semitic," Sam said.

"Sam, don't you read? Arabs are also Semites. Anyway, fuck him."

Marvin was concerned. "Guys, you better go and get the putz out of here before they cut off his schvantz among other things. The authorities will make this place off-limits if that happens. Frankly, it is the only place most of us can unwind. Plus the scenery is nice."

They looked at each and then went to grab Boushanab. Sam got to him first.

"Let me fucking go. That fucking fag was going to fuck me up the ass," Boushanab screamed.

"Boushanab, if you don't get out of here, that bouncer is going to cut off your balls. Now let's go. You'll put your clothes on when we are out of here."

"Fucking let go of me. No one fucks me up the ass."

"Yeah, come on Boushanab. You're drunk. If you hadn't had so much to drink you might have noticed that the she was a he. I mean his clothes are pretty tight and that hose is rather big," Marvin said, trying to lead Boushanab to the door.

Sayeed also tried to shove him out the door.

"You fucking 'rab! Let me go!"

Sayeed let him go and cold-cocked him were he stood. Boushanab dropped like the sack of shit he was.

"Gentlemen, let's get this dickhead out of here ... wait a minute."

Sayeed grabbed Boushanab's clothes and found his wallet. He took out a bunch of bills and walked over to Brunhilda, who was no worse for the wear. The bartender and the bouncer were standing there, also. "Lovely lady, gentlemen, let me apologize for my countryman who has no class, no brains, and obviously no dick. Please accept this payment as an apology from him."

Brunhilda grabbed the money, "Oh amor, don't worry, just make sure he never shows up here again." Sayeed thought about this and asked, "Darling, do you have a camera around here?"

"I have one behind the bar. Why?" asked the bartender as he pulled out a Polaroid.

"I can guarantee he'll never show up again," Sayeed said with a smile.

———— • ————

Boushanab woke up in his apartment, a small dwelling that Boushanab had decorated like a Mexican take on a Hugh Hefner playboy pad. By the small bedside lamp he was able to see a figure sitting in the shadows. He started to get out of bed when he noticed he was still naked.

"What did you do with my fucking clothes, scum bag?"

"That is not the nicest way to talk. One would think that the incident in the bar would have taught you a lesson. And being in your room with your balls intact would at least make you civil," Sayeed said softly.

Boushanab peered into the darkness, "You're the 'rab. I'm going to kill you! He got off the bed with his fists ready to beat the crap out of Sayeed.

"I wouldn't do that."

Boushanab just growled and took a swing. Sayeed had among his many talents a knowledge of street fighting that was unsurpassed.

He rarely struck in anger, but when he had to, he could hold his own. Sayeed ducked under Boushanab's swing and jabbed him just below his sternum. Boushanab went down hard, barely able to catch his breath.

Sayeed went over to him and crouched down beside him. "You are ill-mannered and an embarrassment to all the Americans here. You will never go back to Boy's Town. You will say nothing. There are no fags, wetbacks, or 'rabs. If you talk like that down here again, I will make sure that when—and if—you get home to the States you'll find these snapshots in the hands of your friends and family."

Sayeed showed a snapshot to Boushanab, whose eyes went wide. "How did you get this picture? I never … ?"

"Oh, you did, and Brunhilda says it was a nice snack, but just a small snack. By the way, there are multiple copies, just in case."

With that Sayeed left Boushanab a very contrite and fearful man.

———◆———

Sam, Marvin, and Andy were drinking beers by the pool when Sayeed showed up.

"Well, did that fucker appreciate the art?" Sam laughed.

"I believe he got the point."

Andy asked, "So do you think I'll never have to worry about Boushanab in Boy's Town?"

"I don't think he'll come within ten miles of the place."

"Let me see those, man. I never got to see them," Marvin said curiously. Sayeed handed Marvin the pictures of Boushanab naked in a bed. It appeared there was a woman partially dressed next to him. Her head near his naked crotch and Boushanab's head near her very erect penis.

"Holy Shit," was Marvin's only comment.

Chapter 7

The Body Mysterious

It was the big day. None of the students had actually been in the room that was designated for dissections. The proctors were standing outside the room requiring all the students to wear white coats and to have their dissection tools and dissection atlases with them. They would not let anyone into the room until El Professor showed up. This being a Monday, Valdez showed up fifteen minutes late, smelling like the night before, but at least stable on his feet.

"Vamos aver! Estudiantes, today we come to study the human body on an intimate level. Inside that room," Valdez said, nodding to the wide double doors, "are the mortal remains of people who have generously donated their bodies so you students can learn to be great doctors. We must always remember to respect their contribution when we study in this room." With those words the doors were thrown open and the students entered in anticipation of their first real medical school experience. What they experienced was something akin to a torture chamber.

Arranged on four raised cement slabs were two male and two female bodies. Both sets uncovered, dirty looking, and with a smell that could only be described as sewer squared. Immediately, several students began to gag and cover their faces with their hands as they entered the room.

Sam was proud that he was tolerating the sensory overload as well as he was.

Sayeed's usually olive complexion was pale and sweaty looking. The only person in the entire room absolutely jubilant was Bennie, who was clambering around from body to body.

"Estudiantes, break into four groups. You will each have time on a female and a male."

The students divided themselves into the four groups. The Mexicans converged on one pair of bodies and the Americans on the other pair.

"Jesus Christ, the smell. Do you think this is the way it is at Harvard Med?" Sam cried.

"Only if Harvard was in the third world," Andy said, trying to inspect the body. His eyes widened. "Oh my God," he said, pointing, "is that what I think it is?"

Marvin looked and nodded his head authoritatively. "I'm pretty sure you're right."

"What is it?" Sam asked, looking at small, black ulcers on the skin of the male cadaver. "Is it a disease? Is it catchy?" He instinctively stepped back from the body.

"Yeah, you can get it, but not from this poor bastard," Marvin said.

"Well what is it?"

"Cigarette burns, he was tortured before he died. This guy was probably someone's prisoner before he 'volunteered' his body."

"Oh my God." Andy was white as a sheet.

Bennie joined them, high on his first big medical student experience. "Man! I went to look at the other bodies and the other guy has ligature marks on his neck and I think the other female has a bullet wound in her abdomen. Where do you think these fine volunteers came from?" he asked, jubilant.

"Volunteers? Bennie, are you kidding? These guys were prisoners. Maybe the local authorities, maybe drug runners. Maybe they were trying to cross the border with coyotes and this was someone's idea of a good time. These poor people."

"Attencion, Estudiantes! Come and gather around this cadaver." Valdez leered as he nodded toward the cadaver's very generous and stiff member. "Lupe, he is like a horse, no?" So much for the dignity of the sacrifice of their bodies, Sam thought. Lupe immediately became crimson with embarrassment.

"Class act as always," Sam whispered.

"Amigo, give me the scalpel." One of the proctors came over with a large blade. "I will demonstrate the opening incision."

With that Valdez made a sloppy, but classic "Y" incision. Three of the students dropped like rocks. They were caught by their classmates before bashing their heads. The sound of retching and the smell increased in proportion to the amount of chest that was opened.

"Oh God, this is awful," Sayeed said. He looked like a ghost with a greenish hue. Sweat was pouring off him. "What is that smell? I thought bodies were treated with something before getting buried."

"Maybe that's the problem. These bastards were never buried," Marvin said stoically. He also looked green.

Valdez had finished making the incisions and now looked with satisfaction at the students. "Amigos, the bone cutters." The proctors gave Valdez a large instrument that looked like a bolt cutter. "Vamos aver, look at the connection of the ribs to the sternum." He started snipping through the cartilage of the ribs one by one, each snip making a distinctive snap and causing another student to faint or vomit.

"Ohhh, fuck!" Sayeed ran from the room with his hand over his mouth as some unidentifiable fluid escaped from the cadaver. Valdez looked around at the mayhem he was causing and laughed. "Babies, how do you expect to cut into a live body if you can't handle a dead one?"

"Can I take a closer look Professor?" A lone voice came from the back of the room.

Valdez asked, "Who said that? Come up here."

Bennie made his way through the crowd with a big smile on his face. "Man, look at all the stuff in the body."

Valdez leaned into the chest cavity. "Come closer, gringo." He thrust his hand into the chest and grabbed the heart, lifting it up on its root. "You know what this is?"

"No," said Bennie, grabbing the scalpel that Valdez had laid down, "but can we cut it out and study it some more?" More retching was heard in the room.

"No, not now gringo, but soon," Valdez smiled.

Bennie was staring intently at the corpse's mouth, "Hey Professor Valdez, I thought these bodies were supposed to be dead?"

Valdez looked at Bennie, "Of course they are dead. Are you a moron?"

"Well why is the tongue moving in this one?"

"Of course the tongue isn't moving … "

"Mira, la lengua … ," one of the Mexicans had spotted movement in the corpse's mouth and started shrieking, which had a domino effect on the rest of the students, half of them shoving the others away as they tried to run out of the room.

Valdez was mystified. He looked closer at the mouth.

"Don't get too close Professor Valdez, maybe he is pissed that you opened his chest," Bennie said.

"Don't be such an estupido, the body is dead." Valdez took his fingers and started prying open the mouth that was stiff with rigor mortis. "Chingaree, the jaw is stuck." He put more fingers into the mouth and pried them open with all his strength.

"Motherfucker! Its spirit is coming out to get us," Bennie howled just as a big cockroach crawled out of the mouth.

The class was screaming, punctuated by the sound of many vomiting kids with Valdez laughing his ass off.

"Class dismissed! Estupidos!"

———◆———

Eventually the students were able to deal with the sights and smells of the cadaver room. After their initial visit to the lab, the school sent in fumigators to spray the room and the cadavers. The smell was bad, but masked the rotting aroma of the bodies themselves. Sam wondered how long there would be bodies considering the only refrigeration in the room was a colossal, wheezing, old air conditioner.

Eventually, bodies started taking on an inhuman look, making it easier for the students to forget what they were actually working on. Three days a week Sam, Andy, Marvin, Bennie, and Sayeed would trudge into the room, take off the plastic sheeting, and explore the body for its secrets. Everyday, because of the lack of preservation, the tissue became stiffer and smaller and parts like arteries and nerves less identifiable. The Boys did their best. This was the closest they'd come to an American med school experience.

They set up a procedure for studying parts of the body. It turned out that Sam had a real set of surgical hands. He was able to take a scalpel, tweezers, or clamp and finely dissect small parts of end arteries, almost impossible to identify. Sayeed would wait with two dissector references on a stand in front of him. One of the references would be in English and the other in Spanish. He would trace out the names of the arteries, nerves, and muscles Sam would separate from the decomposing body.

In the meantime, Marvin and Andy would prepare rough sketches with labels of the body parts. Bennie couldn't be held to one place, but even he would help by checking on the dissection of one of the female cadavers for the differences in the anatomy. Bennie turned out to be a true anatomical artist. In the course of time, they got him to re-draw all the pictures and Marvin and Andy would label them.

With the dissection experience, Sam got better at Valdez's slide shows. The "vamos avers," wouldn't cause Sam to draw blanks as much anymore. It was easier to identify body parts in Valdez's line drawings than actually have to trace out the parts in rotting meat.

It was during one of Valdez's slide shows that Garza entered the class.

"Professor Valdez, if I may interrupt the class I have an important announcement."

Valdez, always the ass-kisser when it came to Garza, almost bowed. "Of course Sr. Garza, whatever you need." He moved away from the lectern and Garza grabbed its sides with his beefy hands.

"Estudiantes, I am very pleased to tell you that I have arranged a clinical experience for you at the Social Security Hospital. You will all have rotations once or twice a week in the evening with an excellent doctor working in the *Quarto de Emergencías.*"

There was immediate excitement as the students started applauding. The Americans looked at one another amazed at their good fortune. Even the American medical students didn't have direct patient contact in their first year, let alone the first semester.

"There's gotta be an angle," Marvin muttered.

"Who cares, we're going to see real patients, man. Our first patients!" Sam was so happy. This was his first chance at being a real doctor, albeit a real doctor with no medical knowledge.

"There will be a table set up to measure you all for the new official

UT white coats you will be required to wear. There will also be another table to issue your official hospital name tag. Remember jovenes, you are representing this school. I expect maturity, intelligence, and hard work. There will be consequences for any bad reports. After Professor Valdez's class, report to the courtyard for measurements. The coats are fifty dollars each. Please feel free to buy more than one as they are expected to be clean at all times," Garza smiled.

"Fifty dollars a fucking coat. What a Goddam rip off," Andy said. "I'm going to have to sell a bunch more lipsticks to cover this new expense," he sighed. "Sam, you up for a trip to the Town tonight?"

Before Sam could answer, Marvin broke in. "Andy, Sam really needs to study more. These nocturnal trips are not doing him any good."

"Hey Marvin, I'm right in front of you and my mother is in San Diego," Sam snapped. "I don't need another parent." He turned to Andy and said, "Of course I can, but let's try to make it an earlier night, OK?"

"You got it. I'll see you later." Andy left giving Marvin a dismissive stare.

"Marvin, can you let up on the studying thing? I'm doing much better. I think that cadaver gave me a new life."

"Well," Marvin said, frowning, "just think how much better you could be doing if your evenings were spent nose in book instead of sniffing some hooker perfume."

"Whoa, now that is a fantasy that I think is undeserved. I go to Boy's Town to sell Andy's cosmetics. I talk to the girls, who are very nice and good customers. That, my friend, is as far as it goes. Besides, studying all the time makes Sam a very dull boy. I'm good at the selling game and I enjoy it."

"If that's the case, why not ditch this foreign gig and go back to the States to work as a salesman? You could be making six figures within a couple of years. In four years if you graduate you'll be lucky to crack $10,000 to start. Believe me, as hard as sales is, as a lifestyle it's easier than what you're doing now."

"But I came here to be a doctor, Marvin. Helping Andy is just for the fun of it."

"Sam, you told me about your life in San Diego. You told me about your girl and your days. Let me give you a no-charge analysis."

"OK, what does the Psych Tech think about this Jewboy's life so far?"

"You never had your priorities right. You were smart enough to do the minimum and you were able to achieve the minimum. You could have made it into an American school. Instead you concentrated on the side issues."

"Side issues?" Sam was getting perturbed. Who was Marvin to tell him anything? He wasn't there.

"Instead of studying you went after the girl. Shame of it was, you didn't even put the effort into studying how to get her."

"What the fuck are you talking about?"

"She was never going to be with you, Sam. She wanted a man that was working to be a success, like her father was. What did you tell me, he was one of the top toxicologists in the States? A physician on the teaching staff of a major med school. What else? Oh yeah, a practice in both internal medicine and toxicology, NIH staff consultant to drug companies. What kind of man did she look up to? You didn't think it was a lovesick guy, sitting around feeling sorry for himself, watching too much TV and moping? No Sam, she was looking for a guy like her dad. Someone who was out to accomplish something."

"You're a fucking asshole," Sam said, barely in control of his own emotions. "What's your excuse for being here?"

Marvin gave him a sad little laugh. "Right you are, Sam, we

all fucked up in one way or another. In the end we just didn't have it in us. You probably disappointed her Sam. You're a nice Jewish guy. From what you told me her father and mother probably liked you, but husband or boyfriend material? You weren't serious about yourself, why did you expect her to be serious about you?"

"Fuck you." Sam walked off rip-roaring mad, but who was he angry at? Maybe Marvin was right he thought.

Chapter 8

Learning the Lessons

It was a night like most nights in Boy's Town. The neon lights lit the place up in colors not found in nature. The sounds of the various jukeboxes combined created a white noise event. The patrons were exuberant in their attempts at fleeting happiness.

Sam and Andy arrived just as a patron of Casa Blanca was flung through the front doors, landing with a thud on the dirt street. Sam was about to run over and see how badly the man was hurt. Andy restrained him and very quickly two gentlemen packing revolvers came out of the bar, picked the man up off the street, and put him into a sedan.

"That's good," Andy said with a smile.

"What's good? What do you think those guys are going to do with him?"

"Oh, put him into the local jail. They were cops. They might rough him up a bit, but I'm pretty sure they let these guys sleep it off and then let them out with a fine. Who knows. They might even end up on our dissecting table. Christ, what a thought. The presence of police in the Town has decreased to nada, which works out for us. Let's go sell so we can get the hell out of here."

Sam pulled out the bag of merchandise from his car. He looked in the back seat and wished once again that he had cleared out most of the stuff he had brought down from San Diego. His typewriter (which he doubted he'd ever need), his books (who read here?), even the sake set his father had brought him from Japan sat in the car. He guessed living in the hotel just didn't feel like a permanent place to put away his treasures. He had brought the stuff to make a home here for the years in school. Maybe he'd start looking for an apartment next term.

He walked through the doors of the Casa Blanca and the bartender immediately greeted him.

"Amigo, how's it hangin'?"

"OK. I got stuff for the ladies and I found a new color of lipstick, Red Period. God, I wonder who names this shit? Anyone around to take the stuff?"

"Lola has the night off. She left a message for you, though."

"Yeah?" Sam smiled, "What message?"

"In addition to the usual, she would give you a big introductory discount. Could you come back tomorrow? She did leave money for the stuff that the girls ordered, if you want to give me that stuff?"

Sam looked at the bartender. He was here almost every day that Sam visited and he had introduced Sam to Lola. "Yeah, sure. Frankly the thought of schlepping this stuff back to my hotel is a pain in my ass."

"Schlepping?"

Sam laughed, "Ancient language of my people. It means I'm too lazy to take the stuff back with me. How about a beer?"

The bartender went off to get the drink and Andy walked in.

"Sam, any business done?"

"No, it looks like it's a quiet night. Lola is off and the girls on the floor don't look like any of the regulars. I got payment for the last batch of orders, though."

"Funny, I noticed the same at the other bars. Maybe it's a national day of pelvic rest?"

"Or, maybe it's officially that time of the month."

Andy laughed. "Don't let Marla hear you say that. as it is her time of month. We are all treading very carefully around her right now."

They had a couple of beers, made conversation with the bartender, gathered up the bags and left the bar. Even the street seemed more quiet than usual as they walked over to the car. Sam unlocked it and started loading the sample bags into the trunk.

"What do you have there, señor?" a voice asked from the dark."

Sam jumped from fright. He turned around to see a Mexican wearing mirrored sunglasses and carrying a revolver with a pearl handle.

"Oh, just some presents, nothing more." Sam's voice was very shaky. Andy stood frozen. He knew they were in trouble and his brain had totally shut down.

"Presents, huh. You have a *novía*, a girlfriend, here maybe?"

"Look, who are you?" Sam asked, trying to get some control of the situation. He glanced quickly at Andy who still hadn't moved from the position he was in.

The man pulled out a wallet with a badge and picture ID on it. Sam immediately locked into the words *Servicio Secreto*, Secret Service. "Oh fuck," he thought, "we're going to jail."

"They are presents for a girlfriend, just trinkets."

"You have a girlfriend here among the prostitutas. Let me see what you got her. You know I have a girlfriend too, maybe I will get her the same present you got for your puta girlfriend," he laughed.

"Look, they are nothing, really. Just trinkets."

"Give me the bag please," the federale demanded, his hand reaching towards his gun. Sam thought he was going to piss his pants. Sam turned the bag over. The contents were dumped in the street at the foot of the federale.

He reached down and picked up a packet. "What is this, drugas?" he demanded.

"No, no I swear no drugs. Cosmetics, perfumes, lipsticks. No drugs." Sam was sweating. What was he going to do? Call his parents, the Embassy in Mexico City? Would they let him make a phone call? Phone call, not a phone call, but a long-distance phone call. Oh fuck he was in real trouble. The theme from *Midnight Express* started playing in his mind.

"OK amigo, give me the keys to the car." By this time a couple of other Secret Service men had surrounded Sam and Andy. It was evident from the mirrored sunglasses and pearl handled pistols that they, too, were Secret Service. "This officer is now going to put you in his car and your friend is going to go with the other officer. No trouble from you or your friend, *Entiende?*"

Sam could only nod at this point. He was going to rot for the rest of his life in a Mexican prison. What more was there to say? God, what if he ended up on that cold slab of concrete for his classmates to cut open.

"God." He said, and realized it had come out as a prayer.

———◆———

Hell.

That was the only way to describe the scene before Sam. The ride in the officer's car was a blur. Back roads, dust swirling around the car. His fears worsened when the car headed in the opposite direction from Tampico. He had seen enough movies to get the idea that he was going to be executed somewhere in the wilderness and dumped into a shallow grave. He started sniveling, begging the officer not to "Do It."

The Secret Service agent stared at him through the rear view mirror. "*Silencio*, shut up." The car sped along till Sam saw lights on the horizon.

Where was Andy? He had been placed in another car, which had disappeared. Andy had looked white as a ghost. He hadn't said a word when they had been arrested. Would he ever see Andy again? Maybe they would let them live out their lives sharing the same cell. Christ, they'd be domestic together. Sam began to worry.

The car went through the center of a town that Sam thought was Ciudad Madero, the suburb of Tampico. Was this a good or bad thing? Sam just didn't know. The car stopped in front of the police station and Sam was glad to see that Andy was being taken out of the other car. Thank God he was alive.

They were helped out of the cars and led into the Station. Once there the federale pointed to a dirty blank wall and told them to "assume the position." Rude fingers felt him up paying special attention to his groin area. He started to protest when the original Secret Service agent approached him.

"Amigo, do you have something to hide, like a weapon, maybe?" The officer who was patting him down gave his balls an extra hard squeeze making Sam yelp. "Our officers don't trust squirmy guys," he said.

"I don't have a weapon, just cosmetics, Goddam it."

Andy found his voice and croaked, "Look, can we get a lawyer or pay a fine? We're just students at the new medical school here. I was trying to make a little money for tuition."

"Ahh, you admit you were smuggling, amigo. That is a very serious crime in Mexico."

"Smuggling?" Andy asked. "I just brought stuff down so I could support myself and my family."

The Secret Service guy removed his sunglasses. "Come with me, amigos."

He took them down the hall to a small room with a table and a couple of chairs.

"*Sientese.*"

Sam and Andy sat.

"We have looked through this merchandise you were selling. There are laws in Mexico for selling drugs of any sort. The penalties are severe."

If Andy and Sam were scared when they were arrested, they were absolutely frozen with fear at these words. Sam had read about what the Mexicans did to Americans who were caught with a joint. He couldn't figure out why they would think he was carrying drugs. The bag just had the usual cosmetics and perfume.

"We never carried any drugs. Sam and I don't take drugs, not even marijuana."

"Then what the fuck is this, amigo?" the federale pulled a packet out of the pile of cosmetics. "*Drugas! Que tipo, cocaine, heroina, amphetaminas? Que tipo?*"

Sam stammered, "Look, there is a misunderstanding, those packets aren't drugs."

"What are they then?"

Andy said quietly, "They are for cleaning a woman's private parts."

The federale's mouth dropped open and there was absolute quiet in the room.

"*Chingaree*, you are liars. You will rot in prison for the rest of your sorry lives."

"Please, look at the package. Read it. It's douche."

The federale looked at the packet in his hand. "Chocolate, bullshit. Who makes douche chocolate." He picked up another packet. "Mint?"

Andy looked at him, his uneasiness mounting. "It's supposed to be an aphrodisiac. You know you go down on your woman and it tastes different."

"What the fuck." The federale ripped open the packet and in

classic cop style stuck his pinky into the liquid and tasted it. His eyes went wide, "*Uva?*"

"Grape has been a big hit at Boy's Town. Maybe you want a couple of packets? A present of course," Andy said.

The federale started laughing wildly. "You guys … Busted for selling douche. Sanchez, take these hardened criminals to the cell."

"Wait, it's only cosmetics. Please, just fine us. We won't do it again," Sam cried.

"Amigos, these are dangerous cosmetics and are an insult to Mexican women everywhere. Mexican men like their pussy to taste like a woman. Sanchez take them away." He was still laughing as they were led out of the room.

The last thing Sam saw was the federale grabbing a bunch of packets of douche and shoving them into his pocket.

———•———

Hieronymus Bosch would have felt right at home in the Ciudad Madero Jail. He could have used it as his model for the Hellscape in *The Garden of Earthly Delights.*

They were not taken to a private cell, but to the general lockup. It was a large room with approximately 150 men inside. The officer led Sam and Andy to a wall of bars that separated the main cell from a small desk where the single guard sat. The door to the cell was opened with a large, old fashioned key. Sam was horrified. His only brushes with the law were the occasional traffic ticket. His brain shut down and his heart stopped beating while he wondered why his lungs felt encased in cement.

"Get in there, gringos. Your friends are waiting for you. By the way, I'd stay in the lighted areas … unless you are horny," he laughed and pushed them in.

Most of the prisoners were very drunk, or sick. The floor was covered with vomit, piss, and shit. Many of the men were coughing or losing control of their bladders and bowels. The mix of body fluids pooled in dark puddles on the filthy cement floor.

The cell was unventilated, and the smell of the human waste was so bad that Sam's eyes began watering and his nose began running. The prisoners propped themselves up against the walls or lay directly on the filthy cement floor. No cots or chairs were provided.

The cell was lit by a single low-wattage light bulb in the center of the room. The prisoners cast strange shadows as they shuffled around the cell. The worst were the ones who stayed in the shadows. In the dim light, Sam saw two men performing oral sex on each other in the shadows.

Some of the prisoners appeared to be in agony. Scalp lacerations, extremity lacerations, scrapes, abrasions, and contusions. One man with weathered, coarse features and a nose displaying millions of broken capillaries appeared to have an arm with an extra elbow. Even small movements made the arm take on unnatural angles and caused the man to scream in pain. No one checked on the sick.

Sam and Andy looked for a place to sit down, but there wasn't any clean space. The people were just lying on the filthy floor, usually near their own vomit or blood.

Real life intruded into Sam's imagined transformation into a zombie. "Shit, I've got to take a leak," Sam told Andy. "Where is the toilet?"

"Call the guard, maybe he'll take you out to the can."

They wandered back to the door only to find the guard slouched in his chair fast asleep. No matter how much complaining they did, the guard only snored louder.

"Fuck, I really have to go," Sam said.

Andy was looking off into the distance to a dark area of the cell.

"I think I know where you can go, I just don't think you'll want to," Andy responded.

Sam turned his head in the direction Andy was staring at. "Oh, fuck!"

In the dimness they could make out the base of a toilet on a three-foot platform. It was literally a throne. It was encrusted with feces and myriad other substances. Sam had a feeling that a major portion of the foul smell was coming from the toilet.

"I can't go over there. I'll collapse from the stench." Sam was almost in tears. He was full and needed to go bad.

Andy looked around. "Look, go over into that corner, I can't see a lot, but it looks unoccupied."

Sam was incredulous. "You mean pee on the floor. Are you kidding?"

"I don't see much choice. You can use the toilet or hold it. There is also the ever popular, go in your pants."

"Fuck!" Sam walked over to the corner. He unzipped himself and being careful not to wet his shoes, let loose. He was finishing up when he felt a hand on his shoulder.

"Hey amigo, nice thing you got there … " the drunken voice said. The drunk proceeded to paw at Sam.

"Get the fuck off of me," he shoved at the drunk who was getting more amorous. Sam was having problems getting the guy off him when instantly the guy was gone. Andy had seen what was going on and came to his rescue, slamming the drunk into the wall.

"Let's get away from this corner. I don't think that guy will be bothering you for at least a while," he pointed to the heap on the floor.

Sam was shaking, "Yeah, let's get into the light."

———◆———

Sam and Andy found a patch of relatively clean floor and sat. Sam was still shivering and very quiet.

Andy said, "I'm so sorry to have dragged you into this."

Sam looked up at Andy and said, "It really isn't your fault. I knew what could happen and took a chance. I have fucked up everything in my life by making poor decisions, why not this." He went silent again.

"No, it was my fault. I just needed the money to take care of my family and figured I could do it, study and not take out more loans. Now I'll have to find money to get us a lawyer. I'll get you out of this, Sam."

Sam just nodded. He was bone tired. He couldn't think of anything he could do about anything at this point. He certainly wasn't going to call his parents. "Mom, I need a couple of thousand dollars because I'm in a Mexican jail," followed by the sound of his mother hitting the floor. He'd really fucked up. Marvin was correct. He could never keep his eye on the ball. It had to be a distraction from the real work, not the work itself. Too bad it took an utter disaster to show him the truth about himself.

There was a clamor at the door to the cell. "Hey, gringos. You have friends here. Hurry up."

Andy stood and dragged Sam up. They walked over to the door.

"Hey, we heard about the arrest and came down to see what needed to be done to get you guys out," Sayeed said.

"Yeah man, this is the craziest cell I've ever seen. Is that guy bleeding over there?" Bennie was fascinated by the horror of the place. "Maybe we can practice some medical skills on these guys."

"Bennie, go back out to the car and see about bringing up the food package," Sayeed said.

"Yeah, OK." Bennie disappeared.

"Listen you guys, don't get too worried. We got through to Garza and we think he is going to call some people."

"People," Sam said hopefully, "what people? Like lawyers?"

"I don't know. He didn't sound happy, but I think he realized the downside of having his students in a jail. Not good for advertising in the States."

Bennie showed up with a bag. "They fucking searched it, the idiots," he said with a laugh. "What did they think, I was going to put a file in so you could cut the bars?"

"Did you?" asked Sam.

"No, just a screwdriver. I figured you could break the lock with it."

Sam just shook his head and took the bag from Bennie. "Peanut butter and crackers?"

"The peanut butter doesn't need refrigeration and the crackers will keep forever," said Sayeed.

"So you think we might be here a while?" Andy's face fell. "Listen, can someone go by my house and tell Marla that I'm here, but not to worry."

"Bennie went to the house and told her, Andy," Sayeed said.

"Jesus, your woman has a mouth on her. I couldn't figure out who she was most pissed off at—me, you, or the Mexicans. Anyway she told me to tell you you're a piece of shit and hopes ... wait, let me remember the exact words ... Your asshole has to take the biggest dick in there. She did sound worried though."

"That's my girl," said Andy, "supportive as usual."

Sayeed looked around and then whispered to Sam and Andy, "We gave the guards some pesos to look out for you, take you to the bathroom if you need it ... "

"Where were you an hour ago?" Sam asked, shaking his head.

"We're going back to the hotel and try to put pressure on the school to get this resolved as fast as possible. One of the guys is writing a letter that is going to go to the *New York Times*, critical of the school's support of the Americans. We'll leak it to Garza first. It should make him jump, that's all he needs is bad publicity for the school and his dreams of Global Med School conquest go up in smoke," Sayeed said.

"OK, hopefully we'll see you in a couple of hours."

Sayeed and Bennie took off, leaving Sam and Andy in the dark cell.

Sam was emotionally and physically exhausted. The thought that the school was working on his release did nothing to ease his depression. He couldn't get over his screw-ups. He realized that because he always took the easy way out, he was bound to fail. Andy tried to get him to talk, but he just grunted with each attempt. It was apparent that guilt was killing Andy. "Sam, please talk to me," Andy said, raising both his hands. "I'm sorry, man. What else can I say?" Sam looked at him stone faced and was about to reply when there was another commotion at the door.

"Hey gringos, come over here." It was the federale who arrested them.

"What do you want?" Andy asked. He was in no mood to be friendly to the locals.

"Don't be that way, gringo." The federale took off his sunglasses and spread his arms, "I just want to talk."

"It's your fucking fault we're in here. You know those weren't drugs."

"That is good for you. But, first ... " The federale smiled and called for the guard to bring in large broken-down cardboard boxes, which were passed through the bars to Andy and Sam.

"What are these for?" Sam inquired.

"There are no beds to sleep on here, so I brought the next best thing. The cardboard is clean and will protect you from the filth and dirt on the floor."

Sam laughed, "Great, you're concerned. I guess I should say thank you."

"It would be the polite thing to do," said the federale with a wider smile. "You will like this piece of information even better."

"What information?" asked Andy suspiciously.

"You'll be released and forgotten in the morning."

"What? You're kidding," Sam said.

"In Mexico we have enough problems arresting stupid gringos for drugs. No drugs, no guns, no jail sentence. Now, if you had even a little marijuana, I would have seen you shipped off to the Federal prison. But for possession of douche, I don't have time for it."

"I don't believe it," Andy said angrily. "All this for something we could have walked on."

"Amigo, you should be grateful it worked out this way. Now, enjoy your cardboard."

———————

They took the cardboard and laid it out on the floor under the lights near the door. Andy was so tired that he was snoring in minutes.

Sam lay down, but now sleep was coming hard. They had dodged a bullet. He knew he should be happy, but he also knew he had dodged bullets in the past and still had continued down the same self-destructive path. Would this time be any different? Gradually the world went black and Sam joined Andy asleep on the floor of a Mexican jail cell.

———————

"Gringos, get up!"

Sam shook himself awake. He was disoriented and tried to remember a bad dream he had had. He quickly realized it wasn't a bad dream, it was a bad situation, and he was still in this stinking cell with sunlight streaming through the barred windows that didn't make it any more hospitable.

"Gringos, come on, you've got fifteen minutes to take a piss and wash, then you've got to see the judge."

Andy was up and stretching. He put out a hand and Sam used it to get up. Sam was stiff from sleeping on the hard floor.

They made their way to the door and the guard let them out and led them to the restroom. There was no hot water. They splashed their faces with the icy water that ran brown from the tap.

Their federale poked his head through the doorway. "Come on amigos, we gotta get you out of here." He got them out of the bathroom and led them down the hallway.

"Quite a crowd waiting for you, *sí muchas personas*."

They walked into the comandante's office, who, according to the federale, was like the Police Chief. Suddenly, a flashbulb went off and Sam and Andy were forever immortalized in *El Sol de Tampico*. The article would be about evil American smugglers, caught by the valiant federales. Thankfully the story, with its glorious photo of Sam and Andy, was never picked up by Reuters.

"OK, now get out," the comandante told the photographer who immediately left. He gestured for them to have a seat at the conference table.

Joining them in the comandante's office was Garza and a man they didn't know, who wore a suit.

"You were smuggling goods into Mexico. This is good for at least a year. What do you have to say for yourselves?" asked the comandante.

"Comandante, the American students are not cognizant of Mexican law. They probably didn't realize what they were doing was illegal," Garza said soothingly.

"Bullshit, they knew." The comandante turned to the man in the suit. "*Alcalde*, these gringos have flouted our laws, they deserve a trial and then a stiff sentence."

The alcalde, who turned out to be the Mayor of Ciudad Madero, looked confused.

"Maybe comandante, we should remove the prisoners and discuss this privately," Garza recommended.

"Yes, that is a good idea," the alcalde spoke up.

The comandante ordered, "Guards, put them in the back office and watch that they don't go anywhere."

Sam and Andy were removed.

"What do you think happens now?" Sam asked Andy.

"My guess? I think the comandante is setting the price to keep quiet and let the whole thing die and the mayor is figuring out where he gets his cut."

"Shit, how expensive do you think this is going to get?"

Andy smiled, "Look at you. First you're worried about being in jail and anally raped for the rest of your life. Now you're worried about money. I'd say things are looking up."

"Yeah, I guess we survived. Now how much is survival going to cost us?"

"Enough, but not a hell of a lot. Garza won't allow it. He knows if the fine is high, we go home. Then the other students get the idea that the school doesn't have their backs and they start looking for another paradise. Soon word filters to the States and voilà no students, which means no money coming to Garza. Besides, I think Garza is going to remind the comandante that his business, without the students, is going to decrease, not just over the coming weeks, but over the years."

"What business?"

"The bars, prostitution, maybe even some light drug sales."

"You're kidding," Sam said amazed.

Andy laughed. "While you were mooning over that big Barbie Doll, Lola, I was talking to the bartenders. Someone needed to 'protect' those bars and the girls. In the States it's the Mob, here there is a different kind of Mob. The Town stays relatively safe and no one is totally unhappy."

"I still don't get it. How does he lose business?"

"If they jail us then no American goes to Boy's Town for fear of getting jailed for God knows what charge. The Americans that come down here for school are mostly single men like yourself with some cash in their pockets. They are thirsty and horny. Believe me, the comandante is funding his big retirement account out of the school."

"Christ," Sam said.

"Doubt he'd want anything to do with this," Andy smiled. "Let's chill … "

They heard footsteps down the hall getting closer.

"Game on," Andy said.

The door opened and the alcalde entered.

"You have been unlawful, but due to the respect this town has for Sr. Garza and because this is your first offense, we are letting you go with a fine. We considered banning you from the bars, but Sr. Garza reminded us that this was the only place you could unwind from your studies." He became very stern. "Do not take advantage of our leniency. If the comandante catches you smuggling again you will be put away for a long time."

Andy, looking contrite, said, "We thank you Sr. Alcalde. We will never smuggle in your district again."

Sam, taking Andy's lead said, "Thank you for forgiving us, Alcalde."

"Fifty dollars each, American cash. If you don't have it on you, you may deliver it tomorrow to my office."

Andy gave Sam an "I told you so" wink and a smile.

They walked out into the sunlight, free men. They smelled bad, were hungry, thirsty, and needed some sleep, but realized they were lucky free men.

Out front was Sam's car.

"Shit, no one gave me back my keys," Sam said. "I can't believe I have to go back in there."

"Hey amigos, lose something?" The federale was standing next to the police station, his mirrored sunglasses brilliant in the light. Sam and Andy walked over.

"What do you want?" Sam asked. "I'm sorry we really are out of douche to degrade the moral fiber of Mexican womanhood."

"Oh amigos, you are so funny. I really like you. You are refreshing compared to the *borrachos,* the drunks, I usually deal with."

"Look," Sam said angrily, "I don't think I need friends that are cops. We'll just go over the city line and you won't have to see us or harass us anymore."

"Don't be that way. It's not my fault you got arrested."

"Yeah," Andy said curiously. "If not yours, whose fault was it?"

The federale smiled

"What the fuck." Sam had had enough. He was dirty, tired, and on the brink of a breakdown. "Look, we're going to go get our car keys and go home. And I'd like to try to forget this ever happened."

"*Un momentito,* let me explain. Like I said, I like you and don't want you to be in trouble again."

"Let's go, Andy. I really need a shower. I'll get the keys." Sam turned to go back into the station.

"They are right here, amigos. I protected them for you. Now will you listen? I guarantee it will teach you a lesson about Mexico and keep you out of trouble."

"Fuck, please let's go Andy."

"Sam, it won't hurt to listen to him. We have a minimum of four years down here. I'd like to avoid another trip to this jail or one like it."

The federale nodded. "He knows what he is talking about Sam."

"Talk." Sam gave up. "I'm listening."

"It was the cab drivers."

"What?" said Andy. "The cab drivers? We never even took a cab to get to Boy's Town."

"*Exactamente!*" The federale smiled. "You deprived these men of their daily bread. They considered that rude of guests in this country and reported you. The comandante got wind of this and as he gets a protection fee from the cab drivers, he took notice. You fucked yourselves to save some pesos."

"Fuck!" Sam said.

"Yes you got fucked, but in the end it was your fault. This is a poor country and the workers need every peso they can get. You are rich Americans and as visitors have to pay a user's fee to keep everyone happy. *Entiende?*"

Andy nodded. "We fucked up."

The federale laughed. "Don't worry, amigo. Rule of thumb, make sure you are paying the people that are there to serve. It lubricates everything."

He tossed Sam the car keys. "Thanks, I guess," Sam said as he turned to go to the car.

"No problemo, amigo." The federale started across the street as Sam unlocked the car. He looked inside and was shocked.

"Andy, it's all gone. All my stuff, the typewriter, books, even the sake set my Father gave me."

"Hey," he screamed across the street to the federale, "where is my stuff?"

The federale laughed and said, "See you still haven't learned anything. I need a tip for the lesson I just taught you. Sleep well, amigo." He walked into the police station.

Chapter 9

Doctors ... Us?

ISS Hospital Santa Maria read the sign over the main entrance. It was a typical government hospital in Mexico. The building was an old physical plant out of the 40s and very undersupplied. The one thing it did have was patients. The sick steadily streamed in and out of the doors all day, and all night.

Most of the nurses looked to be about fourteen and the doctors appeared tired. The center of the chaos was the *Cuarto de Emergencias*, or the Emergency Room.

Sam and Marvin were assigned to the ER for Sam's first patient contact. He was very self-conscious of the short white coat and the button-down shirt and tie he was wearing. The pockets of the coat had the stethoscope his father had given him and the reflex hammer. He didn't know how to use either one.

Sam looked at the paper in his pocket. "It says we need to find a Doctor Soto. He's supposed to be our supervisor. I wonder where ... "

There was a loud crash and then a lot of screaming. Sam and Marvin rushed over to the excitement.

They found a crowd gathered around a young man convulsing on the floor. He had been on a stretcher and had fallen off. He was now on the floor seizing and bleeding from a scalp laceration. There were a couple of bystanders screaming for help, but none of the doctors or nurses seemed to be paying attention. The crowd's eyes finally found

Marvin and Sam in their freshly minted white coats, mistaking them for doctors.

"Sam, look for some tongue depressors on that cart … hurry," Marvin cried, already on the floor with the patient, turning him on his side.

Sam exclaimed, "Are you sure you should be doing that?"

"Hurry up, this guy is going to bite his tongue in half." Just then blood spurted from the seizing guy's mouth. Sam thought he was going to vomit or faint or both. "Sam, move!" Marvin's voice brought him back to reality. Sam quickly found the popsicle sticks and handed them to Marvin, who wedged them between the patient's teeth. Marvin had turned the guy over on his side. "Hold this guy's head still. Hopefully the seizure will stop soon."

Soon enough, though it seemed like hours, the patient stopped seizing. Marvin told Sam he wanted to log-roll the patient to the supine position. Sam looked at Marvin like he was speaking Chinese.

"You and I will roll the guy's head and torso back to the lying down position as one unit."

"Why are we doing it this way?" Sam asked.

"Because the guy fell from the stretcher and he could have broken his neck. This is the way we don't add to potential damage. You move a neck fracture and you could cause a spinal cord injury, paralyzing the guy."

"How do you know this stuff, Marvin?" Sam was amazed and grateful that Marvin was around.

Marvin smiled. "As soon as you start working in a hospital, you'll learn this stuff, too. What do think, psych patients don't seize or fall, or both?"

Finally some nurses and a doctor showed up. "What happened here?" the doctor asked.

Marvin explained the situation and the doctor ordered the nurse to get a collar and board for the patient, which they did, securing him into a hard plastic neck collar without moving him and then sliding him onto what looked like a surfboard.

The doctor stood up as did Marvin and Sam. "I'm Dr. Soto. You did a good job here."

"Marvin did everything, I just followed his instructions," said Sam.

"Well, following instructions is good learning so you both get credit," he eyed the white coats. "You are the students from that medical school?"

"Yes we are. This is Marvin Goldberg and I'm Sam Cohen."

"Ahh, *Judios*. You know Maimonides was a doctor and a philosopher. It is fitting you two are here."

While Sam and Marvin could not understand why it mattered that they were Jews, they appreciated that Soto seemed to think they belonged here.

"I take it," Soto said, addressing Marvin, "that you have had some medical training?"

"Psych tech in the Bronx for many years," Marvin replied.

"Good, see that rack over there?" Marvin nodded. "Take the first chart and go see the patient together. You know how to take a history?"

"A psych one," Marvin said hesitantly.

"Well, do the best you can. When you are finished examining the patient, come find me. We will go over the patient together." With that Soto left to deal with another disaster.

Sam was just overjoyed. "My God, Soto is actually going to teach us something practical. We are going to make our first rounds."

Marvin smiled, "Yes we are. Let's go grab a chart."

Sr. Rios was a twenty-five-year-old man in a lot of abdominal pain that had started earlier in the day. He had walked into the ER doubled over. Rios thought it might have been bad shrimp, but even after vomiting his lunch he still was having pain that was increasing. He decided he had no choice but to see a doctor. Not having one he ended up in the ER for the last four hours on a gurney. By this time he had vomited everything that was left in his stomach and was quite dehydrated. He was Sam's and Marvin's first patient.

"Sam, I'll try to take a history. It can't be too different from the psych one, except no inner psyche and a lot of vomit," Marvin smiled nervously.

"You do it and I'm going to listen and make notes." Sam already had out his official looking notebook and pen.

"OK, here goes nothing." They walked over to the gurney.

"Sr. Rios, my name is Dr. Goldberg and this is Dr. Cohen. We are from the Medical School and would like to interview … "

Splat! Rios had vomited bloody, foul looking, slimy gastric contents that had barely missed Marvin's shirt, but did cover his shoes. As Marvin was somewhat of a pro in bodily secretions, having had psych patients use them as weapons, he wasn't that upset. Sam on the other hand was white with shock. His trouser legs were covered with bloody slime and the feel of the hot wetness was making him woozy.

Marvin looked over at Sam, and seeing his situation immediately got a chair. "Sit, and put your head down. Take deep breaths."

"I'm OK, I don't need to sit." Sam's pale, sweaty complexion didn't give Marvin confidence.

"Just sit and take notes," Marvin said confidently. Addressing Sr. Rios he started his questioning. "Sr. Rios how long have you been vomiting?"

"Six or eight hours," Rios moaned.

"Any diarrhea?"

"Sí, with blood."

"Have you had any fever?"

"I don't know."

"Where is the pain?"

Rios moaned again and pointed to his entire belly circling his hand over it.

"Where is the place it hurts the most?" Marvin wanted specific answers.

The hand seemed to hover just under Sr. Rios's breastbone.

Marvin looked at Sam and like the prosecutor in court summed up the guilty party of Sr. Rios's body.

"So we have a (looking at the chart) twenty-five-year-old male with a six to eight hour history of epigastric abdominal pain and bloody vomitus. No fever, chills." (Checking the chart again). "Vital signs stable."

Sam brightened up. "Great, now we do something for this guy?"

"Oh Sam, we haven't even delved into this man's problems," Marvin nodded knowingly.

"But he is obviously suffering. Can't we actually do something?"

"OK, jovenes, you cure this cabron yet?" Dr. Soto had sneaked up behind them, making Sam jump.

"Well Dr. Soto, the patient has abdominal pain, with bloody vomitus and diarrhea. His pain goes into … " Marvin was interrupted by Rios.

"Hey cabron, you been drinking?" Soto asked.

Rios looked sheepish. "Maybe a little, Dr. Soto."

"A little, huh? What, a liter, two? Maybe a couple of cervezas to wash down the tequila?" Soto demanded.

"Maybe a couple of liters and cervezas," Rios said uncomfortably.

"OK jovenes, diagnosis?"

Sam looked lost, but Marvin puffed out his chest and gave his diagnosis.

"Due to the blood and alcohol history he definitely has an erosive gastritis and probably a bleeding gastric ulcer. We need to get a surgeon involved and possibly consider a gastrectomy ... STAT," Marvin said smugly.

Soto looked at Marvin a minute and then started laughing hysterically. He addressed Rios. "Hey cabron, this guy wants one of the butchers to slit you open like a dead fish and remove your *estómago*."

Rios looked panicked. "Slit me open. Gut me. Look, I'll think about it and come back."

"I don't know, the big guy looks pretty smart. Maybe he is right. You certainly will have other problems besides your alcoholism."

"Please Dr. Soto, I don't want to be slit open."

Soto again laughed, "Don't worry, cabron. I'll save you from the gringos." He turned to Sam and Marvin. "Good first attempt, but not so fast on the diagnosis and the surgery. I agree he probably has gastritis, alcoholic gastritis, but I doubt he is bleeding. You also missed another possible diagnosis that has the potential to kill him."

Marvin drew himself up. "But Dr. Soto, the bleeding here is dangerous ... "

"He is not bleeding, but how are you going to prove me wrong?"

Rios chimed in, "But, I am bleeding. I saw the red."

"Prove it, amigos," he said to Marvin and Sam.

"Oh fuck it, here. Cabron, pull down your pants and turn on your side."

"Oh no, not that," cried Rios.

"Yes that," Soto said, pulling on a glove and grabbing some lube and a card. Soto then put his index finger up Rios's anus. "Good sphincter tone, no masses, and prostate is normal size and consistency. You … " he said, nodding at Sam, "put on a glove."

Sam did as he was told.

"Now lube up your index finger and gently push it into the anal canal."

Sam just looked at Soto, "You're kidding?"

Soto laughed again, "Oh sí. One of the joys of the job. Wait until you have a young chica in this position. Heaven. OK come on, I don't have all night."

Sam slowly entered the guy's rectum, cringing, but not as much as the patient.

"Aieee!" yelled Rios.

Soto admonished, "Slowly and gently like with a lady."

"I'm in," Sam said.

"Now feel the anterior wall. Feel the bump? That's the prostate. It's normal. OK now come out."

Sam took his finger out and it was covered with red, bloody looking feces. He thought he was going to be sick.

"Smear the stool on this card." Sam did as Soto said. "Now let's put the magic drops on the card … if there is blood in the stool it will turn blue."

Sam looked intently at the card.

"Can you see the face of Jesus in the shit? Stop staring at it. There is no blue and no blood," Soto said.

Marvin said, "But it is bloody."

Soto smiled, "Joven, your first trick of the trade. Pay attention. Cabron, what were you drinking, before you had red shit."

"Kool-Aid," Rios said.

Soto addressed Sam and Marvin gravely, "Watch this insight into medicine."

He addressed Rios, "I'll bet it was either cherry or strawberry Kool-Aid, sí?"

"How did you know, Doctor?" Rios was amazed.

"Red Kool-Aid colored the shit," Marvin said.

"But when I drink red Kool-Aid, my bowel movements are normal color. So why is his red?" Sam asked.

"Because you didn't have the fast transit time of gastrointestinal distress causing diarrhea so the red color couldn't get degraded in the *intestinos*. In other words what went into his mouth came out really fast, almost intact. He will be OK. We will rehydrate him and put him on something to decrease stomach acid, get blood studies to rule out other problems this cabron may have, and if all is bueno, discharge him. Great case, jovenes!"

Sam realized he had just helped save his first patient; he was no longer a virgin, but an adult with a popped cherry. God, medicine was grand he thought with a big smile.

It was quiet and cool at two a.m. in the dissection lab. School had become more like being in school in the States. Sam wasn't sure this is what an American medical school was like, but at least it was close enough to a college framework based on his experience. It was two weeks before the big practical in anatomy. Valdez would take the cadavers and place numbered pins into the rotting meat. The students would try to identify the piece of meat. Of course, after weeks of the corpses dry rotting, one piece of meat looked like another. He supposed this was just part of medical school in Mexico, so he buckled down without complaining. In one hand he had the dissection manual, and in the other, either a pick, forceps, or scissors. It was long, tedious work and because there was no expert help, it became a guessing game of what body part the pin was positioned in.

At two in the morning he enjoyed the solitude. The dissection lab became a cathedral where he made his apologies to God for not appreciating the second chance he had received to become a doctor.

He traced the aorta leading into the femoral artery and wondered what it would be like to operate on someone who had a problem here. He looked at the inguinal ligament, dissected down into the canal and out the spermatic cord and finally into the scrotum, where he found the structures leading to the testicle.

He smiled. His priority now was learning medicine—his past priority of finding perfect love was a thing of the past, though sometimes he wondered about the wasting away of the organ he had dissected down to. Was living like a monk worth the sacrifice of having zero sex and being lonely?

Sam's mind wandered. He wondered what Leah was doing right now? It must be early afternoon in Jerusalem. Was she in a class? Maybe she was in the library studying or on rounds in some hospital. He couldn't help it as his mind continued to wander to the very real possibility she was on the arm or in the bed of some dark, handsome Israeli. He started packing up his dissection kit. His concentration broken, no more memorization of the muscles of the lower leg would happen. Time to go. He could only hope to sleep dreamlessly and forget how badly he had led his life. He put the sheet plastic over the rotting corpse and walked out of the humid lab turning off the light behind him.

————•◆•————

Sam's sleep was interrupted by a persistent, heavy knock on his door.

"Who's there and what the fuck do you want in the middle of the night?"

"Sr. Sam, it's Carlito. Please let me in!"

"No Carlito, I don't need any male companionship this early in the morning."

"Your parents are on the phone. It's an emergency."

Sam's body went cold. He had just talked to them two weeks ago and all had been well. An emergency? Dad had high blood pressure. Not his heart? "I'm coming."

He threw on his shorts and ran to the door.

———•———

His mother was on the phone.

"Mom, what's wrong? Is it Dad?" He was cold with fear.

"Grandpa died, Sam. Your uncle found him in his bed this morning and couldn't awaken him. They called an ambulance, but by the time he got to the hospital … " She started crying over the phone.

Sam's grandfather had been a fantastic grandfather. His was the classic story of not being the best father, but boy, did he make up for it as a grandfather. His presents and stories were the best, plus he had given Sam an appreciation of how to use a camera. Sam's grandfather, Max, had been a boy when the Tsar tried to conscript him into the Russian Army. This was the Russians' Jewish solution. He decided against it and escaped to Britain where he served in the British Army. After being mustard gassed, he was sent to San Diego for treatment and eventually became a waiter at a top restaurant. Max was a constant in Sam's life.

"When is the funeral, Mom?"

"He is supposed to be buried tomorrow, but if you think you can get back … "

"I'll get back, just wait if you can."

After a few more words to his father Sam hung up. He had to get out of here, but driving the car out of Mexico would take way too long.

He just couldn't leave it here. The Mexican government would construe his leaving the car there as trying to sell it. He needed a way out that caused the least problems. He needed expert advice.

———•———

"Shit, sorry to hear about your grandfather. That's tough. I had a grandfather. He was sort of an a-hole, but he could … "

"Bennie, focus please," Sam begged. "Is there a way out of here without getting into trouble for leaving the car?"

"Oh, that. Well you can't do that technically, but we can get you out on an extra."

"What's an extra?" Sam asked. "Is it legal or will I face 20 years if I get caught?"

"Yeah, there's that." Bennie laughed, but seeing Sam's angry face he controlled himself. "Chances are good you'll get away with it. Most of the old timers down here have gone in and out of Mexico using duplicate visas. It's unfortunate you haven't been here long enough to collect your own set."

"Duplicate visas? What do you mean?"

"A lot of guys cross the border telling the immigration officials that they are going to visit, say Saltillo. So they get the visa and hang around the border town for half a day or so, then walk back into the States. They get over to the next town with a border crossing and do the same. Eventually they have a couple of visas in their names so that if an emergency occurs, like yours, they walk out on one of the visas and are able to leave their car in Mexico. It's great if you want to dump a car here."

As Bennie predicted Sam smoothly crossed the border. He gave Andy the keys to his car and Andy put it in his backyard under a canvas to keep the curious hotel workers away from it.

As soon as Sam walked across the border he made his way to a Denny's and arranged for his parents to pick him up. As promised, he had made it out of Mexico within 24 hours. His grandfather would be buried in the morning.

Chapter **10**

Death of a Dream

The funeral was a somber affair. His aunt had come out from New York and there were a couple of cousins. Sam cried at the gravesite. When he was old enough to understand what his grandfather's emigration entailed he thought of the adventure Grandpa must have lived. What fun, foreign lands, battles, different food and languages. Freedom! Grandpa as a teenager didn't have his parents telling him to clean up his room, come to dinner, or be sure to be somewhere at seven to see the Smiths.

Sam's life had become his grandfather's past. Sure, there weren't guns pointed at him, though there was that danger in Mexico. The foods, the lack of supervision, the different language were all there. What Sam hadn't realized was the loneliness that his grandfather must have felt when he left his family behind. For Sam it was like a piece of his soul had been traumatically amputated. At least Sam was able to have an occasional phone call. Grandpa never saw or heard from his family again. They had been lost in the maelstrom that had been World War One. Sam felt that he had lost the only person who could truly appreciate what he was going through. Maybe dislocation was in his genetics to be a Wandering Jew?

After the burial everyone came back to his parents' house to eat, drink, and talk. Sam's father, with his shirt torn to signify mourning, sat in a traditional low chair. Aside from having red-rimmed eyes he was very happy to see Sam.

"Thank you for getting back here, Sam. I'm sure your grandfather appreciates the effort it must have taken."

"I'm glad I made it."

"We'll talk later, Sam. Don't feel like you have to stick around the house all the time. I'm sure you'll want to see your friends."

"Thanks, Dad. I think right now I'll take a nap and then we'll see."

Sam went down the hall, but instead of going to his room he went into his parents' bedroom and called Leah's house.

Her father answered the phone.

"Hi, it's Sam. How are you?"

"Sam, where are you? The connection is too good to be a call from Mexico."

Sam explained his situation to her father. Making his uttermost effort to sound nonchalant, he asked, "How is Leah doing?"

"You can ask her yourself, Sam. She is also here for a visit. Why don't you come over for a drink after dinner tonight, if you can leave your father. Please send him our condolences."

Sam couldn't believe she was here. Maybe he could go over now? No, her father said tonight. It would be forward. He sounded friendly, even encouraging. Sam's mind was racing, but he was finally able to calm himself down. The trip had taken its toll. The mind may have been willing but the body dragged itself to bed and sleep.

———•◦•———

Sam raced through dinner, making excuses for inhaling the food. His father, knowing the reason, smiled and told him to "get out of here," flipping him the car keys.

Sam was at her house, nervous, short of breath. Forcing himself to calm down he rang the doorbell. What if she refused to see him or was mad that her father had invited him?

The door opened. "Oh Sam, I'm so happy that you're back. I missed you." She hugged him tightly and kissed him. He felt like he had died and gone to heaven. She was very tan and had gained a couple of pounds in a womanly fashion. Her eyes bright with almost a purple hue, she gave him a warm smile. She looked happy and confident in herself.

Leah looked Sam over. "Sam, you lost weight. Isn't the Mexican food any good? But wow, I thought you were in a town that was up in the mountains. Where did you get that tan? You're almost as dark as I am. Are you getting any sleep? You look tired?

Sam was so pleased she noticed the physical changes in him. She must really care. Maybe there was the hope of them getting back together.

"I missed you so much. I kept writing but I never got anything back. I was so worried about you."

"Sam," a booming voice called. "Get in here and let me have a look at you." The doctor called and when he called, you moved. Sam went into the house and was greeted by her mother and father. Her mother came over and gave him a hug and kiss, then looked at him. "You lost weight. Isn't there any food in Mexico or do you just starve yourself to prevent gastrointestinal distress?"

Jews and food he thought. Everyone was a Jewish mother at heart.

"No, just a lot of work and no time to prepare food."

He looked at Leah, still beautiful, vivacious. His heart was pounding so hard he thought they could all hear it. "How are you? It looks like Israel agrees with you."

"Oh Sam, it is wonderful. I've never had such a spiritual, exciting, and satisfying experience. I want to emigrate."

"Emigrate? Isn't that a little drastic? I mean your family and friends are here. You're an American."

She just smiled at him. It was a smile that conveyed knowledge that he wasn't privy to and it depressed him. "How is school? Is it exciting? Have you actually touched a patient yet?"

Her father ushered them all into the living room.

"Tell us about medicine in Mexico. This school you're at. Is it like Guadalajara?"

Sam started talking about most of his adventures in Mexico up to this point. He edited out his jailbird status and his loneliness. He rambled, his story was on autopilot, and his thoughts drifted. He couldn't get over how satisfied and happy she was. The evening went on with tea and cookies and as the hour got late he had hoped that he could have some private time with her, but Leah became fidgety and started suppressing yawns.

"Sam," she apologized, "I'm on a different time zone and need some sleep. We'll get together real soon." She came over and gave him a peck on the cheek and disappeared up the staircase. Sam felt short of breath with frustration. He left her house angry, his shoulders knotting up in spasm, his face hot. Even his eyes hurt and had trouble focusing. Was she avoiding any private time with him? He got into his car to go home.

———⋅———

Shiva, the traditional mourning period for Jews, was coming to a close and Sam was making plans to leave the same way he escaped from Mexico. Sam would start his own collection of visas for emergencies. There was no word from Leah since that first night. He knew it was over, but couldn't face it head on. Better to keep a small fantasy alive than confront reality.

Then Leah called and asked him to come by her house to see her.

"Sam, I'm happy you came over. We hardly got to talk."

She answered the door, and he couldn't get over how beautiful she was. Her smile warmed him, and her voice was a comfort—all thoughts of the other disastrous evening forgotten. "I would have liked that, too. Hey, why don't we go and get a drink somewhere. Like, how about right now?"

"Silly, it's like three in the afternoon. Everyone will think we're alcoholics. Besides, my father wanted to talk to you."

He entered the house happy to see her.

"My father is in his office." She led him deeper into the house. Reluctantly he followed.

"Sam, come in," her father bellowed. "Sit down."

"I'll see you later, Sam," she said and walked away. He watched her go, letting his eyes follow her.

"Sam, I have something for you," he said, drawing Sam back to reality.

"What is that, sir?"

"I have a friend who runs a small ER near downtown. It has a ritzy clientele, but it also gets a lot of ambulance traffic from an adjacent barrio area. Their trauma cases are up so you'd see gunshot wounds and stabbings. Not much vehicular, but you can't have everything."

Sam was confused. "What do you mean I can't have everything?"

"Oh, my friend will hire you as an attendant this summer in his ER. You will help the nurses out, but at the same time the doctors will bring you in on interesting cases to get the general layout of real American medicine. "

Sam couldn't believe his ears. Damn, this was fantastic. He'd be in an American hospital seeing patients with doctors and helping in their care.

"Thank you so much, Sir. I don't know what to say. This is fantastic."

"That ER thing you do in the Mexican hospital, it doesn't sound like there is a lot of formal education." He looked around not finding what he wanted. "Someone out there bring me that package I left in the hallway," he hollered.

A few minutes later Leah came in. "Is this what you wanted, Daddy?"

"Yes, thank you."

She turned to leave. "Stay, darling; we're almost done here and I'm sure you'd like a little time with Sam before he leaves for Mexico."

He turned to Sam. "Open this up," he handed Sam the package.

It was a copy of *Bates' Guide to Physical Exam and History Taking.* "Oh my, it's beautiful," Sam said.

"Well I don't know about beauty, but it is a classic. You should read it from cover to cover and practice on those Mexicans in that ER. By the time you get back here you may understand something of what you will be seeing in my friend's hospital."

Sam was misty eyed as he stood up. "Thank you so much, Sir. This means so much to me."

Her father was pleased but embarrassed at all the emotion. "OK, I don't have any time left for this. Why don't the two of you get out of here and catch up." He looked at his daughter with a knowing look and said, "You really need to catch up."

———•———

Sam took her to a romantic bar. The empty lounge had soft lights and soft music.

"You look fantastic and you have a real Israeli tan," Sam gushed. "Man I missed you. Everyday I thought of you."

She paused, her eyes nervously darting around, not meeting his, though Sam didn't notice. "I missed you too, Sam. How is life down there? Have you made any friends?"

Sam told her about the boys and the classes.

"How do you pronounce it? De-bu-jo?" She forced out a laugh. "It sounds like kindergarten all over again."

"Yeah," he smiled. "But if you color within the lines you are almost guaranteed an M-ai-Bei."

"What's an M-ai-Bei?" she asked curiously.

"It's an M and a B. You get it written on top of your handout sheet if you did well. It stands for Muy Bien. Very Good. It's like an A."

"So even the grading system is fucked up."

Sam thought about it and said, "I guess so, but you get used to it. If it weren't for missing you all the time … "

She squirmed and was having trouble looking him in the eyes, face almost frozen. "Sam, I'm sure you must have a couple of girlfriends down there that keep you company. I mean we have been separated for a while now. Everyone makes new friends, don't they?"

Sam's heart started palpitating and the room's walls felt like they were closing in on him. He felt the blood rush to his face and now his eyes wouldn't focus. He rubbed them ferociously with one hand to bring back clarity. "You're with someone, aren't you?" he said, as he finally faced the reality.

She was silent. She stared down at her hands, which were clasped together, the knuckles white. "His name is Ari. He is a civil engineering student at the Technion. We have been going together for four months. He is wonderful, Sam, and on track with me."

"What about us? I love you. I don't want anyone else but you," Sam bit off.

"Sam, I love you and will always love you, but we can't be

together. There is just too much difference in our needs and goals. We talked about this when we left San Diego. I was honest with you then and I'm being honest with you now." She looked sad, but this time he was sure there were no tears.

"He'd never love you as much as I do! He can never love you as much as I do!"

"He does love me Sam, and what's more I love him and want to be with him. Please be happy for me. I will always be your friend … forever."

She reached out and rested her hand on his, but it felt like a hot poker. His hand jerked back hitting his glass and spilling the drink on him and the table. He stood up and began furiously dabbing with the napkin at the liquid to hide his embarrassment. When he'd cleared as much of the stain as he could, he reached into his pocket, pulled out some bills and threw them on the table. "Let's go," he said angrily.

She got up saying nothing, and they headed for the car. The ride back to her house was silent. She left the car without either of them exchanging another word.

Sam left for Tampico the next day. He never told his parents that she had left his life permanently. That part of his heart had died as he willed his mind to forget her forever.

<hr />

"Vamos aver, Ko-han!"

He went back to the day to day of being a Mexican medical student. The difference this time was that he had foregone nighttime forays into the more interesting side of life in Tampico. He went to classes and as soon as they were finished he rushed back to his room and opened the books. No more late night beer sessions. No more skinny-dipping in the hotel pool to get a rise out of management. He even stopped sneaking around the hotel kitchen to cadge free food from Carlito. His friends started to worry about the opposite turn his actions had taken since he got back. Sam didn't tell any of them about his humiliation at seeing Leah again. Sam knew that for him, the fire burned hottest at the start to the exclusion of everything else. This was his way of instituting a change in his life.

"Ko-han, vamos aver."

"Sí, Professor." Sam stood up and started rattling off the major coronary arteries.

Valdez eyed him. "You prepared for this class, Ko-han? To what do I owe the pleasure? I pray along with your future patients you keep this up."

"Thank you, Professor," Sam beamed.

Valdez eyed him more closely, "but maybe a little more sleep, joven, sí?"

"Sí, Professor."

"*Baratz,* vamos aver … "

Chapter **11**

To Save a Life Is to Save a Whole World

Sam picked up a chart in the *Cuarto de Emergencias* and read "chest pain." Armed with his trusty stethoscope and the first 228 pages of the physical diagnosis book, he went over to find the patient. He prayed that what he was about to encounter wasn't covered on page 229.

Moreno was a fifty-three-year-old male, overweight and short of breath. His gurney was parked in a dark corner in the back of the waiting room. He waited with no cardiac monitor, no IV, no oxygen. The man wasn't even undressed.

He found Moreno clutching his chest, sweating, and having problems talking because he was so short of breath.

"Sr. Moreno, I'm Doctor Cohen. I understand you are having chest pain?"

"Sí, can't breathe. Please, help me."

Sam was a little panicked. This was a case that looked serious and aside from some simple questions about chest pain that were supposed to lead him to a diagnosis, he had no idea what to do with the information he obtained.

"Where is your pain and how long have you had it?"

Moreno pointed to the center of his chest and said two hours. He was looking sweatier by the minute.

"Do you have a history of heart problems or high cholesterol?"

Moreno just gave Sam a blank look. "Please ... " he took shallow breaths, " ... help."

Sam looked around searching for a nurse, and finding no one who wasn't busy with other bleeding or dying patients. He might not know exactly what was going on but he was pretty sure Moreno was about to die.

He found two young girls who were wearing the uniform of attendants. Attendants in this ER meant they were barely out of Junior High School, but he was desperate.

"Quick, one of you find Dr. Soto. Tell him it's an emergency. And get me an oxygen tank and an IV tray."

They just gawked at him. "Run, now!" They did, with one coming back quickly dragging a green tank that had an oxygen mask attached. Sam put the mask on Moreno and then fumbled turning on the oxygen. How much oxygen does a doctor give a patient? He had no idea. Oh well, he cranked it up to the maximum. Maybe too much was better than too little.

Sam saw that some color was returning to Moreno's face. Maybe a small victory? Now if he could just get rid of the pains and sweats.

"Sr. Moreno, I'm going to try to put in a *suero*, an IV to give you pain medication. It's going to sting a bit."

Sam had never even held an angiocath, the needle component of an intravenous line, but he had seen Soto and the nurses do it a bunch of times. He put a rubber tourniquet on Moreno's upper arm and swabbed his inner elbow with alcohol. "Now what?" he thought. Thanking God that Moreno was relatively thin, a large blue pipe showed up. "Great, a big vein, now what?"

He aimed at the vein with the business end of the angiocath and slowly, millimeters of needle per minute entered the skin. Morales screamed and jerked, scaring Sam to death. Sam was now having chest pain.

"Sorry Doctor. I wasn't expecting it," Moreno gasped.

"My fault, I should have warned you." Sam made a mental note, "Tell the patient before you stab him."

Sam tried again and miracle of miracles got a blood return. He quickly hooked in the bag of IV fluid and taped the angiocath down.

Morales was making funny breathing noises and Sam had begun sweating from every pore of his body.

"Por favor, Doctor … ," Moreno whispered as his eyes closed and he slumped on the gurney.

"Oh my God," Sam cried, "he's dead, he went into cardiac arrest."

The two attendants were puzzled at Sam's outburst.

"You help me get him flat and you tell Soto I need him now," Sam ordered. "Fucking school doesn't even teach us what to do with someone who drops dead in front of us," Sam said. He started to remember a basic lifesaving course he had taken one summer in high school.

He opened Moreno's mouth and started breathing into it. "No, this isn't right" he thought. He quickly remembered where the carotid artery was in the neck and tried to find a pulse. No such luck, God fucking damn it, what next?

He slammed his fist down on Moreno's chest once. Tried to find a pulse again, again nada. Sam slammed his fist down again on the chest. No pulse, no response.

Sam assumed the position and started compressing the chest like he thought he remembered. One, two, three … It must be time for a breath. He quickly did another lip lock and breathed into him. Compressions again …

Sam felt a hand clutching his arm and he jumped. Moreno's eyes were open and he was trying to mouth something to Sam. Sam put his head to Moreno's lips. "What happened?" asked Moreno.

Sam looked at him. "Your heart stopped … "

There was a commotion and a lot of shouting as Sam was pushed away from Moreno.

"*Cardiogramma, rapidamente y un presion arterial,*" Soto ordered the nurse who had accompanied him.

Soto turned to Sam. "What happened?"

Sam took a deep breath to calm himself and remember his history skills.

"Fifty-three-year-old male complaining of chest pain and shortness of breath for two hours. He became progressively more short of breath as I was taking the physical and was looking sweatier … "

"Diaphoretic," Soto interrupted.

" … was looking more diaphoretic. I put oxygen on him and started an IV … "

"You started an IV?" Soto again interrupted.

Sam was stricken. "Was that wrong?"

"No, actually it was amazing you got it on the first stab. Congratulations, or as you Judios say, Mazel tov," Soto smiled.

The Nurse handed Soto an EKG, which he read. "Come look at this Sam. See, there are ST elevations in the inferior leads," he said while tracing the lines of the cardiogram with his finger.

Sam was so distressed he had almost killed a patient that he missed the meaning of Soto's words entirely. "I almost killed him?"

Soto looked at Sam sharply, "No Sam, you probably saved this cabron's life." He looked at the nurse at Moreno's arm. "Pressure?'

"110 over 70 Doctor, with a pulse of 72."

Soto looked at the chart. "Moreno, are you still having chest pain?"

Moreno was looking a lot pinker by this time. "Not the same pain, my ribs are very sore."

Soto laughed and nodded to Sam, "That cabron beat you up and broke your ribs. That's why you are still alive. Thank him for the pain." He called to the nurses, "Nitroglycerine and morphine and get a bed in the Cardiac Unit. I need to talk to that *puta* cardiologist, now."

The nurses hustled Moreno out of the ER on his stretcher and Soto turned to Sam. "So, cabron, how does it feel to save your first life?"

Sam was so overwhelmed his hands were shaking and he was trembling.

"I saved his life? I thought I almost killed him."

"No, cabron, if anyone, or in this case, anything, almost killed him it was the institution."

"What do you mean?" Sam said still shaking.

"The institution does not fund the *Cuarto de Emergencias* the way it should. It is the door to the hospital. Almost all the admitted sick come through this place, plus all the patients who can't get clinic appointments. There is not enough room, not enough doctors, nurses, or even support personnel. So what do we do?"

"What do you do?" Sam asked, wide-eyed. He had never seen such crowding and filth apart from the jail where he'd spent the night. There were people who were literally bleeding and vomiting on one another. No privacy existed where people who were being examined were stripped and prodded in front of other patients, visitors, and voyeurs.

"We stack them," Soto said grimly

"Stack them?"

"Yes we stack them in the rooms, the hallways. Hell, I once saw a patient in a bathroom. We do the best we can with the little we have. Most of the time it is like fighting a battle. But today my friend, you became the general and won a war. I think you have done enough for today. Go home, drink muchas cervezas, and get laid. You deserve it."

Sam looked at Soto. He had never felt this way about himself before. Today he had saved a life, and what did he learn in Hebrew school? When you save a life it is like saving an entire world. "If it's OK, I'd like to stay and learn more."

Soto nodded and the two walked down the hallway looking for their next challenge.

Chapter **12**

Breaking With the Past

Life became better for Sam except for the extreme loneliness. He still spent time with the Boys between classes or in the morning by the wall. Rarely did he go over to Andy's with Marvin, Bennie, or Sayeed for beers and bullshit sessions. He found that while Marvin and Sayeed did study, they didn't put in the same hours. He also started spending all his free time in the ER with Soto.

Sam had long finished reading the Physical Diagnosis book, twice. He spent a lot of time doing abdominal exams, because Soto had told him that to be a competent clinician you needed to examine a lot of patients, and examining bellies was an art. "So go and practice, cabron. There are a million putas in here with belly pain and stinky, discharging vaginas. Have fun."

So Sam took advantage. As much as he looked forward to his time at the American hospital, he wondered if he would be able to touch a patient. Here he could touch as much as he wanted, practice all the "simpler procedures" he wanted and Soto always seemed to have time for him.

It turned out that Soto had graduated from a medical school in Monterrey, but had done an internal medicine internship and surgical residency in Lubbock, Texas. They spent hours discussing the politics of American medicine in relationship to an FMG, a foreign medical grad. It wasn't pretty, but Sam tried to remember he was a long way from that and had to be the best in the here and now.

So, what was the problem? He should have been on top of the world.

The answer was that Leah wasn't in his life. His resolution to concentrate on studying medicine to win her back was tough going. Then the game changed after she told him about her new boyfriend, Ari, and her plans to move to Israel for good. Maybe it was time to finally let go of her and move on with his life. A night on the town would do him good. He had been working hard and deserved to have some fun for a change, so he grabbed his keys and headed out to the car.

———•——

The car was cleaned out and he had nothing in his hands. He climbed into the car, counted the cash he had on him, and turned the ignition.

Boy's Town hadn't changed in the least bit. The only change was Sam. Technically he wasn't supposed to be in the Town, but like everything else in Mexico edicts tended to be elastic. He managed to get ten feet away from the car when a familiar figure approached him.

Sam showed his hands and stopped.

"Hey amigo," the federale said. The neon lights reflected on the mirrored lenses of his sunglasses. "What are you selling now? Your body?" he laughed. "Maybe that car? I notice that the ball joints need replacing. Must be the result of our famous Mexican roads."

"I'm not here to sell anything. I'm here to have a beer." Sam wasn't smiling; his thirst could only be quenched in Boy's Town and this asshole was going to ruin it.

"You sure now?" the federale looked at him intently. "You look like a man on a mission."

"You might say that. Am I allowed to spend my money here?"

"As long as you don't try to sell the car, I guess the judge won't mind. I know the chief of police will accept your gringo dollars without a qualm." He made an extensive gesture welcoming Sam into the bar and faded back into the darkness. Sam forced a smile and entered the Casa Blanca.

———•———

"Hey Señor Sam. Welcome back," said the bartender. "Cerveza?"

"Not tonight. Tonight is a night to celebrate. Give me a couple of tequila shots."

"Of course, Sr. Sam." He hurried off to get the salt and lime for Sam.

Sam surveyed the bar looking for … there she was, Lola, as beautiful as ever. Sam opened himself up to her imminent advances.

"Joven, long time." She embraced him, her perfume hitting him like a shot of pure alcohol.

"Hi Lola. Did you miss me?"

"You know I did. I also miss the cosmetics that you brought. Do you have any more of the lipstick?"

"No Lola. I'm out of business thanks to the Government of Ciudad Madero and the Districto Federal. Sorry. Can I buy you a drink?" he asked nervously.

"A drink? My, this is a special occasion." She eyed him. "I know you for months and today out of nowhere you want to buy me a drink."

"Sure, yeah. What's so strange about that? There are men that buy you drinks in here all the time. What's the matter with me?" Sam was getting angry.

"*Calmate* joven, of course you can buy me a drink. I was just curious as to what is new in your life that you honor me so?"

Sam calmed down. He had trouble making eye contact with her, his resolve evaporating quickly. "I want some companionship," he said quietly.

She nodded. "I understand, joven, and I'm honored you want to spend time with me, but I don't think this is what you want or need."

"What? Are you kidding?"

"No joven, you are a student learning to be a doctor. I'm a psychologist of men with many years experience. Trust me on this one. You need sweetness to counter the bitter. I can't supply what you really need and if I try we will not be friends anymore."

Sam was shocked. "I can't believe this. You won't sleep with me? My money isn't good, I have bad breath, you don't fuck gringos … what?"

Lola smiled sadly at Sam. "Ten years ago you would have had my sugar, but now that has fermented into alcohol. It's not what you need." She got up and went into the back.

"Hey Bartender, more tequila," Sam yelled. He was angry and embarrassed at the same time.

The bartender brought him another shot and then a shot after that. Sam was feeling pretty buzzed when he sensed a presence next to him.

The woman was young, pretty, and dark. She had long black hair and beautiful red lips. "Hola Sam, I am Esmeralda. You can call me Esme. Lola asked me to sit with you. She said you'd buy me a drink."

"Lola won't have a drink with me so she sends the second team?" Sam asked drunkenly.

"Second team," she said angrily. "I don't know what that means, but it sounds like an insult. If you do not want the company I will not force myself on you. *Buenas noches, Señor.*" She got off the bar stool and started to walk away.

Sam was embarrassed at his meanness. What an asshole he was. Esme was just trying to be nice.

"Please, don't go. I apologize. I've just had a bad day that became worse this evening. Please let me buy you a drink."

"OK Sam. I am sorry you have had a bad day. Maybe we can talk about it. It isn't very busy here tonight."

———◆———

In the room's dim lighting he could see that she was beautiful, every man's dream. She had slowly taken off his clothes and told him to lie down on a small old bed. Thankfully, the sheets were clean. His heart was beating hard in his chest and he was as erect as he had ever been. He watched as she pulled off her simple top to reveal large, heavy breasts with nipples the size of silver dollars. Then she lowered her skirt. Her waist was small but flared to perfection. Between her legs the dark hair couldn't hide a ripening of her lips. He hesitantly reached for her hand and she smiled, coming to lay down with him. They faced each other and he started to speak, but she quieted him with her lips. His hands massaged her back bringing her even closer to him. Her breasts were soft and hot on her chest. How long had it been? His thoughts went to past women he had shared a bed with that were meaningless but fun experiences. That he had never been intimate with Leah crept about in his thoughts even as his breathing became deeper and his heart pounded. It would have been beautiful, but she didn't feel the same. Oh my God, he felt so good and alive. He didn't know how long they were in this position, but he felt her reach for his ready penis turgid with warm blood. She rolled on top of him and sank onto his erection, sighing. He thought he was going to pop and die right there, but managed to control himself. They looked into each other's eyes as she smiled and started to ride him. In and out, his breath quickening as the pleasure became too intense for words. She moaned and shuddered once, twice, and drove him over the edge emptying every last bit of fluid he had in him as she collapsed on his chest. He held her, stroking her back and face. He closed his eyes, smiling.

———•———

"Amor," he heard an angel speak in his sleep. "Amor, it is a little cold, I'm sorry." Sam felt a wet cool towel at his groin and opened his eyes. She had dressed herself and was now cleaning him. He stretched and became aroused again.

"Oh Esme, you are so wonderful, so beautiful," he said. "Why don't you come back in the bed?" He was smiling.

She stopped wiping him as his erection was growing and playfully swatted it. "Oh Sam, you are a bad boy. You tired me out and it is time for you to go."

He reached for her and she laughed and swatted his hand away. "No more you bad boy. You are very beautiful and I'd like you to come back, but it is enough for tonight."

"Maybe tomorrow?" Sam asked hopefully.

"Sí, come back tomorrow but for tonight maybe you can leave me a present … " She nodded toward the dresser.

The reality intruded into Sam's happiness. He'd just paid for it. She was a hooker and this is how she made money. She had earned it. He had never felt this good after sex with any of the girls he had dated in San Diego. In a flash, he realized that Leah was gone and it was time to move on. His imagined bliss would surely change by the morning, but for now he was happy and calm. He got out of the bed. Finding his pants he took cash out of his pocket and left the bills on the bureau.

"Thank you, Sam," she came over to him and hugged him. "Come back soon," she said as she reached down and felt his hard erection. "Come back when this needs some release again." She kissed him lightly on the cheek and left. Sam headed back into the bar.

⎯⎯⎯•⎯⎯⎯

"Hola joven," Lola called out. "Sí, you look much happier. Lola knows what's good for you. You look like a new man."

Sam blushed, but admitted to himself that Lola had chosen correctly for him. He was feeling a hell of a lot better. "Buy you a beer, Lola?"

She looked at him sharply.

"No, a beer to thank you for your guidance and judgment."

"Well in that case, Bartender, a cerveza for my friend and a brandy for me."

"Tell me about her, Lola."

"Her? Sam, Esmeralda is a sweet girl, but she is not girlfriend material. Please try to remember that and you won't be disappointed. She will always be there for your physical needs, but she is not looking for a boyfriend in the sense that you want a girlfriend."

"Boyfriend, girlfriend? Lola, I just want to know about her. That's all."

There was a quiver of doubt in Sam's chest. Girlfriend? No he didn't need a substitute girlfriend he thought stoically, but the doubt on his motives remained.

Lola downed the brandy and got off the barstool. "Remember, she is to fuck and have fun with. That's all." Lola walked off to the back rooms of the bar.

Chapter 13

Another Road Movie

Sam woke up. The sun was shining and contrary to what he thought last night, he didn't feel guilty, nor did he feel angry.

"Let's call it what it is. It is the antidote to loneliness and it will help me concentrate on my studies and get me one step closer to leaving this country."

He liked that. It was a very medical viewpoint—he needed immunization from the unhappiness he had been feeling. So, even though he had a strong urge to run right back to Boy's Town and get a "booster shot" he grabbed his textbook and started tracing the Krebs cycle for his biochemistry course.

"Acetyl-Co-A goes into what? Oh, citrate." Shit, he only had to memorize the same fucking thing three times, once in high school and twice in college. It was true that a small percentage of beginning med school was a repeat of college. How does this have anything to do with a stabbing victim or a patient with a heart attack?

There was a knock on the door. Fuck, leave me alone he thought. Maybe they'll go away.

The knocking became more persistent and he heard Sayeed shouting. "Sam, open up."

"Christ, I'm coming, cool it on the noise."

Sam opened the door to find not only Sayeed, but Bennie, and Marvin.

"What's up at this ungodly hour boys?"

"It's ten a.m. There is nothing ungodly about it. Good news and bad news."

Sam sighed. Being a veteran of living in Mexico he was now used to the bad news, though it was extremely rare to get good news. "OK, bad news first."

"We have to get out of the country."

"Why do we have to get out of the country? Did all our various tourist visas expire? And what about school?"

"OK," said Bennie, "the good news. The school is closed."

Sam, still neither impressed nor worried, asked, "Why is the school closed?"

Sayeed said, "They are expecting riots over the local elections and they decided they didn't want their tender gringos to get involved in the possible mayhem, arson, and general fun associated with keeping the corrupt in power. Hence, the closing and the possibility of a road trip."

This cheered Sam up. "Road trip, huh. Like where?"

Marvin became animated. "We get you dressed and then hop into my car and go north."

"Now besides the great Estados Unídos what's going on in the north?"

"Brownsville and visual and gastronomical paradise."

"'Splain me, Lucy."

Marvin licked his lips. "Pizza Hut has a five dollar all you can eat lunch buffet. No tortillas, no chiles, just all good second-rate mozzarella and tomato sauce."

Sam laughed. "OK, that covers the gastronomic; what's the visual?"

Bennie got a dreamy look in his eyes. "Texas women. Beautiful,

Southern Belles with a cowgirl twist, blond-haired, big-breasted, hypersexual, Texas women."

Sam didn't have to think twice. "Boys, let's go forth to the promised land."

If you look at a map of North America and find the Great State of Texas and then find the most southern tip of Texas, you'd see that Mexico continues from this point hundreds of miles south. The map would tell you that it is 323 miles from Downtown Tampico to Downtown Brownsville or about six hours driving. It turns out, the map fails to deliver the reality on the ground. Six hours is nothing. You can't get halfway in six hours.

"Goddamit! What is it with these fucking trucks?" Sayeed was at the end of his rope. They had been on the road for five hours and were still at least 200 miles away from the border. It had been beautiful starting out from Tampico. It was sunny with the highway stretching out before them. The traffic was light and the road multi-laned. It wasn't long until the road and the weather turned into a nightmare. Mexican Highway 180, which turned into the two-lane Mexican Highway 101, was the main connection between Tampico and the border. As a result, it had all the truck commerce. The 18-wheelers were slow, but the drivers swung all over the road as if they were drunk, and they weren't charitable in letting the cars pass. It wasn't long before the road itself became one lane each way and made its way into the mountains, where the weather drastically changed. Grey skies soon roiled into black skies, and then the rain fell, changing from a drizzle to buckets.

It was no wonder Sayeed's nerves were frayed. In some areas of the road, the cliff edge appeared mere inches from the tires.

"Man, I hope there is a gas station coming up. We are down to a quarter tank."

"There have to be at least a couple open 24 hours. This is a major route for Mexico. What happens to those trucks that have to get up to the border?" Sam was riding shotgun, but couldn't see more than a few feet in front of them. In addition to the rain, as they increased in altitude the clouds hung so low they obscured the road in a dense fog.

Sam asked, "Sayeed do you want me to drive a while? You can get in back and make with a little shuteye. San Diego gets pretty foggy it would be like ... SHIT!"

An 18-wheeler came out of the fog bank, its headlights bearing down on them head on. Sayeed slammed his foot on the brake, and the tires locked, sending the car into a spin.

"Oh my God, oh my God," Marvin prayed. Bennie started laughing hysterically. "Now I know why my father calls you the best driver in Brooklyn."

Sayeed's hands were shaking. He turned to Sam. "Is the offer to drive still open?"

"Yeah, I guess so."

They barely reached a gas station. Exhausted, they had only the vaguest idea of how much longer the ride was going to be. Trying to get information from the owner of the station was useless. All they could get from him was, "*no mucho.*"

"Man, it's dark. I swear we should have hit the border way before this. I can't even figure out if we are out of the mountains." Sayeed looked a wreck. His hands had a fine shake and his words came out in a slur. It didn't look like his eyes could focus and the muscles in his face were so spastic Sam could see them twitch. This certainly wasn't driving fast in Brooklyn. "Why couldn't they fucking light their highways?"

"You want to camp out till light?" Marvin also had had enough of the ride. He wasn't wild about bouncing over a cliff because road and air looked the same from the car.

"Come on, man. Let's keep going. I can smell those Southern

Belles and what's more there is a pepperoni pizza with my name on it. I'll drive, OK?"

All of them replied, "NO!"

———•———

The border glowed like a jewel in the rapidly brightening sky.

The Boys, weary, smelly, and unshaved had made it. Soon they would have a respite in Paradise. This early in the morning, the traffic was light since most of the illegals chose to take the "unofficial" border crossing. A bleary-eyed overweight *Migracion* officer peered into the car. He smelled strongly of cheap tequila, but who could blame him, posted here all night.

"Gringos?" He slurred.

Sam, feeling he was close enough to the States to gun the car right through this Bozo, said, "We are proud Americans, going home."

The guard laughed, "But you'll be back to use our whores, buy our booze, and leave your dollars. Have a nice day," he said as he waved them through.

"Man," said Marvin. "You told him. Proud of you boy," he said slapping Sam on the back.

"What an asshole," Sam replied dully. They drove ten yards to the next station proudly waving the Stars and Stripes. Sayeed slowed the car to stop in front of the small building. A small floodlight bathed the car in white glare and Sam could see swarms of flying insects playing suicide bomber into the hot bulb. The rest of the sky was inky black with a heavy humidity in the air. It was quiet except for the crickets playing their songs in the brush.

"I want to get out and kiss the ground," said Marvin reverently.

Sayeed said, "Why don't you wait and kiss the floor in the pizza place," and laughed.

"Now that's an asshole," Marvin replied.

"OK, quiet down. Customs is coming," Sam said.

A green-uniformed officer wearing a shiny badge on his chest came out of the building. He was blond, tall, and very muscular. His face was stiff, showing no warmth or welcome to the inhabitants of the car. He came up to the car and immediately switched on his flashlight, shining it into the interior and on their faces.

"Americans?"

"Yes Suh, Officer, Suh. Each and every one of us is," said Bennie in a pseudo-southern-Texan voice. He was happy and manic after too few hours sleep.

"Are you mocking me, Boy?" The Officer was unmistakably angry.

"Oh no Suh. We be saluting yo-ah service to America."

Sam saw the storm coming and felt powerless to stop it. "Sir, he wasn't being disrespectful. He has some mental problems. Please disregard him. We just want to get to the hotel and get some sleep."

Spying Sayeed, the officer asked, "You an Ayrab, Boy?"

"Oh shit." Not the thing to say to Sayeed thought Sam.

"I am an American just like you," declared Sayeed. "What are you trying to say?"

Sam saw the situation going to total shit. "Sayeed, I'm sure the officer meant nothing by it. Why don't we just move on—that pizza won't eat itself." He could only hope that there was still a chance to smooth it over.

The immigration officer set his jaw. "Get out of the car, all of you, and pull out the IDs." He keyed a walkie-talkie. "I got some smart asses out here and need some help." Without delay, several officers in green uniforms filed out of the building like ants from a hole in the ground.

"Fuck, can't anything be easy?" Sam said, pulling out his driver's license.

"Fucking fascist," Sayeed said as he climbed out of the car. "Did you notice he's Irish? They think they own the States, the motherfuckers."

Sam pleaded, "Please shut the fuck up, Sayeed. I just want to get some sleep and eat some pizza and smell an American girl if at all possible. Then I can die a happy man. I don't want to spend the trip in a holding cell."

The officer walked over with another officer who had a Marlboro tucked in the corner of his mouth. "This your car, Boy?" he asked as the cigarette wagged in his mouth.

"Yes Sir, my father's actually," Sam said.

"You got a note saying you have permission to drive this California car in Texas?"

"No Sir, but he gave it to me. We are all going to medical school in Mexico and had some time off, so we decided to visit. Look, we just wanted to get to the hotel and sleep … "

"Lot of kids from California go into Mexico and buy drugs trying to sneak them past the border here. You sneaking drugs, Son?"

"No Sir," Sam said, wiping the sweat from his forehead. "We don't touch drugs. We are just medical students here for a weekend."

Directing his attention to Marvin he said, carefully removing the cigarette from his mouth, cradling it in the notch of his fingers, "Aren't you a bit old and a tad fat to be a medical student? Maybe you are the drug ring leader, huh?"

Bennie had had enough of the officer and not enough sleep. "Look asshole, we are all citizens. Search the fucking car now or let us go."

There was dead silence. Sam felt like he was having a heart attack as he watched the officer become more enraged, the veins in his neck bulging as his face became red and so hot it seemed to Sam that he could feel the heat generated in the car.

"Take these fuckers to the holding cell now," he told one of his fellow officers. "Oh, we will search your piece of shit car, you can be assured of that."

The Boys were herded into a cell and the door was locked.

"Who ends up in a cell twice in a month?" Sam asked, exasperated.

An hour and a half later the door of the cell opened and the immigration officer called to them. "OK, you check out. Get out of here."

He tossed Sam the keys to the car and said, "Car's parked on the side. Load up and get out of here."

Sam was immediately suspicious, "Load up? What do you mean by that?"

The officer laughed, "Next time, make sure your friends watch their mouths."

They all stepped outside into the light of day.

"Oh My God, what did those fucking bastards do to my car?"

The car had had all the interior door panels removed, and the seats had been unbolted from the chassis. It was a clear mess especially since their clothes and toiletries had been unpacked from their bags and emptied into the trunk of the car.

"This trip was a total disaster. How am I going to afford the price to fix all this?"

Sayeed was looking over the damage, "I think five bucks and about a half hour will take care of it." He got to the trunk and looked inside. His expression turned sullen. "My good going-out shirt, those fuck bigots. Oh well, another hour and a half for cleaning of clothes," he smiled. "What time is it?"

Marvin looked at his watch. "About eight-thirty, why?"

"Good. Pizza Place doesn't open for hours. Where do you think the nearest Laundromat is, and is it near a hardware store?"

Sam smiled for the first time. "I guess we can find out."

———•—•———

Sayeed, an expert in all things car, got the tools and went to work while Sam, Marvin, and Bennie washed what could be washed. An hour and a half later they had checked into two rooms in a motel that was at least two notches below a Motel 6, but was reasonably clean (after they switched from one of the rooms that was infested with fire ants) and cheap. They were all snoring ten minutes later.

———•—•———

Ah, America, land of the simple pleasures. Cheap American food like pizza, tacos, fried rice. Only in America.

After finding the Pizza Hut, they gorged themselves until their bellies were bloated to the danger point. A well-lit and relatively clean restaurant with first world public health standards was in itself a simple pleasure. The truth was that none of them had had even a day's worth of distress after any of their meals in Mexico. They had learned that safe eating in Mexico was a matter of where you ate. If you were smart about where and what you were eating, and avoided certain places, you would be fine. None of them had ever been brave enough to sample the mysterious taco meat from the stands that were so popular with the average Mexican.

"God can take me now. I'm ready," Marvin said with a satisfied burp.

"Me too," said Sam. "I can't believe how much I have missed pizza. You'd think with all the Americans running around town now, someone would have the bright idea to actually open a few American restaurants."

"How about the Kentucky," said Sayeed. "It's American." When they first got to Tampico, everyone was amazed that right on the main drag was a Kentucky Fried Chicken, Colonel Sanders and all. The façade of the building was enough to remind them of home. They were quickly disappointed. The old timers at the school reported that there were questionable carcasses seen behind the restaurant that looked nothing like chickens and more like quadrupeds. Soon enough, the Americans were avoiding the place. It seemed only the Mexicans were adventurous enough to eat deep fried rat.

"Man, I can't even move," Sayeed said. "We should go back to the hotel and rest up for tonight."

"Are you kidding?" Bennie got up abruptly from the table. "What time is it?"

"Sometime late in the afternoon. Why?" Sam asked, through a gaping yawn.

"It's time for the best show on Earth, so they tell me. Come on, we got to fly. It all ends at three."

"Bennie, what ends at three?" Marvin asked.

———————

The First National Bank of Texas was established for the border business that sucked in millions of dollars for the shop owners of Little Israel. The early merchants had headed south from the Northeast generations ago to make their fortunes selling trinkets. Over time their business evolved to center on electronics that Mexicans would buy and carry over the border into Mexico. The tax law was different for Mexicans who lived in the Border States. Possibly the Central Government in Mexico was worried about an uprising on the border and eventual loss of territory to the States. The Jews of Texas were wealthy, and the banks were clean, bright, and beautiful.

As beautiful as the buildings were, the women who worked at these banks were more beautiful. Number one in all the land were the women of the First National Bank of Texas. They were legendary.

Mostly tall, blond, and beautifully proportioned, they were true Southern Belles. Ruby red lips, sweet Texas drawls, and ready smiles. They had gorgeous blue eyes and large, proud breasts that strained the fabric that held them in place. Finally, the smell of the women in this bank could only be described as heavenly.

The Boys walked through the doors and were transported back to their hometown banks. There was no piece of the interior that spoke Texas. The walls were the same white plaster and the counters the same marble as in a hundred banks across the US. A giant, open vault door showing rows of safe deposit boxes and bright lighting in front of which was the usual small desk where a customer requested entrance. The air-conditioning kept the place a hermetically sealed environment against the Texas heat and humidity. Even the people seemed non-Texan except for the occasional Stetson, and lizard boots. After a few steps the boys stopped dead in their tracks, their vision collectively inundated by a kaleidoscope of Texan womanhood. These women justified all the rumors. Like goddesses or angels they floated across the marble floor performing their various jobs.

"Good afternoon, Boys. How can the First National Bank of Texas help you this afternoon?"

They all jumped at the voice of the geriatric security guard in the rent-a-cop uniform. "Oh My God, you scared us," Sam said.

"Yes, I get that a lot. Can I direct you anywhere?"

Sam looked at the others with a knowing smile. He guessed that the bank didn't offer horny young men up from Mexican med schools a box seat to watch women.

Stepping forward, Bennie said, "Yes, I'd like to open an account here. Can you direct me to that department?" Suddenly, he had put on the demeanor of a world-class businessman, a look he must have studied on his father growing up. He pulled it off well enough to convince the officer.

"Of course, Sir," replied the guard. "Right over there." He pointed to an old man sitting at a desk in the corner. Bennie looked crestfallen. "Of course, you could see Miss Smith sitting right behind him."

Bennie broke into a smile. "Thank you. I didn't want to bother that gentleman. He looks very busy."

The guard laughed. "Yes, I'm sure he is really busy setting up new accounts with Miss Smith right behind him. Have fun boys and welcome to First National." He watched them make their way to Miss Smith.

"Bennie, who's opening an account?" asked Marvin.

"I am. Look, it usually only takes a minimum to open a checking or savings account and I say it's worth the price of admission. Come on, Boys, let's giddy up."

They walked to new accounts and were greeted by the spectacular Miss Smith.

"Hi there, Boys," she drawled. "How can I help you today?"

Bennie jumped at the invitation. "Well Miss Smith, we are just up from little ol' Mexico and don't know anyone in your spectacular little town. We are looking for a bit of action tonight. Can you recommend anybody?" He smiled, "I mean any place, any place we can go?"

She just smiled absolute sunshine. "Well, Boys, I thought you were here for bank business. What kind of account do you think you need?"

Bennie smiled back and said, "Miss, any account you think will take the longest to open and take up the most of your time."

She laughed and said, "Sit down Mr ... ?"

"Frankle," he said, extending his hand. "Bennie Frankle. I'd be pleased if you called me Bennie."

———•———

At last, Viviene Smith told them that the town had a nightlife of sorts. There was a roadhouse about 10 miles out of town where most of the singles met.

"Bar, music, and singles. It probably isn't up to New York standards, but we also don't charge an arm and a leg for a martini or a cover. Why don't ya'll meet up with us, say around nine?"

Viviene's group of girlfriends, it turned out, had a thing for New York Jew boys. They went back to the hotel and got ready to be the best Jew boys they could.

———•———

The Rattler Bar and Grill was a real Texas roadhouse. In some ways it looked like the Casa Blanca in Madero down to the swinging doors at the entrance and the music coming from within. What it didn't have was the naked woman outlined in neon, but it substituted a neon rattlesnake. The wood of the building was weathered with patches of paint that exposed the dark wood underneath. The boys entered and were assaulted by the Country and Western band playing music that was foreign to them, C&W not being popular in Brooklyn or Sam's area of San Diego. The bar was long and behind it the bartenders served the crowd three deep ordering drinks. The customers were dressed in everything from cowboy wear including 10-gallon hats, to sports jackets over polo shirts and jeans. In the middle of the room a dance floor was crowded with people square dancing or pairing off for a little couple "feeling-up" action.

The Boys were frozen in their tracks by the sight of numerous beautiful Texan women who appeared to be unattached. It seemed that God had a "Texas mold" that he poured basic life forces in to create the Texas woman. All these blond, blue-eyed ladies with hourglass shapes and proud bosoms had Marvin sweating.

"I swear, I must be dead, Sam," he said, gripping Sam's forearm. "Tell me, man, have I died and gone to heaven?"

Sam laughed. "If you're in heaven, then so are the rest of us. Man I have never seen so many potential "Miss Names of the Month" in one place."

Viviene separated herself from the crowd of her girlfriends and walked over to the group. She would have been admitted without hesitation into any club she had wished to join in Manhattan.

"Hey, Boys! Glad you could make it. Come on in and meet my friends." She looked at Bennie. "Hey Bennie, how's it hangin'?"

"It's hangin' fine, Viviene." Bennie was all smiles and reached out to possessively hold her hand. "Wanna dance?"

"Sure thing. Just let me introduce your friends to my girls. Then we can ... " She paused to look him over and said, "Get closer."

The Boys were introduced to the girls and it seemed that no matter what one's physical characteristics were, these girls were happy to have the attention. Soon they were all dancing and as the evening progressed the music got slower and the dancing became slower and much closer. Soon Bennie had disappeared from the dance floor with Viviene, but no one seemed to notice.

The money flowed as they kept buying drinks for the girls. As the girls got friendlier the cash flow diminished markedly.

Sam returned to the bar to buy another round of drinks for the girls. His head was swimming from the alcohol and the euphoria of having his face in the proudest bosom he had ever had the pleasure to be near.

"Fifteen dollars," the bartender shouted, over the din of the bar.

"Sure," Sam shouted back as he reached his hand into his pocket for his wallet. He found only pesos. "Oh shit. Hang on, I'll get some. In the meantime I'll take the drinks over to those girls over there," he said, pointing.

The bartender eyed him and smiled, "Why don't you get the cash first, son."

"Yeah sure," Sam said.

He walked over to Sayeed squeezing through a crowd that was now in violation of the fire department occupancy rules blurting out "'scuse mes" and "sorrys." Sayeed was fused to a voluptuous blond. "Hey man," he tapped on Sayeed's shoulder. "Sayeed!"

Sayeed detached himself. "What's up?" He was all bleary eyed with lipstick smears on his face.

"Need money. You got some I can borrow?"

"Uhh … wait a sec." Sayeed fumbled through his pockets, finally finding his wallet. "Shit, sorry Boss. No money. Maybe we should both go talk to Marvin or Bennie." Sayeed looked around and saw Marvin dancing with a beautiful, plus-sized girl. "Ah, look at Marvin. He looks like he is in heaven."

"Yeah, especially if he wants to breastfeed." Sam began looking for Bennie. "Shit, where is he?"

Sayeed was panic-stricken. "Sam we've got to go find him. You know him, with all the excitement of the day and how he gets. These are new people and that Viviene seems to like him. He could use a girl in his corner—not like the last relationship that landed him here."

"Last relationship?" Sam asked mystified.

"Yeah, I'll tell you about it someday but now I want to make sure he stays out of trouble. Look, go to Marvin and see if he has any cash to pay our bill. Hopefully he has some. If not we're fucked, so run for it. I'm going to search for Bennie."

———•+———

Sam found them near the park.

Viviene was holding Bennie buried in her arms. It was obvious that they had hit it off. Bennie whispered something in Viviene's ear and she responded by giggling softly and then returning to her passionate embrace of him.

Sam thought they looked stunning together under a bright moon with the breeze rustling the leaves. A handsome couple, his dark with her bright—complementary. While he was happy for Bennie, it brought back his sadness and anger at Leah. This is what he wanted, a woman that hugged and kissed and touched and loved and responded to all those things being done to her. Even Andy's Marla showed some sort of love for him. He was pretty sure that even though Andy would have been much happier, on some level, with Marla kvetching back in New York, he must take comfort that she was with him in circumstances that were difficult—especially with two kids.

He heard a final sigh and Viviene and Bennie walked toward the parked cars together.

Sam, once again, walked back to go home alone.

———•+———

The next morning the group woke up and discovered that Bennie hadn't made it back to the motel. They expected to hear from him eventually.

They went over to Denny's for the never-ending pancakes and bottomless coffee.

"I wish we were closer to the border," said Marvin. "Just to be able to eat American food and drink water from a tap and have telephone service every now and then." Marvin was like a pig in shit, crumbs dotting his chin held there by drops of strawberry jam. The maple syrup was drowning his pancakes; the four eggs, sunny-side up, with the toast now soaking in the yolk, and two mugs of creamladen coffee in front of him so he didn't have to wait for a refill.

"Not to mention a little relief from the constant smell of raw sewage. On the other hand I wonder about the distractions we would face. Maybe part of the problem we all had in college was that we were so distracted. There is always something going on in San Diego, movies, concerts, weekends in the mountains or the desert. Who wanted to sit home and study?"

"You're right. I was always doing something to make money. Do you really think that was the difference between those who ended up in Mexico and those who got into Harvard?" Sayeed mused.

Marvin shook his head. "I have been in the hospital environment for ages. I've seen the new doctors from the American schools and the foreign doctors and the American foreign doctors. It is a generalization, but the American grads always seemed so stunted. Medicine is their entire life."

"Isn't that good?" asked Sam. "I mean to be a great doctor don't you have to be totally immersed in medicine?"

Marvin smiled. "You might be right, but in my experience those that were great doctors were those that *lived* life. They understood the drunk, the family man, the child, the adventurer, the saint and sinner alike. Because of their exposure to various segments of the community, those doctors understood how to formulate a treatment that had a better chance of success, because it fit into the life of the patient."

"So to treat you have to understand life. To understand life you have to have lived?" asked Sam.

"Seems so, at least in my experience. I'm sure you can find some Harvard weenies that might disagree."

Had Sam lived a life up to this point? Did putting life on hold while he pined over some girl count as the only life experience? Well in the last months he certainly seemed to be catching up, he thought with a smile.

And speaking of weenies, look what the cat dragged in," Sayeed announced.

Hi guys," said Bennie. He flopped himself on an empty chair and motioned to the waitress. "Sorry about last night. I didn't mean to cut out so early."

The waitress came over and gave everyone a bright Texas smile. "More coffee, boys?" She looked at Bennie. "Coffee and something to eat?"

"Just coffee, thank you." The waitress poured him a cup and went off. "Man, what a night."

Sam asked, "Did everything go OK?"

Bennie smiled at him. "Yeah, I was a little out of my mind. I know the psychiatrists and my father think I'm a basket case, but I don't think that's 100 percent true. I admit I get these periods of depression, but I think everyone does. The manic times, well it's just who I am. I get happy and then I get really happy." He looked at Sam, Marvin, and Sayeed and saw they didn't understand. Hell, he didn't understand himself, but he didn't feel crazy. He just felt more. The more just spilled over into life.

"I don't know, guys. I think I'm normal, at least normal for Bennie. I will tell you this. I met the most wonderful woman last night. She is love and comfort and safety ... "

"Bennie, you've only known her for less than twenty-four hours. How do you know any of this?" Sam saw Bennie's face slump. "Look, maybe I'm wrong, but … "

"No, you aren't wrong Sam. It's just a feeling. I got the same feeling when I met up with you. I knew we would be friends and live through this experience together. I think Viviene and I will live through my time here, also. Who knows, maybe even longer," he said smiling. "In any case have you ever met a better looking woman?" He laughed.

"And don't you forget it." Viviene had entered the Denny's and sneaked up on the boys.

"I never will," said Bennie happily. He gave her a kiss and she returned it demurely.

"What are you doing today, boys?" she asked. "Maybe some shopping and some good American food? There is a great taco place not too far from here."

"Yeah, we need to resupply while we're here in Los Estados Unidos. Shaving cream, razors, soap, condoms," Sayeed said.

"Well, I need to get to work. Bennie is supposed to invite y'all to dinner at my place … "

"Hell girl," said Marvin. "We can take you out unless you want to be alone with that ugly guy over there?"

"We will have time later. No, I'm inviting you home to my parents' house. Y'all like chicken soup and matzo balls right?"

"Texas matzo balls? What are you talking about, girl?" Sam laughed.

"Sam, Viviene is Jewish. Her family was one of the founding families of Little Israel here," Bennie said with a dash of serious in his voice. He worked another creamer into his coffee.

"You're shitting me," said Sayeed.

" … and I have a nice Palestinian-American girl for Bennie's man Friday."

———•———

Dinner was a lovely affair. Viviene's mother was a true Jewish mother with a Texas twang.

"My family has lived in the area since the Civil War. My great-grandparents were merchants who moved away from the competition of the Northeast. They liked the weather and the people. I think they also liked the tolerance of the place. We have white Americans, Asian Americans, African Americans here. We also have Jews, Catholics, Baptists, Mennonites, Mormons, and atheists, plus, probably representatives of hundreds of other groups. We all live here together and get along just fine."

"Who would have known," said Marvin. "Well, your matzo ball soup is better than any I've tasted in the Bronx. I'm stuffed."

"Glad you liked it; the secret is the armadillo skin … "

"What!" Sam howled.

She laughed. "Only kidding, a Jewish Texan joke."

Sayeed and Viviene's friend Maryam walked in off the porch. "Hey guys, did you see Bennie and Viviene? Maryam and I thought we could all go back to that roadhouse for some dancing."

"I don't know but I'm sure they are close by."

———•———

Close they were. They were holding each other tight, kissing, caressing.

"I don't know what it is, but I have never felt as close to anyone as I do to you," said Bennie. "I won't be able to leave tomorrow. I need you in my life."

Viviene smiled. "Bennie I feel the same, but we are just going to have to figure out the separations. I think it is important you complete school. It will give you a sense of independence and accomplishment. I will be here waiting for visits. You can look forward to coming and telling me about your adventures."

"Come with me. I can rent a house and we can be together," Bennie begged.

"Oh," she laughed. "You want me to be that kind of woman."

Bennie flushed with embarrassment at having assumed that she wanted to live with him as much as he wanted to live with her. It was so fast, but he just knew in his soul that they were meant to be together. He wanted her in his life.

Viviene held his face. "Silly, of course I want to be with you and I want to cook for you, walk with you and," she kissed him, "sleep with you every night. But right now I have a job, as do you. We need to take this slower. Plus, maybe you'll meet a nice Mexican girl in Tampico that you'll charm like you charmed me."

"I don't think that could ever happen. If there was another woman attracted to me, she would definitely pale in comparison to you."

She kissed him deeply. "Damn right. Now come with me."

"Where?" asked Bennie.

"You'll see." She led him down a path towards an oasis of trees that was hidden from prying eyes.

Chapter 14

Custom Made Shoes

A week later the "all clear" came from a Mexican med student who was in the States shopping. The school would open again in three days. The main political party was still running the government as they had for most of the modern history of Mexico. Americans would still be welcome to spend their dollars, the police would still be allowed to shake those students down, and cigarettes were still the equivalent of sixteen cents a pack.

The boys made it back to Tampico. It was a tearful goodbye between Viviene and Bennie, but it was also a very hopeful one. It seemed Bennie didn't need the meds as much as he needed to love and be loved. With the sudden appearance of Viviene's love, Bennie had begun to grow up.

For Sam the loneliness persisted. Back in Tampico, he continued to visit Esmeralda. Sam justified all this by convincing himself that he had the choice between anti-depressants, or he could have an hour of pleasure with Esmeralda. It was all bullshit, but now that classes were back in full swing, he was too busy to think it through.

They studied as a group and they studied alone. They had finals in biochemistry, histology, and embryology, but the only thing that really mattered was the practical exam in Anatomy. Valdez was going to try to screw them with those half-rotted cadavers.

Then the cadavers were gone.

———————•◆•———————

"What the fuck?"

The Boys had gathered around midnight in the anatomy lab. By now they all had a great relationship with the security guards. Like everyone else the guards were underpaid and a bottle of the local brandy was all it took to make friends for life. A guard had let them in but there wasn't a cadaver in sight.

Sam looked at the guard. "Where are the bodies? Why aren't they here?"

The guard shrugged and pointed out back.

"Fuck that asshole, Valdez. He put them back in the pools."

When they had first started anatomy lab, Valdez had the students help the proctors pull the bodies from a series of cement pools out behind the mortuary, which contained a poorly mixed solution of formaldehyde and water. There were no pumps to circulate the fluids, so under the direct sun, the liquid would readily evaporate. Occasionally, a groundskeeper would dump more water into the pool when the waterline was low, and the pool was reduced, more or less, to a greenish looking scum. Inevitably, the pool stunk, but the bodies were pretty intact at that point.

Because the proctors, or anyone else at the school, couldn't be bothered to maintain the bodies, they eventually dried and rotted in the minimally air-conditioned room of the lab. "They must be trying to re-hydrate the corpses," Sam said. "Let's get one out of the pool and work on it. After we trace the biliary system, we'll put it back. No one will know the difference." He was desperate for more dissection time and he wasn't going to let Valdez prevent that.

"Man, it's awfully dark out back by the tanks," Marvin said, his voice unsteady. "Do you think trying to wrestle a cadaver out of the tank in the dark is a good idea? I mean, Jesus Christ, what if one of us fell into the tank?"

Sayeed laughed. "Stop being a baby. I'm sure the corpse is not going to mind being banged around getting out of the tank."

"Then let's go," said Sam, leading the way out back to the pool area.

It was pitch-black in the back of the school. Not only was there no security lighting, but the new moon left the sky as dark as ever. They stumbled around with a single flashlight they had obtained from the security guard.

"Where are those fucking ... TANKS?" Sam had inadvertently found one of the tanks by almost falling in. Luckily Sayeed had been right next to him and managed to grab him just as he started falling.

"Shit, who put these tanks in without a cover? It stinks like a huge loose shit! "

"Same person who built an anatomy lab without air-conditioning. Any other dumb questions? If not, let's get the body out and get some studying done," Bennie said. He felt around and eventually found the body hooks on the ground near the tank.

Bennie plunged the hook into the black liquid that was covered with a weird phosphorescent muck. He prodded the depths until he thought he had something. As he strained lifting the body it slipped off the hook. "Goddam it, we need another hook."

Sam eventually found the other hook in the grass and together Bennie and Sam finally managed to hook a body.

"OK now, on a count of three we need to pull one up and slide it onto the grass. It'll be heavy, man. It's waterlogged."

"Yeah, fine ... just let's get moving." Sam was pissed off that all this time was being wasted.

Bennie started counting, "One, Two, and THREE!"

They flipped the weighty object onto the grass in a single heaving motion. As fast as they had landed the corpse, it seemed to come to life, roaring and flopping its body.

"Holy Fuck!" cried Sayeed. Without a second thought, the Boys screamed and ran away from it.

"What in God's name is that," screamed Marvin. "Shit, what is it?"

He moved the flashlight over the awakened corpse and found instead that they had brought up a large alligator that lay with its jaws gaping displaying a thousand glistening teeth. The boys looked at each other and ran for it.

"What do you say we postpone studying for tomorrow night," Bennie suggested.

El Sol de Tampico

Alligator on the Loose at UT. The headlines of the local papers reported the event. While the school was near the tropics and did have lizards around, alligators weren't part of the local fauna. Fortunately Valdez made no connection between the missing alligator and the pool hooks that the Boys had thrown to the ground. Valdez couldn't figure out how the alligator had climbed out.

Truth be told, Valdez didn't even care all that much about the alligator as he was raising him in the tank for another purpose. He wanted to farm the beast for its skin and have one of the locals make him a pair of boots.

Now he was worried that someone would run into the alligator and have his arm torn off or worse. That alligator was a mean SOB. He also didn't want the alligator to be run over by a car. That would ruin all hope of having his boots.

Fortunately for Valdez he had a lot of manpower. Classes were canceled until the alligator was found. He ordered the students to fan out from the school in search of the beast. Instructions were minimal, but mainly said, "Don't hurt the alligator."

"You've got to be kidding," said Sam. "I came here to go to med school, not catch exotic animals."

"Well to be fair, you were the one to set that monster free on an unsuspecting city," Marvin said. Marvin was annoyed. Searching for the alligator in the 85° heat with the 90% humidity wasn't his idea of a good time.

"What do you mean, me? I wasn't the only one trying to study."

"OK guys, maybe we all calm down. Look at this as a blessing. We have an extra couple of days to study till the alligator is found."

"I guess that's true, but it also postpones vacation back in San Diego. I have a job waiting for me."

Sayeed laughed. "Only if that doctor hasn't forgotten you now that you are finished with his daughter."

"Fuck off, Schmuck." Sam was still hurting over Leah's engagement. He had buried his hurt by spending more and more time with Esmeralda. It did salve the wound. They had sex each time he visited her, but they also talked about his frustrations at school, life in Mexico, and Leah. As much as he wanted to know more about her, she resisted. Over time, though, it was inevitable that two young people that were intimate with each other would soon have intimacy on other levels than just sex. With Esme it all happened in a night.

He had been especially hungry for her and instead of Sam's somewhat single-minded pleasure it seemed that Esme, too, needed something more. He went slowly, tender kisses to her face, throat, and breasts led to a trail of caresses on her back, thighs, and finally the kisses to her ready labia. Before, Esme had not allowed this sort of intimacy, though she did willingly give him oral satisfaction. She sighed and her breathing became more ragged as she held his head more tightly in place. Soon she exploded in joy and quickly brought Sam up and reached down to place him in her.

"Come amor, explode in me."

Sam complied and she once again orgasmed followed by his climax. They collapsed in each other's arms trying to catch their collective breath.

"Thank you, Sam, I have never … " She went quiet looking at his face, loving the joy she saw there.

She started talking a little about her home life.

Sam learned that prostitution here was the usual way out of poverty for a family. It was still a Catholic country and while birth control was available it was expensive and the poor couldn't afford it. This meant that the families just got bigger and the poverty increased. When girls in these families reached a certain age, they left their small, rural villages and moved to the cities. Almost all were without education or skills and they ultimately found the Boy's Towns. Here they made money and were able to send some of their savings back to their families. Esme came from a very small town about 100 miles southwest of Tampico, where she was one of eight kids. Her mother had died in childbirth and she had been raised by her older sister. While her father was a decent man, he knew nothing about raising girls and left the running of the household to the kids. When Esme left, he may have known what would happen to her in the big city, but he was powerless to stop it.

Sam felt protective of this girl and soon there were feelings he couldn't deny.

Esme was looking for something, too, and as the weekly meetings became more intimate, she allowed more and more time together. Normally, he knew, there was no such thing as a prostitute with a heart of gold, but Esme and the girls like her were still too young to truly be hardened hookers. They made love like young lovers. Sam was always hard and ready for her and Esme was always open and wanting. While he was excited and impatient to get back to the States, he wished she could come with him. He laughed when he thought about the looks the neighbors would give him if he brought home an impoverished Mexican prostitute. What would his parents say to him if they knew he was even visiting her, let alone falling in love with her?

"Where would I be if I were a motherfucking alligator?" They were parked across the street from the school, Bennie on the hood of the car surveying the land around his 360-degree range of vision. The airport was to the north and the sewage treatment plant was to the east. The rest of the area was a combination of paved and unpaved streets with houses and kids in yards. The open sewers made it look like there were small canals all over Tampico. Bennie was determined to see the alligator close up. He even harbored thoughts of trying to feed it a ticking clock like in *Peter Pan*. Andy had told him he'd report him to Viviene on charges of animal abuse if he tried, though Andy also told him that alligator might go for another of Bennie's appendages instead of an arm or leg. He thought Viviene might not like that, either.

"Let's see, an alligator is a reptile. It likes it cool, but not cold. It probably doesn't like a lot of bright light considering it is in the water a lot. It escaped about one a.m. Hmmm ... Sam how fast do you think an alligator can run?"

Sam said, "How the fuck would I know that?"

"You know, their miles per hour times how many hours and draw a circle around the starting point and search within that circle. Cops do it all the time for escaped convicts."

"Brilliant," Andy said sarcastically.

Andy thought for a second. "Where are the sewage canals located near here? Especially the ones with roads running over them or walkways."

"There is a major canal about a mile from here. You can smell it when the wind is blowing in the right direction. Covered areas? I don't know, but it still sounds like a good place to start."

They piled into Sam's car, ready to go hunting.

"We are a really smart group," Sam said. "Except for one thing."

"And what is that one thing, my genius level friend? I mean that one thing besides being in Mexico studying medicine or facing disease by cutting into cadavers, or maybe the simple things like eating and drinking down here?"

"What do we do when and if we find this alligator?"

Andy stopped in his tracks. "Fuck, Sam, you didn't really expect us to capture this animal. If we find him or her or whatever, one of us will go back and get Valdez and his crew. I'm not getting any closer to that thing than I have to."

Sam nodded thoughtfully. "I am in full agreement."

They continued walking the canal, all nauseated by the smell, bothered by the mosquitos and flies and dripping sweat.

They carried big branches with which they'd probe under the covered part of a canal to see if anything moved. They finally came to an intersection of the canal that wasn't accessible from the road.

"You really think that croc … "

"Alligator," said Marvin.

Sam shook his head. "Whatever. Do you think that alligator got this far?"

"What do I look like, Tarzan?" Andy said tiredly. "Come on, we should get down there and have a look."

"In the shit, are you fucking kidding?" Sam actually was looking at excrement moving down the canal leaving an oily, smelly sheen in the hot sun.

"Look Sam, Marvin and I can't do it. If we even try to get down the bank of the canal we'll end up slipping and going under. It's got to be one of you three, maybe two of you as the canal splits. It will save time to have each go in a different direction."

"But it's shit. My Jewish friend is right. In my case my religion would have me chop off both legs from the contamination." Sayeed said looking at the canal distastefully.

"That's crap and you know it," Bennie said, "but a good try. I read the Koran and it doesn't say anything about shitty canals."

"Fuckhead, when did you read the Koran you Jew Bastard?" Sayeed said indignantly.

"I'd say the same of you, you 'rab," Bennie retorted.

"OK, OK, enough. If I have to listen to you two bickering, I'll have to throw myself into the canal. I'll go. Help me down."

Sam went over the edge of the bank and almost slipped under the water but at the last second he grabbed a root that allowed him to gently go into the water. The stream came up to his crotch and the very thought of the contaminants bathing his penis gave him the heebie-jeebies.

"Ugh, it stinks down here and the bottom is so slimy. I think I'm going to barf."

"Well, you're in a good place to do it. Don't mind us," Andy said with a laugh.

"You're a fuck," Sam responded.

"Wait, take the branch," Bennie said. "You'll need it."

Sam grabbed the branch and started to glide with his feet along the bottom. He slipped once or twice, but managed to stay on his feet with his head above water.

He slowly entered the covered part of the canal. It was pitch-black inside, but he had managed to keep a penlight dry in his shirt pocket. He still couldn't see much, but it kept him from banging into objects.

The canal got darker, the ways slimier, and it appeared that all the wet surfaces now took on an almost phosphorescent glow. God knew what kind of radioactive waste was bathing his balls at this point. He unconsciously tried to elevate himself out of the water.

He didn't see anything besides objects floating on the water. He brushed these away as he proceeded further into the darkness. He shone his light down the branching canals and saw only more filth.

He was 30 feet in when a large floating log appeared in front of him. He gave it a shove, but it wouldn't move. He again tried to shove it out of the way with the branch. Man it was heavy, but he managed to turn it lengthwise so that he could proceed.

The log turned as Sam approached and instantly something glowed when he shined the light on the log. Two bumps flashed and then didn't, then flashed again almost like eyelids blinking."OH FUCK," he screamed and started running and sliding back the other way.

"Sam, you OK?" He heard Marvin in the distance.

Sam had sudden pain in his right buttock, but never stopped running. He arrived in the sunlight screaming he was going to be eaten as he tried to get up the slick canal wall. The alligator was right behind him.

The harder Sam tried to get up the wall the more he slid.

"Help me, I don't want to be McDonalds for this croc!"

"It's an alligator," Marvin cried.

"You fucking asshole I'll haunt you for the rest of your days … "

Arms grabbed him and pulled him up.

"I found it, I found it. I found that fucking beast and lived to tell the tale."

Sam was giddy with adrenaline.

Andy looked at Sam and was very worried. "Bennie, stay here and try to keep an eye on that thing. Join us in the ER when Valdez and crew show up. Sayeed, we're going to drop you at the school. Find Valdez and let him know where the alligator is. Marvin, we have to get Sam to the hospital. Let's get going."

Sam was confused. "Hospital? Why am I going to the hospital? I'm feeling fine."

"I think you're in shock. You're bleeding." Marvin was definitely concerned.

"Bleeding?" Sam did a quick check—arms, legs—all OK. "Where?"

"Your ass." That's when Sam felt a warm stickiness from behind and saw blood dripping from his hindquarters. He promptly fainted.

15

Lord, It's Me, Sam

The Emergency Room was crowded with the usual patients. Vaginal bleed in 16, SOB (shortness of breath) in 5, CP r/o MI (Chest Pain rule out Myocardial Infarction) in 2. This list of conditions could be true for New York, San Diego, Beijing, Madrid, as much as it was true for Tampico, Mexico. When it came down to it, there were few differences among any ERs in the world. Too little staff, too many patients. A very tired looking Dr. Soto was in the middle of a precipitous delivery, made more difficult because the mother was obese and had problems getting her legs sufficiently apart.

"Ahh, gringos. Marvin, grab one drumstick and Bennie grab the other. Andy, you are the cabron with the brats, Sí?"

"Yeah, that's me, but we have a problem ... "

"You want to be a doctor, cabron? Well get used to your problems being the problems in back of the line." Soto noticed Sam looking pasty. "What's the matter, cabron? You don't like the miracle of life?" Soto burst out in laughter at his own wit and Sam promptly vomited and collapsed, only to be caught by Andy before he hit the ground.

"He's hurt, man. He needs medical attention," Andy shouted.

"Whoops," said Soto. He turned to the screaming mother-to-be and said, "Un momento por favor." He went over to the barely conscious Sam, shined the penlight into his eyes and felt for his pulse.

"Lay him over on that gurney. He's fine. Andy, you want to deliver the newest citizen of the Republic of Mexico or what?"

Sam whispered to anyone who could hear, "I'm OK, just get me over to that stretcher. I'll wait. Go deliver the baby." Sam had problems focusing and he was sticky, smelly, and nauseous, but he was mesmerized by the two massive thighs framing a very hairy, swollen vagina with what looked like a purple hairy beach ball coming out of it.

Andy smiled. "If you're sure, Sam?" and laid him down.

"Yeah get over there," he croaked, "how many doctors can say they delivered a beluga whale."

Soto, listening in, shouted at a passing nurse, "Gloves for the doctor. Now you two cabrons," he told Bennie and Marvin, "keep the garage doors open."

Sam focused on Andy's face now inches from a swaying, vibrating set of labia. He couldn't focus, but it looked like Andy would be crushed by two mounds of dark thigh meat. If he wasn't careful.

Soto announced, "Sra. Dominguez this is almost the doctor, Andy. He will deliver your baby today."

Sam tried to concentrate on Soto's presentation, but the thighs were jiggling and all he could think about was quivering flesh Jell-O with a spewing mouth.

"Sra. Dominguez, this very sexy 370 pounder and her 110 pound esposo, like to do IT. You know what IT is, huh jovenes?" Soto smiled diabolically.

Sam slurred weakly, "Yeah Soto, we know babies come from fucking. Can you get on with it. I'm going to barf."

"How do they do IT?" Andy said, looking at Sra. Dominguez.

Soto became very serious. "I know you are un Judio, but have you not read the Bible?"

Sam focused on the growing hairy beach ball, the bile now flooding his mouth. "What does the Bible have to do with this?"

Sra. Dominguez let out a long, drawn out screech.

"Breathe Señora, breathe." Soto turned to Sam just as he vomited on the dirty, tiled floor. "God is the ultimate Engineer," Soto replied, quick stepping away from the gastric contents. "In this case he created the mechanics for where there is a will … "

Marvin completed Soto's thought, " … there is a way."

Soto laughed. "Muy bien … and there has been a way twelve times before. This child is lucky number thirteen. Sí, Señora Dominguez?"

Sra. Dominguez let out another screech, followed by something dark coming out of her very distended and swollen vagina. A steaming, ferrous odor filled the air with the ejaculation of blood, amniotic fluid, feces, and baby.

Soto blasted, "Get in there cabron and catch the little *pendejo*," he shoved Andy further between her monstrous thighs. As soon as he got into a catcher's position, Andy was baptized with a combination of blood, amniotic fluid, and shit. "Fuck me!" yelled Andy.

"Here comes the *cabeza de mierda* now," Soto pointed.

All of a sudden Andy's hands were filled with a blue humanoid thing that was covered with slime and slippery as hell.

"Don't drop the baby," yelled Soto.

Andy bellowed, "It's dead. The baby is dead."

Soto jumped in and grabbed the baby, gave it a whack on the butt, and the baby started screaming and turning bright pink. "Dead my ass, cabron. How do you say it? Mazel tov, Sí," he smiled.

Andy doubled over and vomited, joining Sam in misery.

Soto laughed so hard he was having cramps. "Come on, let's go see Sam." He looked at Andy covered in birth products. "Maybe we get you something cleaner to wear first, you look like … " he theatrically sniffed … "Shit."

———— • ————

"*Chingada Madre*, that pendejo really got you, cabron." Soto was gloved and not too tenderly examining Sam's wound in the busy hallway of the ER. "This happened in the *Canal de Mierda?*"

"Yeah," said Sam weakly.

"*Chupame*," said Soto almost religiously.

Marvin, who had the most experience of the group, asked Soto, "Will we need to explore his rectum for perforation considering the wound's location?"

Soto gave Marvin a deadpan look, "Well, Almost the Doctor Cabrón, I do not think the anatomic position of the wound is even near the anus, but if you care to do a rigid sigmoidoscopy on the pendejo of a friend of yours, be my guest."

Sam's ears perked up, "What do you want to do to my asshole?"

Soto laughed, "Me? Nothing, but your economy size friend wants to *chinga su culo*. You know, fuck your ass."

Sam exclaimed, "Marvin, I swear I'll kill you if you even look at my ass!"

Marvin smiled and said, "I only thought fucking you up the ass might be medically necessary."

"OK, enough cabrónes, I got an ER full of the sick and dying. Which one of you maricons wants to sew him up?"

"Wait, do you think any of these guys have enough experience to … ?"

"Calmate maricon, they will do a fine job and you will be left with a scar that any woman would think is a war wound when she sees it. Bennie, go get some gloves and a set-up. Nurse, get a gallon of lidocaine and a big needle."

The supplies were collected and Bennie was ready. He stuck the needle in Sam's wound and numbed up the tissue.

"Bueno, now you have to irrigate the hell out of it. There is probably shit coating every fucking cell in the wound from the canal water. Sam, it's time for a bath."

It seemed like gallons of saline were poured into Sam's wound. Thankfully, due to the lidocaine the sensation was merely bursts of cold across his gluteus. Soto supervised Bennie's stitching. First layers to close the deep spaces of tissue after the removal of the dead tissue and then the skin. It took over an hour and at the end Bennie was sweating and exhausted.

"Hey man, I did the best I could. It really doesn't look too bad."

Sam nodded, "I'm sure you did. Thanks Bennie, whenever my girlfriend tells me I have a great ass, I'll think of you."

"Hey, why don't you maricons get a room and *chupa la verga*," Soto said. "Sam you need antibiotics." He wrote a script. "Have one of these cabróns check for redness or drainage tomorrow and Bennie can pull the stitches in ten days."

There was a disturbance outside the room. Andy went to check it out when the curtains parted, and Lola and Esmaeralda stormed in.

"What a great *culo*, huh Esme?" Lola laughed.

"Sí, but I think it will be out of commission for awhile, sí Doctor Pene?"

Sam spoke, "Doctor Soto these are … "

"Lola, Esme, *vete a la verga*. Who let you in here?"

"If only we could fuck ourselves we wouldn't need maricons like you," Lola said, tracing her finger along Soto's jaw line.

Andy said to Soto, "I take it you know our friends?"

"Oh, I'm very familiar with Lola and Esme. But I know their bottom halves better than their upper halves from the *Cliníca*.

"*Come caca*," the girls said at once.

"*Chupa Mi Pito*," Soto responded.

"OK, I've had enough. Can I go now?" Sam asked, tired by the day's events.

"Sí, you need someone to help you for the next day or two," Soto looked at Esme. "You going to stay with him?"

"Sí, I will stay."

———•———

Esme moved into Sam's room to take care of him. At first he was resistant but in the end he was grateful to her. To Sam she took to domesticated life like a duck to water. She was a 1950s wife, always present, bringing him his pipe and slippers, always with a smile on her face. It was hard to move around the room and going to sit on the toilet was a nightmare of pain as the hard plastic of the seat put pressure on his wound. Sam was semi-naked most of the time around Esme, but he was especially embarrassed that she had to change his bandages. This didn't seem to bother Esme. She had seen much worse and of course the male body was not a mystery to her.

Sam talked to her about paying for her help, but she refused. She told him there was an unspoken rule among women in her social position. For the women of Boy's Town life outside didn't mix with life inside.

Esme spoke of her parents and brothers and sisters. She spoke of growing up poor, but happy. She said that her father was busy putting food on the table and had to hand over her upbringing to the eldest children. There was no choice. She said there was no money for school and certainly no money for the movies or a TV, but she was able to read because of the nuns at the church. They had let her borrow books to read.

One afternoon Sam was lying on his stomach as Esme was changing his dressing. The soiled gauze was put to the side as she carefully dabbed at the wound with the antiseptic Soto had provided. Sam idly noted that the gauze was showing some remnants of scab and greenish material but really wasn't worried as Esme's voice soon became the center of his attention.

"I was so happy in the lessons the nuns taught. Reading books took me away from my duties at home taking care of my sisters and brothers to a whole new world."

"Why did you leave home, Esme?"

Esme became quiet as she thought about her home. "It was my responsibility to leave otherwise my family would starve."

Sam knew that she sent money home, but this stark reality ... he thought it only happened in the third world, but then where was he now?

"My father didn't want to send me away, but he had my younger siblings to think about. His job was paying less for the amount it cost to feed a growing family. He loved me and wanted me safe with him at home, but what could he do. You know the lifeboat can only allow so many to survive. I was strong. He knew I'd survive on my own. The man told my father he would give him money to feed his children if I would come with him to become a factory girl. My father didn't want to take the money, but it was getting harder and harder to feed his children and he knew winter was coming and he'd need money for heating fuel. He asked the man time and again was the employment safe? The man always replied, it is a good job, safe. Your daughter will be protected in a dorm. Do not worry."

"The man lied to your father," Sam said weakly. Deep inside of him he knew he was part of the evil that Esme lived. He knew though that he was too weak to either give her up or take her away from the Casa Blanca. He became sweaty and hot with guilt almost feeling Esme's eyes boring into him.

"In a way he didn't," Esme said. "I live in a dorm, there is rarely violence at the Casa Blanca, and I do make enough money to send to my family."

Sam heard a pride in her voice that made him feel more ashamed of himself in his weakness. His body was aching with guilt and he felt short of breath.

"I am proud of what I do, Sam. I feed my father, brothers, and sisters and allow them to stay warm. God will forgive me my sins as what I do keeps them alive."

She then laughed as she put a fresh dressing on his wound, "And look, I found a nice man and am helping his *culo* heal."

Though Esme professed happiness, Sam knew he was guilty of a sin.

A day after leaving the hospital, Esme came back from the market only to find Sam burning up with fever and unconscious.

———•———

Lights, followed by darkness, followed by lights. Sam felt her presence, holding his hand, crying over him. His mind was foggy, but what was Leah doing in Tampico? He felt her warm presence and love. He felt a burning kind of pain radiating from his gluteus. Even in his delirious, fevered state, the pain brought him to consciousness. A warm burst across his backside trickling down his anus and scrotum relieving the painful pressure he felt in his wound and filling the bed with a hot bath of putrid smelling liquid. Did his bowels let go? Did he just shit himself? Incapable of addressing the possibility, he lapsed back into sleep.

———•———

Sam heard Esme crying. She was going on and on about Sam dying and it being her fault.

He heard a man's voice say, "Jesus, he's burning up."

And another man, "Look at this wound—it is hot, red, and three times bigger than it was yesterday." It was Andy speaking to Marvin. "I can't get him to answer any questions, he just keeps mumbling how much he loves her."

"We need to get Soto here now. I don't know if it's even safe to move him. That wound probably has a quart of pus in it and the bacteria is probably in his blood," Marvin said worriedly.

"God, it's draining pus between the sutures. That can't be good," Marvin said worriedly.

"Esme," Andy said. "Do you think you can get Soto to come over here?"

She nodded.

"Marvin," he said, "take Esme with you and go get Soto. He tossed Marvin Sam's car keys.

"Oh fuck," yelled Marvin horrified. Sam was having a grand mal seizure on the couch.

Her touch was so cool. Sam knew she would come back to him, love him, give him a family and they'd live their life in a house with a white picket fence. A girl for her and a boy for me. God his ass still hurt … "Baby, stop touching my ass it hurts so much," he screamed.

"*Hijo de perra.*" Soto had not only brought his bag, but had pilfered supplies from the hospital based on Marvin's description. He grabbed his stethoscope and blood pressure cuff and started getting vital signs. He took a thermometer and put it in Sam's rectum.

"His blood pressure is 80 over palp and his heart rate is 130 beats per minute." He took the thermometer out of Sam's rectum and squinted. "Temperature is 40°C, 104° Fahrenheit." He looked at the ice packs Marvin had placed on Sam's head and in his armpits and groin. "Good thinking, Marvin," Soto nodded. "You may have saved your friend's life."

Marvin had seen active cooling once in a psychiatric patient who had developed a reaction to a drug. He thought that it couldn't hurt.

"Hypotension, tachycardia, fever … Do you know what disease this is, jovenes?" Soto asked gravely.

"Fuck, I don't think this is the time for a medical lesson, Soto," Andy exclaimed.

Soto looked up from examining Sam's wound. "If you want to be a doctor Andy, *mi amigo*, any and every time is a medical lesson. This is called septic shock and the mortality is very high unless we do something now."

Andy deflated. He was so scared for his friend and felt powerless.

"Come here. I will show you how to put in the *suero*, the intravenous line." He guided Andy through the steps and got the line going. "Sayeed, you're next," and repeated the lesson with him. He took vials out of the bag and picked his antibiotics. "This to kill one type of bacteria," he said as he drew up fluid from one of the vials. "This one for another type of bacteria," and as he sorted through the bag, "this for luck." He injected the contents of the vials into the lines and set the rate of fluid given from the IV bags.

"Bennie … "

"Yes Soto?" Bennie couldn't believe what he was witnessing. They could be burying Sam by this evening.

"You were the surgeon, sí?"

"I guess I was." Bennie's eyes dulled as he looked at Soto. "Do you think I killed him?"

"No amigo, you are not to blame. It was bad luck and the filth in the water that did this. Now, you are going to save him. A surgeon takes responsibility for his work always. This is true here and true in the States. Remember this if you decide to become a surgeon. You will save your friend."

Bennie stiffened. "What do I have to do?"

———— • ————

Sam was on his stomach. The wound was fiery red with pus seeping from its edges. The skin itself was shiny and stretched, with dark purple streaks running through it.

"First cut the sutures you placed in the skin and take them out," Soto coached Bennie who was gloved and seated next to Sam's prostrate body. He cut the first suture and nothing happened, then cut a second and a third. Like an opening seam the skin edges separated and a very malodorous cream of yellow, red, grey, and black came spilling out.

"Oh my God," Bennie buckled. The stench was overpowering.

"That is the infection that has poisoned your friend. You will see that in releasing this from his body, he will now have a fighting chance. Now take out the rest of the sutures in the skin and we will irrigate the wound."

They bathed the wound in what seemed to be gallons of water and some Betadine, a surgical soap. Soto told them this was not exactly kosher, but felt that with this amount of contamination it would help.

"Crap, his ass is in pieces. How are we going to sew this back together?" Andy asked.

"We don't," Soto replied.

"What do you mean?" Bennie was now sorry he had opened up the wound. "This can't heal."

"It will either granulate in, which means that it will heal by scar tissue formation, or we can close the wound later when the wound stops draining. This is called a closure by secondary intention."

"You mean put in the sutures, but don't tie them now?" Sayeed questioned.

"Yes, this will give Sam a better cosmetic result later." Soto looked at Bennie.

"So cabrón, what is your decision?"

Bennie looked hopeless, but then his face relaxed. "Secondary intention."

Soto smiled and handed Bennie a needle holder with 3-0 Prolene already loaded. "Good decision Doctor Cabrón."

Bennie got to work.

———◆———

Within six hours Sam broke out in a body-encompassing sweat. Soto broke out in a big smile. "Check his temperature. I would be willing to bet it is normal."

Soto took his blood pressure and pulse, "110 over 50 and pulse of 90. Not bad. I think he is going to make it." He saw Sam's eyelids flutter and his body try to move.

———◆———

"Stay with me forever. I understand now and I promise to make you happy and give you whatever you want."

She nodded at him and gave him a sad smile. "I love you Sam, but it is time for you to go back to work and I have to leave. I love you but … "

She faded from his sight as he was being encompassed by a bright light. "Sam, can you hear me?" he heard Bennie call.

Soft crying from Her? No, it was Esme. "Oh Sam, you scared

us." He felt the pressure of her head on his chest and the wetness of her tears.

He saw Soto. "Well cabrón, welcome back."

"What the fuck happened?" he croaked.

Six hours later his fever had totally broken, not to return again. While his butt still hurt like the devil, he was able to hobble around his room, and not long afterward, he could carefully sit on a toilet. He was grateful to be alive, and his fear of not being present to take the Anatomy Practical Final dissipated as the school once again closed for an investigation for the missing alligator.

Esme stayed through the healing. She helped bathe him, cooked for him, did the laundry and cleaned the room. Much to his embarrassment, she also changed his dressings, cleaning away the vile drainage.

He had never felt such love, but he also was angry with himself for not being able to unconditionally offer that love. He had problems with looking at himself that honestly.

When he slept she slept on a mattress that Carlito had liberated from the motel storage space. She never left his side.

Within a week, Esme was reporting that there was no drainage on the bandaging. Sam told her it was time to have Soto look at it.

That afternoon there was a loud banging on the door. The door was opened to find Soto, Bennie, Sayeed, and Marvin all present to see his ass. They had brought a camera to record the event.

"You are not taking a picture of my injured ass," said Sam laughingly, "but I want to see it before the wound is closed. Bring me a mirror." What he saw made him nauseous. The skin edges purple with bright red skin hemorrhages. The laceration's edges retracting, revealing dark crimson tissue underneath still oozing blood and yellow serous fluid. He would have a mother of a scar to remind him of his time in Mexico and he laughed to himself to stay away from reptiles.

"Asshole, we want a record of what everyone has always known: You, Sir, are a double asshole," Bennie said, triumphant. Soto told Bennie that as a reward for excellent work as a surgeon he could do the secondary closure.

The sutures that had been left untied would now be tied closed, bringing the skin edges together for final healing and less scarring.

Soto said, "*Vamos Cabróns*, let's get this mudder done as I have shift in a half hour. Bennie is coming with me and I expect he will tire me out immediately with his *estupído* questions."

Sam felt a pang of jealousy. He could see that Bennie was now a favorite of Soto's and clearly was learning a lot of practical medicine from him. It was amazing to him that between Bennie's relationship with Viviene and his new intense experience with Soto he was a changed man.

Sam assumed the prone position while Bennie put on sterile gloves. Soto removed the dressing.

"Esme, you did a great nursing job," Soto said as he prodded Sam's derrièr feeling for any residual fluctuance, or pus under the skin.

"It was nothing, Doctor. You showed me what to do," Esme said, blushing.

Sam was embarrassed, too. He knew Mexican society frowned on co-habitation, but damn it he wouldn't have made it without her. Soto saw the look on Sam's face and understood.

"Esme, do you like helping people like this?" Soto asked.

"Sí Doctor. I wish … " she trailed off.

"Yes?" Dr. Soto prompted.

"I wish I had been smart enough to go to school to be a nurse."

"Hmmm, yes. I wouldn't sell your intelligence short," he said, thinking. He shook himself. "Come on cabrón, you have been practicing fucking knots. Rapido!"

Bennie painstakingly gathered the ends of the sutures and started hand tying, a skill that took him months to master as no instruments were used, only the finger dexterity of the surgeon. Esme stood behind him, her eyes following the painstaking movements. She noted the sweat and took a loose gauze square and wiped his brow. Bennie was so intent in his work he jolted at her touch, but quickly realized what she was doing.

"Hey, you already have the skill of a scrub nurse," he laughed. "You should listen to Soto about schooling."

Esme had a shy smile, "I only wish ... maybe someday when I make enough money, but for now I'm happy learning with you."

"Esme, don't distract him from his knots. He should be going faster. As for you, well don't stop wishing," Soto interrupted gruffly. "How many knots do you have to tie with Prolene?" Soto asked about the suture material Bennie was tying.

"Five."

"Sam, if this was nylon, how many knots?"

Sam grunted, "As few as possible, this hurts bad."

Bennie told Sam, "Stop squirming, you overgrown baby."

"*Besame culo,*" Sam responded. "Three knots should do it," he said to Soto.

"Correcto, and Marvin: what material did we use inside the wound?"

"How should I know? I couldn't see shit, but it should have been an absorbable. Knowing you, I'm guessing Chromic 4 or 3-0 suture."

"Correcto, again. Jesus Christos, Bennie, the wound will be healed by the time you finish tying those sutures. Anyway gotta fly."

Soto left and Bennie finally finished all his knots. He started to dress the wound, but Esme took over.

"A nurse dresses wounds. You are a doctor."

Bennie looked at Esme and said, "Well thanks for that and I'll let Sam rest, though I did all the work." He smiled and looked at Sam and Esme.

Soto said, "Gotta fly. Come on boys."

They left, leaving Esme to clean up and dress Sam's wound. She gently cleaned the newly joined wound edges with peroxide as she had been taught, slowly getting every inch of tissue. Sam couldn't help it but it felt good, really good, and for the first time since the accident he began to feel a stirring. He became self-conscious, and very uncomfortable lying on his stomach.

Esme finished Sam's dressing. She knew that Sam would soon be able to go back to school, do his own laundry, and cook his own meals. Her hands touched his back, slowly stroking and caressing.

She took off her blouse and bra and laid on his back, her breasts massaging the skin of his back. She kissed his neck. Sam knew this part of their relationship was coming to an end and he wasn't sure he wanted that. He did know he was grateful for the love she had shown him and he also felt the sadness that she had. No longer uncomfortable he slowly turned over and gathered her in his arms. He kissed her urgently and she responded with equal passion, her skirt and undergarments disappeared and they were both naked.

They stopped and looked into each other's eyes. She placed him inside her. The pain of his newly treated wound medicated by the best opiate in the world.

16

What's a Piece of Spoiled Meat?

Sam was ready. He knew all that Valdez had taught them. He had traced the strings of rotting meat in what was once a live human and was now less than a cadaver. He had his pencils, his sharpener, but most importantly he had his brain full of knowledge, knowledge that one day would help him treat patients as a real doctor. He walked over to the wall by the torta truck and met up with Andy, Bennie, Marvin, and Sayeed.

"Ready Boys?" he asked with a confidence he had never had as a college student in San Diego.

"Well I for one would rather be in the hospital with Soto, but yeah I guess I'm ready," Bennie said laughing.

Andy looked grim. "Shit, I hate tests, but I want to get this over with and head back to the States for some R&R."

"Let's do it," Marvin said as the Boys headed for the entrance to the school.

Number forty. Sam was looking at the pin stuck into a piece of meat that was a sickly grey-green color. It was near the liver, but wasn't in the liver. Of course it was hard to tell because one of the students during the dissection had sliced too deep and ended up macerating this area near the liver. Sam wondered if American students at Harvard had the same problems.

He found the blank line beside number forty and wrote common hepatic duct. Why? The only reason he didn't think it was an artery, vein, or nerve for that matter, was the greenish color. Maybe when this woman had been breathing this structure had carried bile. The pin was stuck very near the liver so maybe that was what distinguished it from the common bile duct, which the hepatic duct drained into before it in turn emptied into the duodenum.

Five more pins to go. The heat and humidity was oppressive, as was the smell. "Thank God," he thought, five structures to go and he was done for the semester.

The room went completely dark.

"What the fuck?" yelled Marvin.

The power was out. Between the large wall air conditioner that failed to cool the room and the inadequate wiring that ran a heavy current to the lights, it had all burned and melted. This meant there would be no lights or air conditioner for days.

"Attencíon, no one move. Professor Valdez is coming." The proctors had opened the door and a little light from the windows in the hallway had seeped into the inky humidity.

Soon there was another bustle and Valdez entered through the doorway. "Vamos aver, what is the problem?"

"You can't see the power is out?" Marvin whispered.

"Quiet, he'll hear you," Sam whispered back.

Valdez was conferring with the proctors and then yelled out. "No one move. No one talk or I will fail you on this test."

Valdez came into the room and walked around, often bumping

into the students. "*Hijo de Perra,*" he screamed at any student he encountered. Soon the proctors were back with flashlights.

"Four flashlights, you've got to be kidding. How are we going to see with those?" Andy questioned.

"Vamos aver, two flashlights for each cadaver. You have ten minutes to finish the test." Valdez abruptly turned around bumping into a dissection table and falling into the exposed cavity of a female cadaver, his face near her hollowed out labia. The class was struck dumb. Words could not describe the scene before them.

Valdez picked himself up. He looked completely unkempt. Even in the dim light of the flashlight his tousled appearance struck absolute silence in the class.

"*Diez mínutos!*" He scrambled out of the room, his hair disheveled and sunglasses askew.

Bennie was the first one who lost it, with the rest of the class soon to follow. After a bit, even the proctors joined in.

"Number forty-one," thought Sam. "What could Number forty-one be? Obviously the clitoris. Four more to go and nine minutes," Sam smiled.

———— • ————

In typical Mexican fashion, finding out the grades they received in the classes was a Herculean task in itself. It cost them more days in Mexico and less time for a break in the States.

The old timers insisted you needed to stay in Mexico till *las notas,* or grades, were handed out and the paper *boletín de notas* was stamped with the numerous rubber stamps and impressed foil seals. Some of the students said that they had a safe deposit box in Brownsville just to make sure that if ever the need arose they could prove they took and passed the classes.

Grades followed an American notation more or less. Instead of getting an "A" you got an "MB" pronounced Mā-Bā, short for *Muy Bien.* A "B" was for *Bien,* a "C" an "S" for *Sufficiente,* and interestingly enough an "F" was universal.

According to the old timers, no American so far had obtained an "F." Why? No one really knew except that Garza probably didn't want the bad publicity of an American going back to the States and blabbing to the *New York Times* or *LA Times* that they had gotten a bad grade because they were a gringo. Moreover, the professors didn't earn a lot of money and could be bribed with cash or merchandise.

Sam thought that this only made the Mexican MD even more worthless as the grade could be bought, but Andy disagreed.

"Look, does it really matter what you get as a grade in a class down here?" asked Andy.

"Of course it does. The residencies will see the grades, and … "

"Sam, no residency, hospital, or licensing board will ever even ask for those things. They want to see your scores on the National Medical Board exams. Either you learned anatomy and can prove it by taking and passing a standardized exam, or you didn't. It's that simple."

"So why do I have to even go to these classes? I could be sitting in San Diego and reading the fucking anatomy book."

Andy smiled. "You didn't think the experience of dissecting a rotten corpse wasn't valuable to your education? You are here to take the classes so that Mexico can prove they have medical schools that supply medical education and that medical education has requirements and standards." He paused and took a deep breath. "As much bullshit as we know that is."

"So we are just going through the motions of medical education?"

"Oh, absolutely not," Andy said. "To prepare for the bullshit of the Universidad del Tampico, you are actually preparing for the National Boards in Medicine in the United States of America. Pass those and they give you a license to practice in the Republic of California."

Sam looked at Andy sheepishly. "I guess you're right. I was just hoping you could justify a way to stay in California."

Andy laughed. "Dream on Boy, Dream on.

Was it a waste of time being in this God-forsaken country? Andy's words were stuck in his brain. What would have happened if he hadn't gotten on that plane to Saltillo or maybe decided not to make that phone call to Romney? He knew he would have drifted into a graduate program, no McDonalds for this Jewish boy. He wouldn't have shamed himself or his parents. But, grad school? Would he have put any effort into studying and honing a career? Living in Mexico as a gringo, studying a subject in a different culture, making sure he balanced the necessities of life with the responsibilities of acquiring information necessary to diagnose and treat patients would never have happened in the States. He was as sure of this as he was that his life had been one long ride on easy street. Mom feeding him, Dad making sure he was fed, sheltered, and even entertained. Relationship problems? If it wasn't easy to fix … fuck it, cry over it until the next girl came along. Mexico was like many grades of sandpaper to his soul. The coarse grade of paper was ridding him of the big deficits in his personality. He now knew you had to go out there and deal personally with the important things like sustenance, shelter, education, and health. The fine paper was smoothing the immaturity away. Relationships are for adults, not children that ran away from things that were unpalatable. Day after day this country had changed him from a spoiled little boy to … what? Well, he would see what the final product turned out to be.

As much as Sam wanted to get in the car and start heading back to San Diego, he realized that there was nothing that could hurry the process. They had to wait until the "boss" deemed it appropriate to collect all the students. The answer was days away. He might as well settle in.

In the meantime he was having pleasant days and nights. Soto was allowing them to hang around the ER. He had caught a couple of babies and repaired a beat-up face or two. He was still trying to perfect his knot-tying skills with sutures, but that was coming slowly. Soto gave him a ton of old unsterile suture material and told him bedposts and chair backs made great tying posts on which to practice. He practiced as often as he could.

His nights were filled with passion and comfort. Marvin had graciously moved over to Andy's so that Esme could move in. One afternoon, she brought a bag over and settled in. He loved to watch her diligently make a simple dinner or open a bottle of beer.

Bedtime was playtime and play they did. Lovingly, erotically, and sometimes even a bit on the kinky side. Young lovers at the start of their relationship. He'd wished he could get over the feeling that he was living in a joyous cocoon and one day the real world would intrude. For the time being though he enjoyed his life. He couldn't remember a time he was more content and whole.

This was his new life, danger, adventure, and free sex, as much as he wanted. Esme always supplied whatever his male ego needed. How much better this was than the "nice boy" life he was used to in the States. If he was bothered that he had to share his playmate with other men, he always remembered that he was no longer the possessive Sam who had destroyed his relationship with that bitch Leah. He was free and responsible for himself, and his actions would make him a doctor and a success. He couldn't be stopped by the old morals. He knew that when she went to work at night it should disturb him, but as much as he wanted it to, it didn't ... much.

<hr>

The call went out at 3:12 in the afternoon to immediately report to the school. They were kept waiting four hours when they lined up in alphabetical order to face multiple proctors to get:

- A piece of paper with their grades typed on it
- The piece of paper rubberstamped with the time and date
- A gold foil sticker placed on it, hopefully not covering the grades
- The gold foil sticker embossed as if by a Notary
- Pay $50 for the "expense" of the process of the above four steps

Sam thought, "Ain't Mexico hilarious and predictable?"

<hr>

There was something about "so-long" sex. They were both flushed and drenched with sweat, but they were happy. It was going to be tough tomorrow with Sam in the car heading toward the border, but he would be back.

Sam was catching his breath, enjoying the sight of an Esme, still with a rosy post-orgasmic sheen to her face and breasts.

"Are you excited about starting in the hospital with Soto?"

"*Oh Sí,* Sam. Doctor Soto promised if I studied hard he would make sure I had a place in next semester's nursing classes." A dark frown then replaced the bright smile. "Sam, do you think I can be smart enough to be a nurse?"

Sam looked at her, trying to transfer his newfound confidence in himself. "Yes Esme, you are smart enough and will make a wonderful nurse. You are caring, intuitive, and really just wonderful. Look what you did for me."

"Sam, I really don't think this is the same thing," she said as she playfully stroked his chest.

"It better not be," he laughed and rolled on top of her.

Sam felt relieved that Soto had promised to look after Esme while he was back in the States. She had a new job as a nurse assistant in the ER. Soto would get her prepped to take exams for admission into a nursing school and by the time Sam got back she would be wearing a real ugly uniform of the IMSS hospital with pride. Sam felt good. If they couldn't be together at least she wouldn't be going back to Boy's Town. Soto had promised him.

He looked at her black eyes, red lips, and womanly body with love and gratitude. She had supported him through near death and helped him to forget Leah, at least for the time being.

———•———

Sam had the car all packed and gassed up. He pulled into the courtyard of the school. It was eight a.m. He had to get moving if he wanted to make it over the border before dark. He walked over to the torta truck and ordered his last *café y torta con queso y tomaté* of the semester.

"Hey, give other people some room, maricón," Sayeed squawked.

"Chupame," Sam laughingly replied.

They were all there, Marvin, Bennie, Sayeed, and Andy. All headed back for a couple of months. Sam was going to the hospital in San Diego, Sayeed home to Brooklyn to visit his friends and family, Andy and his family to work the summer term of the Long Island high school where he had been a counselor, and Bennie to Viviene in Brownsville, Texas.

They told each other they would stay in touch over the months, each knowing it wasn't going to happen. All of them needed to decompress in their hometowns. Before any of them could really miss the camaraderie, they'd all be back in Mexico.

They downed the coffee, wrapped the tortas for the road, and started the drive North.

Chapter 17

When in San Diego ... Don't Touch Anything

The three months at home flew by quickly. For Sam the joy of being in an American hospital was never realized. While the people he met and tried to learn from were kind and occasionally attempted to teach, they were too busy for a kid who was going to some Mexican medical school and wasn't attending a real medical school. The "real" was some school that was situated in the United States.

Sam didn't consider himself a medical expert at this point, but the only comparison of patient care he had was to the IMSS hospital in Tampico. He often heard comments from the doctors and nurses alike about the state of medicine in the rest of the world, especially in backward Mexico. The major difference Sam saw was technology.

Mexico was a poor country and just didn't have the money for the latest and greatest technology. The hospitals in the City of Tampico were not fighting over which one was going to be allowed to buy a CT scanner. In San Diego every hospital had plans to buy one at more than a million dollars a pop. The situation in San Diego was so bad that the State government had to step in and referee which hospital was going to buy the most sophisticated machine.

Sam noticed that with the improved technology the doctors spent less time examining and more time ordering tests. Another problem was that every US doctor practiced lawsuit medicine. The more tests you ordered, running up a bill, the more protection you had in a malpractice suit. Mexico didn't have malpractice suits. Whether that was good or bad it certainly let the doctors in Mexico spend more time doctoring than worrying about lawyers.

He did the jobs he was assigned and missed Soto's "cabron!" Sam wasn't given a chance to examine, much less do a supervised procedure on a patient. Even putting on a simple splint or taking a blood pressure could be a point in a malpractice suit. As nice as the doctors he worked with were, they wouldn't take a chance. As such he usually was assigned to stand in a corner and observe the goings on. He wasn't eager to get more involved because of his first and last incident at the hospital.

Sam had been sitting reading at the desk near the ambulance entrance in the ER. Unlike Tampico the hallways were devoid of patients. Here in San Diego patients on gurneys were not allowed to be parked in a hall. Patients waited in the waiting room till a cubicle was available. The exception was ambulance patients, actual emergencies (of which he saw few) and VIPs (patients a hospital administrator called down to take "good care of them"). He once again found himself taking in the physical plant of this ER as it was such a contrast to the ER in Mexico. Instead of the crowded, dirty hallways filled with screaming, bleeding, puking, and shitting patients, hallways here were as quiet as a morgue. The floor so brightly shined that the overhead fluorescent lights could individually be seen reflected on the floor. The walls were painted a flat white and the occasional nurse could be seen gliding between the cubicles in starched whites. Sam almost wished for the contrast of old blood or vomit splatter. That signified a place that was used in the delivery of healthcare.

Suddenly the quiet was broken by the sound of a car driving up at high speed, the brakes squealing. Doors opened followed by the loud thump of something hitting the ground. The car gunned its engine and the tires again squealed as the car left the ambulance port.

Sam ran out the door to see a body, soaked like it had just been in a bath, not moving. He moved to the body that was face down and yelled at the person, "Hey, are you OK?" There was no response. Sam, remembering his first experience in the Tampico ER quickly went back through the ambulance door into the department and yelled for help. He heard multiple footsteps as people came into the hall. "I need help outside," and without checking if he was being followed went back to the body that hadn't moved. Carefully, Sam log-rolled the body and saw a deep bluish-purple colored face with almost black lips. He put his ear near the body's mouth and heard no breathing. His attempt to find a pulse in the neck confirmed that this body was in cardiac arrest. Quickly Sam made a fist and thumped the chest. He again found no pulse and gave the body a couple of mouth-to-mouth breaths followed by chest compressions.

"What do you think you're doing?" a very loud, authoritarian voice called out.

Sam looked up to see the ER doc standing over him. He was a short, wide man with a very ruddy looking face named Moore.

"I heard a thump and came outside to investigate," Sam panted, never breaking the exercise of chest compressions. "I found this person not breathing and in cardiac arrest so I yelled for help and started CPR."

Moore looked around and saw the charge nurse. "Get Dr. Ross and tell him a cardiac arrest is coming into the ER, get the attendants to take over compressions from Mr. Cohen, and get one of the nurses to bag him—now move!"

There was a bustle of action as an attendant took over from Sam and the patient was lifted and put on a stretcher and whisked into the

ER. Silence descended in the ambulance port as only Sam and Moore were left.

Sam was shocked, "But the patient wasn't breathing. I called for help … "

" … and made this hospital liable for whatever the outcome is. There are protocols and Rule #1 is no one goes outside the door to get a patient. We call 911."

"The ER calls 911?" Sam was dumbfounded. "But it would take a minimum of 10 minutes for an ambulance to come and the paramedics to start working the patient. He would be brain dead by then."

"You idiot. Did you notice he was soaked to the bone? He overdosed on heroin somewhere else and his buddies found him dead. Fucking Chicanos throw these assholes in a shower to revive them, which never works. He was brain-dead before he got here in cardiac arrest and you tried to resurrect him. I know most of these bastards are named Jesus, but seriously? Now the hospital may be found responsible for his death."

"I was just … "

"Never touch a body and from now on stay in the corner and keep out of my sight. I never, and I mean never, want to see you touch a patient again. If you didn't have a friend in that asshole of a toxicologist you'd be out of here now. Fucking Americans that go to a Mex med school. Quit now, you will never be a practicing doctor in this country." Moore left Sam out in the ambulance port.

"This is the kind of medicine I'm supposed to practice?" he wondered. "Maybe it's better to be a soulless lawyer."

———— • ————

His social life was very family oriented. He cherished his time with his mother and father, trying to slip back into the old routines he used to have with them. It was somewhat successful, but his personality had changed. His parents had sent their boy to Mexico. A man had come back.

He saw Her father only once during the entire summer. He had met Sam in the hospital to introduce him to the ER chief. The meeting had been friendly, but not a word was said about his daughter, and after an uncomfortable half hour he took his leave and Sam was handed over to the ER staff.

The days passed. Class was supposed to start in two weeks but Sam received a phone call from one of the Americans and it looked like class start was going to be postponed by at least a week. No reason was given, nor was Sam expecting one. It was all part of the game of trying to learn medicine in Mexico.

Finally, word came that classes would probably start within the next seven to ten days. Sam said his teary goodbyes, got into his car, and started down the road heading south.

Chapter 18

Moving On

Sam made it back in four days. He collected another tourist visa to add to his collection and in his sophistication of all things Mexican, had money out and waiting when the Mexican Migracíon Official wanted to look at his belongings a little too closely.

The car held *regalos,* or presents, for Garza. These were tokens to a man who could make the next year easier or harder on a whim. The line that most of the Americans used when personally delivering these presents was "My mother wanted me to give you this token of her esteem and to thank you for taking care of her son or daughter." By now most of the Americans could do this with a straight face.

He had also brought some presents for Soto and of course he had gone overboard finding things that he was sure Esme would love and appreciate. He couldn't wait to kiss her and hold her. He would have gone right to her, but got into Tampico late in the evening and didn't want to disturb her when she was most likely asleep. Morning would come soon enough.

The Holiday Inn accepted the month's rent. Finding an apartment was the next task as student party life was no longer a priority.

He was so tired that he dropped his bags and lay down on the bed to rest a bit. He was deeply asleep within minutes.

He didn't have time to go and find Esme in the morning. Marvin showed up and they decided to have a celebratory breakfast in the hotel. They learned Carlito had been promoted to manager of the restaurant and had decided to change the menu to cater more to American taste. He also redecorated the dining room in what he thought was a more American style. That the restaurant looked like a Denny's was probably more a sad commentary on dining in the States.

"Hey Amigos, you like the new menu and look?"

Before them were real pancakes made of real flour from the States instead of the semi-corn batter ones they used to get, and real Vermont maple syrup.

"Yeah, but how and why? Isn't importing the syrup illegal and where did you get the makings for the batter? It's pure Denny's," Marvin said, his mouth full of gringo breakfast goodness.

"Silly boys, you know I wouldn't do anything that could be found to be illegal." Carlito's eyes darted to his right and left. "I met someone," he said softly.

"A guy?" Sam asked with surprise.

"What do you think, I would switch teams this far out or do you think I'm too ugly to find a man?'

"Calm down. I didn't think you'd be a turncoat to the Mariposa Revolution. As far as ugly, well … I've seen uglier," Sam said with a smile. "Who is he and what does he have to do with pancakes and real maple syrup?"

Carlito blushed. "He is a *piloto*, a pilot, and he is beautiful."

"A gay Mexican pilot. That's got to be a first for Mexicana. Next they'll be offering His and His Weekends in Puerto Vallarta," Marvin said.

"He doesn't work for Mexicana, silly. All the Mexicana pilots are *muchachos*. I am very moral, you know that. I don't fuck children."

"I never said you do," Marvin said hastily. "If he doesn't fly for Mexicana, then for whom? AeroMexico?"

"No, he is a charter pilot and owns his own cargo plane." Carlito giggled. "Isn't that butch? He is beautiful, funny, and best of all has a big *verga*." Carlito laughed again.

Sam, still a little innocent, fell right into it. "Verga? What's that?"

"Sam, you kill me sometimes," Marvin said laughing. "You can't figure it out?"

"Sí, he is an idiota. Verga, you know he has a big salami … a cock."

"Ohhh," Sam blushed.

"He brings in the jarabe, the syrup hidden in the crates of other basura he transports. You know the customs guys. A couple of pesos and a bottle of tequila and they are your friends for life."

"So the manager of the motel knows about this," Marvin said between bites.

"He doesn't care as long as I don't get caught. How do you think I became manager of the restaurant?"

Sam laughed. "Carlito, you are an excellent example of getting ahead in the Mexican workplace."

"Sí, did I tell you about his verga and do you want some more sausage?" Carlito offered.

Chapter **19**

Disease and Harvard

Pathology was the class that actually taught what the various diseases were and what they could do to the human body. Sam was very excited. Finally a class—no, a lab course—that was directly involved in the actual practice of medicine. What happened to heart muscle after infarction? What did the cells of a gastric carcinoma look like? It looked like pathology could be very exciting and financially profitable.

Sam got to the school early and joined Bennie, Sayeed, and Andy at the *torta* truck.

"*Café con leche*," Sam said. "And thus my dependence on caffeine is rejuvenated for the year. Too bad that within the first week, the effect is lost."

"Well Sam, we found just the thing for you. It's perfectly legal in Mexico, but very illegal without a prescription in the States. Late night crams are easy with a simple little pill." Andy looked remarkably stress free considering Marla must have been raging on him since their return to Tampico.

"Why do you look so good?" asked Sam.

"Thank you for the backhanded compliment. I do feel surprisingly good. In fact I feel good, happy, and—most importantly—free."

"You divorced the bitch, didn't you?" Sayeed said. "I'm so happy for you."

Andy smiled. "Careful, that is my beloved wife you are talking about and no, we did not divorce."

"I don't get it," said Marvin. "Then why are you so happy?"

"Marla and I decided, well it was all Marla … decided that it would be better if she and the kids lived in Brownsville. She could enroll the kids in school, talk on the phone, shop, etc. I could live here and come home every three weeks on the weekends for time with my children … "

" … And sex," Bennie said smugly.

"Let's not go that far. This is Marla we are talking about," Andy replied.

"So you are almost a free man," Sam laughed. "A cause for celebration."

"Yes boys, tonight in Boy's Town. First beer is on me."

———•———

Things were about to change. The boys entered the class with the same hubbub as usual. Mexicans on one side, Americans on the other. The proctors were busy collecting names and checking school IDs. The class finally settled down waiting for the professor to enter. The proctors stood at the doors to the class checking their watches. Where was he?

A tall, thin, older man stood up from the first row of seats. He was over six feet tall and couldn't weigh more than 150 pounds. He had grey hair, a wind and sun burned face, and sported a neatly trimmed goatee.

"I am Doctor Anthony Cerene, and no, I am not a native of Mexico," he smiled. "I am here to teach you the fundamental basis of the disease process. It will take a commitment on your part to do quite a lot of reading and we will spend a lot of time in the lab, such as it is, looking at slides. At the end of this class, you should have no problems with the pathology section of the Medical Boards. For those of you who are Mexican, I can guarantee this course will give you a strong basis for your hospital social service. The key," he paused and seemed to look into each and every one's eyes, "will be an absolute commitment to study. Every spare moment you have must be spent looking at and classifying the slides."

Cerene paused and the class was mesmerized. Where had this guy come from? An American teaching in a shithole medical school in Mexico? Christ, he looked like a God.

Cerene sighed, "I'm sure that now with all my inspiring words, most of you are aware of the microscope situation in the school. Sr. Garza has promised me more and better scopes, but I fear that they may not materialize for quite a while. Nevertheless, I have made arrangements for the lab to be open twenty-four hours a day and seven days a week, to give you all time there. Undeniably this will mean less time in Boy's Town for some of you ... " he smirked and the class laughed. "But to achieve the goal of being a doctor you must sacrifice. A final thing ... " He looked down at his roster. "Would the following students stay after class and see me please—Sam Cohen and Andy Blumenkranz. Thank you, now let's start."

"To understand disease one must make sure that one understands the normal working of the cell. We will commence a three day review of the physiology of the cell ... "

As Cerene lectured on, Sam and Andy wondered what Cerene wanted with them. Sam didn't know him and he was pretty sure that Andy didn't, either. On the other hand he was truly excited. This guy sounded like a real teacher and had expectations besides the dibujos and clay models that had been a great part of their basic science education so far. Maybe between Cerene and Soto he could actually become a decent physician.

The bell rang, signaling the end of class. Sam and Andy waited anxiously in their seats for their classmates to file out.

———— • ————

"Blumenkranz and Cohen," Cerene looked at them intently. "It sounds like a law firm, not a Mafioso smuggling ring."

Sam replied, "We are retired, besides I think bringing in lipsticks to sell isn't a crime."

"And," Andy added, "we paid our debt to society. What does this have to do with pathology?"

"Nothing of practicality," said Cerene. "It's just that I have a problem which affects you and the rest of the class and I doubt there is anyone else with the knowledge or the motivation to help the collective us," he said with a smile.

"Look, we were never really smugglers … "

"Maybe you weren't, Sam, but your friend Andy here did a pretty good job. Didn't you, Andy? How long did it take you to figure out the false compartment in that school bus?"

Andy remained silent. Cerene's face lit up.

"You didn't figure it out on your own did you? You had help and I bet I know exactly where you got that help. Interviewing juvenile delinquents at that high school taught you a thing or two. Well Mr. Blumenkranz, the tables are now turned. You're the teacher and your professor needs that same kind of help."

Sam was lost. "What the fuck is he talking about, Andy?"

Andy looked at him. "I think I know what an American is doing here teaching pathology in a shithole med school."

"I can't do this kind of thing myself," said Cerene. "I need someone who can get fifty microscopes across the Mexican border. I can't go into the States and get them, but I bet you can."

"Why doesn't Garza get them?" Andy asked.

"Boys, as wonderful as Sr. Garza was to set up this woefully inadequate school, a philanthropist he is not. I can get the scopes for about $100 apiece. He will pay that much but unfortunately La Republíca wants its due. The tax is about $125 per scope." He smiled. "Crazy, isn't it?"

Sam was suspicious. "Why do you care about the scopes? You have lived here long enough and must realize the Mexicans could give a shit whether you actually teach us anything or not."

Cerene's face fell. He was old, but suddenly he looked ten years older. "I have sinned. The ability to practice medicine is a great gift and I squandered it. That was only my first sin. The second was that I broke the Sixth Commandment. There was a woman, a patient of mine, whom I killed through arrogance and inattention. God may forgive me, but I will never forgive myself. Maybe teaching you will help atone for my sins."

———◆———

Anthony Cerene, MD was first in his class at Harvard. A brilliant diagnostician he was named the youngest researcher at Harvard in oncology. He later earned a PhD in Oncogenic genetics and virology. On track to become a major researcher, there was a good chance he would become head of the National Institutes of Health in Washington one day.

Dr. Anthony Cerene had one small problem. He was addicted to hallucinogens. He was unmistakably smart enough to know better, but Anthony's brilliance was due to his brain always being on. Day and night he continuously thought about new and obscure solutions to oncological problems. He didn't sleep, didn't really eat, and couldn't sit still.

About the same time Anthony was at Harvard a small group of doctors were interested in the human mind achieving another level of being. In 1960, Anthony met with a PhD psychologist to find help for his constantly active mind. Tim, the PhD, said he had an answer. The answer was three little letters, LSD. For the first time in a long time Anthony knew periods of peace. Anthony believed that treating patients and doing research under the influence of hallucinogens made him the best there was. He was "treated" by Tim over the next three years.

Anthony became more and more addicted to Tim's treatment, spending more and more time in another world. His clinical and research skills suffered. The university attempted multiple times to warn Anthony, but ended up firing him. The firing was too late. Anthony's last patient, a forty-three-year-old mother of two, came in complaining of shortness of breath and chest pain. She had been on a business trip and was flying back from Los Angeles when she noticed some pain in her leg. She never mentioned this to Anthony, but to be fair, no one thought Anthony would have picked up on any of the fine points of the patient history as he was high as a kite.

Anthony admitted her to rule out cardiac chest pain, never exploring the possibility that she had a pulmonary embolism or putting her on the blood thinner, heparin. She died five hours later of a massive saddle embolism. Malpractice suits were easier to avoid in those days and the weight of Harvard Medical School covered up Anthony's mistake.

Meanwhile, Tim's research was shut down by Harvard. Tim disappeared into Mexico to continue his experiments with psychoactive drugs. The psychedelic revolution continued.

Anthony followed Tim Leary to Mexico. Three years later LSD was banned in the States.

Anthony started his own lab in Mexico and made LSD. He

began visiting the States to preach once again about the benefits of mind expansion. He also quietly smuggled the product of his lab to happy patrons north of the border. One day after giving his lecture a long-haired man with a Sancho Panza moustache came up to him. He told Anthony he was very impressed with his lecture and with him. The man and his friends had gone into Mexico to try various mind-expanding substances, but were always disappointed because the quality was so uneven.

Anthony was very proud of his quality control and offered the man a sample. The man thanked him and two days later showed up at Anthony's hotel. He asked Anthony if he would consider a partnership. Anthony could bring the product across the border and the man would buy it for converts to the cause. Anthony quickly agreed as money was always a problem.

In 1969, Anthony drove into the United States in his old Ford truck. He met the man in order to hand over the product when a floodlight prematurely went off, showing police and DEA agents ready for an arrest.

Anthony ran to his truck and managed to get back across the border without getting caught. On that day he realized that he needed to clean up his act, which he did, but he never set foot in his homeland again.

———— ◆ ————

The room was quiet.

Andy and Sam didn't know what to say. Finally, Andy looked at Cerene and said, "We need to figure this out. Fifty microscopes will take up a lot of room and we need them here in one trip and as fast as we can. Do you have the money, and the pick-up location of the scopes?"

Cerene brightened. "Give me twenty-four hours notice of when you plan to move them, and I will make arrangements."

Sam said, "One more thing. Garza is not to know who moved the scopes. He has too much on us as it is."

"Agreed. I'll see you tomorrow. Make sure to read Chapters Five and Six by then."

———— • ————

"How are we going to do this?" Sam asked. "That bus of yours doesn't have enough room in the hidden compartments."

"I really don't know. That last brush with the federales hasn't exactly made me feel confident about our smuggling abilities. You are right, though. I just don't have enough room in the bus's compartments for more than fifteen to twenty scopes. Plus, let's face it, even the student scopes need some care. I can't just cram them into odd spaces. And that road with my shocks … I'll lose a couple right there."

"Well, I guess we'll have to think on it. What do you think of Cerene?"

"Now that is an interesting story in itself. On the one hand I guess we have a world-class teacher to get us ready for the pathology part of the boards. On the other hand we have a "so-he-says" ex-drug addict that isn't averse to asking his students to do something dangerous and illegal. Hmmm … I think I like his chutzpah. There is something familiar about him. I just can't put my finger on it."

Sam asked, "Did you meet him on Long Island, maybe read about him?"

"I don't remember. Maybe it will come back to me. I'm going back to the house and start cracking the Path book. Want to come?"

"No, I still haven't seen Esme. I have to go find her."

"Sam, you sure that's a good idea?" Andy looked concerned.

"Andy, she is sweet and loving and I want to be with her. I'll see you later."

Chapter 20

Love Lost (Again)

Sam headed for the apartment Esme shared with four of the other girls who worked at Casa Blanca. It was a cement box that had three other apartments filled with poor couples with kids in all sizes and states of dirtiness. There was always the background music of screaming infants, barking dogs, or domestic violence. Esme had once told him that the girls were happy they worked at night, because they didn't have to hear the screams the wives made as their husbands beat them.

He parked, ran up the stairs and knocked on the door.

"Sí?" a voice inquired from behind the door.

"*Esme esta?*" Sam asked. "*Yo soy Sam un amigo de ella*, I'm Sam a friend of hers."

"She isn't here. She moved out three weeks ago," the voice said.

Sam was confused. "What do you mean she moved out? You sure? Her name is Esme, black hair … "

" … and what part of moved out don't you understand, Sam?" The door opened and a young girl that Sam had seen in the Town emerged. Like most of the girls she looked quite different in the daylight without make-up and the neon lighting.

"She moved out, disappeared. Vanished into the mist. Do you understand any of that English? Why are you here?" she asked suspiciously. Their apartments had none of the tinsel glamour of the zone. The girls wore minimal make-up and the skimpy costumes of the Town were kept in the Town. Some of the girls had learned to keep their secret identities secret the hard way. Those who were not discreet had faced harassment in the neighborhood, even eviction. One poor girl had been recognized by a previous customer, who had taken her willingness in the Town as an invitation. She was found raped and killed. This happened years ago, but the lesson had stuck.

"I just got back from the States and wanted to see her."

"You know we don't entertain men in our home," she said, looking around outside to see who was watching them. "You need to get out of here."

"But I have to find her. Do you know where she might have gone? Maybe she left a message. Can I come in and check her room?"

"She came home one day, packed her toothbrush and spare dress, and left. She left nothing in the house, now get out of here before the neighbors notice and you ruin this place for the rest of us." She slammed the door in Sam's face.

He was very worried. Where had she gone? He left not knowing how he was going to get through the next hours till night.

***

Marvin came back with a mission. It was a scam that still needed a solution to help all the Americans in Tampico. He would almost guarantee them all a medical career and get them out of this hellhole once and for all. The scam would turn American-foreign medical education on its ass.

The problem was twofold and he needed solutions on both sides of the border. In Mexico he definitely needed the Boys, at least Andy and Sam, to work on Garza. This might be the easier of the two parts, but who would work the problem in the States? They needed someone who understood money and had some power. Unfortunately the list of people he knew in that position was zero and he doubted his friends had a bigger list. Maybe someone political?

He'd talk to Andy. If they wanted to leave Mexico they needed to move on the rumor.

———◆———

Night had finally fallen and Sam was headed for the Town. He no longer worried about federales, smuggling contraband, or anything else. Boy's Town was a part of his world for better or worse. He knew his friends there and he knew who to stay away from. He almost thought he was more comfortable in the Town than he was in San Diego.

The neon lights were the same as were the dirt streets, the smells and the drunks staggering from bar to bar. The jukeboxes could be heard playing up and down the streets and the skinless heads of the donkeys, pigs, steers, and whatever else they used for taco meat still stared, eye sockets empty and gaping. Nothing had changed. Sam parked and went into the Casa Blanca.

The bartender saw him and smiled. "*Sr. Sam, como estas?* Long time no see. Cerveza?"

"Yeah, that would be great." Sam looked around and didn't see any of the regular girls. "Say, is Lola around?"

The bartender shook his head. "You know, I haven't seen her tonight, but that doesn't mean a lot as I just got here myself. Why don't you relax and drink that down and I'll go in the back and see if she's here."

"Thanks, Man. I appreciate it."

Sam tried to relax, but he found himself oddly agitated. He thought that, no matter what, Esme couldn't be far. She wouldn't leave town knowing he was coming back. He didn't expect her back at Casa Blanca, but she still had friends here. One of them would know where she was.

The bartender approached Sam. "Another cerveza?"

"No, I'm good. Lola back there?"

"No, she isn't in but she left a message for you. One of the girls back there said that Lola told her if you came into the bar to tell you "She's gone, and it's for the best." The bartender shook his head. "Do you have any idea what that means?"

Sam sat in shock. "Where is Lola? I need to see her right away." Sam got up and started toward the back, but the bartender grabbed him by the arm.

"Hey Sr. Sam, you know you have to be invited back there by one of the girls. Anyway, she isn't back there I swear. The girl that gave me the message didn't know what it meant, either."

Sam looked frantic. "Please, you have to help me. I need to find Esme."

The bartender was confused, "Wait, I thought you said you wanted Lola. Esme is a different matter."

Sam relaxed. "Yeah, sorry my fault. I need Esme. Can you tell her I'm here and want to see her?"

"I wish I could Sr. Sam, but Esme hasn't worked here in months. I haven't seen that girl since … hmm, let me see. Yeah, since you were hurt. Man that was something with that croc … "

Sam's world was rapidly falling apart. "It was an alligator." He turned and walked out of the bar.

Andy looked at Marvin with wonder. "You're shitting me. It can't be."

"The source was good. This guy was in his fourth year at La Guad and was mighty pissed that he didn't get to reap the benefits," Marvin took a long pull on his beer.

"Well, how do you think we can use this info to convert Garza to the cause? I for one don't want to spend an extra minute down here. God, Marla may actually give me one night of sex, maybe even a blow job if this works."

Marvin had a mouthful of beer and started laughing so hard he sprayed his beer all over the table. "Yes, I agree, Andy, we have to make sure this gets done so you can get that blow job you richly deserve."

Andy's eyes had a distant look. "We need someone powerful and with political connections in the States, huh."

"I can't see any way around it. If we walk into the hospitals they'll just laugh us out the door. We need some muscle."

"I think I might know the right person, but I need an expert on this guy. Let's meet tomorrow. I need to do a little research and in the meantime you think about the Garza end ... though I think I have an idea there, too. In fact one that might take care of a certain problem that I'm trying to work on with Sam. So now I have two people to talk to. Tomorrow is going to be a busy day."

———•———

Sam had no idea where Lola lived. He didn't even have an idea as to how she looked without all the "enhancements." He cruised Esme's neighborhood. The streets were typical of lower class neighborhoods in Tampico and Ciudad Madero. Only the main street was paved, the rest of the feeder streets were dirt and potholes filled with mud and water. There was the faint stench of the public sewer canals and the flea-bitten dogs that roved in packs and were forever barking at anything that moved. Overhead electrical wires were strung between oily looking wooden poles. Some of the wires looked like they were strung dangerously close to the ground. Everywhere there were people on the street, talking to their neighbors over balcony walls or fences. Sam even passed an occasional ice cream truck, its ringing bells happily announcing it had product to sell. Sam stopped on most of the small streets and asked for Lola, but blank stares were all he got. No one knew of a beautiful blond woman with a Coke-bottle figure and perfect makeup. After two hours with the streetlights starting to fade out he finally gave up and headed for the motel.

He entered the motel bone-tired. Much too tired to study pathology or any other subject that he'd promised himself he'd keep up on. There was a smoky smell and a glow as he walked into the otherwise dark room. It came from someone sitting on his bed smoking a cigarette. It was Lola.

"*Hola Joven*, I hear you are trying to find me?"

Sam ran over to her and grabbed her arm. "Where is she? Where is Esme?'

"Let go of me! You're hurting me."

Sam was angry and afraid. He didn't realize that he had grabbed her in anger and immediately released her.

"That's better, *Amor*. Sit down. I will tell you some things you need to know. Things that she wanted to keep from you."

"Where is she, Lola? Please tell me."

"Joven, she went away to re-start her life. Esme couldn't believe that an American studying to be a doctor could love someone like her. When she found she was pregnant she knew she had to leave."

Sam was in shock. "She is pregnant? Lola, I have to be with her, where is she? Please tell me." He got up to start after her, but Lola pulled him down.

"Joven," she smiled sadly, "she was pregnant. In the profession, pregnancy is an occupational hazard. Despite the teachings of the Church the women of the Towns know how to take care of the problem."

"I ... I don't understand." Sam was in shock. He was going to be a father, but what was Lola telling him?

"She had an abortion, joven. She couldn't burden you with this and she knew you would come to hate her, so she left."

Sam couldn't speak. He could only sob. Lola put her arms around him and hugged him to her chest. "*Mi Niño, no llores. No llores, Amor.* She stroked him, letting him cry himself out in her arms.

———•———

The sun came through the window. Sam opened his eyes. Was it a nightmare? He found himself naked, covered only by a thin sheet. "Lola!" But she wasn't there. He stretched. He needed to find her, but how? Lola must know something.

The door opened and in came Lola, but not the Lola he was used to. She had no make-up on and she was wearing a simple dress, her fabulous figure hidden in its looseness. Sam fixed his eyes on her.

"Not as beautiful as Lola of the Casa Blanca, eh? A little older too. Disappointed? I see I am not getting the response I used to get from you." She laughed, pointing at his groin.

Sam blushed and quickly put the sheet around his waist. "Where did she go, Lola? I need to find her. I love her."

"I don't know where she went, joven. I didn't make those arrangements ... "

"But you know who did, don't you?" he demanded angrily.

"I may, but I want you to think for a moment and no man can do that with a woman he desires in the room," she smiled.

"I don't desire you," he said indignantly.

"Maybe not the way I look now," she said tiredly, "but the

thought of Lola seems to have risen the spirit." She pointed at his growing erection.

"Get dressed after a cold shower. I will fetch us some café and we will talk, an old experienced woman to a young man."

She walked out the door.

———•———

Sam did as she suggested. He showered, though not with cold water, shaved and dressed. He then started packing his bag.

Lola silently walked into the room with coffee and tortas. "You are packing for nothing, *Amor*. Stop and have breakfast with this old woman."

Sam continued packing an overnight bag. He didn't even look up. "You are not helping me and I need to find her as soon as possible. Maybe if I beg on my knees and have money in my hands her roommate will tell me which way she headed?"

She looked sad. "I sometimes forget what it is to be young and burning with love and innocence. Esme picked correctly. You would have been perfect for her except your worlds could never meet."

He finally looked up from his task and gave her an angry look. "I don't give a fuck about our separate worlds. Where is she?"

She slapped him. "Sit down and listen, Child, or you will never hear where she went."

Sam was stunned. He didn't move a muscle, but his body was tense with a demand to hit back. His mind blank he took some long, deep breaths, and slowly sat down.

"That is better," Lola said. "You are a romantic, joven, living in a very romantic country."

"Romantic? Women are not treated well here and I don't think towns of whores are romantic," Sam said hotly.

"Is that what you think of Esme, as a whore?"

Sam's face fell, "No, I … "

"No, I know you don't. You look at her as a woman who loved and made love to you. Someone who took care of you when you were sick, became a vessel for your spent passion, cooked for you and cleaned for you. In the end she would have made a real man out of you except for one thing. You couldn't fulfill your happiness with her. She realized that and unselfishly left. Are there many women in the States who did anything near this to make you feel loved?"

The woman who broke his heart, long ago in San Diego, immediately came to his mind. He had loved her almost desperately, but not even a fraction of that was returned. It was the deepest relationship he had ever had. None of the other one-night stands or casual dates even went that far.

"No, Esme was a true love, even for the short time we had together." He looked at her urgently. "Lola, that's why I have to find her. I will never have a love like this again."

"No Joven, you will find a love similar in your world. Esme knew she would never be able to survive in the States, in California. She knew she would always be afraid that her origins would be discovered and you would hate her for it."

Sam knew in his heart she was right. He still needed to know Esme would be alright. That she would have some sort of future besides a Boy's Town in another city. "Lola, I have to make sure."

Lola smiled. "Ask your friend, the doctor. He can give you the assurance you need."

———— •• ————

"You fucking bastard, why did you let her go away?" Sam was angry and he didn't care where he shouted it.

Soto was in the middle of suturing up a lip in the IMSS ER. He looked up calmly and smiled at Sam.

"So Lola once again proves that women have big mouths, sí cabron?"

The last cabron was the last straw. Sam grabbed Soto and hit him in the face. Soto went down, blood dripping from his mouth.

"You fucking bastard, why? You knew how important she was to me."

"Jesus, calm down cabron. She wanted to leave and I agreed with her. You would never have taken her back with you to the States."

Sam went to slug Soto again, but three security guards in mall cop uniforms had grabbed him. Soto got off the floor and walked over to Sam while wiping the blood from his lip.

"Shit! Do I need stitches, you asshole?"

Sam was still breathing fast, but the adrenalin in him was decreasing. "Why did she leave and why did she … ?" Sam choked.

Soto looked at him. "Finished hitting, Sam?"

Sam nodded, suddenly very tired. Soto motioned to the guards to let him go.

"Come on," Soto said and led Sam to an on-call room with a bunk, desk light, and desk.

"Sit down and no hitting." Soto opened a drawer, pulled out a pack of cigarettes, and lit two up. He gave one to Sam. "When you left she suspected she was pregnant, so of course she came to me. I've known Esme for some time." Soto looked up at Sam, taking a drag off the cigarette, "but not in that way," he assured Sam. "She was a nice child, forced by her circumstances into Boy's Town. She was different. She never became hard or bitter and took it as her lot in life. She tried to be as comforting as possible and tried to be as decent as she could."

"She helped me, loved me. I don't know if I would have survived without her. I owe her so much," Sam said sadly.

"Yes, and I understand your love for her and she knew that you loved her, but it is a love based on gratitude. This kind of love would never survive life in the US, your friends there, your colleagues in the hospital, and especially your parents. Esme is love, that is true, but she is not sophisticated and certainly not educated. Eventually her being with you would have desolated you both."

"But the baby..." Sam cried.

"Forget it. You are very lucky she did what she did and she will have an easier future. Look Sam, you are at a stage of life where you are learning how to take care of yourself. You are in no position to take care of a family. Neither is Esme. Single motherhood is harsh down here. There is no help; she would have been on the street with a starving brat."

"I could have helped," Sam said quietly.

"Where, from the States? You are not this stupid."

Sam had utterly collapsed in front of Soto's eyes.

"Sam ... "

"Yeah."

"Don't worry about Esme. I loved her, too. I couldn't see her in another Boy's Town, especially not after the nursing job she did with you."

"So where is she?" Sam asked hopefully.

"I won't tell you where, but I have a friend who owes me. He runs a hospital with a nursing school. He will make sure she gets the background education and then attends nursing school. He placed her as a nanny with a nice couple and she will have time to study."

"That's great, but why can't I see her?"

"Because, you can't confuse her or yourself any longer. You both are on different tracks and have different destinies. It will be a pleasant memory for both of you."

———•———

Sam walked out of the ER into the sunlight.

Around him people were streaming into the front doors of the hospital. These people had problems that had bigger consequences than his little ones. He realized that but he still felt empty inside. This was a great adventure he had embarked on. He wished he had someone to share it with, but Leah had rejected him, and Esme had, in the end, probably done the right thing for both of them.

He would always love her, but maybe his experience with her could count as a first life saved. Instead of living in impoverished servitude, Esme would become a great nurse. She had saved him and one day would help someone else in need. He was confused and maybe the logic didn't make sense, but as Soto said, it was a pleasant memory. Now it was time to go back to work. He turned on his heel and strode back into the ER. "Let's see now. Who can I help and who can help me become a better doctor," he asked himself.

Chapter 21

Of Airplanes and the Promised Land

"I think I've figured it out. I just need the cooperation of a friend's new squeeze."

Marvin looked at Andy and Sam, saying, "Well, I might have the answer to some of the political problems. It might be a reach, but fortunately most of the kids down here have parents and a lot of those parents have money. I think we need to let the students in on our little project."

"I agree, but even with the student body support we need something Garza needs and is willing to trade for."

Marvin smiled. "You know, being back in the States and having to play by the rules of the medical establishment is going to be boring after this."

"Boring maybe but I can guarantee very stressful. The American establishment hates us and will never accept us as competent physicians. We are just starting the fight to achieve what we came down here for."

Andy shook his head. "It will never be boring, Marvin, and Sam is right on his second point. If you think the Mexicans are morally bankrupt you know our future colleagues in the American medical establishment are just as bankrupt, probably more morally bankrupt as most of them want to create edifices with their names on them. Americans do it bigger and with more finesse. My guess is that most of our future will be involved with defending our right to practice medicine within an establishment that never wanted the competition. It will be challenging."

They smiled at each other while drinking down their beers.

———•———

Andy found Carlito in the hotel kitchen counting linens. "Hey Carlito, how are you doing?"

"Hola Andy, how are you?" He asked as he continued counting inventory.

"Fine, and how's that new love of yours?"

Carlito stopped and smiled shyly. "He is fantastic. So sweet, so romantic, and what a *verga!*"

"Uh yeah, I'm sure that's very important. Remind me, he's a pilot with a private aircraft, right?"

"Sí, twin engine for charter passengers and cargo. He usually flies from Houston into the Tampico airport, sometimes to the airstrip in Madero. Depends how much hassle his passengers don't want," he said with a laugh.

Now Andy's interest was really peaked. He laughed. "What do you mean by passengers who don't want a hassle? I've never seen anything down here that didn't involve a hassle of some sort?"

Carlito looked around anxiously. "Oh Andy," he whispered, "I've said too much. Forget what I said."

Andy smiled and put an arm around Carlito, "Buddy, we are all friends here. You know I'm not a federale."

"Sí, you are a graduate of the carcel, the jail." Carlito looked around again. "Sometimes his passengers don't want a lot of attention to the baggage or cargo they bring in or out. Madero's officials can be persuaded to look the other way. You know with the proper *propina* you can make a lot of friends."

"*Propina* is a tip right? Like in a bribe?"

"Andy," Carlito said knowingly, "my friend would never break the law with a bribe. A tip is a friendly present for good service, and my friend and his passengers can be very grateful for good service."

Andy was elated. A pilot with an understanding of the local economy, who operated in a city where law enforcement needed the support of outside economic stimuli. Maybe Marvin was right. Maybe he would miss all this illegal manipulation of the system.

Andy started doing the math in his head. "Say $100 per scope in the US. That would mean, with the duty that scope would cost about $225 in Mexico. Say we added on even $75 bucks per scope that's $175, a savings of $50 per scope or $2,500. Maybe the newly formed Student Association clips $750 from the pot ... nah, too early. Besides this was an experiment. Shit, I've got to talk to his boyfriend."

"Carlito, we'd love to meet him. What's his name?"

"His name is Henry. It's a shit name, but that *verga* ... "

"Maybe you and Henry would like to meet us for a drink at the Casa Blanca?"

Carlito looked like he was floored. "You want to go out together?"

"Yeah, we'd love to. Why don't you tell me when Henry flies in and we can pick an evening. You don't mind if Marvin and Sam come with us?"

Carlito was so excited. Andy guessed that the gay social life wasn't quite the same as on the Lower West Side. Now he needed to deal with Cerene. Cerene needed to be more involved and get Garza much more involved too.

As they stepped out of the motel, Andy was whistling a happy tune. Sam, unable to share in his elation even though they had nearly secured an aircraft, launched into his tale of losing Esme.

"Sam, I liked Esme," Andy said. "There was no doubt in my mind she helped you and loved you. I would even say she was good for you. I was rooting for you, I guess in a tragic way, when you went after her after we got back, but … "

Sam looked at the floor, "The 'but' is the problem isn't it?"

"Yes, the 'but' is the problem. You know as well as I that when we get back to the States there will be a million problems waiting for us. Esme would be the equivalent of another half a million problems. Look, for starters your parents are nice liberal people, but they aren't ready for you to arrive with an uneducated girl from the middle of nowhere. Now what happens if either of you lets it slip that she was a hooker?"

"I can't even imagine."

Andy put an arm around him. "Mourn her, mourn the relationship, and even though you don't believe it now be thankful that she decided to make a fresh start. Now I hate to tread on your sadness, but we have work to do."

Andy proceeded to tell Sam his plan and the recent rumors that were coming out of La Guad.

Sam was joyous. "You're telling me that La Guad is so afraid of competition from other med schools, that they are actually sending away their third and fourth year classes? All the Americans are going to be in the States? You mean … "

Andy laughed, "Yeah. it means that unless we want to be the only gringos left in Mexico, we better get Garza to see the financial advantage of sending us away."

"What financial advantage?"

"God, you can be so dense sometimes, Sam. If Garza allowed

third and fourth year hospital rotations in the States for credit here, he no longer has to pay IMSS for the privilege of hosting his students. He doesn't really need to pay clinical doctors to teach in the hospital and he doesn't need to deal with the gringos and their demands on a daily basis. Know what the most glorious aspect of all this is for him?"

"What?"

"We end up paying tuition for minimal services and all he has to do is hand out a piece of paper in two and a half years saying we are doctors.

"What about the Mexican students?"

"Who cares, and believe me Garza will care even less. We need to drop the rumor on him."

"How?"

"The Americans are all trying to make a deal with La Guad for entrance into the third year class. He'll immediately call the National University and ask for any new policies La Guad put out."

"Why won't he call the chief at La Guad and find out?"

"Remember, Garza took away potential high-paying customers from La Guad when he opened this school. They won't talk to him."

"So the minute he finds out from the National University they are allowing all rotations to be done in the States he will think that La Guad is trying to steal students back."

"We have to force this along, and I mean fast. The students at La Guad are probably already trying to get rotations. We need to do the same or the American hospitals will start catching on and either close positions or charge for them. Soon all the foreign medical schools that are using Americans as a cash cow will be allowing their students to get rotations in the States. If the Medical Association catches on and works fast enough we might as well go home."

"What do you mean?" asked Sam.

"Buddy, no matter what the American Medical Association has been telling you, there are not enough docs in the US. We need to produce a hell of a lot more, but can't. Not enough med schools and too much resistance by the medical establishment to create new ones."

Sam looked at Andy, "Resistance?"

"Sure, future competition in the workplace. Here's a great example. You know Brooklyn would be the tenth largest city in the United States if it wasn't a part of the City of New York, right?"

"Yeah, so what?"

"Did you know there are only two pediatric surgeons practicing in Brooklyn? They split the Borough in half taking all the Peds cases."

"Shit," Sam said amazed, "they must be making gazillions."

"One is rumored to be so rich he has a stake in oil tankers. I doubt he wants any more competition."

"We need to work on Garza. We need to pay him off with a deal he wants badly, but can't get on his own. I think I have an answer for that, also."

"So let's go see him."

"First we have to see Cerene. We'll use his problem as the experiment to solve the bigger problem."

———•———

"I'm pretty sure we can do it," Andy told Cerene, "but it's gonna cost a slight fee." They had taken Cerene poolside at the motel. Sam and Andy, with input from Marvin, had run over the plan again and again refining it as they went along. About four a.m. Andy thought the plan was set as long as they got the cooperation of Carlito and his verga boy.

"Now we need to figure out the second issue that has come up," Andy said.

Sam's eyes were red and gritty from the lack of sleep and too many cervezas. "Issue? What issue is that?"

Marvin nodded knowingly, "And here I thought we had finally taught you how to think like a criminal. Don't you want something for Passover boychik?"

Sam thought, "I want … " His face looked at Marvin in amazement.

Marvin looked at Andy and said, "Sam clicks his ruby red slippers together and … "

Sam breathed, "I go home."

Chapter 22

Tab A into Slot B

Cerene laughed, "Don't look at me. I don't have the money for this, but Garza might if you can come in significantly cheaper than if he tried to buy the scopes here. Also on my end I need those scopes ASAP."

"OK, you get us an appointment with Garza. We will present the deal, then you excuse yourself."

Cerene was confused. "I disappear? Don't you want me there to put pressure on Garza or just for moral support?"

Sam said, "Professor Cerene, after we take care of your small problem, we need a little time with Garza to discuss the future of his school and financing his dreams while granting ours."

"The future, huh. Anything I should invest in now?"

"No, though I think you might be guaranteed future employment if all works out."

"I'll set something up."

———◆———

Boy's Town was hopping. Everyone was in a great mood. The smoke was thick and the noise was loud. The Shriner's were in town. Sam couldn't believe it—Mexican Shriners—what would they think of next?

Sam, Andy, and Marvin were at the bar waiting for Carlito and Henry to show up.

"Can you believe the noise?" said Andy.

Marvin smiled, "You've never been in a hotel with a Shriners Convention? This is tame. Give it a couple of hours, then you'll see the action."

"I bet the girls are already counting their money. I've never seen a hornier group of middle-aged men … Duck!" A Shriner had tried to paw Lola, but she just grabbed his hand knocking him off balance into a table that launched beer bottles and nachos.

"Hi Lola," Sam shouted out.

"Fucking Shriners, every year the same fucking thing," Lola huffed.

Andy brought Sam and Marvin back to the business at hand. "I think I can work this deal, if we can get cooperation from Garza and his buddy the Chief of Police of Madero. I just hope Henry is as head over heels in love with Carlito as Carlito is with Henry."

"Why?" Marvin was curious.

"Simple. Henry needs a stake in Mexico for this to be worth it to him. Besides, who knows if Carlito's verga is big enough to keep Henry interested," he laughed.

The prospects were good. Andy was already smelling the States as Carlito and Henry walked into the bar "dolled up," their hands on each other's asses.

"Hola, Amigos! Henry this is Sam, Andy, and Marvin, my friends."

"Hi," Henry said, looking around. "Shit, Shriners!" He swerved as another drunken Shriner lost his footing almost crashing into him. He was truly beautiful. Six foot two, with broad shoulders, flat abdomen, and muscular arms. His teeth were pearly white and his curly hair was jet black. Judging from his outfit it was clear he was very proud of his verga.

"Hi Henry, pleasure to meet you. Carlito has told us a lot about you. Where do you hail from?" Sam asked, shaking Henry's hand.

"I was born and raised in Phoenix, but the past few years I have been running an air charter service out of Texas."

"That must be nice. We have friends in Brownsville and I have never met a friendlier group than Texans. How did you learn to fly? Jesus, watch it!" Sam shoved a Shriner that was trying to balance four beers and a couple of tequila chasers on a tray that was too close to Andy's head.

"Air Force. Uncle Sam taught me," Henry replied as he kept a wary lookout for more flying objects.

Marvin and Andy looked at each other, and Henry laughed.

"I can be quite butch when I have to and we are not all card-carrying members of the lifestyle."

Marvin became flustered, "We didn't mean anything by it. It's just that ... "

"Don't sweat it. Carlito told me you were good guys. I just kept it very quiet when I was serving. Besides, you wouldn't believe how many of the brass like a little dick once in a while."

They all laughed. "Why don't we have a round," Andy suggested.

"I'll get this round," Henry said. "I hear you're all poor students. I also understand that you may have some work for me."

Andy looked at Henry and smiled. "We may. But first, a toast to new friends!"

They all downed their beers and started talking business just as a 300 pounder in a very ornate fez crashed into their table.

———— • ————

Henry leaned back in his chair, their table now kindling at their feet. "My God, you can do this?"

Andy also stretched and then took a swig of beer. "I think we can. Even if Garza lets all the gringos go back to the States he still wants areas to expand his business. His business now is medical and my guess is that he is quietly trying to line up physicians to staff a private hospital."

Sam didn't understand this part. "What is a private hospital?"

Carlito piped up: "Sí, it makes sense. Sam, in the States the hospitals all take various insurance and if you are old you give the hospital government insurance."

"You mean Medicare," Marvin said.

"Sí. We don't really have this here and in any case the hospitals are not required to take any insurance. A lot of doctors in Mexico, especially if they have a reputation, set up their own *clinícas*. These are really hospitals."

"Garza is a man with connections," Andy added.

"Sí," Carlito said. "Maybe he makes a deal with a *Cirujano Plastico*, you know for faces and *tetas y culo*. Tits and ass, like the song. He builds a hospital for plastic surgery and makes it a cash business taking a percentage of the fees."

"I get it," Sam said. "He is like the silent partner and cleans up."

"OK, OK, wonderful lecture on the horrible medical system here. How does this involve me?" Andy noticed that Henry was hungrily trying to catch Carlito's eye. He knew the evening was about over and needed to make the pitch.

Andy said, "It's simple. A hospital is not just a building. It is a building with a lot of specialized expensive equipment, costing two to three times as much in Mexico as in the States. Garza would just love to be able to buy the equipment in the States, and pay a small markup in transportation costs and bribes. He would still end up ahead."

Henry smiled big. "Transport costs. That's where I come in, right?"

"Yes it is," said Sam.

Henry got worried. "But the customs guys at the airport?"

"Ah, the beauty of it all. Garza is friends with the chief of police who runs the customs guys and will, let's say, look the other way as long as he is looking straight at the money." Andy laughed, "Can you imagine how long you'll be hauling in equipment and re-supplying the hospital once it is built?"

"Man, I may have to get a bigger plane."

Carlito looked cross. "Hey, what about me?"

Sam smiled and said, "Oh, this is the beautiful part. You set up your own business with Henry. Along with Garza's supplies I don't see why part of the cargo can't be fresh American foodstuffs and other luxury items that get mixed up with Garza's stuff. The food can be re-sold to the motels and restaurants around here. I'm sure you two boys can work something out. Here is the real beauty of it. Garza is paying your bribes."

Now Carlito looked hungry. "Henry, do you think we should go somewhere and talk about this?"

Henry got up from his chair and grabbed Carlito's hand. "Yeah, let's go talk."

They took off, but not before Henry turned and shook Andy's hand. "Set it up ASAP. I want to give it a whirl."

——————

Classes continued and the pressure was on. In addition to studying, Sam had to help Andy find a place in Texas that could supply scopes. He also still wanted to get in enough ER time with Soto.

After his tussle with Soto over Esme, Sam had nervously entered the ER. He wouldn't have been surprised if he was thrown out of the place or if Soto had instructed him to stand in a corner and watch the cases. He found Soto coming out of an exam room, scrubs sprayed with blood and a large unidentifiable coffee-ground like liquid on his pants, probably bloody gastric contents.

Soto immediately put up his fists and scowled. "Hey cabron, you want a rematch?"

"I'm here to apologize and to thank you for helping Esme. I was upset and was looking for someone to blame. Instead of understanding the situation and being grateful that you were here, I was ready to murder you. I just came by to tell you this."

Sam turned to exit the ER. He had said his piece, and while he still ached over a girl he loved, he had come to terms with it. Now he had at least attempted to make amends with a person who had tried his best to teach him. If he had anyone to be mad at, it was himself. Sam wondered if he would ever mature.

"Hey cabron, where do you think you're going. I've got patients here in need of a doctor. Get your ass over to the chart rack and pick up the next one."

Sam turned around and saw Soto's smiling face. Soto looked at him and said, "Hey what are friends for but to beat the shit out of. Besides, you punch like a girl. Now go get to work." Soto looked down at himself. "I think I need to go change."

Sam, forever grateful, went over to the chart rack and set to work.

⸻

The first flight or "The Experiment," as it was to be called, would bring in twenty microscopes. Everyone thought this would be the safest course. They figured that if the customs inspectors were to make a stink, the loss of twenty scopes was explainable and tolerable.

Sam and Bennie had enlisted Viviene to make false documents. She had initially been reluctant to get involved, but she soon realized that the documentation would end up in Mexico and that would kill any paper trail as far as the American customs agents were concerned. Because her family was involved in Little Israel Viviene had experience with bills of lading from the United States to Mexico. She also had copies of the tax stamps and the other bells and whistles Mexicans loved on their documents. In the end her reluctance was trumped by her love of Bennie. She would do anything for him and his friends. Besides, this was the most excitement she had experienced in her hometown of Brownsville since she was six years old and she found out that Little Bobby was built quite differently than her.

Samples of the official documents were brought down by Henry so that Sayeed could get a good look at them.

Sayeed inspected them for about fifteen minutes, sometimes with a magnifying glass. "We don't want you to memorize them. We just want to know if they can be reproduced. So, can they?" Henry demanded anxiously.

"Sure, piece of cake. I'm surprised that there is no embossment. The Mexicans love the silver and gold foil embossing stamps. I guess with the amount of papers that it takes to bring a condom into the country, prettifying the papers is impractical. All we have to do is make a couple of rubber stamps. That'll cost about $50 to a guy I know to keep it quiet. Add about another $50 to make a pad of 'fill in the blank' documents that we can produce in case customs noses around."

Sam looked relieved. "Well, I hope we never have to use them, but I'm glad of the $100 insurance policy, as is Henry, I'm sure. When do you think we can have this ready?"

"I'll pack up these forms with instructions and Henry will take them up to Brownsville where Viviene will airmail them to this guy in Brooklyn. It should take him a week. We should have the blanks and the rubber stamps within two weeks."

Sam went to talk to Cerene who wasn't happy about the two plus week delay getting the scopes, but agreed that it was better to be safe than sorry. He would order his proctors to do the hand off from Henry whenever the plane landed. Cerene thought it would be less conspicuous for Mexicans to pick up the merchandise from the plane and Sam agreed, but Sam thought it might also be good to be at the airport and keep an eye on the proctors. Marvin and Andy agreed wholeheartedly.

So, the big night came. Henry wasn't wild about a night flight into Madero since the facility was little more than a landing strip, but he agreed that it would be quiet and safe. Furthermore, he was a good pilot and he had made the run before at night for other clients.

The plane touched down at 10 p.m. The weather had started changing and it was cold in the evenings. Tonight was moonless and there was only starlight on the landing strip. The engines stopped and the hatch opened. Henry was outlined in the lighted interior and beyond the airport fence Sam and Andy waited nervously. It turned out they had no reason to worry. A truck drove up, the proctors jumped out and helped Henry move the boxes of scopes from the plane into the truck and the truck disappeared down the road. Not one official from the Mexican customs agency bothered to leave the warm office that housed them. A new service to the Universidad de Tampico was born. Over time they were importing luxury foodstuffs, as well as components for x-ray machines in much the same way. Sam and Andy kept a record of the types of cargo that were brought in for Garza. It was their "just in case" documents. They even kept a copy in Viviene's bank, as added insurance.

———◆———

The shipments arrived without a problem, and soon enough, Cerene had his beautiful scopes. Garza was so happy at the prices he paid for the scopes he decided to install electrical supply strips and benches in a newly painted classroom. He also installed sinks and bought slides and in general tried to make a pleasant, dirt-free lab for pathology study.

Cerene was a skilled and responsible teacher. Pathology class was truly one that the US couldn't surpass. One day Cerene said he had a surprise for the class. He had contacted the morgue for the federales in the government building and they were willing for him to conduct an autopsy on one of their minor cases.

Sam asked, "What's a minor case? In the States that's jaywalking."

"I heard that," Cerene called out. "Here a minor case is one they don't think was from criminal intent. It might be a known suicide, a drowning, electrocution … that sort of thing."

Andy rang out happily, "That is so cool."

"Right you are young man. It is cool. Do you Bozos realize that as second year students in the States you wouldn't get within two miles of an official police autopsy? Anyway, I'll be guest pathologist tomorrow for anyone interested." He paused, giving the class the dead eye, "and you all should be interested. Everyone read Chapter 36 in anticipation so we don't have to waste too much time with bullshit. Class dismissed. Andy stay behind."

"What the fuck do you think he wants?" Marvin asked Andy.

"How should I know," Andy said nervously.

Sam said, "Maybe he wants to ship his product into the States now. He must have figured out 'illegal in, maybe illegal out'. What's the sentence for importing drugs into the States nowadays? Is Nixon's War on Drugs still in effect?"

"Don't know, maybe Carter lusts in his heart for acid along with pussy. I guess there is only one way to find out."

Andy got up and headed toward Cerene.

Sam was sick and tired of looking for a place to live, but even in a best-case scenario he would be here for another two semesters. He was fed up with the hotel and as much as he loved Marvin, they both needed privacy, especially now. Yesterday had been the straw that broke the camel's back.

Sam headed back to the room from pathology class after picking up some items including his bi-monthly box of Tenuate-Dospan, the amphetamine-like drug to keep him awake for studying. His habit was worrying him. He was reassured that he wouldn't get addicted to the stuff because he hated the way it made him feel. The pharmacology class had studied amphetamines and the course of addiction wasn't pretty. Of course Tenuate really wasn't an amphetamine, but it seemed close enough. There were just not enough hours at night for study and sleep and he had long become immune to strong coffee and *No-Doze* which he and the other students bought by the caseload in Brownsville. (Sam found he could drink coffee or pop *No-Doze* at any time of the day and still be snoring an hour later.) No, Tenuate was the only thing that helped. The local pharmacist encouraged the students at UT to buy from him by giving them a 10% Tenuate/UT discount. The students complied. Besides, it took a weight-loss prescription to buy the stuff in the States and no responsible MD would give Sam a prescription to stay awake. The Physicians' Desk Reference, the medication bible, said it was illegal to do so. Tenuate had become the Mexican forbidden fruit.

Sam got the Tenuate, then stopped at a *torta* stand for a quick lunch. He was very excited to witness the next day's autopsy and wanted to get to the required reading. He got to the door of his room and tried to open it, but was stopped by the inner security latch.

"What the fuck? Marvin, are you in there?" Sam was impatient. "Open the fucking door!"

Sam heard giggling and moaning. What the hell was going on?

He rattled the door aggressively. "Who the fuck is in there? I'm going to call security."

Now Sam heard a rustling of … cotton on polyester? Maybe bedsprings? With more moans and giggling. Finally he heard Marvin yell out a loud, "OH! GOD!

Sam started trying to break the door down. "Marvin, I'm coming. Are you having chest pain?" Sam was very worried. Marvin was overweight, ate shit, and was old. Sam had learned enough from Soto to know Marvin was at severe risk for a coronary event.

"Marvin, try to take deep breaths and lie still, I'm coming," he said as he again banged against the door.

"I'm cumming too … stop banging. No, not you *Amor!*" Marvin sounded really out of breath. Sam froze … it couldn't be … yuck!

Very soon the giggling decreased and the bedsprings stopped squeaking. The door opened and one of the young hotel maids, pretty, petite, and blushing ran out of the room, clothes askew. She smiled and nodded while adjusting a bra strap. She said "*Perdoneme,*" and ran off.

Sam walked into the room to find Marvin looking like a perverted version of a Rubens nude, half covered with the bed sheet.

"Hey, Buddy. How's it hangin'?" he asked.

"What the fuck do you think you're doing?" Sam was pissed and disgusted.

"I think you know what I was doing. If not come sit over here and I'll explain. You see the birds … "

"Don't be disgusting, Marvin. She was young enough to be your daughter. How could you take advantage of her? What did you do, pay her?"

Marvin was quiet for a moment. "Sam … how could you ask that question considering everything you've been through? Anyway, it really is none of your business, but in an attempt to try to bring you out of that quasi-religious, middle-class morality you seem to cling to when it's convenient for you, what if I did?"

It was now Sam's turn to be quiet. He looked at Marvin. "It's been pretty lonely here for you, hasn't it?"

"Well, thanks for noticing that, best friend," Marvin said sarcastically. "I'm in my early 40s, not good-looking, overweight, and I have never been married or had a lasting relationship with a woman." He paused as if gathering his thoughts. "Here I have an advantage that I don't have in the States. I'm American. As an American I'm perceived as generous to the women. I'm kind and not into the machismo thing, which to the girls I'm with is heaven. I know: they've told me. They don't look at me as a failed, broken down psych attendant. Here, I'm a doctor. I deserve the one advantage."

"But Marvin, she is so young."

Marvin smiled, "Sam, she is legal, even in the States. I know it's a cliché, but old men really do want young women. So, that is my explanation of the girls. Paying the girls is another thing. Bella is similar to Esme. She comes from a small town south of here and is trying to help support a family of seven. She got this job, but it doesn't really pay her enough. She showed me pictures of her family. I wanted to help, so I give her some money. She has never asked for it. I think she really likes me and I know I like her."

"So you'd take her back to the States, but you fought me on Esme? You hypocritical bastard."

"Sam," Marvin said tiredly, "I have no one left in the States, therefore I have no baggage. If Bella and I want to go back together, we will be just another couple in a big city."

"I'm going to get some air. If there is a return bout before I get back, do you own a tie?"

"A tie, no, but I'll hang my boxers from the doorknob," he laughed.

So Sam was off to look at his fifth apartment, this one located on the Madero bus line. He hoped this place was decent. All the other apartments had been in decrepit buildings that smelled and leaked.

Sam got off the bus at a dusty crossroad and walked over to a house. Typical of Tampico it was built of reinforced concrete and had a flat roof. This house appeared to have new construction as a second floor and an outside staircase that tilted towards the ground with no bannister. Not a deal breaker ... he hadn't found a floor here that was true. He walked into the yard and saw the usual chickens walking around, but to his surprise, there also were two turkeys and three pigs. "Man, a farm." He knocked on the door and was greeted with the noise of running, noisy kids.

"*Hola, hablas Ingles?*"

"Yes, we speak English," a teen-aged girl replied.

"Are your parents here? I'm interested in seeing the apartment they are renting."

There was movement inside the house, and soon a beautiful Mexican woman appeared at the door. She had long raven hair and was wearing a blouse opened enough to show deep cleavage. It was hard for Sam to look at anything else. "*Si?*"

"*Apartamento?*" Sam inquired.

"Oh, you want to see the apartment?" her voice was very husky.

"Yes, I'm a student at the medical school and am looking for a quiet apartment."

"It is a very quiet street. Let me show you upstairs." She went into her house to grab the key and they walked up the tilted staircase together. A tree shaded part of the stairs, and when they entered the apartment it looked new and clean. A perfect place with a nice breeze from cross-circulation.

"You can see it has a full kitchen with a refrigerator, and a bathroom with a shower and tub. Water and electricity are included in the rent. I come in every day and do some cleaning and I will do your laundry for a small extra charge."

This alone was music to Sam's ears. He rarely had time to wash his clothes in Tampico's one laundromat. "You have hot water from your own tank." She showed him its outside location near the propane tank that it used as fuel.

"I love it. When is it available?" Sam heard footsteps on the stairs and a policeman walked in.

"*Quien es*, who is this?" he asked.

The woman said, "This is my husband." She explained to the officer that Sam was interested in the apartment.

"*No drugas?*" The officer asked.

Sam was startled but answered, "No Sir, I don't use drugs."

"*Cerveza?*"

"Beer, yes I like beer and alcohol. Is that a problem?"

The officer motioned for Sam to come downstairs. Sam looked at the officer's wife. "Go downstairs with him."

He went into the house and the officer handed him a cold one. In broken English the officer said, "Welcome, I am Miguel Cervantes. You stay apartment?"

"I'd like to."

"OK," Miguel smiled, "remember no drugs."

Sam smiled, "no drugs."

Miguel then smiled real wide. "And *no jode mi esposa*," he said as he fingered his gun.

Sam's eyes went wide. "*Absolutamente*, no wife."

Miguel put out his hand and Sam grabbed it. "*Bueno y* welcome."

Chapter 23

Cause of Death

The basement of the police headquarters was a dank, dimly lit area. If one were quiet, one could hear rats scampering about looking for odd pieces of tissue left on the floor post-autopsy. It was certainly a great setting for a horror film.

The students, all in the UT white coats, filed into the large room that was the main autopsy area. Much like the school's anatomy room, this place was also poorly air-conditioned and stunk. The walls were spattered with fluids: brown, possibly coagulated blood, green, maybe bile, and yellow, well who the hell knew. The stainless steel tables were discolored and rusting.

On the table was a covered form that Sam thought might be a body. This being Mexico, God alone knew what was really under there. Sam had come by himself from his new apartment and found Marvin, Bennie, and Sayeed all excited at seeing a real autopsy take place. Even Marvin, with his hospital experience, had never seen one. At this time in the States most hospitals were not doing them because they were expensive and insurance didn't pay.

"Where is Andy?" Sam asked.

"I don't know. Sayeed and I swung around his house to see if he wanted a ride, but Marla, in her usual welcoming manner, told us that Andy had left and that we should—and I quote here—"Get the fuck off my lawn unless you want your dicks cut shorter than they already are."

Sayeed laughed. "That woman has a mouth on her that a sailor would love. Poor Andy. As far as I know, he's never even been on a boat."

Cerene finally entered the room and following in his wake was Andy, gowned up in a vinyl apron over surgical scrubs.

Bennie was taking pleasure in seeing his friend. "Would you look at him. A Star is Born. Where can I get an outfit like that?"

Cerene called for attention. "Class, I would like to introduce you to our guest pathologist today, Mr. Andy Blumenkranz. He will demonstrate autopsy technique."

"What does Andy know about autopsies besides what he watched on medical TV shows?" whispered Bennie.

"As far as I know, nothing," Sam said.

"Mr. Blumenkranz has had extensive experience as a coroner's assistant. He has participated in at least 50 necropsies and has some experience in courtroom testifying. Ladies and Gentleman, I hand you over to Mr. Blumenkranz.

"What the fuck? Andy worked in the coroner's office? I thought he was a high school counselor?" Sayeed was amazed. "Why didn't he tell us?"

"Well, when his demonstration is over, he has a lot of 'splainin to do," Sam said.

Andy lifted the cover off the body. Unlike the cadavers at school, this one was in relatively good shape and didn't have the rotting edges of skin that their med school cadavers had had.

Andy started, "Subject is a caucasian male, 210 pounds, 5 foot 11 inches," Andy said, checking the scale attached to the autopsy table, and the measure on the table. He continued describing external features of the body including supernumerary nipples, moles, and scars.

Cerene interjected at this point about the need for detail in a court of law as an identifier of the body and how sometimes a case could hang on the smallest point, like a deformed toe or an old scar on the back.

Andy picked up a scalpel and looked at Cerene. "You sure you want me to do this?"

"Proceed, Mr. Blumenkranz. Impress us," Cerene said with a smile.

"A standard "Y" incision was made exposing the chest cavity … ," Andy continued. Unlike the first time the class was exposed to a cadaver, not even one student flinched. Exposure to the ER and the cadaver lab had made them immune to the stink, sounds, and look of dead flesh being pulled apart. In fact the class got closer trying to see details of the dissection.

Andy went through the chest organs, carefully cutting them out and weighing them. He then opened the abdomen and started doing the same. "The right kidney notes a hematoma with a three-centimeter laceration near the inferior pole. The pedicle appears to also be lacerated with about 750 cc of blood … ," he reached into the pelvis and then inserted a suction catheter in the area. Blood flowed into a canister and stopped around the 750 mark. Andy made no comment of the cause or the outcome from this finding. He continued to methodically go through every section of the body including removing the top of the skull and pulling out the brain.

Cerene interjected here and there, but on the whole let Andy perform the dissection. Andy finally finished.

"Excellent, Mr. Blumenkranz. Truly excellent work. What are your conclusions?"

Andy looked blankly at Cerene. "You know I can't make the autopsy conclusions."

Cerene smiled. "Why not?"

"We haven't done toxicological or microscopic slides. Legally I can't give an opinion yet as to cause of death."

Cerene looked at the class. "What Mr. Blumenkranz has said is very important. Autopsies are legal procedures and they are also educational procedures. No stone should be left unturned in uncovering the true reason for a death. In this poor bastard's case I dare say that a knife to the flank lacerating the renal artery and causing probable exsanguination is probably a very good guess as to diagnosis." He turned to Andy. "Thank you Mr. Blumenkranz, for a very complete and interesting presentation."

The class applauded Andy.

———◆◆———

The group of friends left the dark, dank morgue for the equally dark, dank bar across the street from the Police HQ. They chose a table away from the inebriated cops who were holding onto the bar railing for dear life. Sam wanted as much space as possible from these guys, as their shiny revolvers looked like they were slipping out of their holsters. Sam felt that a bullet ending his med school career by accidental discharge of pistol was not a great situation.

"Where did you learn that?" Sam questioned. "You never told us you were a pathologist in a past life."

"Far from it," said Andy. "In fact it is a part of my life I almost wish I'd forgotten.

"You're kidding. In fact it sounded so professional I'm surprised you never got into an American school," Sayeed said.

Andy was quiet, thinking. "I was in an American medical school and then I wasn't."

"What!" the rest exclaimed.

"I was in med school way before Marla. She never knew about it.

I was enrolled in a Doctoral Program in Pathology at the university. My thesis related to research on breast cancer tumors. It was really great stuff and may even have led to a cure one day. The professors were so pleased they even recommended that I apply to the MD program," Andy reminisced.

"Shit, what happened? No one gets kicked out of med school. I mean you should have been a PhD by now." Marvin was amazed.

"Yeah, just a small problem. I needed money and went along with things I shouldn't have. I looked the other way when I should have said something. It cost me the career I wanted so damn badly, and it taught me a valuable lesson. Never compromise. The research was important and I treated it like a meal ticket. I deserved what I got.

"I had just graduated college," Andy continued.

He had wanted to be a cancer researcher and had studied biology and physiology in college. Everyone's hands were held out for money in cancer research. There was money from the government and money from the charitable organizations. The most money was from the pharmacological firms. Millions were available for chemotherapy research to fight cancers. They didn't care what kind of cancer it was, just as long as it was a catchy cancer. What were the catchiest cancers? Prostate for men and breast for women.

Andy's department was working on the genetics of certain types of breast cancers. Andy's boss was a brilliant researcher, and everyone said he had the best chance of discovering a cure. Unfortunately, he also had a very messy private life. It made him easy to manipulate, and in turn made it easy for him to compromise his entire staff.

The researcher, a typical nerd, had the usual problems. He wasn't attractive to women, he was depressed, and he looked at himself as someone who never had any excitement in his life. He was brilliant and jealous of the doctors who worked around him at the medical school.

They were making money, buying snazzy sports cars, and got the nurses in bed on a regular basis. He couldn't get a woman in bed with him unless he paid for it.

One of the smaller drug companies was out to make itself into a big drug company by coming out with a revolutionary cancer drug, and found the perfect researcher in Andy's boss. They fed him more and more money for the research he was doing to find either a drug to kill the cancer or slow it way down. Andy was in the middle of the research. While he was not a PhD he was extremely talented and was a definite contributor to testing and theory for the research.

Andy's boss, the PhD, now had more money than he knew what to do with. He worked his crew mercilessly and it looked like they might be on to a new treatment. Dr. PhD was ecstatic. He envisioned being at the Nobel Prize award ceremony in Stockholm and having the women and riches of his dreams. "Why not start now?" he thought. The money was there and the drug company was more than happy with the research.

He moved into a better apartment, bought a Porsche, and soon had a better grade of hooker. He discovered self-medication in the form of cocaine. What he didn't realize was the drug company knew about this and kept a confidential record.

Andy, for his part, was working his ass off. He also thought they were on the right track. His main worry at this point was his boss's instability. The boss was still a genius, and Andy was appreciative to be working with him, but it was obvious he was doing coke and he disappeared for long stretches of time, only to return looking like he had been on a weekend bender.

It was around this time that the first failed experiments started. Andy, the good scientist, made the notes and tried to change parameters. There were still areas that looked good and the notes came back from his boss and the drug company praising him for his efforts. Andy never heard anything about the failed part of the experiments, but he kept working.

One day, his experiment showed a definite ability for a drug to reduce tumor size. He was in heaven and thought maybe this was it. He reported to his boss, who seemed more unstable than ever, cautioning that the results were early and he would need to follow progress in his animal trials.

His boss wanted to push through now and go directly to clinical trial, and called the drug company who was in full agreement. They wanted to call a press conference and notify the world about their cure for cancer.

Andy told his boss that it was still early, but his boss handed him a large wad of money and told him to go back to the lab. Andy had great misgivings, but the money and the excitement that this could possibly be "IT," allowed his conscience to quiet, continue the work, and have fun with the money.

Five days later the first of the animals died post-treatment. Autopsy showed massive liver and kidney failure. Within seven days all the animals were dead. Andy was beside himself. He finally located his boss, who had just come back from a hotel after a great time with a $2,000 hooker and some prime coke.

He looked over Andy's results and said he'd deal with it. He was sure that it wasn't the new med causing this catastrophe, but something else Andy had done. The boss would repeat the experiments and let the drug company know.

Andy waited days for an announcement that this was not the drug the world had anticipated. In fact an announcement was made by the drug company that they would seek expedited permission to start human trials. Andy vomited. He couldn't allow this to happen as he was sure there would be patients killed by this drug.

He went to the school's Office of Research and spoke to the dean who didn't seem to take Andy seriously. The dean spoke of Andy's relative inexperience and his boss's reputation as a preeminent researcher. Andy got angry and tried to show him the test results. For those efforts, he got a warning about spreading rumors and exposing confidential reports.

Andy didn't know what to do next. He was still young and idealistic. He didn't want people to die and he was not going to let this experiment go forward. He went to the *Times* and, as an anonymous source, recounted all the events in the lab.

The school was investigated by the CDER, a division of the FDA, and was cited for not closely supervising research. The drug company's stock went down and the company eventually declared bankruptcy when federal investigators found that they had paid to manipulate data. His boss ended up doing time for embezzlement of funds and cocaine possession.

Andy's name was never leaked, but he was called into the dean of the medical school's office. It was found that besides being part of the tainted research, Andy had accepted money from his boss over and above his meager salary as a research assistant. The money the boss had given him in cash was recorded somewhere in the books and it made it look like Andy had been in on the fraud. Andy didn't know what to say. He knew that worse than this cash payment would be the fact that he went over the head of the research dean and reported his findings to a newspaper. He would never have a chance again in academia. Andy thought that one day maybe he could still do research on his own. The dean dashed these dreams when he told Andy he had tainted himself and would have no place in a research institution. Andy cleared out his desk that afternoon.

" ... And that was the story of my aborted career as a cancer researcher. Over time I realized that as much as I loved the research I preferred to take care of patients directly. I wanted to go to medical school and use my knowledge of research to choose treatment modalities based on the unadulterated findings of the scientists and not the hyped-up profit-driven research of the drug companies."

"How did Cerene find out about your pathology skill?" Sam asked.

Andy smiled wistfully. "He was in the same department as I was."

Sayeed was thunderstruck. "Wait, Cerene was at … "

Andy shook his head, " … Harvard. Yeah, I used to wear crimson."

"Mudderfucker," cried Sam.

"Yeah, mudderfucker," Andy agreed.

Chapter **24**

The Deal

Classes continued with the addition of one Andy Blumenkranz as assistant to the professor. The Boys were very lucky. Andy's knowledge was encyclopedic and his teaching ability was amazing. Cerene was very pleased. Maybe the gringos would have problems passing the boards in other medical subjects, but he knew they'd all be top scorers in pathology.

———◆———

Social life diminished as the study schedule increased. It was like the entire gringo class had finally realized that they would soon have to prove that being in Mexico had not been a big mistake. That the medical authority had relegated them to the trash heap as a tragic mistake. Most of the class just wanted to fit into the life they had dreamed for themselves a year and a half ago. Only a few, like Sam, were still white-hot angry at the turn of events in their lives. These students had discovered the truth about a medical career. The tests and the requirements that the gringos had failed had no correlation with the skills that a doctor needed. Memorizing the Krebs Cycle or knowing the equation for acceleration by gravity mattered little to the sick or dying.

Sam thought, "What was that old joke? What do you call the last man in his class in medical school? Of course the answer was 'doctor'."

So, study they all did. In addition, negotiations were going on very quietly behind the scenes on two fronts.

Garza had heard rumors about a new Guadalajara policy for the gringos. The moment La Guad started letting their gringos go to the States all his students and probably the gringos of every other Mexican med school would flock to La Guad. Because every school was accredited by the National University, there would be no problems transferring credits between the schools. Garza knew if he did not change his school policy he would have a school that was populated with discounted tuition Mexicans. Still, with the arrival of Andy and Cerene, Garza thought there might be a deal in the works. Better to string Andy along and see what riches might be in the offing.

"What do you want, I am very busy today." Garza stuck to his usual script when dealing with the gringos.

"*Jefe*, I am concerned about the future of our esteemed school … "

"Cut the crap Blumenkranz, what are the gringos trying to get out of now?"

"Nothing Sir, it's just that La Guad is now offering us a chance to study … "

"Yes I know, in Estados Unidos. You want the same. Well this school runs on a budget and that budget allows only for expenditures toward improvements for the good of the students. I don't have money to ask UNAM to study the advisability of *extranjeros* studying in the States. Money goes to finding good professors like Professor Cerene and for equipment like microscopes. Also, we have committed to building a great hospital for all the *mexicanos y gringos* to continue their clinicals in. This costs mucho pesos."

Bingo, Andy thought. The bastard had already heard about La Guad and figured out the deal. Now to just get him to approve it.

Garza had come to the same conclusion Andy had. Less students physically present in the third and fourth years meant instead of paying exorbitant fees to the IMSS hospital and building a general hospital, he could collect tuition and fees from students who were not there. This was a dream come true, money for doing nothing. That money would at least start the new private hospital's physical plant. Maybe, Garza thought, there was more?"

"Jefe, the gringos have a plan to help you build a great hospital and stock it with the finest equipment. What's more, it will all be for the Mexican students to obtain the best clinical education. The best part is you will pay American prices to build and equip and not have to worry about those pricey markups the government unfairly charges to bring equipment here."

Garza smiled, the deal already made. Now for the details. "Go on," he replied.

Andy and Garza started working out the details of sending everyone back to the States for their clinicals and in turn helping Garza build a private hospital with the latest equipment at cut-rate prices. That was when crisis struck.

Chapter 25

To Save a Life Is Like Saving a Whole World

The evening birds were singing their last songs before roosting for the night. Dusk was approaching and the weather was cool and crisp.

Bennie was walking with a song in his heart. After years of being "Crazy Bennie," the crazy Bennie was now just a fun Bennie as he had finally stabilized his life. Even Sayeed realized that there was no longer a real necessity for a Bennie babysitter.

For Sayeed this was a tough time. His father had taught him to be an honest man and while there were times during his adult life that he had stretched the rules, he had never screwed a friend. Bennie's father, Mr. Frankle, had been a rock in his life, offering mentorship, friendship, financial comfort, and most of all the opportunity to meet and help "raise" his son, Bennie. Bennie had gone from being his biggest headache to his closest friend. He was proud if he had anything to do with Bennie's stabilization. He was happy that Bennie had found Viviene and that Bennie had discovered his love of medicine. Bennie wanted to permanently move to the Brownsville area and open a clinic for the poor. He had asked Sayeed to become a partner with him. To Sayeed it seemed like a natural continuation of the friendship, but unlike Bennie, he didn't have a Viviene. Bennie just laughed and said, "Brother, we got two years of rotations and then residencies. My guess is you'll have a harem of nurses to pick from. Let's put this part of your future on hold."

Sayeed agreed happily. He did have plenty of time.

Bennie hadn't told Sayeed his other plan. Bennie believed that deep down Sayeed was still insecure about certain aspects of his life, but then again who wasn't. He was walking to the public phone to talk to his father. The "politically important person" Andy needed was Mr. Frankle. Bennie had persuaded him to use his philanthropic ties to open New York hospitals to the third and fourth year students at UT. Mr. Frankle had agreed and Bennie was on his way to get information on the last of those negotiations. His hand went to his coat pocket and felt the small box containing a token representing his promise to himself. "I'll make sure that all her days are happy and filled with love," he thought. That was when the lights went out and all he had was searing pain.

———◆———

Sam was working with Soto, sewing up a girl who had the misfortune of putting both arms through a plate glass window. She had lacerations to both arms so Sam and Soto double-teamed her.

"Ta-da, winner and still champion, Da Gringo Doctor! What's the matter, Soto? Getting old?" Sam crowed.

"Chupame, cabron!"

"Tut-tut, you know we don't allow language like that in Man's Best Hospital," said Sam.

"That is why I love working here. How do you *mariposas* say it? Here I'm free to be!"

"Yeah, free to be a dickhead," Sam laughed.

There was bedlam with strobe lights and sirens at the ambulance entrance. All of a sudden a lot of uniformed people filled the hallway.

Soto looked at Sam, "I think they are playing our fucking theme song, cabrón. Care to join me?"

"You know it," Sam said eagerly.

"Vamos aver," said Soto and led the way.

Sam caught up and gave Soto a dirty look. "Don't ever say that to me again!"

———————•———————

The Trauma Room was mass chaos. Mexico hadn't even started the Trauma Center proposition the States had, so trauma was brought in directly from the street with no notice to the hospital and most of the time with no pre-hospital stabilization having been done.

Sam had read articles on the trauma system that had been published in San Francisco. The articles talked about the training of paramedics who were taught about stabilization in the field and the Golden Hour in trauma. He knew he would see none of this in Tampico's IMSS hospital. Already minutes behind, Soto would have to start stabilizing the patient even before anything besides a perfunctory exam could be done. Sam quickly put on gloves and elbowed his way across the gurney opposite Soto.

"What the fuck happened to this guy?" Soto asked the ambulance driver while starting a large IV in the victim's arm. "Sam, get me some vital signs." Sam grabbed a pressure cuff.

"He was walking across the street and a drunk truck driver nailed him. There was blood all over the place," the ambulance driver said.

Soto got the IV in and started to place a hard collar on the victim's neck. If the victim had a broken neck and he was still neurologically intact, meaning the spinal cord hadn't been damaged, this would prevent the neck from moving and causing more damage. "Sam, what's his BP?"

"Fuck, wait. OK, 200 systolic, pulse 40, and respiratory rate 12 and irregular. Wait, that can't be right."

"Double fuck, anyone see Muñoz?"

A nurse said, "I think he is in a call room, asleep."

Soto asked, "Is he sober?"

The nurse discreetly said, "I think he is ill."

"*Hijo de puta*, we're going to have to do this by ourselves. Sam get your ass over here." Soto yelled to the nurse to bring him the head package.

"Sam, look at the patient's eyes, what do you see?"

Sam looked at the patient's face but saw only a traumatically swollen face with ecchymosis and blood. The eyelids were closed and swollen. Blood had collected within the lids making them fat and purple. "The lids are swollen … "

"Shithead, open them and check pupillary reflexes, get on the ball."

Sam grabbed his penlight and pried the lids open. The left eye had a small pupil and when he shined a light it constricted even more. The right eye was a different story. When he looked at that pupil it was grossly dilated and shining a light in it did nothing.

"Oh my God … " Sam stammered.

"See cabron, reading does make you a better doctor. What did you discover?"

Sam calmed himself. "He has an epidural hematoma."

"How do you know that?" Soto interrogated him as he was placing another IV in the victim, while motioning to the nurse to get another set of vitals.

"He has Cushings triad … "

"Which is … ?" Soto questioned."

"Hypertension, bradycardia, and irregular respiration."

"Bueno," said Soto satisfied, "and what did you see in the eyes?"

"A blown pupil, he's herniating, and going to die. We need a neurosurgeon."

Soto grimaced, "Yes and we have one, drunk in a call room. Congratulations, you just graduated and are now a neurosurgeon."

"What the fuck are you talking about … ? I don't know how … "

"Yeah, that's why I'm here. Remember, teach one do one. I'm the teach one, you are the do one. Which side is the epidural?"

"Right side … "

"Get a razor and prep the right temple area and face … hurry cabron. If this guy has a chance to live and still be able to fuck we gotta move."

Sam grabbed a wet towel and razor from the nurse and started to wipe away the blood and shave the victim's hair. He hadn't really looked at the face, but now he was seeing it for the first time. "Oh my God, I can't do this." He dropped the razor in horror.

"What's the matter, you can't stop now," Soto shouted as he was in the middle of putting a central line into the victim's subclavian vein below the collar bone.

"Soto, it's Bennie!"

———— ● ————

Sam backed off from the gurney, horrified. He had witnessed traumatic death in the ER at the IMSS. Some patients died peacefully of old age, some died painfully from cancer, and some died of trauma. Sam had been able to deal with this in a detached manner. They were all patients, patients that a doctor tried to save. Patients that even in death a doctor could learn from. Never had Sam had a friend at death's door. He couldn't look at Bennie's face, nor could he touch Bennie's body.

"Cabron, don't you dare leave this room. If you do I'll fucking find you and cut off your balls!"

"I can't Soto, he is my friend. I'll fuck up and he'll die. I'll fuck up like I've done every other important thing in my life."

Soto looked at him. "Maybe the old San Diego Sam was a fuck up. Not the one who was reborn in this shithole. You not only won't fuck up, you will give your friend his only chance to live. If you don't he will be in the ground by tomorrow. How will you feel then?"

Sam was visibly terrified. He was shaking.

"He is a patient, a patient in trouble. You are a doctor and if you don't know this already you can leave. Doctors save patients with their last ounce of energy. That is the profession. Know this or leave and enjoy being a bum in San Diego."

Soto's words hit Sam like he had been slapped. He wanted to be a hero. That was why he was here in this godforsaken place.

"What do I do?"

Soto ordered, "Nurse, sterile gloves for Doctor Cohen, and open the head pack."

Sam gloved up and then opened the inner sterile packing of the package. In it was an old-fashioned manual crank drill and a single bit. "What the fuck is this?" To Sam this looked like something Torquemada might have used during the Spanish Inquisition.

"Cabron, it's your friend's only chance. Now listen carefully. Put the bit in the drill and make sure it's in there tight and locked. Can't have the bit wobble."

Sam did what Soto said with shaking hands.

"Hey Pendejo, those hands are good to strum the clit, not so good for neurosurgery," Soto smiled. "Calm down, por favor. Now take two fingers and measure a line anterior to the ear and then a line superior to the ear. Where these two lines intersect is where you drill. Scalpel to Dr.

Cohen, please. Now cut the skin down to the bone. Don't worry about how much it bleeds."

Sam did as he was told and the blood started flowing down Bennie's head like a rushing river.

"You need to make that incision bigger. Look at the bit—it needs to have space. Remember 'big incision, big surgeon.'"

Sam looked at the bit. It was big and would make a big hole in Bennie's head. "Soto, you sure? This is going to make a quarter-sized hole."

"I'm sure cabron. Now cut. You're wasting time."

Sam did as he was told. The blood flowed and flowed.

"Now pick up the drill and start cranking."

The drill bit into the skull's bone with a sickening crack. Soon pieces of bone mixed with the flowing blood, the hole getting deeper and deeper. Sam thought he smelled burning meat, but that couldn't be true.

"Cabron, stop when you feel a 'give'—if you go further than that, well there goes the violin lessons, entíendes?"

"Thanks for the advice," and the pressure of the bone's resistance gave way. Sam froze immediately. "I'm through, what now?"

"Back out the drill, make sure you are backing out, not advancing."

Sam slowly did as he was told. As he pulled out the drill the blood flow increased with dark blood and clots.

"I'm getting a lot of bleeding here, Soto! What now?" Sam felt his pulse rise and he had an urge to piss his pants.

"Now the life saver. Put your finger in the hole and scoop out as many clots as you can. Hurry."

"But Bennie's brain … "

"Yeah, his brain is in there and getting more squashed by the second, so hurry up. Nurse, start cephalexin, *immediatamente*."

Sam started scooping and scooping, big clots and blood pouring down onto the sheets, getting on his scrubs and running down to the floor until there was no more. He heard a groan and saw some movement.

"Bennie, Bennie can you hear me?"

Sam got close to Bennie's face. "Bennie, answer me."

"Why are you fucking shouting?" came a weak reply. "What the fuck happened?"

Sam, charged with emotion, said "A truck hit you, but I think you're going to be alright."

"A truck hit me? Shit, where are my clothes?"

"Bennie, you don't need them … "

"Yes I do, find the box in my pocket and tell Viviene I love her."

Bennie closed his eyes as the monitors started screaming.

"What's happening now?" Sam cried out.

"Blood pressure is dropping, look at his belly," Soto said, concerned.

Sam looked and saw that Bennie's abdomen was distended and there was a large area of purple bruising to the left upper abdomen and flank.

"Spleen?"

Soto nodded, "Probably. He needs the OR now. Get the O negative blood and meet us in the OR Stat." Soto looked around. "Get Hernandez and have him meet me in the OR. He's a good surgeon and thank God a teetotaler. Sam, change into fresh scrubs and join us in the OR. You can observe."

Soto and Sam ran their separate ways.

———◆———

In the end, Bennie survived. Sam went to see him in the recovery room every spare minute he had. He watched him sleep, he watched the monitors, he watched for signs of infection. He had been lucky that

Soto's friend Hernandez turned out to be a Chicago-trained surgeon who did most of his residency at Cook County. He told Sam that in his last year as chief resident he had doubts about coming back to Mexico. He had been well trained at the County and on his outside rotations in the private suburban hospitals. He had the most modern equipment to work with, but every time he rotated back to the County, he was reminded of the hospitals in Mexico. Old hospitals, not the cleanest, and a mass of suffering humanity. It was strange he said. He always felt more alive at the County, doing good work not because of the machines, but in spite of the machines. This made him use his brain and his surgical skills. Hernandez told Sam, "You'll see, the rough education will make you a better doctor. Besides, do you really think there is any second year medical student in the States who's done burr holes to decompress an epidural hematoma, cabron?" Hernandez laughed and after clapping Sam on the back, he walked off.

Sam rode in the ambulance with Bennie to the airport. Mr. Frankle had wanted to have an air ambulance take Bennie to New York Medical Center, but Bennie refused. Bennie got on the phone with his father and they talked and then talked a lot more.

So Sam found himself flying to Corpus Christie, just up the coast from Brownsville to an anxiously waiting Viviene, Mr. Frankle, and a rabbi from Viviene's synagogue. Sayeed flew with them and carried a small, slightly damaged box. Who else were going to be the Best Men!

Chapter 26

On the Road Again

They gathered at the wall, sipping coffee and munching tortas. Each adopted his familiar posture—Marvin leaning, Andy sitting, Sayeed standing, Sam semi-reclining, and Bennie pacing to let off energy.

Word had gone out that Garza wanted to see all the gringos before they took off for vacation. As usual Garza kept them waiting for close to two hours. They didn't care. Andy was sure the deal was done and they would be free to do rotations in the States. They would only have to come back every six months for exams. Andy thought this was reasonable because it established a paper trail that they had been enrolled for all four years.

"So, how is Bennie recovering?" Marvin asked.

"Great. Garza let him take bullshit finals in the hospital and send them back to him. Viviene and her father got the teaching hospital in McAllen to take him on for his rotations. I've never seen Bennie happier. Their fathers are buying some land for them to homestead and Bennie said that it will be the future site of his 'Crazy Clinic' for undocumented farm workers."

"It sounds great. I'm sure he and Viviene will be producing little Jewish cowboys before too long," Andy said, and they all chuckled.

"So, Marvin and I will be rotating at Bronx Hospital. Marvin thinks he can get you in, Sam."

"That would be nice, but I think I'll try for San Diego first. There are fewer Californians down here than New Yorkers, so maybe there will be a place."

"Well, keep it in mind," said Marvin. "We can even room together. It will be like Tampico, North."

Sam laughed. "How's the maid situation in the Bronx?"

"Attencion, attencion ... "

Here it comes thought Sam—freedom.

"Come up for your packets when your name is called ... "

"Jesus, not even a fond farewell from Garza," Sayeed said sarcastically. "You'd think he'd at least kiss us for all the money he is going to make for doing nothing over the next two years."

Marvin chuckled. "Just be thankful you'll only be coming back here for a few days at a time. You can kiss him when you hand over your tuition check."

"*Ko-haan!*"

"That's me," he said as he ran over to get his packet. Next step, freedom and learning how to be an American doctor. Sam got his packet, a shiny white paper folder with the red crest of the school consisting of return schedules for tests and instructions for the subjects he needed to find clerkships for. He doubted he would ever miss this place, but he knew he would miss the people that had shared the struggle with him. Sam thought about the typical Harvard grad and what thoughts that third year must have felt as he left those hallowed halls of sterility and intense academic competition. Both the gringos and the Harvard students must have felt fear and excitement starting in new hospitals, learning surgery, internal medicine, pediatrics, and all the other clinical sciences. He supposed that the difference was when you were from Harvard you already knew you were accepted. Would he spend the next two years being told to stay in the corner? Would the nurses look at him like he was an interloper? Would he constantly hear them whisper, "not good enough" or even worse, "not good at all?"

Well, he had four days of driving to worry about next steps. In the meantime he took one last look at the still-unfinished building where he became more of a man and closer to being a doctor. He got into his car and started down the road. One thing he knew for sure, Jesus would be on every radio station he tuned into.

About the Author

Doctor Irv Danesh was born in Brooklyn, N.Y. Before he started kindergarten he and his family had schlepped to five new homes because of his father's jobs. This was to be a recurrent theme in his life. Like the main character of his novel, *Doctor Taco*, Irv just didn't concentrate well in college. Women, and the lack of them, had a lot to do with that. After the rejections for admission to medical schools in the States arrived, Irv joined the Diaspora of similar, slacker pre-meds, and journeyed south of the Border.

Two years of cultural and academic re-education enabled Irv to trek back to the promised land of Brooklyn. More specifically, Irv was nurtured at the world's largest community hospital, Brookdale Medical Center. This mega-hospital provided him enough stab wounds, gunshot wounds, blunt trauma, and general patient stupidity to regale his friends with stories for years to come.

After two years of surgical training, he decided he didn't want to spend the rest of his life removing gallbladders or doing bariatric surgery. Being somewhat of an adrenalin junkie, he was in the right place at the right time to snag a residency at Thomas Jefferson University Hospital in the new field of Emergency Medicine. He has practiced in-inner city emergency departments for twenty-six years.

Dr. Irv's job statistically has a high rate of burnout. He fought through two of these periods—the first by moving to Boston and serving as an Assistant Professor of Emergency Medicine at the Tufts School of Medicine.

He later continued his career as Associate Director of Emergency Medicine at the Lawrence General Hospital. It was here that he had his second period of burnout. He again was in the right place at the right time, helping birth USA Network's *Royal Pains*. Irv started as Medical Consultant, advancing over three seasons to Co-Producer. His MacGyver-like vignettes such as skull drilling, fishhook chest wall stabilizing, and other pseudo-medical procedures would never be allowed in conventional AMA approved medicine. Then again, Dr. Irv marches to his own drummer.

He wrote *Doctor Taco* as a fictional account of the great American student exodus to Mexico in the 1970s. Many of the scenarios are true, but needed to be altered to maintain privacy, sometimes his own. He hopes that you enjoy reading this story.

Dr. Irv lives in Marblehead, Massachusetts with his lovely and grammatically correct wife, and their dog, Harry. He loves the change of seasons except for the winter, which he curses every year.

His four artistic sons all left for other parts of Massachusetts and N.Y.

All in all, he would rather be in South Beach.

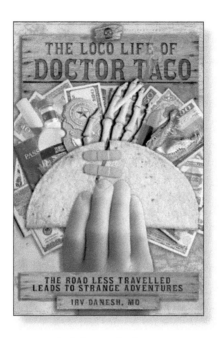

The Loco Life of Doctor Taco
The Road Less Travelled
Leads to Strange Adventures

Dr. Irv Danesh

www.doctortacobook.com

Publisher: SDP Publishing

Also available in ebook format

TO PURCHASE:
Amazon.com
BarnesAndNoble.com
SDPPublishing.com

 **SDP Publishing**

www.SDPPublishing.com
Contact us at: info@SDPPublishing.com